M000033522

The Gathering Dark

~◆~ *Quest of Fire* ~◆~

BRETT ARMSTRONG

EXPANSE
BOOKS

2020© Brett Armstrong

Published by Expanse Books, an imprint of
Scrivenings Press LLC
15 Lucky Lane
Morrilton, Arkansas 72110
https://ScriveningsPress.com

Printed in the United States of America

Paperback ISBN 978-1-64917-030-9
eBook ISBN 978-1-64917-031-6

Library of Congress Control Number: 2020940042

Cover by Diane Turpin, www.dianeturpindesigns.com

Artwork by Eric Dotseth.

(Note: This book was previously published by Mantle Rock Publishing LLC and was re-published when MRP was acquired by Scrivenings Press LLC in 2020.)

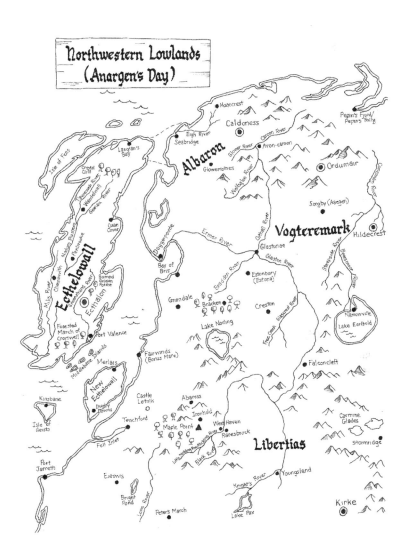

This book is dedicated the glory of God without Whom there are no words worthy of writing, and the memory of my uncle, Meredith William (Butch) Carroll, who taught me so much with so little time.

ACKNOWLEDGMENTS

Without doubt, I must thank my longsuffering wife and immeasurably supportive parents who stand both on the frontlines and supply lines of my writing endeavors. Without them I could not brave the literary worlds I encounter.

My publisher, Kathy Cretsinger and editors Erin Howard, Kathy McKinsey, and Pam Harris for believing in and tirelessly working to shape *The Gathering Dark*.

The unremittingly optimistic Eric Dotseth for hearing out my crazy story-ideas and then giving them form in illustration.

Also Marsha Brock, my high school creative writing teacher, who let me have the freedom to take my first steps into this story-world while in her classroom.

PROLOGUE

A HEAVY RAIN beat down on Jason, but there was nothing he could do about that. The sky was an unforgiving swirl of iron and argent hues, refusing to entertain the notion of respite. It had been so all day.

Nearby, a flivver honked its horn at a horse and its rider. The latter having careened across the car's path.

Muttering a curse under his breath, Jason made a dash across the incongruous lattice of street stones to the nearest building open to the public. Through the veil of rainfall, he could scarce glimpse the building's name etched on a wooden sign that swung wild in the storm's bluster. Without a moment's delay, he pulled open the door and ducked into the Black River Inn.

Far from imposing, the squat, grey stone building was only three stories, dwarfed by many of the structures around it. A quick scan of its interior told Jason why. It looked like a page from a codex on the history of a long past era. Banners bearing the emblems of a variety of foreign regions that ceased to exist decades ago hung along the walls. The layout was more in line with an old wayfaring tavern than a modern hotel or inn of the great burghs such as this one. A fair number of people were present, garbed, as far as Jason could tell, in attire befitting the current period. Some seemed to be examining the quaint relics of the past as well.

Running his hands through his hair, a steady trickle dribbled down onto his soaked vest and slacks. He sucked in a breath, his sprint through the streets caught up with him. Jason was only a mile or so from what passed for home, but the way the rain hammered the roof above, like a smith at his forge, coming in here was the wisest choice.

As Jason crossed the threshold, a wave of anxiety crashed upon him. He scanned the room for anyone who might recognize him. Drenched to his thin frame's core and being seventeen, he was certainly not expected in a place like this. Not alone at least. Maybe in one of the new factories springing up, but not in a traveler's inn at the edge of the city. The city limits were temptingly close, and he ached to get back on the other side of them as soon as possible. Jason wasn't welcome in Brackenburgh.

His fears of drawing attention were unfounded. No one gave him a moment's consideration. In fact, everyone's eyes seemed directed towards the back of the room. A small group of patrons was gathered, oblivious of anything else going on in the large, open room.

Taking a few tentative steps in that direction, Jason tapped a waitress on the arm and asked, "May I have a drink?"

The pale young woman turned, her dark hair and deep green eyes startling him. Ruddy lips, which immediately drew his eye, set themselves into an easy smile. "Of course, right away, sir."

Before he could enquire about the price or make his choice of beverage known, she hurried off, the maroon skirt she wore swishing as she walked. Sighing, Jason noted that in her wake she left a faintly aromatic scent. Cinnamon?

He cast a few more furtive glances around the room. No one was watching, but he didn't want to seem too out of place. Rather than linger where he stood in the open, he wove through the long tables to one near the clustered patrons and against the right wall. Keeping his back to the wall, he dropped onto a bench.

Rubbing his face, he wondered what he would do when he got out of this bizarre place. After the rain stopped, he didn't think he could bring himself to go home. Not yet.

A few minutes later, the servant girl returned with a glass full of milk. "Your drink, sir."

From her tone, Jason guessed the girl was amused to be calling him "sir," given she looked about his age. Probably doubled her pleasure to bring a kid's drink to him. Jason smirked and mumbled, "Thanks."

Across the room some boisterous laughter erupted from the patrons. The waitress seemed distressed by this. Her large eyes glistened with a sadness and the smile she had worn wilted, becoming an intense frown.

"What's going on?" Jason asked, eyeing her expression with interest. He took a sip from the glass. The milk was nice and warm, precisely what he needed.

To Jason's surprise, some of the waitress's sorrow melted away, like a brief summer shower replaced by a shy sun. "The owner is telling stories again. He's quite a weaver of tales," she informed him.

"Oh? They do seem to be enjoying it," Jason stated as he took another drink of milk and tried to not be obvious about looking at the girl. There was something about the way her eyes gleamed, the way her hair fell, the set of her full lips when she smiled.

"Since you've never heard any before, you should listen," she said. "They are like no author today would tell!"

Until the girl beamed a smile that was solely for him, Jason had no intention of listening to an old innkeeper's ramblings. Now he found it impossible to refuse her urging. "Sure," he began, "I will, if you come along?"

Her eyes narrowed a fraction, as if in suspicion. She put a hand on her hip and smirked. "I've heard them a few times, but after you've listened, perhaps we'll have something to talk about."

"Your terms seem agreeable," Jason answered with pretentious pomp. Standing, he gave a slight bow and added, "Jason Landsby, in your service."

The girl laughed aloud and offered a hand to shake. "Aria."

Gripping her hand with care, he gave it a shake. "Well, if you grant me your leave, Aria, I have some stories to hear."

She walked off to tend to another patron's needs, but her eyes stayed on Jason and his on her. Aria nodded to the end of the room. Draining the last of his milk, Jason stalked over to the gathered listeners. He'd already forgotten his soaked clothes and darker reasons for being in town.

On the back wall hung the last of the aged banners: bright white with a golden lion on it. Or perhaps it was a lamb with a star behind it? Either way, after a few seconds of staring at it, Jason thought he remembered what it stood for. There were legends. Most called them fables.

Long ago, thousands of years past, there had been a king, the High King of all the countries of the world. No one remembered what the king looked like, and many couldn't bring to reckoning a single word or decree from this king. In more recent times there had been an order of Knights who served that king and had long lived in these lands. By now even they had all but disappeared. As had chivalry and castles and all manner of relics from the darker ages past. It was an interesting antique tapestry to hang.

From the banner, Jason's eyes drifted down to take in the central figure of the gathering. The innkeeper was a grizzled man. Salt and steel hair, short and bristly, capped a head dominated by a long unruly beard. Lively sage eyes, deeply set, roved from person to person as he spoke. He wore a thick, brown duster over pristine white shirt and brown slacks. With old age, he had not thickened in the middle, more the spindly type. Most memorable was the embroidered emblem on his sleek, alabaster shirt. The same emblem as the banner. He spoke with great animation, his hands having lives of their own.

"What is everyone laughing over?" Jason enquired of the stocky man standing nearest him. The man, with a tooth-bearing grin and cheeks reddened by mirth, answered, "This one claims to have seen the legendary High King in person! He's a shriveled old sot, to be sure. But you can't see a myth."

Jason nodded. "Yeah, what a loon." The man's words intrigued him though. Watching the innkeeper, he noted the old man didn't have sloppy speech from too much drinking. His movements were too controlled for a fit of madness. More peculiar, he did appear diminished, as though collapsed from a greater volume by age and wear. His eyes were as sharp as any soldier's bayonet.

While Jason watched in this way, those eyes found him and stopped. The storyteller stared right at him, running him through, it felt. Jason swallowed, uncomfortable under the gaze.

"You there," the old man said, pointing to Jason. "I have not seen you before. Where do you hail from?"

Everyone turned their attention from the storyteller to Jason, who managed to get off a quick reply. "Um, I'm from here, sir, Brackenburgh."

The man nodded. "Explains why I would not have met you. We only get travelers here. Are you on a journey, lad?"

"You could say that," Jason replied.

A smile, warm and quiet, spread over the old man's thin lips. "Good. What's your name then?"

"Jason Landsby," he responded, glancing at each of the onlookers, examining what they made of this attention being paid to him.

"Jason, would you be interested in hearing the story of a journey I'm familiar with?"

Surveying those around him, Jason looked last at the man beside him, who shrugged. Swallowing with difficulty again, he fought the urge to squirm. "Sure. That's what I came for."

With a keen chuckle, the old man said, "Getting soaked in this horrid storm just to hear a tale from me? I shall begin straightaway then!"

He paused and with a more thoughtful tone added, "I must warn you, this tale is not mine. It began days long past in a land far from here, but it is one which I'm certain is true." His gaze sweeping across the audience, once more the story-teller, the innkeeper, began demure, as if imparting a close-held secret. "This journey, like so many, began with a lad no older than Jason, seventeen to be precise, stepping foot on to a new road. His journey began late one night in his home village, where he had an encounter with the High King . . ."

1

A NEW ROAD

WHEN THE HAND reached out to help him up, it was like he'd been thrown in a furnace. One burning so high and with such intensity, Anargen couldn't imagine how he wasn't incinerated in an instant. The light had already been so bright he could scarcely open his eyes, but this was more. This fire crept into his skin, tracing out his entire frame, burning him not from outward in but inward out. Anargen couldn't close his eyes though the sensation intensified.

Then, as suddenly as it had begun, the brilliant light filling his vision faded. In its place was the world he knew. Around him was a small gathering of people. Most of them were talking amongst themselves and not aware of what had just transpired.

Standing from a kneel, he felt wholly consumed. Everything within the light and fire had burned away. Now there was a newness, a different edge to everything about him. As though light touched everything around him more solidly. It felt . . . good.

Sounds of familiar voices in a low conversation drifted to him. Anargen tried not to give in to curiosity and listen in. Despite his intentions, he couldn't help overhearing the final words spoken between Anargen's best friend, Caeserus, and Knight Errant Cinaed.

Sir Cinaed's deep voice was remarkably soft in tone. "In three days you will have your conferral ceremony. We will discuss this further afterwards. Till then, meditate on this and obey the Great King's will."

Caeserus nodded, a bit of reservation hindering his movements. It reminded Anargen of a horse wanting to race off as soon as the stall is opened to him but, barred by his rider, must stay where it stood. A few moments later, Caeserus stalked through the building's simple wooden doors and into the night. He did not look back as he left.

"Can I help you with something, Anargen?"

The teen took a step back and stared blankly at the imposing form of Sir Cinaed, unsure of what to say. Cinaed was at least fifty with broad shoulders betraying an innate and honed strength of limbs and sinews few could boast. He wore the ornate and formidable armor of his order. *Palatini Lucis Aeternae* or the Knights of Light as they were more generally referred to in these days.

Dark days, in which many erroneously questioned what it was the Knights' light revealed. Anargen had never been amongst those who doubted their purpose. From a time before his memory of life was fully formed, he had been in attendance for the meetings in this Hall. First with his mother and later with his father as well. Each parent was a member of the Order, devoted to their duties. Even now they were off on errands for the Hall, seeking out and acquiring provisions necessary for its upkeep.

"Anargen?" Cinaed's thick eyebrows were lifted in concern.

"Sorry, sir. I had the vision tonight. Of the High King. And I, well, what do I do?"

"Have you now? That is good news indeed. You pledged your fealty to the High King?"

"Yes, sir. Whatever service I may render my Lord, I will."

These words came out steadier, almost zealous in their pronouncement.

Cinaed's large hand clasped Anargen's shoulder. "Very well, my lad. I will tell you what I just told your friend, Caeserus. In three days, I will hold a council with some of the elder Knights of the Hall. They will then examine you to ensure your oath is sure and you truly discharge your duties in a fitting manner before our king. Then you will be given your first task. For the moment, you should ponder on what Quest the Great King has for you. You know what the Quest refers to, correct?"

"Oh! Um, yes. It is the act, or set of acts, which defines the life of a Knight." Displeased with the formal taste of his answer, Anargen added, "It's the goal a Knight is to work towards. Upon completing it, he may rest from labor and join the High King in his Hall."

"That is a good answer, Anargen. But you must also remember, it is not the completion of your Quest which has earned you a spot at the High King's table. He chose you, specifically, and on your confession of him as your king, he has now reserved your place." Cinaed seemed to be finished and then added in a gentler, less instructive tone, "Remember this when things seem to go awry while striving to complete your Quest."

Anargen nodded emphatically, repeating the words to commit them to memory as if carving each one in stone. "When all goes awry."

Sir Cinaed smiled. It must have been a relief having a willing learner. "Well then, you better be getting home." He nodded toward the exit. "Your mother and father could return any time and will be glad to hear this news. Give them my regards."

"I will, sir. May you have a good night as well." Anargen gave a shallow bow and hurried out of the Hall and out into the warm night beyond.

Once outside, he expected the late summer air might dispel some of what he was feeling.

It was as if the world had undergone a metamorphosis. Each

breath of air tasted sweeter. Each sound was sharper. Every contour to the world around him was more defined. Did all Knights feel this way? Did it ever diminish? How could anyone be sleeping in such a world?

These and a thousand other questions swirled in an unavoidable dance around him. Popping up, disappearing, and then reappearing before he'd handled the last. This village he had known his whole life appeared so much the same and yet fundamentally altered. True enough, terrible things could lurk in the dark, but tonight he feared none of them. Perhaps he would if he knew what stalked in the woods of the world.

All too soon his pleasurable stroll was ended by his arrival at the darkened doorway to his stone and stick home. Stepping inside, he fumbled about for a well-used lantern. Lighting it, he blinked as the lantern cast about the confines of the room a tiny aura of luminance. Just enough to find his way to his rough straw bed with its brown, woolen covers.

Dropping onto the familiar pallet, he sat, too engrossed with the events of the day to sleep just yet. He watched the lantern flames die down and let his mind's eye rove over the expansive landscape of the Lowlands, wandering in search of a place he'd never seen, where land and sky touched. He recalled it was said of that place, "High atop a plateau is founded the City of Light, the home of the Great King, which stands magnificently overlooking all the realms."

Wondering after the magnificent city, Anargen found his way into a restful slumber.

2

WAKING DREAMS

AHEAD STRETCHED two long and divergent paths. One was beautiful, lined with tiger lilies and lush trees with a soft dirt road in its midst. A pale cool mist drifted across the ground with ethereal affection. It looked very much like the road nearest his home.

The other was consumed in a bright, warm light which comforted him, called to him, and held at its center a road paved in stone. Where either led, he could not see, and his heart yearned for both. There was no knowing whether the paths should ever again meet.

The thought of abandoning either pained him, yet a resolute voice within him spoke to him. Or perhaps it was without? Both?

Soon it was all around, calling him to the brilliant path, though it led to a more arduous walk. After some deliberation, Anargen waved a parting farewell to the lovely road with flowers and entered the light, walking down the stone path and letting the soothing voice which called him guide his footfalls —

A solid rapping on the door of the cottage snapped Anargen out of sleep before he could discover any more of where the way led. He blinked, forcing his eyes to focus on the reality summoning him.

Soon the rapping on the door became a steady banging.

Anargen stumbled to the door. It was still dark and he could indeed feel the coolness of the night air circling throughout the cottage's large common area. The lantern he'd used to find his way had smoldered out.

Frowning, he squinted towards the door as if he could see through it. Another pound on it drew him the final paces, and he opened the door slowly.

Immediately, he was shoved out of the way by the awaiting visitor. Startled, Anargen whirled around to see Caeserus standing in the midst of his home. Visible only for the light of a full moon without.

"Caeserus? What are you —?"

"I'm here to ask you for some help. I'm leaving Black River tonight," Caeserus announced as he cast furtive glances around the room.

Anargen shook his head, trying to clear away the fuzziness and grasp what had just been said. "What? You're leaving tonight? Why?"

"I had a vision when I became a Knight. I and three others left here for a faraway city." Anargen's friend paused and stepped forward to look him in the eyes. "I think you were one of them."

There was no wavering, no doubt in his demeanor or tone. Anargen struggled to get his bearings and reason the matter out, "You said you're leaving tonight? Sir Cinaed asked that we come before the elder Knights after three days. We can't just leave before speaking with them."

The other teen let out a derisive snort as his tall, thin frame relaxed enough to lean with a posture of nonchalance against the stones of Anargen's hearth. His light blue eyes were buried beneath thick brows. "All they will tell us is that we should seek the king's will and let him guide us to our Quest. Or worse still, they'll try to tell us we have to stay near the lodge until we receive all the further 'guidance' we need. Well, I know the king's will and received all the guidance I need!"

"What's the rush to leave then? Could it hurt to wait and at least hear what the elders say? After all, if it is the Great King's desire for you to leave, particularly with these three other Knights, shouldn't they confirm your convictions?"

A frown was as much an answer as Anargen got for a few moments. Caeserus was not one to back down from a verbal battle and never easily persuaded. It was somewhat a surprise for Anargen to find Caeserus struggling for a response. Anargen watched his friend with wariness, readying himself for another sharp retort.

Caeserus ran his long, bony fingers through his bristly ashen hair as if racked with indecision. The muscles within his thin, squared jaw tensed and relaxed a few times. Anargen wondered in that brief span if this was all still a dream. It seemed plausible.

Suddenly, Caeserus jerked into motion from his contemplative position. Through gritted teeth he muttered, "Fine. I'll wait. Just be ready to leave the morning after. They're going to confirm my vision, and we need to get out of this place as soon as possible."

It was then Anargen noticed the short sword tethered by a thin leather strap to his friend's side. Caeserus had been working on it for some time in his apprenticeship to Anargen's father.

On edge, Anargen nodded without fully comprehending what he was conceding to and held open the door for his friend to exit.

Caeserus returned a curt nod and announced with a brisk tempo, "I'll see you tomorrow." Then, just as startling as in his arrival, Caeserus departed, leaving Anargen wide awake and markedly confused.

Pushing closed the door and stumbling to his bed, he dropped with a new heaviness onto his sleeping mat, sending coarse fibers of straw onto the loose dirt floor.

What would Caeserus need that sword for? He had been working on it for months.

Has he been planning on this since then? Does he believe so sincerely he's had a vision from the Great King?

Strands of straw and folds of the coarse blanket crumpled in Anargen's hands as they tightened. All he could do was stare off into the dark of his family home.

What if Caeserus really has received a vision?

Anargen's forehead creased, sending his dark hair into his eyes. Clearing the rogue strands, he noticed in his rush to answer the rapping on his door, he had knocked the bound parchments which served as his journal to the floor. On occasion, he would jot down tales he heard from others in town or, more often, those stories which he imagined. Important events and thoughts, sketches, and other pressing details of life joined his stories and went into the worn book.

Picking it up and holding it firm in one hand, he rubbed his face and found the stubbly beginnings of a beard. As he weighed the option of opening the book and perhaps recording the bemusing swirl of events in the trusted book, he realized with sudden and definite clarity a fact he could not have considered before Caeserus's visit.

What if my dream tonight was a vision as well and I am meant to leave this place?

Unsettled by the thought, Anargen put the book down and stretched out on his bed, trying — with little success — to return to sleep. The once inviting bed had become too hard and scratchy for him to find any comfort. Sleep eluded him some hours, and the little he caught was full of restless energy.

3

BLOSSOM BEMUSING

THE SUN'S warm rays rested with light insistence on Anargen's face, beckoning him to wake. Unable to resist, he opened his groggy eyes. As he sat up, he stretched his sleep-tensed muscles and blinked as awareness flooded back to him. Looking around the large common room cottage, he wondered if the events of the night before could really be true. From within he could feel a subtle reassuring touch that was from beyond himself. He smiled. "I'm a Knight of Light now."

Standing, he continued to stretch and looked through the window over his bed. Anargen had to squint. Already his father's field was exuberant with the brilliance of the noon sun. The long shadows stretching from the stalks of corn reminded Anargen of fingers to some great hand. Everything was growing well, and for the moment no woodland dwellers had come to visit the crops. It was a pleasant sight.

Then, sudden and complete realization overtook him. It was past noon!

His father had left him specific instructions to tend his shop in town till around three in the afternoon and then use the remaining hours of daylight looking to the verdant garden Anargen had just been admiring.

Needing no further encouraging than his father's displeasure, Anargen rushed from his house. By instinct, he grabbed the pouch containing the heavy iron keys to his father's shop before dashing down the same path he'd walked the night before.

Emerald trees and jagged, tan stones rushed past Anargen as he charged townward fast as he could run. Glewdyn, Anargen's father, rarely received grumbles for the hours he kept. As the master blacksmith in town, Glewdyn had a few apprentices and steady demand for his quality work.

Despite an intense devotion to his craft, Glewdyn never wanted the vocation that provided for his family. Nature and the growing of things, poor or excellent, captivated him far more than the hot, smelly bellows of his smithy. The clatter of iron on iron did not entice Anargen any more than his father.

Fortunately Anargen wasn't forced to follow in his footsteps. Instead of being apprenticed to his father, Anargen indulged in his own passion, telling stories. Such pursuits conflicted with the productive necessities of his village and thus left him in a predicament. Presumably he would have a family someday, so he needed a trade to provide for them.

Few children had the benefit of the tutelage Anargen had received. As guardians of light and memory of the past, the Knight Hall offered lessons in reading, writing, and a basic introduction to the sciences and mathematics. Anargen fully exhausted the Hall's library long ago, as had a number of his friends. One of whom was Caeserus.

Ahead, Anargen could see the shop and imagined his childhood friend would tease him for his tardiness. Following the single, ancient road that divided the village into two halves, Anargen found no difficulty navigating the street at this hour.

Nearing his father's shop, he could make out a lone figure waiting by its doorway, apparently conflicted over whether to stay longer or depart. It certainly was not Caeserus.

Cloaked in a russet robe, the figure made a hesitant turn to walk away from both the shop and the approaching Anargen.

Coaxing still more speed from his legs, Anargen huffed out, "Wait! I'm coming!"

The potential patron halted. Less than a minute later, he was at his father's shop and looking on the patient soul who needed the services of a blacksmith. Anargen's eyes widened with surprise.

Awaiting his arrival was Seren, a girl his age with hair dark and long like the river running through the region. The first day Anargen saw Seren, really saw her, was at a festival last summer in the nearest town of any size, West Haven. Anargen was participating in an archery contest and on his last shot of the tournament one of his friends, Bertinand, bumped his elbow, sending the shot wide.

Anargen ran over to retrieve the arrow from a basket it had skewered and reached it in time to see Seren bending over to pick it up. At that moment, the sun caught her long tresses in just the right way to reveal the tinges of red hidden in them, like precious copper in a mine. When her warm, cocoa eyes found his, the words of apology he had planned to offer were lost. She was a marvel. The contrast of her pallid skin with her dark hair were reminiscent of his favorite treat, blackberries and cream. The fragrance of honeysuckles in bloom clung to the air around her.

At length, he had managed to mumble, "I'm sorry about that. My friend bumped me."

She merely handed him the arrow and went back to tending her family's booth. Anargen's heart almost went still with dejection.

After he went home, Anargen drafted a letter of apology and found her home some distance from Black River. No one was there, so he left it on her doorstep, sure he'd never know her. The next day, Anargen had found a letter from her on his family's doorstep:

Anargen,

I do not accept your apology, because I do not see the need of it. One lost ear of corn gained me your letter. Likewise, one lost contest gains you mine. Life is filled with losses that are full of greater gains.

Fondly,

Seren

Rather than approach her in person, Anargen had written a reply letter, and the practice persisted for weeks. Since then a friendship had blossomed, but Anargen carried quiet hope for more.

"Anargen, I'm glad you made it," Seren greeted, looking at him like she could already tell he'd overslept. "I was beginning to worry something had closed the smithy."

Fussing a bit with his hair, which he suspected of giving away his dereliction, Anargen replied, "No, all is well. At least now it is."

There must have been some unsuppressed remnants of his excitement to see her tingeing his words because a coy smile turned up one side of her mouth. "It seems it is," she agreed with a soft lilt.

A few seconds ticked away with Anargen digesting each of her words like prize morsels. She raised her eyebrows and asked with a little giggle, "Are you okay?"

"Oh! Yes, yes," he replied hastily. "What brings you to my father's shop?" He removed the ring of jangling keys from his satchel and began eyeing them for the one to the smithy. The keys clanked against one another, like a crude wind chime. In his haste to open the shop, Anargen barely noticed Seren rubbing one of her pale arms as she delayed answering.

A moment later, he had the key in the lock and the tumblers clicked loudly. Giving the heavy, sycamore door a push, he stepped aside and gestured for her to enter first.

"Thank you," she responded and slipped inside.

Anargen followed and noticed she was looking around as if

concerned someone was hiding inside. When she turned, Anargen saw she was gnawing on her bottom lip, and she offered him a tight smile. "It's chillier in here than I expected."

"It's usually quite warm, I, uh, just haven't stoked the forge's fire yet." He silently berated himself for ushering her into such a dark, cold place. Heading over to the shop's lone window, he undid the burlap flap there and let more of the late morning sun stream in. Next to handle was the fire.

"Sorry to be bustling about so," Anargen grunted as he hefted a few of the biggest logs from their pile. Tossing them into the pit for the fire, he sucked in a deep breath before returning for more wood. He tried not to let his eyes linger too long on Seren, knowing it would unsettle his thoughts. Anargen hoped the extra focus would keep him from embarrassing himself in front of her. "Is there something you need?" he inquired, picking up his question from earlier and feeling he failed miserably at sounding casual as he did so.

"I'm not sure," she said almost wistfully, her brows furrowed.

Something was bothering her. She never struggled for words like this.

"I, well, my mother —" she began.

About that time, Anargen, his eyes still holding onto her wavering expression, clipped a table edge with the end of a log in the stack he carried. The log wrenched free of his grasp and rolled across the floor to Seren's feet.

"Argh, sorry," he called out and dithered for an instant over whether to set the logs he still had down or toss them into the pit. By the time he opted for the latter and got to the escaped log, Seren had already picked it up and effortlessly offered it to him.

"Sorry about that," he reiterated, swallowing overloud. "I'm a bit clumsy today." He left off, "Because the girl of my dreams is standing two feet from me."

"Clumsier than usual?" she asked with a smirk. There was a teasing edge to her voice but something more in her warm eyes.

"Yeah, I would say so," he admitted, lingering there close to her, feeling drawn to the spot like a magnet does iron.

A new sort of smile formed on Seren's lips. Conspiratorial? She seemed suddenly awake as if from a daze and said, "My mother needs our mattock and plow blade repaired. She hoped your father would be here to work on them."

There was a note of regret at the end that caused a complementing chord of Anargen's heart to be strummed. Without either of the tools it could seriously hamper her family's food stores. "I can do it."

An immediate flowering of hope, stark and beautiful, was evident in her demeanor, forcing Anargen to catch himself and amend, "I mean, I should be able to. If you don't mind a novice working on them?"

"That would be wonderful! Thank you, Anargen," she said and looked as if she might have hugged him had a sizable log not been draped across his arms. "The tools are at home. I can retrieve them —"

"No, no, it's okay," he interrupted as he finally tossed the troublesome bit of timber into the fire pit. "I can come get them later, around dusk? It's the least I can do after making you wait for me."

She nodded. "That would be lovely."

Again, a tense silence followed, or it felt so for Anargen, which was unusual. Anargen scrambled to find something to keep Seren there a little longer and came upon an obvious bit of news, "I missed telling you! I pledged myself to the High King last night."

"You did?" Seren replied, genuine surprise overtaking whatever remained in her gaze.

"The vision just came to me. I'm to be a Knight of Light. The ceremony is in two nights," he recalled.

"That's wonderful. You've wanted this for so long," she replied, a genuineness to her smile that made her all the lovelier in Anargen's estimation. "What must you do after that?"

Anargen shrugged. "I'm not sure. Every Knight has a great Quest that is pursued throughout life. Sometimes they are simple, never roving far or doing great deeds. Sometimes," a sudden lump in his throat as the memory of the night before struck him again, "fantastic, roving far and changing the Lowlands indefinitely."

As he watched, Seren's face fell. Something he had said troubled her, perhaps his tone? Anargen's brows furrowed, and he inquired, sheepish, "Seren?"

"I need to go," she replied quietly, her gaze dropping to the floor. "Thank you again, Anargen."

Seren turned to leave, and Anargen was gripped by guilt's accusation that he had hurt her some way. Instinctively, his hand shot out and grabbed hers. "Wait!" he pleaded.

The suddenness of her stop and the wide set of her eyes jarred Anargen back to his senses. He had never been so bold as to hold her hand before. It felt soft and warm and welcome as he ever imagined. More.

Immediately he dropped his hold, shame scorching his cheeks. "Sorry, I just — I didn't want you to leave looking so sad. I've said something upsetting, haven't I?"

For a moment, Seren hesitated, looking at him with a thoughtful knit to her brows. Slow and cautious, she faced him and took his hand in hers. "No. You were fine. But I need to tell you something. You remember my mother has always wished I would return to our home in Stormridge?"

Anargen nodded, though it was partly reflexive, because he was still marveling over how gently she held his hand in hers. Wait! Was she telling him she was leaving for good?

"Well," Seren continued, a little catch in her voice. "She has decided to accept that I don't want to go back. I want to find a suitor here and build my life in Black River instead. My mother finally realized my life would be so much more wonderful if I stayed."

A light pressure was applied to Anargen's hand, conducting

the reality of what Seren was implying to him. If his cheeks hadn't been reddened before, they certainly were now. His heart raced, as if it needed to roam the whole world to make sure it was indeed the same world he had always known and not some fantastical dream. The journey must have taken Anargen's heart too long, because Seren started to release his hand and murmured, "Anargen?"

He looked into her eyes and saw the anxiety there. She thought he was distraught over this. Again, as though a negative force of pain in her needed a canceling positive from him, he acted on impulse and leaned forward to kiss her.

It hadn't occurred to him she might resist or step back. Not until it was too late anyway. Which was good, because had he, he never would've tried, and he wouldn't have known how soft her lips were and how sweet the sensation of such an embrace could become when she returned that pressure. Far better than he imagined.

Though it lasted only precious seconds, when he opened his eyes, a new pleasure and warmth radiated through him as he saw that conspiratorial smile from earlier on Seren's face restored.

This is what love looks like.

"I'm glad you are pleased too," she noted with a light laugh then stepped back. "I'll see you tonight at dusk?"

"At dusk," he confirmed, feeling like even the vast canyons of Kernsgulch could not keep him from doing so.

"Good," she replied and then leaned forward and brushed his cheek with the gentlest of kisses. "Till then," she whispered, the scent of honeysuckle encircling Anargen.

Then she walked to the door, waved, and was gone.

Drawing in a shaky breath, Anargen found a stool to drop onto. Was this whole week a midsummer's dream? Touching his cheek, which still coursed with warmness from the kiss, he hoped not.

4

INQUISITIVE

TRYING to work after Seren left was futile. Every thought clung to her face, her smile, the anticipation of the evening ahead and days to come. Anargen could not even bring himself to light the fire in the forge.

An hour or more passed. No one came. Caeserus had broken his word and wasn't going to show. Glewdyn's other apprentice was notably absent as well. Arnauld was a man from Ecthelowall in his thirties, whom Anargen's father had offered an apprenticeship after he came starving to the Knight Hall one chilly, winter night. Not much else was known of his past, though he often mumbled reverent tunes about the sea and rubbed at a bit of amber slung from a leather cord around his neck.

Whatever kept everyone away, the solitude and Anargen's overactive imagination weren't benefitting him. Though filled with goodness, never had his life felt so upended. Standing suddenly, he resolved to take his mind off the pleasant torments by reading in the Knight Hall.

When he entered the Hall, he found it incredibly still and somewhat stuffy. The large glass windows high above his head let in plenty of light and heat from the summer day. Anargen watched as dust motes twirled in a lackadaisical dance through the bright white beams pouring over every surface of the room.

Seeing no one to speak to for permission, Anargen headed deeper into the building, following a hall that led to the library of sorts. En route, he passed by an open room on his right, and a few steps later, he paused to peer back. He had just passed the dueling room.

Anargen peered down the hall toward the modest library. He had already read all the books in the Hall's collections. What he had never done was handle a Spiritsword. The blade wielded by Knights of Light, said to be imbued with power from the High King. Many legends circulated bestowing honor or disparaging the prowess of the Spiritsword and its wielders.

Shaking his head, Anargen reminded himself this was supposed to be a calming exercise, not practice in being daring. A few purposeful strides put him in the library. Black River's Hall held a collection both impressive and modest. Impressive for the size of the village but nothing compared to the great libraries of the world. Seren had told Anargen about one in Stormridge which held a copy of every work of literature and philosophy ever recorded in the Lowlands. That bit of information had set Anargen's mind reeling over what such a grand place must be like.

But this wasn't Stormridge, so Anargen fetched a well perused copy of the history of the region. Black River was one of a collection of villages in the County of Walhonde. Walhonde in turn belonged to the country of Libertias.

Libertias had been forged when Ecthelowall's grip on the lands, so distant from its heartland, had become choking. The rebellion had been devastating for both sides by accounts, but at its end, Libertias was born. Ruled by a council of counts with the most powerful count given the added title viscount, Libertias had lasted for more than a century now.

Once Anargen had thought to ask Arnauld what he felt about Libertias, given his Ecthelish descent. Looking up from a spade he was crafting with a quizzical expression, Arnauld had replied, "You mean this speck of a village is in the great land of Libertias?"

After that, Anargen didn't venture to ask Arnauld many questions of any sort. Though he understood the underlying commentary. Black River was not a prosperous city like many in Libertias. Even West Haven and Raresbruck, twin cities and jewels of Walhonde, were nothing to the greater world beyond. If there were no mines in Walhonde, Anargen often wondered if the whole region would disappear from maps of the Lowlands.

A couple hours passed as Anargen re-read the familiar stories and histories. It was to no avail though. Anxious energy still coursed through him and of all the things to be obsessing over, now he could not get the room with the Spiritsword out of his mind.

Huffing out a sigh, Anargen slammed shut the book and crept back along the hall. Heart thrumming, he ducked into the doorway and drew a steadying breath.

In the long room's quiet enclosure was an array of swords laid out for use in practice by Knights of the Hall. Anyone might come in for shelter or a meal or simply to learn from the wisest Knights. Only Knights who had dedicated themselves to the Hall's work and pledged to come in an hour of need and defense could obtain the title Knight of the Hall. Among the twelve or so in Black River were Anargen's father and mother and Sir Cinaed.

The swords along the wall were not his father's work, but rather were delivered from afar. Though a blacksmith, Glewdyn rarely received orders for swords. Most of what came through the shop were requests for farming tools to be fixed or for various other wares of daily living. In fact, one of Glewdyn's most prized works was crafting an ornate brass tea set for a newly married couple. Many were surprised the large, tough hands of Glewdyn could produce such intricate patterns.

Somewhere amongst the handful of blades of varying size,

shape, and make would be one special sword, a *Machaira Tou
Pneuma*, Spiritsword. The very words of the High King were
inscribed upon it. No other sword had ever existed to be its
equal.

Though Anargen had never seen it or even tried to touch
one, it was said when a Knight took hold of its hilt, the Spiritsword would take on a life of its own. Fire would catch on the
blade and burn till released, though it neither burned the holder
nor charred the sword or softened it. It was afire without being
consumed.

Or so it was told. Legends also said only Knights saw such a
thing take place. In more ancient times, many could see the
effect, but now, something was different. There were whispered
stories of darker lands where the High King's rule had never
been accepted still having such a keen awareness of the blades'
powers. This, of course, induced riotous laughter amongst those
who doubted the verity of the stories about the Spiritswords.
Anargen had always taken it to be something like seeing stars in
the day. Where there is already some light, it is more difficult to
notice a star. But against the night sky they gleam like precious
gems in indigo mines.

Anargen licked his lips which were suddenly dry. He had
been in this room before, but never before as a Knight, or at
least one soon to be confirmed as a Knight. Knowing the stories,
the idea of getting to witness the marvel of the Spiritsword was
like the inescapable pull of gravity for him.

He made his way over to a grouping of swords. None of
them looked particularly magnificent or capable of the wonders
ascribed to a Spiritsword. Several had some inscriptions on their
blades.

Gnawing on his lip for a moment, Anargen spared one more
glance to ensure he was alone and then grabbed a sword and
jerked it from its pine rack before he could talk himself out of
it. A silly thing to do. The blade got stuck halfway out because
of the poor angle. Anargen spent the next several seconds

tugging at the blade as he was overcome with anxiety and frustration.

When he realized it would do no good, he took a deep breath and freed it from the groove it was cutting into the rack's wood and slid it out the rest of the way. Holding it up, he stared intently.

Nothing happened.

He got into a guard stance, mimicking what he had observed of other Knights. Muscles tensed, he stood as rigid and still as possible, holding the pose till he felt the gentle burn of his muscles tiring.

Nothing happened.

He swung the sword around.

There was a slight rush of air and nothing more.

Sighing, Anargen went through an entire series of slashes, guards, and stabs. Battling invisible opponents, he parried and countered, sortied and delivered finishing blows. One imaginary foe after another fell to the sword.

At length, he was breathing heavily and had only three swords left to choose from. Even as he put back his most recent choice, he noticed it. One sword, slightly longer, double-edged and gleaming with an argent nobility. Well-polished, it was adorned in so many characters of small and precise script, Anargen could scarcely read them. A padded leather hilt showed little use and in the cross-guard and pommel were carvings of a lion, or was it a radiant lamb?

In an instant, his heart knew what his mind was more slowly coming to accept. This was a Spiritsword. The one he had been looking for all this time. He drew near slowly, in fear. Not fear as of a snake that could strike an incautious palm, but a reverent fear.

Swallowing and gnawing on his lip, he reached out with ginger fingers to brush the hilt of the Spiritsword. For a split second Anargen thought he could feel heat rising off the blade and hear a crackle.

"Are you sure you're ready to handle such a sword?" someone enquired from behind.

Stunned, Anargen whirled round to find Sir Cinaed watching him with a thoughtful expression. "Don't let me stop you. For one so young and new to the Order, you have excellent form," Sir Cinaed's deep voice intoned.

Immediately the teen tensed from neck to knees. Stiffened by reluctance, Anargen turned around and hid both hands behind his back. "Thank you, sir."

All Anargen wanted to do was slip out. His cheeks grew warm and he had little doubt they looked like they were on fire. Given his intention to sneak and observe the Spiritsword, the irony wasn't lost on him.

Sir Cinaed crossed the room and placed a large hand on Anargen's shoulder and gave it a squeeze. "What brought you in here? I don't believe I have ever seen you practicing before."

Anargen offered a rueful smile but really didn't know what to say. He wasn't sure what the punishment for something like this would be. The truth burst out on the breakers of a sigh. "I wanted to see what the legends speak of."

To Anargen's surprise, Sir Cinaed grinned broadly. "We prefer an experienced Knight be present when first learning to wield a Spiritsword, but I'm proud of your inquisitiveness. Nightfall is approaching, so I must attend to other matters. Another time, however, I can instruct you myself."

"That would be fantastic." the words had just left Anargen's mouth in an excited rush when he realized all of what Sir Cinaed had said. "Seren! I'll be late!"

The young Knight started to run past Sir Cinaed but skidded to a halt and whirled around. "I'm sorry, sir. I'm running late!"

A deep, rumbling chuckle echoed in the room as Sir Cinaed noted, "Seren is much lovelier company than me." The mirth gave way to a sudden somber note in conclusion. "Just keep a keen eye. Always."

5

STRANGELY MET

NIGHT WAS heavy on the land when Anargen made the trek back from Seren's home, toting her family's tools. Cutting it close on the time, Anargen arrived to see Seren waiting outside. Fortunately, he had the presence of mind to harvest a few tiger lilies on the way to see her. He had remembered they were her favorite flower. Seren's smile was his reward.

Rather than simply give him the tools, Seren took him with her to the edge of her family's lands which ended in a wide meadow. They sat on a hillock that looked out over the land in all directions. Anargen would have been a wretched liar to say he hadn't been nervous about things being different between them. Though it was what he'd always wanted, it was new. Much like his newness to Knighthood.

Seren, of course, picked up on his anxieties and took his hand. "You know, I read a Knight's chronicle of his Quest once in Stormridge. He said, 'The future is only that which the Great King has prepared us for, by way of all that is past.'"

Awed by the apt words, Anargen had looked at her and said, "You are beautiful." And immediately after wanted to throw himself off the hill, because he'd meant to say that of her words.

Seren only giggled and said, "Don't look so stricken. I'm glad you see beauty in me. I see it in you too, Anargen."

That was when they shared their second kiss.

Three hours had passed since he received the kiss, but his lips still lingered on its welcome warmth. Parting from Seren had been a challenge but one Anargen knew he needed to master. He had to get the tools to his father's shop and drop them off for the morning and still make the trek home. Black River was hardly a den of thieves and unsavory types, but it was not without dangers in the darkest hours of night. Such an hour was upon the land. No one save Anargen was likely to be awake.

Anargen had not made it halfway through the village, however, when he saw light coming from the Knight Hall's lower windows. That meant many candles remained lit, and there must be a number of people there this night. Including Cinaed.

Suddenly, Anargen remembered the great bear of a Knight's understanding and felt a pang of guilt. A singular thought gripped him: "I should apologize for rushing out on him."

Anargen walked with furtive footfalls up to the doors of the Hall. Opening them slowly, he hoped he wouldn't disturb whatever proceedings were taking place inside. The Hall's gathering chamber was empty of people but filled with the shining envoys of the many candles.

Rather than turn back, Anargen pressed forward till at last he heard a pair of hushed voices discussing something. Approaching with all the more caution, he found Sir Cinaed in the library standing with his arms crossed over his chest. In one hand he gripped a letter as he scowled down at something.

Peeking in against his better judgment, Anargen saw a short, stout figure robed in a thick, dark cloak standing opposite Cinaed. The Knight Errant seemed displeased with the visitor, whose countenance Anargen could only imagine.

This stranger was too small to be a man, but much too large to be a child. What's more, the fabric which made up his cloak appeared to be richly textured, smooth and soft, rather than the woolen stuff Anargen was accustomed to. Coupled with its rich indigo coloring, the cloak suggested this was someone of importance or means. Then Anargen caught a glimpse of a gauntlet-shod hand, ornate and bejeweled, waving deferentially at Cinaed.

Who are you, stranger?

The whole time Anargen had fixated on the little man, but as he looked at Sir Cinaed, he felt a jolt of anxiety. Cinaed's usual ease of manner and jovial nature seemed buried beneath a thousand layers of emotions Anargen could only guess after. Some of the words were lost to mumbling, but Cinaed's expression darkened into what Anargen took to be bitterness. A few more terse utterances were issued from the dour facsimile of Cinaed.

Turning to creep away, Anargen was almost to the end of the hall when he stumbled, dumping the iron keys from his pocket. They hit the floor with a hideous clang.

Frozen where he stood, Anargen heard stirring in the library. Scooping up his keys, he sprinted out of the Hall, headed for his house. The last bits of the conversation he understood cycled through his mind many times over: "I will bring this matter before the Great King once more. Go or stay, I'm sure you will have your answer by this time tomorrow."

6

STANDING ON CEREMONY

TWIGS SNAPPED underfoot as Anargen strode through the forest. Normally he tried to be quieter, but night had fallen, and he was not alone.

"Are you sure this is the way?" Seren asked, glancing back the way they'd come.

Anargen just grinned. The woods around Black River tended to be dense. Most of its paths were just deer trails. For the uninitiated, they would seem labyrinthine. "Absolutely. My father has taken me through here often. Have some faith."

She reached out and gave his hand a squeeze. "If there are any who wander without being lost, I'm sure it is you. Lead the way."

It was nice being able to show her something for a change. "Okay, stay close. We'll be coming up on the river bank soon. Watch out for roots too, they'll trip you up."

"Oh, I see. Don't want to fall in. With all that coal on the bottom, the river is dark enough during the day."

"The current isn't very fast, but it's definitely not how you want this night to end." He laughed.

"How do you want this night to end?" she asked, innocence in her voice.

Honestly, he didn't want it to end, ever. "Any way except returning you home sopping wet. I'm sure your mother is grateful for the tools, but that would probably ruin me in her eyes."

"Oh, no it wouldn't. It couldn't undo all that good. The craftsmanship was impressive. You're more a blacksmith than you admit."

"Ha! From the look of shock on Arnauld's face when I'd finished, you'd think I'm never in that shop." Anargen half-turned and imitated the expression. Something close to how a rock would look surprised.

"Well, you really aren't there often," she pointed out chuckling. "Didn't you even leave early today to bring the tools?"

"Yes, but really it was you who suggested I show you these woods. So, I think it might be you who kept me from returning to my duties."

"Oh," she huffed in mock fluster and gave him a shove. As she did, she pitched forward suddenly with a squeal of surprise.

Anargen spun and caught her. For a few seconds, he held her like that, his heart racing, ready to catch her many times over. He helped her back to steady footing. Though not with any haste, he enjoyed the closeness more than was proper.

"Thank you," she whispered.

"My pleasure." Feeling his awkward nature strangling him for what to do or say next, he cleared his throat. "Like I said, watch out for roots."

A smirk crept up on Seren's lips. "Duly noted." Linking her arm in his, she laid her head against him and said, "Though it's probably best I stay close."

"I agree." Against his will, his heartbeat raced faster. It wouldn't be so embarrassing were Seren's ear not so near to hear the change. Strangely, the rhythm calmed considerably after a minute or so more walking with her. There was something so easy about it. Soothing.

He needed it with the maelstrom of abnormal happenings

this week. All day he'd dreaded Sir Cinaed showing up, or worse his strange little visitor. Seren made all of it seem so far away.

By the time they reached the water's edge, it had to be an hour till midnight. "Here we are," he said gesturing to a small jetty. "The best place to view the stars in Walhonde."

From the way Seren's mouth hung open, eyes wide, he knew she agreed. The river was wide here and the already dark waters were as deep an indigo as the sky. In the gentle current it reflected all the starry host above. Fireflies blinked in and out of existence among the trees of the opposite shore and hovered near enough to touch. Standing on the dock, it appeared the stars were all around them.

"You never see anything like this in Stormridge," she murmured.

"You never see anything like this anywhere," he wanted to say. But he could sooner move a mountain than speak so freely. "Really? Didn't you see the stars there?"

"Well, of course. But not like this. Not half of this," she said as he helped her sit down on the weathered boards.

Dropping down beside her, he slipped his feet in the water next to hers. "Do you see any stars you recognize from there?"

After a few seconds, she nodded and pointed to the right. "That group is known as Bellafortis the Gryphon. And a little bit below is Dolosus the Wyvern. The two are supposed to be always locked in battle. 'Valor and deceit, war without respite, Battle of all souls, mirroring their strife.'"

Anargen raised his brows and Seren blushed. "It's something a poet from home wrote about them. It's much longer but that's the part I remember best. Though the myth actually comes from Ecthelowall, not Stormridge. It's tied to their ancient line of monarchs somehow. A lot of the fabric of Libertias's society is still very much . . ."

She splashed some water at him, "Anargen, are you listening?"

"Oh, yes. I'm sorry," Anargen replied. In truth, he was only half aware of what she'd said. Her poetry and the beauty of being with her here had distracted him. It was clear from her eyes. She'd fallen down the same hole into a new, other-world as him.

Amidst the gentle thrum of summer's night-pulse, he snuck another lingering kiss. In it he needn't keep wondering whether he had taken the dive so much sooner than her after all.

❖

MORNING CAME TOO SOON. He groaned and rolled out of bed. "Please, please let dreams be only dreams!"

As it had every night, the dream of the pleasant path and the sunlit road returned. Every time he had to take the sunlit one. On waking today, he feared his home and Seren somehow lay along the other. Choosing to leave now felt impossible. After a year's pursuit of Seren's affection and experiencing its wonderful reality, forming lasting scars would be unavoidable.

Whatever happened in the ceremony would decide his future. Anargen knew he should accept the elders' guidance, because he could not trust his own judgment now. It was too conflicted.

Unwilling to find confirmation of his fears, Anargen went outside the cottage to bring in some crops. He should have been gathering them over the past few days. Overall, most of the garden's goods were still prime for the picking and would keep till his father got back. Should Anargen not be there in the coming days.

Stopping where he stood, he braced himself against the frame of the house's door. The sack he'd stowed the garden's gleanings in was still hanging heavy from his other hand.

"How can I leave this behind?"

After several seconds standing there with no clear answer, Anargen noticed growing by the cottage a particularly beautiful bloom. It was as radiant a tiger lily as any he'd seen.

His first impulse was to deliver this flower straightway to his beloved Seren. A fresh swell of pain mounted up and crashed over him like a rough surf pounding the shore. When the initial pain receded, it left in its wake a frothy ache.

How could he tell her what is really going on? Visions, dreams, secret meetings. Could she understand it if even he didn't?

Faced with little alternative, Anargen allowed himself to believe Caeserus's visit, his dreams, and even witnessing the odd encounter between Cinaed and the diminutive figure must in some way be intertwined. Things happen for a reason, even if that reason is not readily or willfully apparent.

That meant he must also come to grips with the likelihood of his imminent departure from Black River and from Seren. Perhaps forever.

Anargen gnawed on his bottom lip. Logic and his convictions said one thing, but accepting the direction they led would wound him as few things in life ever had.

Stalking back into the house, Anargen sat on his bed once more, wondering if sleeping his pain away would be possible. Knowing he could not sleep even if he thought it could.

There was no hiding from it. His choice and its outcome were too important.

He had to think of something. Some way to ensure that even if he traveled far from here, his fledgling courtship of Seren would endure.

Still following this desire and all the thoughts it brought, his eyes happened on his journal. It was lying on the floor as it often was by morning. The page it was opened to was a page he'd chosen to sketch an image onto. This one was of his father, wearing the full suit of armor granted to the Knight Order. Inscribed in an artistic script beside the suit's breastplate was the ancient name for the full suit: *Panoplia tou Theos*.

Anargen had faithfully replicated the armor's features. The High King's symbol, the lion, embossed on each pauldron. The vine, a symbol of the King and His people united with its twenty-four leaves down each arm. On every article of the armor was the faint hint of the ancient lettering of the Order. Drawn almost two years ago, each detail was replicated, though it lacked the fiery pall he had never seen.

He drew this picture the day his father joined the Order and a short time before Glewdyn was named a Knight of the Hall. It was the most vivid and imposing portrait Anargen had made of his family members. He had only the faintest inkling at the time of its comfort during those long periods of separation between himself and his father. Caught in the eddy of wistfulness, realization struck Anargen. A plan coalesced before him which could assure Seren knew his love for her.

Love?

Yes, even in the brief expanse in which he was permitted to explore that possibility in earnest, Anargen knew he loved Seren. A solid passion, neither distance nor time had dictated and therefore could not diminish.

By late afternoon, Anargen finished his work, packed his satchel, and left. His first destination was the shop, which he had only a vague sense of regret for having not opened yet. When he arrived there, neither his father's apprentices nor Seren were there to greet him. Instead, Sir Cinaed stood squarely in his path as he approached.

"Hello there, Anargen. It's good to finally see you this day." Cinaed's baritone voice sounded gentle. "I have been waiting to deliver you news of when your conferral will take place."

A slow nod was the best Anargen could manage as he tried not to look guilty. This was the first he'd seen Cinaed since two nights ago.

"It will be in about three hours," Sir Cinaed stated with nothing but congeniality. "I know this is not the usual hour to hold such a ceremony, but neither you nor Caeserus are to be considered common amongst Knights. For better or worse, the elders and I have already found there remains for you both a Quest far greater than is normal for those of this small region."

Anargen found himself swallowing hard. His grey-green eyes could scarce meet the Knight Errant's.

Cinaed placed a hand on Anargen's back. His tone became gentler still. "Don't worry, lad. Your father and mother will be informed of your choice. The Great King is faithful. He has not chosen any task for you that he hasn't found you and formed you fully for."

The teen pieced together a smile. Anargen hadn't even given conscious consideration of what his departure would mean for his family. An only child of two parents who had borne him late in life, his parents had raised him with unwavering love. Beyond a deep respect, he felt as if they were the closest of friends. Leaving now, before they returned, might mean never seeing them again in the Lowlands. Moreover, it was not lost on Anargen that Sir Cinaed's sentiments were the same as Seren's comforts two nights ago. If less elegant than the philosopher she had quoted.

Noticing Anargen's brooding, Cinaed wisely bade Anargen a farewell and reminded him once more of his anticipation that this night would reveal goodly things awaiting him.

After Sir Cinaed had walked off, Anargen tried to go about his day. He opened the shop and even took a few orders from villagers. Some avowed to attend his conferral ceremony later that evening. Others simply expressed hope their orders would be filled before too many days passed. "Your shop's hours have been oddly out of sorts the past few days," one man noted. A couple prickly comments about both the master smith and his apprentices slacking at their labors rifled with Anargen's emotions still further.

For his part, Anargen kept a rigid calm and managed to offer token assurances all would be well. He made sure to scribble down the orders of the iratest customers in larger print. On the off chance they could read, it might convince them their work would be highest priority.

After the early press of patrons, the remaining two hours

before his conferral ceremony were markedly quiet. As was usual with time's passing when one was unwilling to allow a single second's departure, the two hours melted into what seemed like a half hour's breadth.

Time for introspection was at an end, and he was no more at ease with the impending direction of his fate than when he awoke. Amidst it all, Anargen was aware of sensation, deep within his heart, soft and comforting. As of a father's reassuring hand on the shoulder of his son. Holding tight to its soothing, he exited his father's shop, locked it tight, and headed with slow, purposeful steps towards the Knight Hall.

7

MIRTHLESS MATTER

WITHIN THE KNIGHT Hall there were no special banners or lavish decorations commemorating the impending event. No additional candles were lit or mood-altering effects sought after for the main room's atmosphere. Still, there was a kind of excitement present.

A surge of nervousness flooded Anargen. There were more people than expected. Moreover, he realized they were all dressed in their finest outfits. How had he forgotten to dress in something better than his common clothes? Anargen swallowed back the ill ease choking him and walked towards the front, seeking out Sir Cinaed.

Still more surprises awaited Anargen. Beside Cinaed stood his other good friend, Bertinand. From snippets of their conversation, it seemed Bertinand, too, had become a Knight within the past three days. His conferral was this evening as well.

Bertinand was by nature a humorist. Though sometimes his sense of comedy fell flat with Anargen. Not to mention, Anargen was aware Bertinand had some feelings for Seren. Watching him now, he seemed his usual buoyant self.

In stark contrast to Bertinand's enthusiasm was Caeserus. Relieved, Anargen called out to him, "You're here!"

His friend did not reply as he came to stand nearby. A cool concentration radiated from Caeserus. Shrugging off the reticence, Anargen decided not to disturb his friend's thoughts. Fortunately, the interim was short, and the proceedings began.

The three teens stood before the elders of the Hall in a row and quietly heard them out on some preliminary questions and statements. Most of which were meant to calm their nerves and assure them this was just a formality. Ceremony to display for others the wonder of the vision they had seen.

Among the elders seated before them was Sir Darius, stern as mountain stone. He was about to ask a question directed at Anargen when Sir Cinaed strode forward to stand before everyone. "Fellow *Palatini Lucis Aeternae*, friends, citizens of Black River." He waited for the whispers over his interruption to fade.

"I come to you on a night celebrating the oaths of loyalty these three youths have pledged to the High King of all the realms. Fond memories of my own admittance into this Order come to mind. As do my first memories of standing before you to be honored as this hall's captain and the caretaker of your trust."

Anargen glanced over at Caeserus and Bertinand. This was not at all the conventional order to the ceremony. Though it would be fair to say Sir Cinaed was not an utterly conventional man.

Focusing on the Knight Errant, Anargen tried not to notice so many eyes on him. It felt as though they searched for some chink in his resolve to keep to his new oaths. The task was made easier, because Sir Cinaed's next words drew everyone's attention: "Which is why I find it most prudent, though it pains me dearly, to announce my departure. I am leaving Black River to travel north, where the High King leads me to fulfill a great purpose."

Whispers drifted between listeners, but Sir Cinaed did not wait for them to abate this time. "Would that I could tell you of it in full, but the nature of this journey necessitates I be spare with details. Accompanying me on this task are these three young ones before you and one other. We know not when we shall pass this way again. Rather than fill this night with trite ceremony and formality, I invite you to heartily encourage each one of us in our work for our Lord King. Let us emblaze this night of good cheer and fellowship into all our memories forevermore."

Several seconds passed before Sir Darius began clapping. Soon the room was filled with shouts and cheers. People rose from their seats and came away from the back walls as if prisoners set free. There was so much joy to behold. But Anargen found one pair of eyes in which no sign of pleasure could be found. One set of eyes which looked panicked.

Seren!

Before he could take another breath, those eyes had squeezed shut as tears began to flow. She pushed through the crowd and dashed out into the night.

Anargen felt paralyzed. None of this had happened as it should have, as he had expected. He had guessed he would be leaving soon, but tomorrow? With so little certainty of return?

It felt as though he had been pummeled to dust. In his numbness, he stumbled forward a few steps and almost tripped off the platform.

A strong hand reached out and gripped Anargen's shoulder, keeping him from falling. When Anargen looked back on his helper, he found Sir Cinaed looking at him with a thoughtful expression. The older man said, "Careful. Follow her tonight, but make sure you are in the village square to join us in the morning."

Having said that, the hand let up its hold on Anargen and without consciously telling himself to do so, he was off. He pushed through the crowds of well-wishers and out the door. In the twilight, he spotted Seren a few dozen yards away.

"Seren, wait!" he called out, but she kept walking. Running half the distance between them, he tried again. "Seren, wait!"

This time Seren hesitated for a few crucial seconds and then stopped altogether, waiting for him.

Catching up and then passing her stand in between her and her destination, he fought to get his breath. Try as he might, he all but gaped at her. She was wearing makeup and a long gown made of a soft blue fabric with a sheer white drape. It clung to her bodice as if a precise fitting. This had to be the regalest outfit she owned. Seren was beauty itself.

Anargen's eyes dropped to the ground, and he gnawed at his lip for a moment. "I don't want to leave you," he settled on at last, a sigh escaping. His chest felt tight, crowded with all the thoughts and emotions he desperately needed to express but could not coax into words.

If he hoped Seren would understand the deeper sentiments behind what he'd actually said, her scowl revealed she veered far from it. "You could have fooled me. How long have you known you were going to leave? Since you became a Knight? Before?"

Shaking his head and holding his hands up in a futile gesture of palliation, he replied, "No, no. I didn't know till today. Well, Caeserus came and . . ."

Heat radiated from her stare, and though it seared Anargen, he knew it was consuming her far more ferociously. "So, you just decided on a whim to rush off then?"

Anargen let his hands fall at his sides, and he sighed again. "No," he answered softly and then fell silent. Navigating this encounter was like being a ship in a vicious squall.

After several seconds passed, Seren said, "I should go."

As she moved to leave, Anargen reached out for her hand and grabbed hold of it. "Seren!"

She stopped without resistance. Her eyes shimmered with the tears ready to descend in their torrents again. There was hope in them. It was enough to sober Anargen from his conflicted daze. He reached into his bag and produced the letter he had written for her. "I won't try to force you to stay, but, please, read this before you go."

Eyeing him with an expression of underwhelming enthusiasm, she took the letter and opened it. The faint crinkle of the parchment could be heard as she gripped the letter ever tighter. All too soon she was at the end and looked up at him with a civil war being fought behind her gaze. "You love me."

"I do," he answered, swallowing to fight the tightness in his throat. "It has never been my intention to hurt you. I don't want to leave you."

"Then don't," she said, taking a step closer to him and taking his hand in hers again. "Stay. Anargen, it's you I want. Of all the would-be suitors pursuing me and places I could be, it's you I want."

The ache building in his chest was a maelstrom of happiness and bitterness in equally matched concerts. In the wake of one's bluster, the other would interlude and ravage what the other could not effect. Pleasure and pain, potent as he had ever partaken.

"You have no idea how much I've wanted to hear those words from you, but I don't have a choice."

"Of course you have a choice," she pleaded, squeezing his hand tighter.

"Not in the way you think," he replied, looking down at the ground. He let her pull back her hand. "I pledged my loyalty—my life—to the High King. I belong to him as a servant. It would destroy me to go back on my oaths."

"And what if it destroys me to lose you?" Seren countered quietly.

Another swell of pain broke over Anargen. Looking away at the trees, dark, jagged spires in the gathering twilight, he bit at his lip. In the night, even the most familiar sights could hold menace. Conversely, a little light could change things utterly. A little beacon of such light shown through sorrow's gale. "You don't have to lose me or me you. Even if I have to go, my love will linger here for you."

"So, you want me to wait for you?" Her brows furrowed in

frustration. "How long should I wait with no word of your life or death?" Shaking her head, Seren's expression hardened. "How long before I begin to go mad with thoughts of you giving your love to another girl from exotic lands afar? Or of you falling at the hands of some foe? How many others' genuine love should I spurn for the promise of yours?"

"No one could ever replace you," Anargen replied, his voice as steady and solid as rock. Conviction was at last shoring up his words.

"That's what you say now, but—"

"You think I would go back on my word?"

Seren gave a slight shrug and looked off towards the direction of her home. "No. Maybe? Ugh. You've never seen anything beyond Black River."

The accusation struck hard. Anargen studied her for a moment. "Not with my eyes. But every time I've spoken to you, I've glimpsed what lies beyond.

"Seren, you'll hear my love in the words of the letters I'll send, and," he produced the drawing he'd made earlier as well, "I'll let you see my love with every sight I capture."

For several moments, she regarded the picture with an unreadable expression. "It's lovely," she said, whisper-soft.

"So are you," he replied, reaching for her hand again.

This time she did not let him touch it. She backed away. Keeping her eyes averted, she said, "Goodnight, Sir Anargen."

What Anargen expected to come was a hammer's blow, a shattering, crushing pain. Instead, he felt numb, drained. He watched Seren till she was out of sight and then walked home and collapsed on his bed, devastated.

8

GONE

EARLY AS HE COULD BEAR, Anargen set out from his childhood home. He catalogued details of every little thing on the trek to town. Inscribing all in his memory should he never again pass this way. Pain from his encounter with Seren and the melancholy of his departure mingled to make the trip a miserable one.

As Anargen entered the town square, he took in a sharp breath. A small crowd was milling around. The other Knights were already on their mounts and had hitched a small wagon to a pair of additional horses. With a bit of straining, Anargen could see the cart's driver was yet another friend of his, Terrillian. A few years Anargen's senior both physically and as a Knight, it had been some time since the two had spoken. Terrillian looked much the same as the last time he'd talked with Anargen: shaved head, stern demeanor, bony features, and dark eyes that rarely seemed to open at more than slits.

Some judged Terrillian to be standoffish and cold on first approaching him, but for those who knew him, it was only half the coin. Terrillian was inexorably focused. Already working in the regional mines, he had earned a reputation for being a hard worker. Filling his quotas and then some every day. On occasion, he was prone to relaxing into the same humor Bertinand enjoyed. When he smiled, it was without doubt genuine.

No one had mentioned Terrillian would be coming, though Caeserus had said his dream involved four young Knights. Or was it four Knights? If so, they had one more Knight than necessary. Perhaps they didn't need Anargen to go after all.

At the moment the thought seized him, Sir Cinaed turned around and caught sight of Anargen. The youth's body tensed under the gaze. A quiet expression of recognition and expectation from Sir Cinaed told Anargen his first instincts about the composition of the group in Caeserus's dream was the right one.

Guess there is no escaping this. I'm leaving Black River today.

Taking in another breath, Anargen scanned the crowd, trying not to hope for his eyes to lay hold of one person in particular and knowing it was impossible not to at the same time.

She's not here.

He scanned twice more, peering as far as he could in each direction, just in case.

No. I've lost her.

A feeling of release lifted much of the weight on him. Anargen carried the wounds of sorrow and regret yet was mended by devotion to the High King. By accepting it, there was a sense of destiny's touch highlighting every facet of this journey. Indeed, now that he let himself look down this road, he felt a surge of strength and comfort wash over him. Fear would not crush him. Anargen would fulfill his oath. Though the shadow of guilt lurked at the edge of this new excitement, he ignored it.

The crowd was still thick around Sir Cinaed, who was taking his trusty chestnut bay horse, Swiftfoot. Anargen could also see the wagon was being loaded with a few more supplies and was to be pulled by a pair of darker Bretons. Terrillian leaned down from it, slugging Bertinand in the arm playfully as he went. Next to them, Caeserus was stiff, regal, above it all.

Anargen grimaced. He had never ridden a horse before. It had always seemed so inconsequential. Now he could almost taste the dirt he'd be eating as he faced serious embarrassment. No one would be much impressed or reassured by a Knight walking off beside his horse, but seeing one fall off would be remembered in jokes for years to come.

His teeth ground at each other, and he looked away from his looming humiliation. Standing to the side, beside Glewdyn's smithy, was Arnauld. "Oh, yeah," Anargen said aloud to no one in particular. Making his way over, Anargen was still several steps away when Arnauld's expression changed. The look wasn't a welcoming one.

Reaching his side, Anargen spoke in a low voice. "I'm sorry for the suddenness of this departure. But I do have to go."

Arnauld crossed his sinewy arms over his chest. His head was shorn, and he had a ruddy, rough beard which grew in short, tangled coils around his jaw, but most memorable were his piercing, green eyes. The muscles in his arms tightened. "Hmph, I'm not concerned with you leaving, but losing Caeserus is a blow. Your father promised this smithy to me, and it looks like I'll be inheriting a bereft shell."

It took an incredible amount of effort for Anargen to rein in all the diverse and visceral responses which came to mind. Somehow, he remembered where he was, what the day was, and how he could not be bothered by ingratitude. Clenching his fists at his sides, Anargen managed to suppress all but what passed for a look of surprise.

Of course, why should it be a surprise Arnauld had no respect for him? Given how much distance Anargen had always put between himself and the smithy. It may have been insulting to the man to be offered a prize Anargen had so boldly rejected. Now he was leaving, and Arnauld would be here holding what he had called a "shell" together.

Gentler for his thoughts, Anargen's replied, "Father won't be much longer in returning. You certainly would not be wanting for help in discharging your duties while he is here."

There was a fractional narrowing of Arnauld's eyes. "If your father ever returns." There was a peculiar edge to his words. Just as quick as it came, he buried it beneath another string of comments. "Perhaps, he has gotten sucked into going off gallivanting as you and Caeserus have. One never knows."

Anargen spared a glance towards the other Knights and the crowd.

They're almost ready to leave. Better make this fast.

What those words should be escaped Anargen initially. He wanted to say something sincere, but he suspected that could lead to an altercation. Rather than work at angles, Anargen just produced the shop's keys and said, "May the High King's light shine upon you, even on your darkest days. Goodbye, Arnauld."

The keys had no more clanked into Arnauld's weathered palm than Anargen remembered he wanted to ask Arnauld about handling the letters for Seren. Arnauld responded to the blessing with a grunt and curt nod. He slipped into the shop and, without another glance back, the door to the shop slammed shut.

"Guess that opportunity is lost," Anargen muttered. Perhaps he didn't need a courier in town. Seren didn't exactly leave an open door either the night before.

In spite of himself, Anargen again looked around at those gathered.

No Seren. Time to go anyway.

With heavy steps, Anargen made his way towards Sir Cinaed. As he sieved through the ranks, people realized it was him. A gauntlet of congratulations, well wishes, slaps on the back, and a few leers fell upon him. By the time the crowd parted, Anargen was smiling but had an icy lump forming in his deepest recesses.

"Good morning, Anargen. Are you ready to go?" Sir Cinaed

asked from a short distance. A faint hint of concern was present in the way he regarded the youth.

Anargen's mouth had long since gone dry, so as he stood there, he had a hard time choking out the words. "I'm ready." In some sense of the word.

Another hand clapped Anargen on the back. He whirled around to find Sir Darius grinning at him. Darius was breaking drastically from his usually minimalist pallet of emotional colors. "This is quite something, Anargen. You will be bringing honor to your family, this town, and most of all, to our Great King."

"Yes," Anargen answered, stiffly, still having trouble adjusting to the new Darius he was meeting. "It is a great honor, humbling." Anargen tried to cover his awkwardness by looking away from Darius. At that moment, his eyes found her.

Seren was standing amidst the crowd. She looked like she wanted to get closer but couldn't push past everyone. Her eyes caught his, and they both just stood, locked to one another for what felt like a very long time. Yet when their eyes did drop, it did not feel long enough. Darius was still standing there, potentially oblivious to what transpired.

It's now or never.

Reaching into the sack he carried, Anargen pulled out the parchments bearing a letter to Seren he'd written early this morning. Clearing his throat, Anargen asked, "Sir Darius, could you carry these to Seren? She is the dark-haired girl, there." He pointed to her as discretely as he was able.

The elder Knight looked at each young person and nodded, intrigue the only reaction showing through on his face. "I can. Do you want me to do so now?"

"Yes, please, if you could," Anargen replied, feeling guilty for asking but unable to not risk doing so.

"Just a moment," he said and began working around the edges of the crowd.

"It's time to go, Anargen," Sir Cinaed said from Anargen's side, having walked up to fill the void Sir Darius left.

"I know, just . . ." Anargen could see Darius had slipped to Seren's side and was giving her the parchments. She took them with apparent reluctance, not even really looking at them, and glanced at Anargen. There was a haunted look about her.

She broke the gaze quickly and heard Darius say something. Her ruddy lips moved in a short burst, and he nodded. Darius filtered his way back through the crowd with more forcefulness than Seren would have felt comfortable using. "Need a moment," Anargen finished.

By now, Sir Cinaed had tracked Anargen's line of sight to Seren and could see Sir Darius coming. The Knight Errant pursed his lips and rumbled out something Anargen couldn't quite understand. "Very well," was what registered audibly. "Be quick though. We haven't half as much time as you imagine."

The large man shuffled over to join the other Knights. The others were looking at Anargen expectantly, and the best Anargen could offer was a weak grin in response. In a few seconds, the crowd would also be staring at him and wondering after the handoff Darius was even now making to him.

Against rational judgment, Anargen spared a final glance at Seren and then put her letter to him in his satchel. "Thank you," he whispered to Sir Darius. The other man looked at him uncomprehending and leaned as if to better hear. "Thank you," Anargen reiterated louder.

This time Darius got the message and gave a nod, the air of decorum once more descending on him. "May the Great King's light be upon your path," he intoned.

"On yours as well," Anargen replied over his shoulder as he turned and hurried over to join the others. The crowd was indeed focused on him, the straggler, and Anargen felt the searing heat of their stares on his back. He didn't dare look back or even slow. He was at his horse and reaching to leap up on it before he had even fully considered he didn't really know how to climb up. *Help me, Great King.*

Grasping in the air, his hands fumbled, found the straps of

the saddle, and he was pulling up and, with a little extra wobble which drew some amused laughs, he was on the horse. Holding the reins his hands shook ever so slightly. Not that Anargen really worried over it, the important thing was he wasn't falling off or lying on the ground failing to climb at all. All in all, far better than he'd hoped.

There was a rewarding rush of adrenaline carried on the wave of relief, and he felt so euphoric. Anargen even felt willing to look back, laughter and gossip he'd be leaving behind of no concern for the moment.

His view atop the horse gave him a better vantage, and he easily spotted Seren. But as he did, he found she was looking at him with a worried expression, trying to mouth something to him. Her pain cut through Anargen's buoyancy like a warm knife through butter. He couldn't quite make out what she was saying. A second later, someone much larger than Seren stepped into his line of sight, blocking his view of her.

Annoyed, Anargen thought about getting down and going to her when Sir Cinaed bellowed, drawing Anargen's attention to the imposing Knight: "Farewell, dear ones. May the Great King's light ever shine upon you and the town of Black River!"

The other Knights spurred their horses on, a trot quickly becoming a gallop. Anargen looked back around again. Already the crowd was clapping and cheering. In all the commotion and enthusiasm, he still could not see Seren. There was no way of knowing if she was even in the same spot or amongst the throng at all.

Gnawing on his bottom lip, Anargen felt the pull of the other Knights' departure and knew he already had to catch up. Amongst his minimal bits of riding knowledge was at least the ability to spur his horse on. Doing so there was a slight jerk as the horse took off faster than he intended. Anargen wobbled in the saddle, forced to look ahead lest he fall off.

All around the road, the landscape streamed past. Ahead he was closing in on the others, who weren't as far as he imagined.

At his back, fading from hearing and sight, was a raucous cheer raised by his dramatic exit. Somewhere in the midst had to be Seren, who had desperately wanted to say something. He had her letter, but had she changed her mind about what it said? For the better or the worse?

It was too late now. He could not go back. Catching up to the others, his horse slowed of its own accord, keeping pace with the other Knights' mounts. Silent and fervent, Anargen said his goodbye to Seren, his absent family, and to his home. Trying not to let the emotion of it all cripple him, he set his eyes on the road and the journey ahead.

9

THE FIRST LEG

"Taking the first step was hard. Every step after, I watch in awe to see where my foot will fall. There is so much to discover. Far beyond what I had imagined."

- ANARGEN'S JOURNEY JOURNAL,
SUMMER 1605 M.E.

AFTER THREE HOURS OF RIDING, the pace slowed. Rolling hillocks around Black River gave way to the mountains on the edges of Walhonde's borders. Most of their travel had been spent in a wide valley. Cinaed kept them on a road well demarked that wound towards the base of a mountain known as Maple Point.

The whole area was covered in a dense sweet gum and maple forests. In summer it was green and plain, but in the fall, it was called the Mountains of Fire. At that time of year, all around the landscape blazed with leaves of yellow, orange, red, and burgundy. Anargen had never witnessed this for himself, having only traveled this far a few times in the seventeen years of his life. A shame he would never see it now.

The group was getting close to the regional mines, upon

which Black River and Walhonde were so dependent. They were still an hour away via the pass between Maple Point and its nearest sister mountain, Elwell's Knob. Beyond the pass awaited the mining town, Ironfork. Anargen expected they would take their first rest there.

It was quite a surprise when Sir Cinaed rode up to a sparse stand of Elm trees. "Okay, lads, let's stop here for a moment. Go, fill up your skins at the river."

Bertinand was the first to dismount and made for the River Middling. A clear mountain stream, it eventually forked into the Black and Little Middling Rivers several miles away. Terrillian wasn't far behind Bertinand, calling out, "He said, 'Fill your skins', not take a dunk you lout!"

"I'd be more worried about him dunking you," Caeserus called out after them, laughing. It was the first time Anargen had seen him happy since the night he'd shown up demanding they leave Black River.

Caeserus looked over at Anargen, who was still struggling to get his horse fully stopped, and said, "Come on, quit playing around. I think we're looking at a fantastic chance to douse Bertinand in the river and get a little revenge for when he lost you the tournament at the summer harvest last year!"

Anargen's first meeting with Seren flared before his mind's eye with painful clarity. He could hardly say he begrudged Bertinand for it. More importantly, Anargen didn't know if he could rein in his horse enough to dismount. "You go ahead," he answered with a strained chuckle, discretely battling to keep his horse from wandering aimlessly away. "I'll be along in just a moment."

"Hmm, all right, but I make no promises about waiting. If the opportunity presents itself . . ." Caeserus shrugged and dropped to the ground without effort. A few seconds later his horse was tethered to the nearest tree and he was off after his quarry. This left Anargen to more openly flounder with his steed.

The painted horse was impressive, well-muscled, with a

smooth gait and calm demeanor. Its creamy white and brown coat patterns reminded Anargen of snow on Black River's trees during winter. But the horse, for all its graces, was beyond his control. "Come on, now," he pleaded. "Good boy, let's get you to the tree, and you can have some delicious grass."

Not even bothering to snort in dismissal of Anargen's pleas, the horse simply meandered further from the tree. It was headed to where Sir Cinaed had steered his mount and was watching the antics of the three other teens. The older Knight caught their approach and moved to intercept them. "Whoa," he instructed Anargen's mount, and the animal faithfully obeyed him. Patting it on the muzzle, Sir Cinaed smiled broadly to the horse but grew stern as he looked at Anargen. "Having some troubles with Patch, are you?"

"Patch?" Anargen asked then glanced down at the horse. "Oh, this horse? Maybe a little. To be honest I don't have much riding experience." Anargen flashed an innocent grin, still concerned his horse would be taken of a whim to go trotting off somewhere else.

"I see," the older man said, as if amused by the entendre of his words. Cinaed shifted in his saddle, redirecting his horse to come alongside Anargen. "Let me help you out, lad. The way you're handling the horse is just short of abuse."

"Oh!" Anargen said, momentarily horrified. Just long enough to see the other furrow his brow with a quiet amusement, tipping Anargen off he was exaggerating. "So, what is my first lesson?" Anargen quickly recovered.

"Well, for starters, you're holding the reins wrong," he said, grasping the worn leather straps and rearranging them for Anargen so that they looped over the backs of Anargen's palms. Tugging on them, he said, "See?"

"Yeah, thanks," Anargen said, abashed at missing something so basic.

"You know how to start and stop a horse's gait?" Sir Cinaed's voice sounded as though it was a rhetorical question.

Anargen's head dropped, and he stared down at Patch. "No, not really. I know I have to squeeze his sides?"

"Close, but watch me," Cinaed instructed, demonstrating in a few looping lopes with his horse starting, stopping, and adjusting its pace. After this, he shared some general tips with Anargen and had the youth practice some of the lessons to modest success.

"You'll get the hang of it in time." Sir Cinaed reassured. "Patch is a forgiving horse."

"A gift for which I have you to thank?" Anargen replied, calming and even enjoying the exercise having gained new bearings on it all. The other Knight gave a slight nod in reply. Quiet settled in, and Anargen, for want of something to say, asked, "I take it we'll be traveling by horse a long way?"

"Long enough," Sir Cinaed answered, immediately guarded. "We'll be going to the far north, so we have a lot of ground to cover in general before fall sets in."

"Oh. A long trip, over a long time," Anargen murmured to himself, thinking on his unopened letter from Seren for the first time. Still in his bag, he dreaded opening it.

"You looked reluctant to leave earlier," Sir Cinaed commented into Anargen's wistful thoughts. "Seren wasn't willing to live in wait for you, was she?"

Rose hues bloomed over Anargen's cheeks. "I, uh, well, I don't know. I don't suppose so. I mean, she gave me this letter, but I haven't read it yet." Anargen reached into his bag and produced the letter, turning it over and over in display.

There was a pause of a few seconds, and Sir Cinaed took in a heavy breath. "The Great King will show you what is best. But from my experience, tying yourself to anything, or anyone, pulling against the direction our High King leads you will only serve to hinder you from fulfilling your oath to him and bring you great sorrow. Tread carefully, Anargen."

Swallowing against the constricting of his throat, Anargen answered, "Thank you, Sir." Anargen placed the letter, with ginger care, back into his satchel and looked up at Sir Cinaed, unsure what to do or say.

The Knight Errant glanced up at the sky, the wrinkles on his forehead bunching. "Today is a good day for travel. We'll use what of it we can. Go round up the others. We need to be on our way."

Anargen nodded and put his new knowledge of horses to the test. Bringing Patch around, he directed him over to where the other Knights had begun relaxing. Bertinand still appeared mostly dry, though his hair was damp, as was Terrillian's. The two were still picking at one another as Anargen approached, perhaps just waiting for the right moment to pounce and launch the other into the river. Caeserus, however, was absolutely dry and leaning against a tree, arms crossed over his chest. It looked to Anargen as if Caeserus was glowering at him.

Sparing a glance at the harmless battle going on closer to the river, Anargen opted to investigate the source of Caeserus's baleful stare. He dropped to the ground with at least some dignity intact and tethered Patch to a tree. Taking his water skin with him, he headed over to where Caeserus stood. Before Anargen reached his friend, the other snapped free from the tree and asked, "What did Sir Cinaed want with you?"

"Just giving me some advice for the trip," Anargen answered with a shrug. Though Caeserus had been his friend since they were both kids, Anargen drew the line at revealing his incompetence with a horse and failing to make sense out of his first love.

"Did he?" Caeserus replied, walking towards Anargen. "Like where exactly we're going?"

"No, nothing like that," Anargen answered, tensing as the other stalked towards him. "I guess he did at least mention it would be a long journey, take a couple months at least."

From the tightening around his eyes and the firm set of his mouth, Anargen doubted Caeserus liked the answer. Confirming Anargen's suspicions, the other spit and said, "What does he think he's doing, carrying us off on some personal errand for months. My vision was about a quest we have to be on now!"

Anargen wanted to ask what Caeserus was talking about, but whether it was guidance from the High King or unease about the simmering bitterness in his friend, he resisted the urge. "Sir Cinaed asked me to get everyone ready to move on. I'll go get the others."

"You do that," Caeserus seethed and then, as Anargen slunk past, he slapped Anargen's upper arm. In a gentler tone he said, "Hey, sorry. Just let me know if you find out anything, okay?"

"Yeah, sure," Anargen agreed readily and tried his best to not rush off, much as he desperately wanted to after the encounter. Once he was a sufficient distance from his friend, he glanced back at Caeserus and saw him walking at a sluggish pace towards his horse. Caeserus's hands were folded behind his head, a sign he was conflicted about something.

"I suppose we're all having our little conflicts," Anargen mumbled to himself. As he turned around, he managed to just catch a glimpse of Terrillian heaving Bertinand into the river shallows. Anargen smirked as water splashed everywhere and the air in the quiet little vale was filled with Terrillian's laughter and Bertinand's threats of vengeance. Anargen regretted having to tell them they needed to move on.

He filled his skin with water, upriver from Bertinand's place of defeat, and then they were on their way again, though marginally quieter than before. The individual tension in the group was already beginning to work against them. Anargen could only guess what the next months would be like.

◇────────────◇

THE TREK through the mountain pass was uneventful and largely absent of conversation. For his chicanery, Terrillian had to give up his spot on the wagon to Bertinand. From Sir

Cinaed's amused expression upon seeing a sopping wet Bertinand, it was fairly evident the censure wasn't permanent.

It was a shame for Anargen there was so little distraction. Even the landscape became uninteresting. A path had been carved down into the foot of Maple Point, allowing swifter passage but leaving the road a pale grey corridor of roughhewn stone. Too high to see over, too low to create a tunnel-passage sensation or evoke awe. All this meant Anargen had time to think. To brood over whether he should open Seren's letter or not. To wonder what that last look at his departure meant. Could have meant. Should have meant.

Do I write her now? Would she want me to? Will the letters get to her?

Anargen hadn't been able to set up a specific courier before leaving. He could just let the established courier system care for his letters. It risked Seren's over-protective brother intercepting them. Though at this point it seemed silly to worry over what he thought. Seren herself might take his letters and burn them without reading.

The whole thing was too painful to dwell on. So Anargen tried to think of something, anything else. Except the only thing holding his attention against the thoughts of Seren was nearly as vexing, if for different reasons.

Why did Caeserus act so offended? What was his vision of if not the Quest they were on now?

The stone walls on either side abruptly fell away and rolling hills again dominated the landscape. Sitting at the base of one of those hillocks was Ironfork. Almost immediately, Anargen's sense of awe and excitement was tempered by the fuller picture of what he saw. All the surrounding hills were covered in the impressive array of green sentinels. Come fall, the green would give way to the fiery display for which the region was named. Around Ironfork and the mine, there was no such forestry visible. Only a dark, muddied plain, stained black by the coal dust and fragments drawn from the vein running under Maple Point.

Anargen glanced at Terrillian who was riding a few yards behind. Terrillian's jaw tensed and relaxed as he ground his teeth together.

Unsure what to say, Anargen stared at the town as they reached the valley it was staked upon. They passed a group of miners hauling carts of coal from the mine. Each man was covered in a thick, black grime from sweat and coal dust. Anargen waved, giving them a tight smile. "Hale day," he called to them. If the miners noticed him, they didn't show it. The men kept their eyes on the path ahead of them, their whole bodies tensed and quivering as if ready to collapse.

Trying to distract himself from the miners by focusing on the town was pointless. None of the buildings stood out, except one tall building sitting on the lone hill in Ironfork. It was drab grey stone, but once it must have been alabaster, with dark tiles. Evocative of an architecture used in the Ancient Era and revivalist imitations.

"A bit ostentatious, isn't it?" Anargen muttered, mostly to himself.

"You have no idea," Terrillian huffed, pulling Anargen's attention back to his friend. Terrillian's countenance darkened and tightened still further. "The mining guild owns this worthless county."

Keeping quiet, Anargen knew his face had betrayed his surprise over Terrillian's assessment. Did no one else regret leaving Black River?

"The guild built that 'town center' a few years ago. The mayor of Ironfork graciously agreed to let them use 'some' of the space in it for its purposes." Terrillian snorted. "The whole thing sits just outside Walhonde's borders so the guild doesn't pay an excise to Walhonde, but the mines are in Walhonde and the miners, so we pay Walhonde's stiff taxes and the guild gets around county-to-county tariffs."

"That's absurd," Caeserus vented, coming up beside them. "How do they get away with this?"

"They own us, that's how," Terrillian said with a shrug, throwing a hand up and letting it crash down at his side. "We barely earn enough to fully pay our housing and meal allotments. The mayor of Ironfork works the mines the same as the rest of us. No one wants to have their debts given to collectors."

"What about the county reeve? Couldn't he do something to stop it?" Anargen asked, as he watched dark faced men with picks shuffling towards the mines.

"Pfft, he and all of Walhonde are in the guild's pockets. Look, the town hall even has the guild's banner hanging off it."

Anargen's sage eyes scrutinized the building closer, and sure enough, there hanging centrally over the entrance was a black tapestry with grey borders. A pick axe and maul were copper-colored and centered over a gold rose. Each color symbolized a different mineral or metal the guild prospected. Anargen's face scrunched up on one side, feeling ill at ease with the flagrant show of favor to the guild. He understood the guilds were important and mining particularly, but at what cost?

"So," Caeserus spoke up, seeming to have concluded something of the sudden, "Does that mean you technically belong to them?"

"Technically," Terrillian replied with a scowl. "I was supposed to be coming back to the mines tomorrow."

"Are you staying here then?" Bertinand asked, ruffling the dry and stiffening fabric of his garments.

Before Terrillian could answer, Sir Cinaed dropped back and with a stern voice said, "Leave that matter to me. You four should take our coin bag and get enough supplies for another week of travel. Afterwards, wait for me at the town's inn."

"This place has its own inn?" Bertinand asked, doubtful.

"Yeah, it's on the other side of the Watcher's Nest," Terrillian answered. When the other young Knights returned blank stares, he elaborated, "The hill the guild headquarters sits on." He pointed to it for good measure.

"Wait, I thought they got 'some' space. But it's a guild headquarters? Isn't it primarily a town hall?" Caeserus questioned, a fresh hesitancy creeping into his tone.

"The guild headquarters oversees town affairs," Sir Cinaed replied, a grimness to his words.

"Isn't that illegal or at least unethical?" Bertinand questioned, glancing from person to person.

"If by illegal and unethical you mean corrupt, yes. Absolutely," Cinaed replied.

"Like most of Walhonde," Caeserus said and then spat. Anargen flinched at the display but found the sight of the guild's dominance over the lives of those it should be championing more galling with every minute.

Cinaed shook his head and rumbled, "You lads have a lot to learn about the Lowlands beyond Walhonde's borders. Hard and corrupt as officials may be here, there are far more wicked things to be found beyond this county's borders."

Along the way to the Watcher's Nest, they passed worn workers toting carts of coal like beasts of burden. Hovels was a generous term for the spotty homes built for the workers. Impossible to believe, they looked worse up close. "What could be worse than this?" Anargen mumbled to himself.

Sir Cinaed did not waste time on a formal dismissal of the teens. He was already off and travelling up the hill's road to the guild headquarters. Everyone watched until the Knight Errant reached the hill's crest.

Caeserus spoke first. "You didn't know Sir Cinaed was bringing us here to secure your contract release?" He continued to watch Sir Cinaed with a thoughtful expression, but Anargen could detect a slight change in his voice.

When Terrillian hesitated to answer, Caeserus cocked an eyebrow and looked over at the other young Knight. "Ah, no, I didn't," Terrillian admitted. "To be honest, I had hoped to never see this place again."

"Interesting . . ." Caeserus assessed, letting his words trail off into quiet musings.

"Maybe Sir Cinaed wanted to get a legal and proper release for you?" Anargen proffered. "You could have a bounty placed on you or a lien set against your family's lands otherwise, right?"

"Oh, well, yeah. I suppose so," Terrillian answered, seeming a bit reluctant.

"You know," Caeserus interjected. "Most guild offices like this would be international posts, wouldn't they?"

"I guess so," Terrillian replied. "Sometimes we would see foreigners visit the headquarters. What does that have—"

"Do they lodge there over night?" Caeserus pressed.

"Well, they sure didn't bunk with us in our huts," Terrillian snapped back.

"What is this about?" Anargen asked, trying to mask his own ire with only modest success.

Caeserus held up his hands. "Just thinking through some things."

What was Caeserus getting at?

Anargen's friend rarely gushed, but he didn't tend to play things this close to the chest either. None of it felt right. On top of it all, Anargen had the strangest feeling of being watched.

10

AN UNFORESEEN EXCHANGE

"We came for supplies, but there's something more. I can't help feeling trouble is coming for being in Ironfork."

—ANARGEN'S JOURNEY JOURNAL,
SUMMER 1605 M.E.

INSIDE THE TRADING POST, there were several different points of transaction available around the room, with a larger central counter sitting near the back.

"What is this, Terrillian?" Caeserus asked. His brows furrowed as he waved his hand in the air to clear the smoke swirling like a temptress's dance. His other hand rested on the hilt of his Spiritsword.

Terrillian answered without any apology in his voice. "This is the official company trading post, but most miners make so little, 'other' markets have moved in as well. The company looks the other way, most of the time."

"Most of the time?" Caeserus quipped with intrigue. "Isn't this all illegal?"

"All of this town is 'illegal'," Terrillian grumbled. "No one seems to complain much about any of it so long as coal and money flow out of here."

"Take it easy." Caeserus held his hands up in defense. "I just needed to know where we've gotten to with all of our gold for the trip."

Anargen's eyes widened, and he glanced around them. They were still close to the doorway, but it seemed an incredibly bold statement to blurt out in such a place. Only a few people even seemed aware of them. One, the large man behind the official counter, and one other man conducting some business in the room's corner.

The latter fellow wore a dingy grey cloak caked with dirt. He held his gaze on them just long enough to make Anargen uncomfortable. "Maybe we should be more discreet," Anargen advised, looking away before the other man had. "Or at least be about it more quickly?"

"Yeah, I'm starving," Bertinand stated, without apology." Did you see what Sir Cinaed packed for food? I say we get to it before he has the chance to fill our cart with more nonsense."

"He has to go negotiate Terrillian's release from contract," Caeserus reminded him. "He'll be gone for hours."

"I seriously doubt that," Bertinand replied. "You've seen the guy, right? Six foot two, two hundred plus pounds of 'Get out of my way?' I'm thinking they'll be happy to let Terrillian go."

Anargen didn't know if Bertinand meant for it to be funny, but Anargen couldn't help chuckling. He tried to suppress it, but it came out as a snort instead.

Caeserus snickered, "I thought Bertinand was the 'ham' here," and jabbed Anargen in the arm.

"Ugh, you're both terrible with jokes." Terrillian sighed. "But Bertinand is right. Sir Cinaed's idea of food wasn't the best I've ever eaten. Of course, neither is the food here, but at least it'll be a step up."

"Relax," Caeserus urged. "We're Knights now. We can handle ourselves." He cracked his knuckles meaningfully.

"Yeah," Terrillian said eyeing Caeserus, "and we really don't need to worry too much. There isn't that much gold."

"What do you mean?" both Caeserus and Anargen asked at the same time. "We're on a quest that spans Libertias, maybe beyond. How little do we have?" Caeserus pressed, concern and suspicion rising with his tone.

Anargen looked around. This time his hairs stood on end, as he felt the eerie, ethereal touch of another's gaze. No one was staring, not even the grey watcher, though it looked to Anargen like he was wearing a smirk. The discomfort intensified.

"I mean, we have enough for this trip and maybe one other. Less if we have to stay in an inn," Terrillian stated, weighing the pouch of gold coins in his hand. "We might make it to the coast if we forage, hunt, and stay to the wilderness the whole way," he added with a shrug and tossed Caeserus the coin bag for him to make his own assessment.

Weighing it with bouncy lifts and drops, Caeserus's brows knit in puzzlement. "This makes no sense."

"No, what makes no sense is us, still standing here, not getting some decent food," Bertinand intoned, shoving Caeserus towards the counter in the back.

Anargen tensed, waiting for Caeserus to explode on the other teen, but he just huffed out a sigh and grumbled, "Fine, let's get the stuff and get out of here." Caeserus pushed back against Bertinand, and for a brief second it seemed as though the furor Anargen expected would materialize as Caeserus added, "You can explain to Sir Cinaed why we've no more gold left and have sacks filled with pastries though."

A snort ripped free from Terrillian's lips, and he said, "Ha, pastries. Right, keep dreaming. This is still Walhonde County, not Stormridge."

Attempting to distract himself, Anargen took in a sweeping view of the room. Off to the far-right corner there appeared to be gambling and currency exchanges. He tried to not linger long in looking on them. He had heard stories of the terrible price such things carried. Here in a place of desperation though, Anargen was surprised there weren't more taking a taste of luck's liquor.

Opposite the gambling den was a table devoted to selling odd and exotic wares, most of which looked like pilfered scraps of equipment or minerals from the mine. Anargen might have had a poor angle, but he thought he saw a pickax among the offerings a man placed on the table.

Just beyond that on the left side of the room was the literal liquor-seller. The most raucous and enthusiastic customers were there, many of them miners still covered in black coal dust and ready to collapse from over-patronage. The other little sellers and bargaining areas constituted the remainder of the room's contents.

As the Knights approached the market keeper, from behind the counter a large dog, with mangy hair and eyes wild as any wolf's, bared its teeth and growled. Its master was a rotund man with an unruly beard. He wore a leather vest over a sullied white tunic and looked to be as amused at his approaching customers as his pet. "Quiet, Barrow," he boomed once the Knights stopped in front of him. "What do you need?"

"We need some supplies—" Caeserus began.

"Do you now? I wonder where you might find those around these parts?" the merchant chided, a mock thoughtful expression fading before the effect could even play out.

"Pardon?" Caeserus replied.

"Beat it, kids, I'm not here to hold anyone's hands. Buy something or shove off."

"I'm trying to, you spawn of—"

Terrillian eased forward and pushed Caeserus to the side. "Hello, Geoff. We need ten pounds of salted meat. The good stuff too. None of your muskrat knockoff. We'll also need some of your wife's hardtack and some curing salt. Oh and the closest thing to a pastry you can pass off."

"Terrillian, isn't it?" Geoff answered, his demeanor softening a fraction. "What are you doing with these soft hands?"

"Does it matter?" Terrillian countered. "You aren't in the habit of turning down gold, are you?"

"Aye, that I'm not. But you aren't in the habit of having enough to buy a fourth of the order you're needing."

For a moment, Terrillian just stood there, staring at Geoff, scrutinizing the plump merchant's hardened face. Terrillian crossed his arms over his chest and looked down his nose at the man. At last, he added, "Show him the gold, Sir Caeserus."

The expression Caeserus shot Terrillian looked like he wanted to say, "Get another servant boy." But Caeserus complied all the same, foisting the bag on to the counter and letting some gold spill out.

Geoff snatched up a coin and spun it around, observing the knotted laurel and the eagle, symbols of Libertias. He checked both sides of the coin before grunting and producing a mallet. He dropped the coin on the counter and shot Terrillian a look. Suddenly Geoff smashed the mallet onto the coin with enough force to shake the solid looking poplar counter.

He picked up the flattened disc, examined it closer, and grunted again. "Sir Caeserus, you say? Is this whelp a page of the junior militiamen or something?"

"I'm a Knight in the Order of the High King of all the realms," Caeserus fumed.

The dog behind the counter growled a warning. Neither display phased Geoff. "Been a while since anyone stuck out his chest over that claim in these parts. Where's your armor, 'Knight'?"

Caeserus looked away, gnawing on his lip. Terrillian spoke up again on his behalf. "We've not received any yet. We're passing through on a trip north." The last detail was only a guess, but Terrillian played it off as a valuable secret, vague as it was.

"What've you gotten yourself into now, boy?" Geoff asked,

shaking his head. Terrillian only shrugged, which produced the perplexing effect of a sort of weariness in Geoff. The hefty trader sighed. "Very well. Bring your horses around back. I assume you do have horses?"

A smirk turned up one corner of Terrillian's mouth. "We do. But we'll take the goods upfront here all the same. No offense, but if you tried to sneak muskrat in our sacks, I'd have to come back and let some of your other patrons know you're in the habit of doing so."

Geoff's eyes narrowed a degree. "I'm not swindling you, boy. There are bandits in these parts. The sort who would cut you open and spill your guts just to get their jollies. Sometimes they come here to sell their prizes and tell tales of what they've done."

"Thanks for the tip, we'll be on guard. Again, all the same, it would be better to look above the board on this trip. We're Knights of Light and all."

Stroking his bushy beard, Geoff grumbled, "Very well and for your information, muskrats happen to be a bit scarce right now."

"Downgraded to river rats, eh?" Terrillian jibed.

"Keep talking and the price will go up," Geoff said with a sneer.

Terrillian held up his hands and smiled. With some reluctance, Geoff began rummaging in some sacks and produced their order. Once the transaction was complete, Terrillian gave a nod and said, "A pleasure as always, Geoff."

The trader seemed to be brooding. "You children remember what I said. It's a dangerous world for soft hands playing dress up."

Terrillian pushed Caeserus along towards the door to the outside. A sufficient distance away, Caeserus asked, "How do you stand him, let alone make friends?"

"Geoff doesn't make friends with anyone. But he does give you respect if you push back the right way."

Anargen could guess his face reflected the same surprise as

Caeserus's. From their banter, the two had seemed to get along well enough. Perhaps Anargen had something to learn of "well enough" outside friendly little Black River. He took one last appreciative look on the place as the group neared the door to the outside. Anargen saw the young man in grey. He was watching them, but suddenly his attention shifted.

Following his line of sight back to Geoff, Anargen saw the merchant was staring back at the grey-clad patron. Anargen's gaze returned to the grey watcher, except, he was gone.

Making no effort to conceal his search, Anargen spun to look all around the room, but there was no sign of him. The hairs on the back of Anargen's neck stood on end.

"Everything good, Anargen?" Terrillian asked as Anargen continued to stare into the darkened corner he knew the grey watcher had been sitting in only moments earlier. Anargen couldn't resist the urge to scowl. He felt like he was going mad.

"Hello, Anargen?" Caeserus waved a hand an inch in front of Anargen's face, which Anargen was happily ready to bat aside. "What is going on with you?"

"Must be the mess with Seren," Bertinand said. "She probably broke his heart."

Every ounce of distractedness and wonderment over the eerie behavior of the grey-cloaked man evaporated in an instant. In its place was a shame and indignation that sent burning flares into his cheeks. Knowing he'd blushed in that way in front of the others only made the whole thing even more galling.

"What are you talking about?" Caeserus asked. "Anargen finally got up the nerve to talk to her and she rejected him?"

"Well, he's here with us, isn't he?" Bertinand said with a shrug. "Do you think he'd leave a girl like her if he had a say?"

Anargen could see his friend adding up the instances of hesitation on Anargen's part and assigning them to his infatuation with Seren. Either way, admitting he held any flame for Seren might further drive a wedge between him and Caeserus.

By contrast, Bertinand suddenly seemed to have eyes wide

with some unspoken thought. An emotion. Hope? Was he hoping things had gone poorly so he could court her?

Before anyone else could weigh in further, Anargen snapped, "She didn't reject me. Before I left she gave me a letter. We're going to keep in touch that way."

Anargen had gauged both friends well. Bertinand deflated some, and Caeserus looked annoyed. The latter rolled his eyes and said, "Come on, you better tell me you aren't planning to turn back now."

A furrowing of the brows was the most positive expression Anargen could manage. "No. I wouldn't go back on my oath to the Great King."

"Good," Caeserus said, though it was clear he was skeptical.

"Erhm, well," Terrillian interrupted, "I think we better get going. Sir Cinaed is probably already waiting by the city gate or half way to the coast by now."

It was clear to Anargen that Terrillian was trying to cobble together some kind of distraction, to keep the group intact. Such a thing seemed impossible to imagine given no more conversation ever caught root till well after they reached the inn and stood in wait for Sir Cinaed.

Another twenty minutes, roughly, passed before Sir Cinaed rode up to the waiting youths. At first he said nothing, just eyed each of them with a somber wariness. When he did speak, he sounded tired. "So, you have the supplies we need?"

No one answered at first, with varying reasons behind it. Now that Sir Cinaed was standing in front of them, their extravagant purchases no longer seemed as justified. Caeserus was the first to find his voice. "Yes, we got ten pounds of cured meat, some hardtack, and curing salt to use on the game we hunt."

"Expecting we would be sticking to the wilderness for the duration of the journey?" Cinaed asked, a bushy brow raised. He held up an open hand to Terrillian, waiting for the money pouch's return. The bag was lobbed to him with half-hearted enthusiasm.

Like the younger bearers of the bag, the moment he got it, Cinaed tested its weight. A crease formed on his forehead as he took on a look of shock. "How much did this cost?"

"Half," Terrillian reported, as though in utter failure. "Geoff's prices aren't reasonable, but he's the least crooked merchant here."

"Geoff of Convington?" Cinaed asked, surprise turning into something akin to suspicion.

"I think so," Terrillian replied, his posture stiffening for an impending rebuke. "Though I've never asked Geoff where he's from."

"If we didn't have so little money for such a long trip, this wouldn't be an issue," Caeserus accused, bringing his horse around closer to Cinaed's and levelling an incisive glare at the man.

On impulse, Anargen rushed to Cinaed's defense. "Is the small sum we're travelling with because we're avoiding bandits?"

Cinaed's brows lifted. "Bandits? No, not bandits in particular, though I suppose were any to be in the areas we will travel a light coin pouch might be a passive deterrent to attention."

"According to Geoff, this region is riddled with bandits. I think they help prop up Geoff's business too," Terrillian assessed rather glumly.

Anargen wondered after his friend's hesitance to suspect Geoff of ill intentions. A camaraderie amongst those consigned to the world of the mines?

"Did he?" Cinaed mused, glancing back in the direction of the town market square. "Something to keep in mind and pass on to the other Knights we meet." From his tone, Cinaed didn't seem reluctant at all to think Geoff shifty. "For now, I'm afraid all we can do is be on our way with as much care as we can manage." Spurring his horse forward, Cinaed seemed to expect the other Knights to fall in line.

"When do we find out what this trip is really about?"

Caeserus chided and reached out to grab Cinaed's arm before the larger man could turn to ride the other way.

Anargen gaped at the sudden brazenness of his friend. From the initial silence, he thought Sir Cinaed was stunned as well, but the Knight Errant showed no signs of surprise or preparation for a fierce rebuttal. His lips were pursed as he studied Caeserus with a calm but stern intrigue.

Seconds passed and Caeserus's hand dropped to his side. Cinaed answered him, "You'll find out soon enough the importance of our current task." Gentle and firm, the reply was far more respectful than Caeserus's attitude warranted.

"When is that exactly? We're supposed to be on a quest from the High King. The one from my vision," Caeserus added, his voice ringing with poignancy.

"We are on a quest from the High King," Cinaed countered, squaring his shoulders and coming to face Caeserus directly. The Knight Errant seemed to double in size and bearing. "We cannot speak of such things in detail for the moment. One cannot be too trusting of the idle ears around us. Once we are a safe distance away, I will speak more freely with all of you." His hazel eyes roved over each Knight in turn. "For now, we will press on in our journey."

The response hardly seemed to mollify Caeserus. All the less so for what had to be an intentional distinction Cinaed had made between the quest they were on and that of Caeserus's vision. Or was it only Anargen's imagining? He wasn't privy to all of the details of Caeserus's vision, or even many of them, only the involvement of four Knights. For Caeserus's obsession, it must be of dire consequence. Meaning, perhaps Sir Cinaed's was all the more so.

Without waiting for further questions to be voiced, Cinaed added, "And our benefactor on this trip will be revealed as well. Suffice it to say we will have more money available to us than we need. And fewer opportunities to use it to our benefit than you will like."

Cinaed leveled a pointed look of challenge at Caeserus.

"You may come along as planned or if you so fear me making ill use of your time, you are free to pursue your own path at your own risk."

From the look of consternation on Caeserus's face as Cinaed began riding away, the young Knight had not found anything resolved, much less to his liking. Terrillian, in turn, had already fallen in behind Cinaed, and Bertinand seemed to waver on the knife's edge of doing so as well.

Anargen tried not to gape at his friend. Caeserus had gotten Anargen into this quest, so perhaps it was only fair to let his friend direct it. Though that felt somewhat like a betrayal of his allegiance to the High King. The High King's will was to be followed over all others, even a close friend like Caeserus. It occurred to Anargen, it might feel the same way for Caeserus regarding his vision being set aside.

Sighing, Anargen wanted to make some sort of move, but found himself unable to convince himself that if he did, Caeserus would not ride off on his own. A disastrous misstep for the young Knight, whatever his ambitions and boasts.

Already Cinaed and Terrillian were fading from sight. Too much deliberation and none of them would be going along.

Bertinand was about to turn his horse to follow after Cinaed when, from his steeping, Caeserus emerged with a wry grin. "What are you muddling over? Our captain said to be on our way, let's not dawdle!"

The very next second, Caeserus's horse shot off in pursuit of Cinaed and Terrillian, leaving Bertinand and Anargen to gape at one another.

Sudden turns of view were not in Caeserus's repertoire of normal behaviors. Certainly not on this matter. Before Bertinand could add his questions on top of Anargen's, Anargen shrugged to the other Knight and pulled his horse around to pursue the others at a gallop. A moment later, Bertinand joined him.

Some people in the village looked at them oddly as they rode past, clearly as puzzled over the Knights' behavior as Anargen found himself feeling. One among them, though, stood out to Anargen and set his heart thudding a little faster. The grey watcher from the market was among those observing with bemused eyes. Cinaed's comment about "idle ears" suddenly hit Anargen with more force, and he strained in his saddle to look back without changing momentum. Was that man smiling? A chill rippled through Anargen and threatened to unsteady his hold on the reins.

Facing forward again, Anargen considered going back. He could determine the meaning of the shifty man's behavior. However, something kept him on course, placing more and more distance between him and the concerns swirling up in him over the man.

11

THE FALLEN

"Would that we have half the strength of fellowship as Caeserus's dream implied. Then such a terrible thing would never have befallen us."

– ANARGEN'S JOURNEY JOURNAL,
SUMMER 1605 M.E.

DAYS PASSED WITHOUT INCIDENT, becoming a week of peaceful coexistence. They passed rolling, green knolls, a large river valley, and a wide, bumpy plateau.

At present, they were traveling rather slow through a minor mountain range. Anargen took advantage of the languid pace to mentally settle on what to write in letters home. A few miles back he'd plucked some flowers to press and from them draw pictures for Seren. Assuming she would want them.

A scowl worked its way onto his face.

Somehow sensing his melancholy, Bertinand came up beside him and slapped him on the arm, then pointed back to Caeserus. "That goof thinks Kirke is the greatest city in Libertias!"

From a few yards back Caeserus called, "It's the capital, of course it's the greatest!"

Anargen just stared back at his friend. "Uh, okay."

Shaking his head, Bertinand said, "No, it isn't. Stormridge is way more important. I would've thought someone courting Seren would know that."

Intended or not, the words struck Anargen like a blow to his jaw. For several seconds he eyed Bertinand cooly, unable to reply. He could almost feel the weight of the unread letter in his bag. For all he wanted to say, he didn't know what Seren had wanted him to know. How would hiding from its contents change her feelings?

Sir Cinaed came to an inadvertent rescue by calling out for everyone to halt. Bertinand rode on ahead and dismounted, picking up his silly banter with Caeserus. Hanging back, Anargen was the last of the group to step forward to claim what amounted to a lunch, the final stores of their hardtack and strips of cured pork from Ironfork and some blueberries Anargen had managed to find along the way.

Things were easier for Anargen once everyone was finished eating. A huge, old oak tree near their camp had long twisted roots which shot out at every angle and boughs that covered at least ten feet in every direction with a blanket of shade. It was the perfect place to take a rest, even the tree itself seemed to sit in comfort on the top of its knoll. Each teen picked a different side.

In the distance, one could see for a mile or more into the remainder of the hilly region. There was a faint breeze, on it was the heavy scent of honeysuckle, thickly present in the area. Were that not Seren's scent, Anargen might have been able to relax. The others certainly seemed to, Anargen even heard Bertinand mumble drowsily, "This is a veritable holiday."

When Cinaed finally approached them, he seemed ready to deliver some important news. The stern set of his brows slipped when he saw the absurd look of contentment on Bertinand's face. His eyes were shut, and he wore a big grin.

Adopting a grave tone, Cinaed began. "All right, lads. We are about eight miles from the nearest town along our route. I will ride ahead and secure sleeping quarters, supplies, and other essentials for the remainder of the journey. To do so before dark, I will need you all to follow the route I marked on this parchment." At this he produced a thin, worn roll, which looked to be a well-used map. He tossed it to Terrillian who snagged it out of the air before Caeserus could do so.

Cutting off a match to determine who would be first to peruse its content, Cinaed spoke up. "I'm leaving Terrillian in charge while I am away today. Please, come quickly and follow the path precisely. I will be waiting for you."

A few discordant notes of snoring broke into Cinaed's solemn charge. Bertinand was asleep. "Since this is only the first leg of our journey, please do not leave anyone behind," he added, shaking his head. "May the Great King's light guide you on the way."

With these things said, Cinaed untethered his horse's reins from the wagon and mounted Swiftfoot once more. Nodding towards his young brethren, he was off, galloping at a pace to earn his horse its name.

In his wake, he kicked up much of the dust that had been lying idle on the ground in the intensifying heat of the day. Already it was much warmer than the entirety of the past week, and Anargen came to realize this was not going to be a pleasant little jaunt. Eight miles on this hilly terrain would take till after nightfall with the wagon, assuming they all got along and did not quarrel. Probably why Sir Cinaed hedged his bets and rode ahead.

Terrillian gave the group another fifteen minutes after Cinaed had departed before climbing on the wagon and calling out, "Alright, everyone up. We'd better get going."

Anargen walked over and leaned against the pine buggy,

bracing himself for some contention over the leader role. His anxieties proved unfounded as Caeserus simply went to cajole Bertinand into getting on the move. The other teen continued singing soft, if dissonant, notes of sleep.

Caeserus tapped his boot lightly against the flat of Bertinand's feet. No noticeable effect was obtained. Rolling his eyes, Caeserus looked back at the others. Snickering Anargen shrugged. Looking up he saw Terrillian giving Caeserus a wave that meant, "Keep trying."

This time Caeserus tapped a little more forcefully.

Still no reaction.

A few raps on the shoulder.

Nothing.

Beyond the point of annoyance, Caeserus threw his hands into the air. "Maybe we should leave him? We've been heading due north for a while now, he can follow. When he wakes up, he'll learn not to take naps in the middle of the most important journey of his life."

To that point Anargen had been chuckling at the spectacle. His friend's suggestion drew him up short. Caeserus wasn't above leaving anyone behind. It made him think of how close he'd come to lingering in Black River. Would he have been written off for loving his home and family. For loving Seren?

Shaking his head, Anargen called out, "No, remember when I took you all out to find the berries a few days back? We almost lost him then, better not to risk it now."

"Fine," Caeserus replied, his words heavier with exasperation than a mountain with stone. Turning, he uncorked his skin full of water and poured half the contents of the leathery sack on Bertinand's head.

Shocked and soaked, a groggy Bertinand jumped to his feet and looked around like he'd been lit on fire instead of doused. Then his eyes fell on Caeserus taking a sip of his water and grinning with a brazen smugness. Without an intelligible word,

Bertinand charged the other teen, tackling the thinner Caeserus from behind.

Anargen rubbed the bridge of his nose as they rolled about struggling in a wrestling contest. His annoyance began to drift to concern as the pair's scuffle brought them to the edge of the steep hill's slope. His voice caught in his throat as he debated whether to speak up or not. The decision wasn't long available.

Together the pair went over the side. From the curvature and angle Anargen had, it looked as if they'd plunged off a cliff. Seconds passed with neither Knight returning. Anargen jogged over to examine the sudden drop off, hoping to find a lull. Looking over its crest Anargen's sage eyes grew wide. From the side of their approach the hill had been much more sloping. Here it was far steeper, almost sheer.

Far down the slope he could see his friends tumbling to the roots of the hill, their arms flailing as they failed to stop their descent. Neither seemed capable of stopping their downward careen.

Horrified, Anargen shouted to Terrillian, "They've fallen down the hill! It's very steep. I'll have to try to get down there to them." He started to edge down the hill and stopped himself, thinking better of it. "What does the map look like?"

Terrillian had already jumped down from the wagon and rushed over. Handing Anargen the map, he peered over and grimaced. "I think they've stopped, but they're not moving."

Pouring over the map fast as he could, what Anargen saw was far from simple. It was a winding path, likely meant to be a safe and easy route for the wagon to pass along. Staring out over the hillside once more, Anargen could now see that this area was made of pronounced, jade-colored peaks and low valleys in alternation. Taking in a deep breath, he tried to figure out where the map fit into the terrain he saw. A mile or two away, the path on the map appeared to pass through a valley lull in the hills.

Anargen turned to face Terrillian and said, "Look, the path Sir Cinaed mapped out for us passes through a low spot a few miles from here. If you can get the cart and our horses to there, I think I can get down this hill and help Caeserus and Bertinand. We'll meet up and get back underway before Sir Cinaed realizes something has happened."

After a few moments of thought, Terrillian nodded in agreement. He took the map and dashed over to the wagon. "I'll meet you there. Are you sure you can get down the hill?"

"I think so. Just concentrate on keeping the cart and horses on track with these roads, I'm guessing they won't be the most navigable we've seen."

Terrillian nodded and then held up a finger. Reaching into the wagon, he produced the Spiritsword. He tossed it to Anargen and said, "You should hang onto it. Who knows what you'll find down there."

Raising the sword in its scabbard in salute, Anargen began edging down the hill. Navigating the slope in a wide, criss-crossing path, he did his best to keep from looking at the bottom of the hill. It would serve no one's good to suffer a fit of vertigo and plunge to its bottom as well.

As he progressed down the hill, he found signs of where they had dug their hands into the soil as they rolled or tried to grab hold of some plant in order to slow the tumble. In the end, these attempts only served to slow Anargen's pace as he had to work around them to keep from slipping. Finally he reached the base of the steep knoll.

Once there, looking up, he could not see the tree under which they'd found shade and despaired of the chance that his friends could even have survived the fall. The King's favor alone could have rescued them from that plummet.

As Anargen walked towards an embankment of trees, a small stream collected from several of the hillsides and ran along the length of the valley floor. The stream had a steep, rock-strewn bank. Even before reaching its edge, Anargen could hear moaning.

At the sound of it, his heart's pace grew frantic, and he

rushed into the thicket. There, by the stream, he saw Caeserus and Bertinand. Caeserus was propped against the stones on the shallow creek's bank, and Bertinand sat upright in the middle of the clear, cool water. They were cleaning their wounds.

Hurrying down the side of the stream, Anargen was careful not to slip on the moss-covered stones. Eight minutes after the debacle started, he made it to his friends.

Before Anargen could ask, Bertinand set about informing him, "I only have a few scratches and a couple bruises, but I think Caeserus twisted his ankle or worse—" Bertinand paused to shoot a pointed look in Caeserus's direction. The other ignored him, so Bertinand continued, "—as we fell. I don't know if he'll be able to make it from here without some help."

Bertinand's voice was low, and looking over at Caeserus, Anargen could see why he felt so guilty. Caeserus had escaped with fewer scratches, but two things were clearly noticeable from looking at his friend's expression. From the way Caeserus clenched his teeth and gingerly rubbed at his leg, he had a sharp pain there. It was also equally clear from the way he glowered at Bertinand that he held him fully responsible.

Neither seemed capable of making a long journey, but if Terrillian made it to their meeting spot and they were nowhere to be found, he wouldn't wait long before searching for them. Getting separated for long in this wilderness put their very lives in danger.

Anargen needed to get his friends moving and now.

Closing his eyes, he mouthed a plea for aid to the Great King of Light. As he opened his eyes, he squared his shoulders for the immediate task. Before he could bid them to rise, Bertinand was already standing and saying, "We have to get moving before we lose too much of the day. Cinaed expects us there by dark." His tone still held some remorse, but his own resolution was hard to miss, as was Caeserus's respondent snort of distaste at Bertinand's assessment.

"Caeserus, he's right. If we're going to make it all, we need to get you into the wagon before nightfall. Our chances are slim otherwise."

The firmness in Anargen's voice, coupled with his sense of urgency, seemed enough to distract Caeserus from his pain and spite. He strained out, "It's worth trying. Help me up from here."

Anargen and Bertinand each took one of their friend's arms and began to slowly walk. Just walking was a feat amidst slipping on the lichen strewn stones and poignant ripostes of thorny bushes.

It took some doing, but they managed to get halfway up the creek bed's slope. Gnarled trees and thorny brambles besotted it and Bertinand pointed out, "It might be easier if we just followed the stream bed. These last few feet look kind of steep."

"No," Anargen said and kept them moving upward. "I've looked over the area, and if we can get out into the open, I think I can guide us to the meeting spot. If we follow the stream, who knows where we could find ourselves? Besides . . . it is . . . only . . . a . . . few feet . . . further!"

With those final struggle laden words, the group made it up the steep embankment of the stream and back to the more level surface of the valley floor. The going was awkward, but they had no choice.

Into the sound of gravel being ground under foot, the trampling of damp vegetation, and the labored sound of Caeserus's breathing, Bertinand spoke up. In a straightforward tone, like he had solved a riddle, he said, "You know, we're idiots." The other two Knights eyed him like he was insane. Caeserus looked ready to slug him.

Bertinand wasn't fazed. "What are we doing? A bunch of twits like us are going to go to set everything right? We can't even go down a hillside."

Anargen felt the muscles in Caeserus's arm tense and he tightened his grip on his shoulder, telling him to stop. It wasn't enough deterrent. Caeserus pressed down hard on Anargen's shoulder, turned, and hopping on his good foot, gave Bertinand a light shove. Light because in his precarious balance he couldn't put more force behind it. Definitely not the extent of Caeserus's aims.

"Show some respect!" he snapped, his face stern. "The Great King gave me a vision of the journey, our journey. We are going to succeed. So cut the self-effacing nonsense and just keep walking."

It looked like Bertinand was seconds from pummeling Caeserus, but guilty as he already felt, it was doubtful he'd act on it. Doubtful, but not impossible. "You know," Anargen began. "I'd imagine the point of a journey is to take one from where they are to where they need to be."

Bertinand shook his head and raised his arms as if to remove the burden of confusion he carried. "What in the Lowlands does that mean? Of course you go on a journey to get somewhere."

Caeserus snorted and hobbled back into position for Anargen to help him again. Anargen smiled, pleased that Caeserus was calmed for the moment. He could explain to Bertinand the deep meaning in his words later. They had a rendezvous to make, and time was not their most abundant asset. Silly, but he hoped they made it through this so he could tell Seren about it in a letter.

12

HIGHWAYMEN

"I looked on his face aghast. Being not many years older than me, I wondered how we could come to such a point. One misstep and life would end on the knife's edge of our tenuous conflict."

- ANARGEN'S JOURNEY JOURNAL,
SUMMER 1605 M.E.

THE JOURNEY that followed was of similar difficulty. Caeserus, wracked with pain, offered little help in transporting his lanky frame over the two miles of uneven terrain. Several breaks were needed, and it had taken nearly an hour and a half for each mile trekked.

With the day fading, Anargen was about to suggest they consider sending either him or Bertinand on to bring Terrillian back to pick them all up when he heard a laugh. Faint, but it stuck out in the stillness of the woods. "Do you hear that?" he whispered to the others.

Bertinand and Caeserus looked at him and quieted whatever contest of cruel words was happening in hushed tones. "Voices. Are we near a road?" Caeserus asked.

There was no mistaking the sounds of people ahead. If the

traces of boisterous conversation to be heard was any indication, there were at least three.

"Finally," Bertinand groaned from under Caeserus's arm. Small beads of sweat clung to his forehead, even though the riverbed in this valley was quite cool and only getting cooler as the day wore on towards late evening.

Caeserus grumbled something in reply, probably reminding Bertinand he didn't have the worst of it. At least Anargen hoped his injured friend wasn't still trying to blame Bertinand for what happened. It was every bit as much Caeserus's fault after all. Though the way Caeserus complained at first, one would have thought Bertinand had simply pushed him off a cliff.

In fact, when Anargen had tried to resolve an acute outbreak of virulence in the dispute, it had earned him a fierce scowl from Caeserus, and the trio had been in silence ever since. Maybe it wasn't Anargen's place to arbitrate, or maybe it was. Whatever the case, it had been more important to keep them moving than to worry about hurting a friend's feelings.

The sounds of the three other people nearby grew louder and more distinct. They were just beyond Anargen and the others, higher up and further away from the riverbed they had been following. It looked like a thicket of blackberries and multi-flora rose had grown up around some willows and river birch to form a natural wall of tangled thorns.

Feeling too exhausted from effort to waste the speech, Anargen nodded towards a place a few yards ahead where they could climb out onto this "road" without as much effort. Bertinand grunted in response, and Caeserus seemed to push off faster on the slick stones with his good leg. At least until they heard something unexpected.

"You have the wagon, away with you then," Terrillian's voice echoed to them. None of the three youths moved a step further. A continual murmur from the creek muted what they heard, but Terrillian should have been more than a mile ahead at least.

Entranced, Anargen slipped out from helping Caeserus and

crept up the embankment. Peering through the brambles, he could see the wagon. Terrillian sat atop the driver's seat, his hands palm up as though deflecting an accusation. It took some careful maneuvering to not get skewered by the thorns, but Anargen managed to shift quietly amongst the blackberry vines to see those Terrillian addressed.

Highwaymen by the look of them. A rather large oafish one with a club and an average size older man with a dagger stood to the side in the relaxed stance of a victor looking on the vanquished. Then, from beyond where Anargen could see, came a reply to Terrillian's plea: "Keep quiet, child. I know there was another with you. A Knight. When he returns, then my business will be concluded."

Anargen twisted to see if he could get a view of the speaker. A pair of thorns, unnoticed, dug into his flesh for the trouble. It was no use. The speaker was too far to the right with the tangle of multi-flora rose and blackberries acting as an impenetrable wall there. He was well-spoken for a bandit.

Beginning to back away, Anargen froze as some old twigs crunched under foot. The two bandits in sight didn't seem to notice, but the hidden speaker snapped, "What was that?"

The other two men looked around in a clueless manner. Anargen didn't dare breathe.

"Call back the others from down the road," the mystery bandit commanded, his voice heavy with disdain. "We are moving on. Let the Knight find us elsewhere."

As the other two bandits scurried off out of sight to the left of Anargen's vision, the speaking bandit finally stepped into view. Anargen's chest tightened with anxiety and guilt when he saw that the bandit was dressed in grey. The grey watcher!

Less concerned about the scratches he'd endure, Anargen backed out as quickly and quietly as he could. Once out, he trotted back to the others.

"What did you see?" Bertinand asked in a strained whisper. "You look like you've seen a ghost."

"There are bandits, and one was a man who had followed us around back in Ironfork," Anargen answered, his voice sounding hollow even to him.

"That grey lurker?" Caeserus asked, a hard edge to his voice.

"Yes," Anargen replied in a softer tone. He resisted the urge to ask why Caeserus hadn't mentioned the man following them either.

"That jerk merchant warned there were bandits," Bertinand commented, louder than Anargen would have liked.

"So did Sir Cinaed," Anargen retorted through his teeth. "And none of it matters because it won't change this situation."

Before Bertinand could launch a volley of sarcastic retorts, Caeserus spoke up. "How many bandits were there? Did they seem well-trained?"

With a shrug, Anargen answered, "I don't know how many. I saw three and the leader called for more after he heard a noise."

"Was the noise you?" Bertinand quipped dryly.

Choosing to ignore Bertinand's snide question, Anargen continued. "They're about to move on to find a better spot to ambush us. Or at least Sir Cinaed. The grey one seems to want him specifically."

Caeserus expression became thoughtful. "So, how trained do they seem?"

Anargen shook his head and held up his hands in incredulity. "How trained? Who knows? They all seemed fairly ragged besides the grey one." With a shudder, he added, "His voice was deep and cold as the grave."

"Good," Caeserus said, straightening up some at Bertinand's expense. "He sounds like he already belongs there."

"Man, are you crazed?" Bertinand asked from under Caeserus's arm, jostling him as he repositioned his grip. "We're going to kill him? We'll be lucky if we can drag you past them without being captured and killed ourselves."

Glancing down at him, Caeserus bit back. "What then? We

let them take the wagon, supplies, and, oh yeah, Terrillian, our friend, and just keep moving?"

Bertinand looked to be seething under Caeserus's reproachful gaze. Taking in a quick breath, Anargen commented, "He's right, we can't leave Terrillian, but I don't see the two of us dragging you over and stopping those bandits. Ragged or not, they're bound to be more deft in combat."

"You will be surprised then," Caeserus countered. "Just get me to their flank and I will fend them off."

"Yeah, you're insane," Bertinand stated without humor. "Or your sense was knocked out of you in that fall."

Closing his eyes, Anargen tried to come up with something, but nothing rational came to mind. Under his breath he pleaded, "Perhaps we need more than reason right now. Help us, Great King."

Seeing Caeserus and Bertinand about to exchange blows again, Anargen pulled the Spiritsword and its scabbard over his head and said, "Caeserus, follow me. You will have your chance to back your words. Bertinand and I will come around the opposite side of the thieves, free Terrillian, and then come to your aid."

As he strode over, he could see Bertinand gaping. Whether it was bluster before or not, Caeserus leaned on Anargen and accepted his aid when Anargen offered.

They had only made it a few steps when Bertinand piped up, "I don't have my sword."

Anargen and Caeserus both gaped at him. The other teen quickly finished, "I dropped it when I went down the hill, I think."

A heavy sigh of annoyance rolled out from deep in Caeserus's chest. "Fine, take the Spiritsword. Just give me something."

"Take my sword," Anargen said, glaring at Bertinand.

By the time it hit Anargen he had no weapon for attack or defense, the exchange was done and Anargen's friends were in position. He drew in a steadying breath. There was no time left. No turning back.

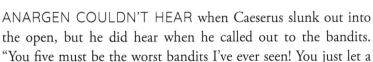

ANARGEN COULDN'T HEAR when Caeserus slunk out into the open, but he did hear when he called out to the bandits. "You five must be the worst bandits I've ever seen! You just let a hobbled child like me sneak up on you. And you have what? One sword among you? Terrillian, did you really let a pack of dirty bums with sticks and butter knives con you into thinking they were highwaymen?"

Only the grey bandit had a sword. Good to know.

Beside Anargen, Bertinand grabbed his arm and squeezed hard. When Anargen looked at his friend, a dagger was being offered to him, or rather a small knife. "Didn't want to tell Caeserus I had this. Thought he'd say I deserve to use this in the fight. Not much of a weapon, but it should make cutting ropes easier than a sword would."

Fighting a grin, Anargen took the knife. Then Bertinand gave a nod and charged out from their cover with far more agility and stealth than Anargen expected. A couple heartbeats' space later, Anargen followed after.

The moment he burst out into the path, Anargen was immediately struck by how much brighter it was on the road than it was lower down by the stream. The hot afternoon sun bore down hard on him, and a lot of dust had been kicked up in the air, forcing him to squint.

Down the road, three figures had converged around Caeserus in a triangle. None dared get close. Even though it was clear from Caeserus's unsteady stance only one strike would be possible before he fell, none of the three, two bearing daggers and one with a club, wanted to be the one who drew the sword's blow. Caeserus was also fortunate to be taller than the men circling him. His longer reach made the danger of the sword he wielded all the more menacing to the bandits.

Of greater concern than the three surrounding Caeserus was the grey highwayman who was halfway across the distance. His slow, guarded approach was like a predator stalking its prey. Behind him, near the wagon where Terrillian was still tied up, stood a large, oafish one with what looked more like a knobby tree limb in this light than the club Anargen had identified it to be before. He could easily have made a swat at Caeserus without much personal risk but was likely not trusted to make such deft strikes. The brute hadn't even noticed Bertinand creeping up behind him.

Anargen slunk in a half crouch over towards the wagon and was about two paces away when he heard a crunch. Bertinand had stepped into a pile of dried branches on the ground. The sound drew the attention of the man in grey immediately, though his large companion took a moment longer to realize what was happening.

For a moment, Anargen found himself frozen in place, while his heart took flight at a furious pace. Bertinand, however, was in motion less than a second after alerting the pair of bandits to his presence. Straightening and charging, Bertinand didn't even bother to unsheathe the sword and instead brought it, scabbard and all, around to crash into the side of the bigger man's head.

The blow barely staggered the massive man, and from his expression, Bertinand may have only succeeded in rousing a dormant bear. This was not lost on the grey-wearer whose eyes shifted instinctively towards their prize and stopped on Anargen. There was a cool recognition there. No anger or perverse pleasure, only the eyes of the hunter finding his prey.

In all the occasions Anargen had imagined himself on an adventure, facing such a fight—under-armed, outnumbered, with the stakes his life—he had always assumed time would slow for him. The moment of decisive action would stretch, and somehow he would enter a kind of battle mindset. But all he felt was the sun on him as before and the tension in his muscles as they ached to act. When the grey man started towards him, Anargen found himself reacting as if this were any other moment in his life instead of a pivotal one.

Closing the remaining steps to the wagon, Anargen leapt on. Brandishing the dagger, he tried to cut Terrillian's ropes but found the grey bandit had closed the gap so quickly he was about to spring onto the wagon himself.

Dropping the dagger next to Terrillian, Anargen jumped into the back of the wagon, knowing his only hope was that the bandits, having captured the wagon and bound Terrillian, did not bother to remove Terrillian's sword from in back.

Pushing through the scattered supplies, Anargen found he had a dull ache in his leg and noticed he'd shattered a bottle and had a minor cut on his shin. Or he hoped it was minor as blood began to run down his leg.

Numbly his hands fumbled over the things spread around him till he spotted the squat broadsword lying near the far side of the wagon. Gasping in relief, he reached for it only to recoil in horror as the wagon's fabric cover was punctured by a sword.

The sword withdrew and in its void Anargen could see the grey man peering through the hole he'd made in the taut fabric. A wicked gleam entered his eye when he saw Anargen still weaponless and already injured, though he must have believed he had delivered the blow. The bandit made for the back of the wagon.

Wasting no further time, Anargen reached the sword and yanked it up into a hasty guard just in time for the bandit to leap into the wagon and bring down a hammering blow that almost shattered Anargen's defense. Had the other man realized Anargen would be armed, he might have put forward the effort needed to do so.

Anargen instinctively seized the momentary advantage of the other man's surprise and pushed him off with a great heave. Adrenaline had started coursing through him, and he suddenly felt the speed he had missed earlier entering his limbs.

As the grey bandit stumbled backward and very nearly fell to his back over a wood chest with dried foodstuffs inside, Anargen leaned forward and swung his sword round in a diagonal blow. The other man deflected but at the cost of his footing and went tumbling out the back of the wagon to the ground.

For a breath's space, Anargen relished his triumph. He had high ground on the other man. This was his first fight, and he had turned the tables decisively.

His pride withered when the bandit seemed to recognize Anargen was at least skilled enough to make a fight of things with such an advantage and made a dash back around the wagon. Terrillian would be an easy mark, bound as he still was, though in the back of his mind Anargen knew Bertinand would be in danger as well. Which friend did he risk losing, and which should he aid?

Thinking Bertinand to have at least some hope, Anargen elected to spin around and climb back into the driver's section. He found an anxious Terrillian struggling to cut his ropes with the dagger he'd retrieved even as he watched the grey bandit charging toward Bertinand, who was just ducking a swipe from the bear-like bandit's stick.

Bertinand smacked the man's flanks with the broad side of his still sheathed sword and when the man stumbled, half-turned by his own over-committed strike, Bertinand gave him a swift kick, sending him tumbling to the ground. Anargen couldn't believe it was his friend deftly handling the brute.

Beside him, Terrillian cried out, "Bertinand, on your right!"

Both Anargen and Bertinand's attention veered to the grey bandit who was leaping into a powerful slash. Faster than Anargen could believe possible, Bertinand threw up his sword in guard, and the other blade bit into the scabbard's leather with an audible "thuk."

There was a momentary respite as each tugged to free his

sword. Lashing out first, the grey bandit back-handed Bertinand, sending the youth stumbling back. As he did, the bandit jerked free his sword, cutting off the clasp keeping Bertinand's scabbard in place. The loose housing for the sword fell away, and Anargen had no words for what happened next.

By now the larger bandit had righted himself and charged forward with a bellow. With surprising agility, the smaller grey bandit stepped aside, as if anticipating the other's action and allowed him to come at Bertinand.

Anargen watched as his friend, off guard, could only swing his sword round in a desperate attempt to ward the man off. When he did, light flashed along the length of the sword and what looked like tongues of fire leapt off the tip, searing the chest of the bandit.

Screeching with pain, the massive man clutched his chest and dropped to the ground by the briers. No one else moved.

Gradually fire began to wind its way along the sword in Bertinand's hand. Burning, but consuming neither sword nor wielder. The breath caught in Anargen's chest, and he dropped down from the wagon absently, as if drawn to the brilliant blaze.

The legends are true . . .

Quite reasonably, the grey bandit began backing away from the sight towards Anargen, though with his eyes still fixed on the Spiritsword. To Anargen's surprise, he caught the sound of a whisper, firm but soothing. And though he did it as if in a dream, he obeyed the familiar yet mysterious voice and bounded a few paces forward and brought the pommel of his sword around to crash into the back of the grey bandit's head.

With a garbled cry of surprise, the chief highwayman collapsed to the ground, unconscious. That was when things became truly peculiar.

Even as he fell to the ground, strangled cries of the wounded tore from the throats of the other bandits up the road who had been circling Caeserus. One among them lay on the ground, unmoving, and Caeserus was half collapsed, his left knee and hand on the ground holding him up as he waved his sword defensively.

Around him, both of the remaining men fell to the ground clutching their heads and lay there whimpering. Caeserus could be seen wincing as he turned to regard each one in turn. He then raised back up to rest on both haunches and shrugged to Anargen and Bertinand.

It's over?

"What just happened?" Terrillian asked, looking over the scene.

"They all just fell unconscious," Anargen confirmed as much for himself as his friend. Anargen's gaze roved from the downed grey bandit to Bertinand.

At some point Bertinand had dropped the Spiritsword and was just staring at the big man he had burned with it. The bandit lay very still, out cold just like the others, though his breathing was so faint he looked dead.

"Hey, some help here," Caeserus called, motioning for the others to come get him.

Snapping out of his trance, Anargen nodded for Terrillian, who had drifted beside Bertinand, to follow. Bertinand still hadn't moved, and Anargen worried he was going into shock. It could have been how the other teen was processing things though.

Anargen and Terrillian got Caeserus to the wagon before dragging their downed foes over to the edge of the road. One of them, the man already defeated by Caeserus, had a nasty looking gash on his shoulder, and Anargen couldn't feel his breath. He hadn't yet grown pale from blood loss, so it was hard for Anargen to say whether the man was dead. Certainly he was not in the best of conditions.

Seized by concern, Anargen rent some of the fabric from the man's shirt and tied it around the wound, though he couldn't be sure how tight to make it.

Once all of the thieves were gathered, Caeserus said, "I

suppose you are opposed to us dispatching of these fiends while we have a chance?" He was looking at the bandaged man but clearly addressing Anargen.

"There is no honor in killing a man you've already rendered unconscious," Bertinand replied rather hollowly, coming out of his stupor but still not facing them as he picked up the Spiritsword gingerly and restored it to its damaged scabbard.

The comments from each surprised Anargen. There was such a contrast between Caeserus's gruff, matter-of-fact intonation with the haunted sound of Bertinand's sudden response. Neither friend sounded like himself, but none of what just transpired was remotely normal for Anargen either.

"We should at least bind them," Terrillian assessed, and without waiting for agreement, set about gathering all of the rope used on him and present in the wagon.

In ten minutes all of the bandits were tied up and the four Knights struck out. Caeserus drove the wagon and the other three Knights walked until they found the missing horses a few miles down the road munching some grass and drinking from the stream. A welcome discovery, but even with the horses it would be a challenge to reach Abarros before dark.

"So, what are we going to tell Sir Cinaed?" Bertinand asked after about an hour of the trip. It was a question Anargen had reluctantly considered before but resisted asking.

"The truth, I would imagine," Terrillian replied rather diffidently. "He needs to know the bandits are a real threat and not just a story from Geoff."

Remembering the icy way the grey bandit looked at them while in Ironfork, Anargen shuddered and spoke up, adding, "And that this was planned from the moment we entered Ironfork. The one in grey followed us around before we left. Probably tracked us all the way here."

"No," Caeserus asserted. "We aren't telling Sir Cinaed anything about this. If he asks, we lost control of the wagon and that's how we each got injured and lost some supplies."

"Why are we lying about this?" Anargen asked, caught off guard by the chill emanating from his friend's hardened eyes.

"Because we don't need him looking at us like we're dumb little children. Or worse yet he might try to send us back to Black River. I had a vision, remember? We can't let the High King down," Caeserus replied, vehemence creeping into his voice.

"Sir Cinaed isn't stupid, and I don't think he would do something to thwart a quest from our king," Terrillian demurred, clearly thinking about something else.

"I don't trust him," Caeserus asserted, invoking a hush over them all that lasted a few tense minutes.

"Why not?" Bertinand asked, with the cadence a person might use to enquire about what ingredients were in a stew.

"He tells us nothing!" Caeserus snapped. "Just rode off without us to a place miles away and asked us to find our own way there. What sort of mentor does that?"

No one gave reply. As much as Anargen wanted to answer, he could tell Caeserus wasn't interested in logic at any rate.

"He did leave us to get attacked by the bandits," Bertinand agreed, adding his contribution to a day of ceaseless surprises and ill turns for Anargen. The other rubbed his head as if fighting off a headache. "If we hadn't been separated, I guess we would have all been taken."

"Exactly," Caeserus agreed. "I say until he is open with us, we have no reason to do the same with him."

"This is crazy," Anargen mumbled, softer than he intended because he was still stunned to be hearing it.

Apparently he had been loud enough for Caeserus to hear him. "Is it? This whole thing is supposed to be our quest, but before we left, a stranger met several times with Sir Cinaed. He refused to tell anyone, even the elders at the Hall, what the meetings regarded.

"Tell me, is it crazy to be suspicious of someone who hides things from even his closest allies?"

There wasn't a good answer for that sort of reasoning. It still felt wrong, but Anargen could not get the memory of the clandestine meeting between Cinaed and that stranger to dissipate. It sat boldly before his imagination, conjuring still more wild and worrisome visions of what it could mean.

Into Anargen's silence, Bertinand interjected, "We should decide this together. I vote we keep this to ourselves. Terrillian?"

Though his expression was hard for Anargen to read, Terrillian sounded confident when he answered. "We were hasty to act in the first place and it almost cost us dearly. Hearing what Caeserus had to say, it seems just as hasty to spill everything out until we know the container it is going into."

"It's settled then," Caeserus announced.

"No it isn't, "Bertinand spoke up. "I said we should decide 'together.' This is 'our quest,' so we all have to agree to this."

Bertinand turned a meaningful gaze to Anargen, and the others did the same with varying emotions undergirding them. As much as he tried not to, Anargen swallowed rather loudly. "I . . . do not object. We will tell Sir Cinaed when the time is right."

If anyone was pleased by this answer, Anargen couldn't tell. Inside his stomach roiled and felt heavy as if a huge stone had been dropped into it.

Without further word the group pressed on. The invisible weight bore down on Anargen. He kept alongside the others, but it was as if a gulf had opened between them. It widened all the more as one thought kept adding pressure in the back of his mind. How could he face Cinaed?

13

ABARROS AND THE GIFTS OF FIRE

"It felt as though its weight and texture were known to me my entire life. As though I held my birthright."

– ANARGEN'S JOURNEY JOURNAL,
LATE SUMMER 1605 M.E.

WAITING at Abarros's gates was Sir Cinaed, who descended on the teens like a concerned mother hen. Caeserus related the tale of their troubles, requiring only Anargen's silence to fulfill his complicity. Sir Cinaed regarded them all with such concern, Anargen found it difficult to keep eye contact as he ushered them to a small inn for their lodging that night. Anargen sensed there was an edge to Sir Cinaed. Whether it was guilt for leaving them behind yesterday or perceiving the teens' deception, Anargen could not say.

The next morning, much of whatever gloom held over the great Knight passed. He roused Anargen and the others from deep sleeps early to go out to the stables on the opposite side of the town. Trekking through town before sunrise felt like slogging through chest high river-mud to Anargen, until he saw what Sir Cinaed had in wait for them.

Like diamonds among dirty rocks gleamed several pieces of silver armor within a large, hay-lined wagon. Though spying them from a distance, Anargen could make out a few intricate engravings on the plate mail surfaces. He ached to ask about the display, but years of learning propriety kept his question caught midway between mind and mouth.

Bertinand had no such qualms with speaking his thoughts. "What's with the armor, is that for us?"

Sir Cinaed chuckled. His mirth was so profound that every part of his bearing silently beamed with the amusement. "Of course, lads. It would be difficult to be proper Knights if you were never trusted to put on the armor of our Order."

Anargen wasn't the first to step towards the silvery stack. Terrillian won that honor. Halfway across the space, Anargen remembered Caeserus and rushed back to help his friend. He got there just in time to hear Caeserus grumble under his breath. "Fantastic that we get this now when we needed it yesterday."

Sparing a glance at Sir Cinaed, Anargen could tell the older Knight hadn't overheard the comment. From the way Caeserus seemed annoyed to put an arm around him for support, Anargen had to wonder if he was meant to hear either. A couple seconds passed as he weighed out internally whether to talk to Caeserus about it and decided against it. Undoubtedly Caeserus was tired and sore from the previous day's misfortunes. A more pragmatic part of Anargen's mind also knew fighting would only draw Cinaed's attention.

Once he'd delivered Caeserus to the armor stack, his friend muttered, "Thanks." Before Anargen could offer to help with donning the armor, Caeserus waved him away.

Being the last to take his armor, Anargen saw no reason not to pause and take it in. Nearby, Terrillian and Bertinand were already donning theirs.

Reaching out and letting his fingers brush along the smooth, almost reflective, surface of the cuirass, he marveled that with so many engravings it did not feel coarse or bumpy. It didn't even feel cool, though wisps of fog and early morning dew still clung to the land. Beside him, Anargen faintly noted the heavy footsteps.

"It is called *Thorax Dikaiosyne* in the ancient language of the Order. In our tongue, we call it 'Righteousness'," Sir Cinaed informed Anargen, his voice and tone softer than the young Knight was accustomed to hearing from him. "Nothing will penetrate the breastplate our Great King imparts."

As Anargen glanced up at Sir Cinaed, he caught sight of the gleam in the other man's eyes. The quiet reverence. It sent a shiver of awe through Anargen. For decades. Sir Cinaed had worn a similar suit of armor, but he held it with such high regard, it was as if the whole thing still felt new to him.

"And this," the Knight Errant pointed to the full-face helm beside the cuirass and said, "is *Perikephalia Sosterios.* Salvation. No blow has ever pierced it while Knight-worn. In long past days, when tales of witches and sorcery abounded, it was said to keep a Knight's thoughts from being twisted by those cunning in such arts."

"There are such things as witches and sorcerers? I thought they were just stories people told?" Anargen asked lightly.

"There is far worse in this world. Remember that," Sir Cinaed answered, all hint of good humor buried in solemnity.

By this point, Anargen noticed the others had stopped at varying stages of putting on the armor and were listening to Sir Cinaed as well. The older Knight must have been aware, too, because he began to speak louder, though he didn't turn his head to acknowledge his increased audience.

"And these boots, the *Evaggelion Eirene*, carried the first Knights on feet swifter than the wind itself to announce to rebels the Good News of Peace with the High King. They will do the same for you.

"Holding all together is the *Aletheia.* A belt that if held in place will ensure no element of your armor can be removed and you will not be moved by any opponent."

Sir Cinaed looked at Anargen and nodded towards the armor. It took a second for Anargen to understand this meant he needed to pick it up. Scooping it all in his arms, it felt heavier than the materials it was all comprised of.

In a breath's space after, Sir Cinaed tore aside a layer of hay, revealing four kite shields of varying size and shape. Anargen had not noticed before, but everyone's armor was slightly different, as if fitted to each of them. The observation was interrupted by Sir Cinaed booming, "And these shields. They are the *Thyreos Pistis*. Faith. No arrow or bolt has passed through its surface. No fire or acid can burn through to injure the Knight who allows it to be his defense."

The older Knight gestured for them to all take up their proper shield. Anargen took the time as the others picked a shield to get his armor on. Even once on, it did not feel cumbersome. In fact, in all the years working with his father at the smithy, he had not encountered such an alloy. Nor could he quite understand how natural this armor felt to wear.

After a handful of minutes, the others stepped away, and Anargen claimed the shield he would have if he had gone first. A heavy, tall shield, with the King's lion and vines on it. He had scarce pulled its straps onto his forearm when Sir Cinaed ripped away another layer of straw and beamed at what he had uncovered.

Anargen's heart picked up its rhythm. Four Spiritswords and scabbards lay atop the remaining strands of straw. When they had left Black River with only one, he had wondered if he would ever get to use one. Now it was clear he was destined to wield his own.

Once more each youth picked out a sword and its scabbard. More surprising to Anargen than the variations in the shields was the variation in the swords. Caeserus picked a long, narrow blade; Terrillian, a heavy-looking two-handed sword; and Bertinand, a short broadsword. The remaining sword was somewhere between Caeserus and Terrillian's. Long as or longer than Caeserus's but still able to be wielded in one hand if chosen.

Anargen rubbed the smooth leather on the hilt and took in the gleaming argent surfaces of the hilt and pommel. On the pommel was engraved the symbol of the Great King that could look like lion or lamb, depending on how you viewed it. Holding it as though it were fragile and extremely valuable, one of which he knew was true, Anargen frowned. Whereas his choice of shield felt right, this choice of sword felt beyond him. Any notion of using a Spiritsword for so long felt like a fanciful flight. This reality had become tinged with those same sentiments.

"Eh-hem," Sir Cinaed called, clearing his throat to gather the teens' attentions. Though when Anargen looked up, he realized he had been the only one not looking at Sir Cinaed already. For his part, the kind-hearted bear of a Knight offered Anargen a wry grin and then addressed all four youths. "Now you each have a Spiritsword. *Machaira tou Pneuma.*"

Without warning, and quicker than Anargen could imagine a man of Cinaed's size and age could, the Knight Errant pulled free his Spiritsword from its sheath and swung it around with one hand in a wide sweeping arc. As he did, the blade blazed with a fire double in intensity of both heat and luminance to what the teens had witnessed battling the highwaymen.

Unconsciously, Anargen took a step back in surprise but then moved closer. Though he couldn't explain it, it was as if the sword whispered to him. The tongues of flame encircling the blade seemed to reach towards him. Initially indistinct, the whisper Anargen thought he was imagining was growing more focused, clearer, sharper.

Into this trance, Sir Cinaed boomed, "There is no craft in this world to create the Spiritsword's equal. It will shatter any spear, overcome any shield, break every sword it encounters. No armor can resist it, no sorcery disenchants it, no gale's bluster snuffs out its flame, and no darkness will overtake you with this blade in hand. Know it. Practice daily. Let it be as familiar to you as your own arm and the words it imparts as memorable as your own waking thoughts."

For a few moments longer, Sir Cinaed brandished the blade, turning it over in the air before re-sheathing it. Once he had, Caeserus immediately spoke up. "Begging your pardon, Sir Cinaed, but if all that is true, why does anyone doubt the High King's reality? Why would anyone stand against the Knights of Light?"

"And how could they?" Bertinand chimed in, eyeing his sword with a faint anxiety in his eyes.

This smoothed some of the lines evidencing Sir Cinaed's pleasure and pride over the Spiritsword. He looked on Caeserus and Bertinand like a parent consoling a hurt child. "The swords themselves are made by the hands of men as any other. It is the words of the High King, inscribed on the blade, which make the Spiritsword wonderful. In the hands of one who has truly pledged his fealty to the High King, the blade shows itself as magnificent as I've described. For all others, however, it is merely another sword.

"Be careful, all of you. While doubt and reason may serve you in some hours, if left to usurp your faith and fealty to the High King, only ruin awaits. In time and devoted practice, you will hear our Great King's voice speaking to you, guiding your thoughts and actions as He wills."

Clapping his hands together with a sound that reverberated across the rolling meadow, Sir Cinaed concluded by saying, "From now on you will all be practicing with the full armor and Spiritsword daily. We begin now."

Once more he drew the sword, but this time he waited for the teens to do the same and began walking them through a series of stances, guards, ripostes, blocks, attacks, and forms to fill the entire day. It wasn't until night was upon them and their blades glowed with faint traces of flames, particularly on the lettering of the High King's words, that Sir Cinaed told them it was time to rest for the day and led them all back into the city.

Collapsing exhausted onto his bunk, Anargen, having removed all the rest of his armor, could not quite part with the Spiritsword. As he lay curled under the rough linens, he kept the sword partially unsheathed and tried to read the inscriptions on the blade deep into the night. When sleep overtook him, his dreams and reality seemed less distinct from one another than ever before.

◇────────────────◇

"ALRIGHT LADS, we're about eight miles from Abarros," Sir Cinaed called out before dawn. Moving from teen to teen he roused and herded them out, not unlike sheep.

Once again, Anargen was slower than the others, lingering too long in examining each bit of armor as he donned it. The others were all outside already. Anargen pulled on his second gauntlet and charged out carrying his helmet under arm. When he got outside he saw all the others wore theirs and tried to pull his on.

As he adjusted it, he came to stand with the group. Eyes full of mischief, Bertinand turned and rapped his bare knuckles against the helmet Anargen had just donned. "Ow!" he shook his hand.

"I like this armor all the more," Anargen chuckled and gave Bertinand a shove.

"If the children are ready," Cinaed called in mock reproof. "You must be sure to listen to my orders at every turn." Cinaed hoisted one last crate on the wagon. "We are on a quest of great importance, one which will shape the rest of your lives. Pay attention and keep focused."

Anargen noticed Caeserus and Terrillian were suddenly less interested in prepping their horses. Not that he could blame them. Any morsels of information about what lay ahead were prized by all of them.

Continuing as though he was unaware of their interest, Sir Cinaed added, "It wasn't by coincidence you were given arms and armor yesterday. The nearer we come to our destination, the greater the danger will be. In a week's journey, we will reach the port to ferry us to regions far beyond Libertias. Remember, no matter the distance or the circumstance, the Great King will be guarding us with his light. Look now and see the sign of it for yourselves."

Drawing his sword, the moment the flames caught on it, Sir Cinaed walked to Caeserus and touched his sword to the teen's pauldron. Little tongues of the sword's blaze crept onto the armor and began tracing intricate patterns of inscriptions that had not been visible till that moment.

Next, Sir Cinaed touched Terrillian, then Anargen, and Bertinand. All four suits of armor burned with a low fire that seemed more light than heat. In fact, Anargen couldn't say he felt the heat at all, nor did the fire seem inclined to catch to anything but the engravings on the armor. The result was a faint glow on their silvery mail that in the predawn reminded Anargen ever so strongly of lamplight.

Awestruck, Anargen was the first to look to Sir Cinaed for answers. The older Knight smirked, "You have seen my armor's sheen and likely thought it some work of my own craft or my station earned me this power. Well, you've been wrong to think so.

"As Knights we are all granted equal resources and benevolence from the Great King. His light is in you now, so your own armor, sword, and shield will burn with that light. Do not strive to hide this light, instead let it be seen by all who will see it. Not all will, but those who do you may yet draw to the High King's service as well."

Staring at every tiny turn and sweep of lettering on his rerebrace, Anargen whispered, "Thank you, my King." He had never imagined he would ever actually possess such wondrous things. The armor was more than magical. He could feel so in his very bones.

"Ha, and to think this comes without cost," Caeserus said as he admired the vambraces which had been given as part of the righteous cuirass. "Glewdyn was a generous blacksmith, but even he never gave entire suits of armor for free."

Cinaed shook his head. "Not free, young Knight. A terrible price had to be paid for you to wear these. Remember, the High King has bestowed these upon you out of his abundance of charity."

"Right, sorry, Sir," Caeserus said, his voice carrying a genuine note of ruefulness.

"Mmm." Cinaed hoisted a couple more bags onto the wagon. Hefty bags, too, by the look of them. In a lower voice, almost to himself, he added, "Wear them well."

Pausing a few minutes longer to let the young Knights further study their wondrous gifts, Cinaed took in a deep breath and released it slowly. "Now, step away from the wagon and bid it farewell. We will not be requiring it for the remainder of the journey. You each have your horse and the provisions you will need to carry to reach the next stop in our trip."

"What?" Caeserus asked, looking at Sir Cinaed and then the others. "Why did we load the wagon if we aren't taking it?"

A somberness tinged Sir Cinaed's reply. "Gifts for Black River. Some amongst the town are suffering privations. The harvest won't be sufficient for all." The elder Knight glanced at Anargen and Terrillian for just a second, then looked away to the wagon and slapped a heavy hand against its pine frame. "Besides, this would only have slowed us, and we haven't time to waste. So, all of you, mount up and let's be on our way!"

"Care to race, hobbles?" Bertinand called out to Caeserus and then dashed on, intermittently wobbling and looking back smugly.

"You'll regret that!" Caeserus bellowed back and took off. It seemed the injuries from before weren't so troubling to him now. If it surprised Sir Cinaed as much as it did Anargen, the older Knight didn't show it. A moment later he was following the pair on Swiftfoot, while Terrillian and Anargen had each gotten mounted.

Anargen huffed and patted Patch on the head. He had wanted to ask after the look he had received from his mentor. So far as he knew, his father's crops and proceeds from the smithy were more than enough to carry his family through the winter. Could it be Arnauld's fields failing? Seren's?

Somehow the latter seemed to fit best with the look.

An ache was beginning to form in his chest as Anargen spurred on his horse. He looked over at Terrillian, hoping to talk away his worries with him. Something in Terrillian's expression stopped him.

Realization struck Anargen. Poor harvests were how Terrillian had come to be in the mines. His family once had more land and livestock than all the other teens put together. At least until Terrillian's father, a soldier for Libertias' militia, died in a pirate raid on Lanyon's Mooring in the far north. The family never recovered from the loss, and a painful decline to financial ruin ensued. The last blow was when Terrillian entered the mines.

"Terrillian, I'm sorry," Anargen began.

"It's always something, you know?" Terrillian interrupted him. "Just when Cinaed starts to tell us a bit, we are suddenly in a rush." He levelled hard eyes at Anargen. "I'm beginning to think Caeserus was right to question him."

With that, Terrillian gave his horse a nudge to pick up pace forcing Anargen to catch up. As he followed after, Anargen remembered Terrillian used to drive away burglars and bandits who sought to purloin the few chickens in his family's flock. The roosters were particularly endangered for the popularity of cock fights in other nearby villages. When Anargen asked about fighting off thieves, Terrillian had said, "You have to be desperate to defend what others are desperate to take."

Through hardships, Terrillian had become level-headed. This left Anargen in a difficult spot. Was his friends' discomfort with Sir Cinaed's secrecy well founded?

Hours like this made Anargen miss speaking with Seren even more. She was always his window to the outside world. Quoting great philosophers, giving context to things beyond Black River's expanse. Her letter remained on his person, unopened. Just the thought of what could be inside . . .

Writing might help him sort it out. Though Seren may never read the letter, writing her seemed to pull things together for him. He would have to pass the letter on to a courier before leaving the lands of Libertias. There was no knowing the secret place Sir Cinaed led them towards. Though Anargen could guess at the port Cinaed had chosen. Bonus Mare was the last port in this region that would offer vessels traveling to destinations of considerable distance.

The port got its name from the steady breezes which made the seas nearby pleasurable to sail. Arnauld had mentioned it many times in his reminiscing about the life he'd lost.

Anargen looked ahead to see his friends already caught up in rambunctious riding, pushing one another, and galloping off in fits of racing. Sir Cinaed kept just far enough back to watch them. Struck by the scene, Anargen had two goals to complete by the time they reached Bonus Mare. First was the letter for Seren and second, pry from Sir Cinaed where it was they were going.

14

A STRANGE WARNING

"Something is changing. It is on the wind and tide. It is in us. A sleeping energy is awakened and rages against a foe I cannot see and know I cannot escape."

-ANARGEN'S JOURNEY JOURNAL,
LATE SUMMER 1605 M.E.

ANARGEN LAY ON HIS BED, recording a few more things about Bonus Mare in his journal, then set down the quill. Terrillian was already asleep in the next bunk and was snoring lightly. Anargen didn't bother checking on Caeserus or Bertinand. At the moment it was the dark waters in the distance that drew his eyes.

Through the glass window beside his bunk, Anargen could see out into the city and beyond to the sea. What he had written to Seren of this place was incomplete. The darkling beauty of the waters under the waxing moon and stars completed the breathtaking character of this place. At one time Anargen likened Seren's dark hair and soft, pale skin to blackberries and cream. Now that he had seen the luminous pallor of the moon on these dark waters, he knew a more potent simile for her beauty.

Anargen had never before wanted to live outside Black River. "If only you were here too."

A gust, seemingly from out at sea, struck the window, shaking its frame and startling Anargen. The faint howl of the breeze trying to find its way in through the glass persisted for some time. Long enough to make Anargen feel uncomfortable, though he didn't know why.

"Even the winds oppose us."

Shaking his head, he tried to push the silly thought from his head and rolled over in his bunk, stretching out to sleep. There was more to his ill ease than the oddly potent winds. After he had returned from mailing his letter for Seren, Sir Cinaed had scolded him for slipping away. The elder Knight insisted they all remain inside until the next morning. Transport to docks further north could be arranged then.

The decision raised eyebrows among all the teens, but no one challenged the command. Something about the journey was changing, and everyone could sense it. The further out into the world they rode, the nights grew more restless and darker. As though they were roving beyond the reach of a candle into shadows. Anargen could not escape Sir Cinaed's most urgent words. "Whatever happens from now forward, stay together. All of you. Everything depends on it."

FIRST INTERLOGUE

OF A SUDDEN, the old man paused and looked around at Jason and the rest of the audience. After a few seconds, he reached down to a burlap sack beside him and pulled out a tattered, old parchment, yellowed and flimsy with such age it might well have been the storyteller's birth record or family heraldry.

"This," the old innkeeper croaked, "is the letter Anargen wrote to his beloved Seren on the night he arrived at Bonus Mare. Most of you know it as the town of Fairwinds today. This is the first of a number of his letters I have come to possess. I hope you will not mind, on occasion, letting Anargen speak for me in telling this tale."

Out of the corner of his eye, Jason saw Aria stiffen. Though her face remained impassive, her posture was clearly tensed. Whatever was about to be read worried her, though Jason couldn't fathom why other than for sake of embarrassment. Few of the other listeners seemed to believe a word of what he said.

Now that he was looking, Jason could spot at least two others in the room watching and listening to the old man with something more than amusement or idle interest. Dressed in expensive black suits, heat radiated from their glares.

Just before the innkeeper began to read the letter, one of the two men stood up, his skin reddening. "Are you really about to read that farce? How dare you sit here and tell your stories as fact. You've been warned about spreading mistruths. Whether you are deaf or just ignorant, you will not deceive these people."

Like most of those in the group of listeners, Jason gaped at the sharp criticisms.

What is with him? Why take the stories so personally?

"And you have a strange definition of fact, when I hold a letter from one of my lies in my hand," the old innkeeper deflected without betraying any annoyance over the accusations. "Camden, your warnings have been heard, but given I have evidence my stories are not just my own fantasy, I do not heed your hot air."

The man, Camden, turned in haste to leave, causing his stool to catch around one leg and send him stumbling. He was back on his feet in seconds and spun to face any detractors. He snapped, "You're a fool. The mayor and his council aren't going to overlook your corruption of Brackenburgh's citizenry any longer. I will see to it personally."

With that, Camden grabbed the other suited man by the arm and towed him to the door of the inn. Stepping out into the rainstorm the pair disappeared down the gloomy streets beyond. A gust of wind banged the door against the wall, causing it to slam shut.

Jason realized his fingers had a tight grip on his chair's arms and relaxed his hold. Brackenburgh's people weren't known for courtesy, but he had never seen such an outburst over a tall-tale before. When he looked back to the old man, the storyteller appeared unflustered.

After sighing, the innkeeper smiled for everyone. "Well, back to this letter.

Aurigids 1st- Bonus Mare
  Dear Seren,

I hope this letter finds you well. This journey already wearies me and leaves me parched for waters of home, for the smell of the forest honeysuckle, the sounds of mockingbirds in the morning. Seeing those I love.

There is not much time to write. There is so much to tell.

Yesterday, we arrived in Bonus Mare. Even at night restless sailors and warehouse porters roam the streets. An entire district of the city is devoted to housing goods ferried from all over Libertias and beyond. Here, lamplights burn vigilant through the night, not to be doused and refilled till morning's light. The city has an ethereal quality for it.

Sir Cinaed thought it best if we were up early to visit one of the two Knight Halls within the city. He explained to us how over the centuries the Knights of Light have fractured into different suborders or chapters which operate autonomously of each other — for the most part. This happened for a variety of reasons, some just and others a product of the curse of darkness.

Different suborders can be readily recognized by the color of the tunics over their armor. The tunic, unlike the armor, is utterly common. Befitting the distinctions and divisions men imposed upon the Order founded by the High King. Sir Cinaed told us he refuses to wear any suborder's colors out of respect for all, though he vehemently disagrees with the practices of some chapters. The Knight Hall we were taken to was of a similar chapter to our familiar Hall in Black River.

Their hall was lavishly decorated. Tapestries were of fine linen, in vibrant hues. Candelabras formed from bronze adorned the tables and windows to the Hall were not only glass, but of colored glass to give the Hall an inner vibrancy. The color was a deep blue, matching the suborder's colors.

From ceilings, vaulted above us, dangle ornately crafted chandeliers, which have more than a score of candles lit each day to give light to not only the floor of entry, but also a second floor, high above the first! On this secondary level was their library. Though we did not venture to its shelves, Sir Cinaed assures us it is of comparable size to Black River's. A comfort, even if a prideful one.

As most buildings in Bonus Mare, it is composed of a grainy stone with a faintly tan tinge. The stone made the building seem sturdy and imposing, uniform in construction. It is little wonder the number of Knights there far exceeds Black River.

Regrettably, we had our explorations cut short. Sir Cinaed centered most of the day's efforts on practicing our technique. We focused on hearing the voice of the High King as we used our Spiritsword and divinely imbued armor. It felt good to practice and for once I was not timid in showing my abilities. What's more, I heard the High King's voice clearly today. He told me not to fear what lies ahead. All I cannot see, he can. It was amazing, Seren!

With our intense practice I nearly didn't get to mail this letter. Fortunately, I have slipped out for a short time and found a capable courier to bring it homeward.

While on the way to the courier's post, I was privileged to see the true beauty of the seaside for myself. It is midday and the wind is coming in from the sea, setting the fronds and leaves of the trees to dancing. In harmony with the gentle rustling is the quizzically quiet roar of the waves coming to crash against the shore. The rhythm it carries is as soothing a song as I can imagine. Around the coast the water is a glassy green and from the bustling of fishermen the waters must be filled with a bounty of fish.

Over it all is a deep blue sky with giant fluffy clouds hovering where sky and sea meet. They look like ships sailing to port. It has taken great effort for me to not walk down to the beach to feel the waves. I think I finally understand why Arnauld misses it so, scorned though he was by it.

You would love the way the sun's rays dance gently across the crests of the waves in the distance. One day we will both see it.

The courier wants this letter. I added a pressed lily from our travels. Should it fade in its travels, it is white with fuchsia or lavender (I cannot choose which) strokes on the interior of each petal. The form is exquisite for its arbitrary curves, each one supple in its own way. Dotting it are dark little spots like the stars in the night sky.

It's so lovely it struck me to write you this poem:

'As I gaze at stars above,
My thoughts wonder to my dear love,
And rest sweetly there in that embrace,
If but to hope she looks upon the same.'

I hope dearly you find these words fittingly sweet. You deserve far more than I can offer and it pains me still to be away, but the more I learn of being a Knight and hear my King's voice, the more I feel certain I have chosen the right course to follow. I hope you can understand.

With limitless affection,
Anargen"

Taking in a breath after reading through the relatively long letter, the storyteller reached for a cup of tea he had sitting at ready. After taking a good long swig, he looked at his audience. "Things become interesting hereafter."

15

FANGS IN THE NIGHT

"I had never known such dreariness, such decay as this moment. Is this the fate of Black River? Of us too?"

- ANARGEN'S JOURNEY JOURNAL, 1605 M.E.

ANARGEN DUCKED a low hanging tree limb. As he passed under it, he felt its gnarled branches rake over his back like fingers through hair. Spurring his horse on a little faster, he worked his way past the offending tree. Rain continued to fall on the stand of trees in a steady downpour. It was as though the Knights were walking through curtains of rain suspended before them rather than it simply falling from the sky.

After days journeying across a rolling plain of tall, verdant grasses, Anargen should have been glad for this forest. It was, after all, far more evocative of the home he'd left behind. Before entering it, however, the wind took on a boisterous bluster, buffeting them as if trying to push them back to the coast. Then came the rains, which persisted ever since. Today marked a full day of rain. A full day of rain in a wood lacking most of the beauty to which Anargen was accustomed. This stand of spindly ironwoods and other gangly trees was bereft of most of its leaves already. Coarse bushes and thorny vines filled out the spaces and complicated the passage. The scent of multi-flora rose was heavy here, almost sickly sweet.

Somewhere in the distance a limb broke loose and crashed with a muted cry to the ground below. Anargen wanted to spur his horse on faster, but the forest passage was too narrow.

At the head of a single file column, Sir Cinaed cut the path. Into the dark, he trilled the notes of a song.

"Will you be home, will our wait ever end?
What friend may we seek, for our hearts' rends?"

Cinaed's voice was clear and mellifluous, the best Anargen had ever heard. But the song was about a family waiting for a father who would never come home. It was the saddest song Walhonde's mountains ever bore.

"When all our journeys' ways mend,
Will you be home again?
Will you be home again?"

The songs words pierced between the plates of Anargen's armor. Passing his mail coat unopposed to strike his heart. Memories of a fire, warm and low in his home's hearth beset him. His father's laughter as he told familiar stories with fresh mirth. Mother cooking a savory stew from the autumn garden gleanings.

Then there was something new to the scene. Seren's smile. Her hand soft and sure in his own as they sat by the fire. It was no longer memory but a longing. Hiraeth. Cinaed's song was more than words now, it was in his very bones.

Anargen shook his head and refocused his thoughts on where he was. In the unfamiliar wood, dark and cold, riding to the unknown. The storm masked the sky and only the luminance of their armor afforded any light.

Amidst the sea of dreariness, the rain drops sticking to their armor did not extinguish the faint flames. As the drops slid down, they glowed. Ahead, Sir Cinaed looked like a body of earthbound stars gliding through the ebon night.

Of a sudden, the song and stellar migration halted, hovering in wait. Sir Cinaed had reached a wider point in the path. The sound of rain striking the softened soil was like the roar of a small waterfall. Over it, Sir Cinaed boomed, "We're only a mile or so from a village. We'll stay there the night and head out tomorrow. Pair up so you don't get lost, the path becomes rather winding soon."

At his back, Anargen heard Terrillian and Bertinand talking jovially. Moments later, they trotted past him, following Sir Cinaed, who was ready to be on the way. That meant Anargen would be riding beside Caeserus.

A heaviness overtook Anargen. It occurred to him he had not been able to speak to Caeserus for some time. Whether this was by choice or chance, he could not be sure. A malingering cloud of ire seemed to be hovering over his friend of late. Perhaps Anargen should have investigated into the source sooner.

Spurring his horse a few steps forward, he came alongside Caeserus, who noticed Anargen's approach and asked, "Finally ready to go?" He goaded his horse, forcing Anargen to hurry Patch on to keep in step.

Swallowing his unease, Anargen looked over at his friend and cleared his throat. Voice soft, he enquired, "How is your ankle doing? Is it fully recovered?" Anargen's expression of congeniality was forgery. He regretted the clunky and unnecessary question, but he found it difficult to choose a topic to start with. This sudden awkwardness when conversing with his friend was new and frustrating.

The other Knight did not respond, not even acknowledging Anargen with a glance. After a dozen more paces, Anargen spoke up again, louder. "How are you, Caeserus?"

"You mean besides being soaking wet, riding through the forest-the-world-forgot, in the middle of a moonless night? I'm doing fantastic." He urged his horse on to a faster gait and banked, following the pair of Knights ahead around a sudden turn in course.

After another such correction, Anargen endeavored to reply, the sting from Caeserus's sardonic response still fresh. "I see. Fortunately we should be at our destination soon. I wonder what the village will be like."

Caeserus looked at Anargen with a thoughtful expression. "Judging from the path so far, it will probably be a scattered cluster of shanties and hovels. If we're lucky they might have a scrap of bread to share between us all too." He spurred his horse on and turned his eyes to the path ahead.

Anargen opened his mouth to speak, thought better of it, started again, and found words eluded him. Never had he experienced such open hostility from his friend.

What is vexing Caeserus?

"At least, we'll be out of the rain," Caeserus added, his voice mellowed by a pensive note.

"Yeah." Anargen's thoughts drifted for a moment, to a place of simplicity far removed. "My father always taught me to appreciate rain. It helps with the harvest, allows for growth.

"What do you think they are doing in Black River right now? I imagine the fall harvest will soon be under way," Anargen said, a sudden swell of homesickness crashing over him.

"I don't know and can't say I really care." Caeserus's brows were set on edge like a whetstone, sharpening the gaze he leveled at Anargen. "I haven't thought of that place once since we left it. And if I'm able, I won't be doing so again."

The answer struck Anargen like a physical blow to his jaw. He had never imagined his friend could have so vehement a distaste for the mutual home of their youth. Was Caeserus's life so hard, so forlorn, he truly wished never to recount Black River's existence again?

As the clop of the horses' hooves marked an increasing span of silence, the more certain Anargen became he shouldn't press further. Trying a new route, he asked with mock enthusiasm, "I see, then how do you find our journey to be so far? Could you have imagined we would ever travel this far?"

Caeserus turned his attention in full to Anargen, a contemplative scowl developing on his face. Hopefully he sought a less volatile answer. "The distance is irrelevant, though I had hoped to see places of greater interest." Pausing, he pursed his lips and added under his breath, "If I had my way, though, I would have more of the questions in this journey answered. Sir Cinaed seems unwilling to tell us anything of what this quest is meant to accomplish. Where we're ultimately going among them."

"He discloses what we need to know as time and conditions allow," Anargen countered, his voice losing the warmth he'd forced into it before.

"Hmm. If we were called to this quest and the Great King has assured our success, then what harm is there in sharing with us the details? I for one am not going to turn back just because something ahead is dangerous or difficult."

Nodding, Anargen regarded Caeserus with some confusion. Wasn't he the one who had the vision of this quest? Was he doubting it now?

"Nor will I," Anargen replied. "But for now, what harm is there in being patient? Remember, if we are destined to do something on the High King's behalf, we will get there regardless of whether we know where we are led or not. Sometimes one has to be content with the status of squire rather than that of duke."

Caeserus scowled. "And perhaps you don't know half as much as you think, Anargen. You aren't the only one who has read the books at the Knight Hall and who listened to the elders. Instead of thinking so much about the past and Black River, you should try being of some good here and now."

Had Caeserus drawn his sword and run Anargen through, it would have hurt no more than these words. A flash of lightning, all too near, followed soon after by the crash of thunder, spoke the last word between them.

Anargen blinked a few times and closed his eyes as he tried to readjust to the dark after the flash. At length, he opened them again and through the sheeting rain thought he saw the cluster of bleary gleams that were the other three Knights several paces ahead. Caeserus, too, had hurried off, leaving Anargen behind. "Maybe you're right," he mumbled to himself. "Maybe it is time to let go of home."

Following at a distance, a shudder tore through Anargen's body. The deeper into the woods the Knights had trekked, the lighter the rain became but the more piercing the chill grew. Near the end of their journey for the night, Anargen was growing acutely aware of this. It had been days since he had slept properly. Dreams of terrible things he could never quite perceive, haunted his nights, draining him during the day. After this rain and Caeserus's harsh rebuke, exhaustion was near.

Another clap of thunder, like a hammer on a forge, followed a second flash of lightning, all too close. In that brief moment, however, Anargen saw it. The village was just ahead. Unlike most towns, its wall was only a split-rail fence. He could only assume this was because being surrounded by such dense forest rendered anything more excessive.

"Welcome to Bracken, lads," Sir Cinaed announced.

The town was dark except for a few lanterns hanging off the eaves of what must have been the inn. It was only in the brief glimpses afforded by still more lightning strikes that Anargen was able to see the rest of the town.

Built in a clearing that by now was a muddied wreck, it had no other plants to lend it beauty. The village was smaller than Black River and of an older, quaint nature. All of the buildings, nine or so total, were uniformly of spindly, wooden construction. In the gloom, the buildings looked heavily weather beaten, aged past prime.

Though one aspect of the village stuck out to Anargen as truly unusual. Where were the people?

It was true a village this small, in weather so foul, would scarcely have a soul stirring without the buildings, yet within these shells no sign of activity could be seen. No candles or oil lanterns burning within. No smoke rose from chimneys signaling hearths prepared to ferry them through this dark and dreary day. An eerie stillness clung to this small village. Only a pair of horses, tethered out in the rain, gave voice to the town's life. They neighed with displeasure, unable to escape the continuing downpour.

"Whew. This place is kind of dead, isn't it?" Bertinand asked bluntly. Anargen looked at him, gaze reproachful, as did Caeserus. Sir Cinaed did not speak. He seemed lost in thought.

Into the relative quiet amongst the Knights, Bertinand again spoke up, this time thoughtful:

> *"Doors locked tight,*
> *Fear's full height,*
> *Glimmering white,*
> *Dread fangs in the night,*
> *New Moon's bane,*
> *Full Moon's gain . . .*

"Kind of creepy, huh?"

A shiver ran down the length of Anargen's spine and spread to all his limbs. Terrillian, on the other hand, snorted and shot back, "I remember that one. I used to tell my little sister that at night. She would be white as a ghost all night and keep checking to make sure nothing was coming to get her."

Bertinand chuckled, and Caeserus snickered. Caeserus had a pair of younger sisters and a brother. Likely as not, he had frightened them on a fair share of occasions. It was impossible for Anargen to keep from wondering how they must be taking their brother's sudden departure. Did Caeserus miss them?

It surprised Anargen to realize he was the only Knight present who had no siblings. Perhaps that was why he had never heard the mischievous poetaster's concoction. And, perhaps, why he missed Black River so much more. He had to live with the guilt of abandoning his parents in their old age to the care of no one. Anargen felt like an anomaly.

Even more vexing, he couldn't fight down his unease with the nonchalance his friends possessed. Only minutes into his stay and already Anargen could not wait to put Bracken to his back for good.

Caeserus spoke up just then. "Well, what are we waiting for? It's still raining and I for one am tired of freezing only yards from buildings with hearths to warm myself by!"

"Yeah, I could certainly make myself comfortable around a warm fire right now. Shall we?" Bertinand added in a cheerful voice.

As they dismounted and lashed their horses to the hitch, Cinaed spoke wistfully, almost whispering. "This area was first inhabited nearly a hundred and fifty years ago. At the time all that grew here was scraggly brambles and bracken. Hence, its name."

"Not much has changed," Bertinand pointed out, looking around.

But Cinaed must not have noticed. He was like a man bewitched. "Over the years, the town grew from a family homestead to include a handful of other homes and this inn.

"You would not know it now, but in my youth, Bracken was beautiful. I passed through during the spring. Roses of Sharon were in bloom and from the midst of the commanding pines and firs, they looked like besotted warriors doting over beloved maidens. Time has never besmirched Bracken's dual prides: Homes and hearts open to all travelers."

Sir Cinaed's expression darkened. "It has been years since I have passed through, and it seems the mirth has left this place. I want you to be on your guards."

Having given time enough for his words to take hold of their hearts, Sir Cinaed nodded to the large building behind him. "This is the village inn and tavern. We have no business needing the scrutiny of any wayfarers, so do not venture out once in.

"Follow me."

Caeserus and Terrillian were the first to comply, passing through the dark portal of the door without hesitation. Not wishing to be last in, Anargen followed after, his steps a little uncertain and his senses alert and anxious for what awaited within the dark building. Much of his awkward gait was an attempt to keep bearings on Bertinand. His friend was certainly not above cheap spook tactics. Whatever his plan, Anargen was not going to be caught unaware.

Whether it was Anargen's constant scrutiny or a burgeoning sense of propriety, Bertinand followed in silence. The faint aura of the armor each Knight wore cast a pallid glow about them such that they could make out the general nature of the inn.

If the outside of the inn had seemed dark, it was only a staging for the depth of the shadows within. A single candle burned on the desk of the innkeeper. There were three other doorways in the little entry room. One led left, another right, and the last led back behind a large desk. Behind the latter stood a tall thin man, utterly absorbed in a book he had opened, a ledger of some kind judging from its size.

The man showed no signs of noticing them, even as they all shivered and shook out the rain drenched portions of their garments. Anargen glanced down the left passage, seeing at its end another faint light, one of the lanterns they had seen from outside. The pitiful glow barely managed to illuminate a trio of surly looking figures, each poised around the inn's bar. Large tankers were like dull studs on the countertop. The tavern patrons also appeared oblivious the Knights had entered.

So much for priding themselves on "open hearts."

Turning his attention back to the forefront, Anargen noticed

Sir Cinaed's jaw was clenched, the muscles taut. He spoke a moment later. "Ehem, innkeeper, sir, might we speak with you?"

Languid in every movement the innkeeper didn't bother to look up as he replied, "Speak. This is the Bracken Inn. Welcome."

Hearing the man speak was as unpleasant as if he had uttered curses. His voice was a lilting lily at the start and descended to be coarse as sand strewn with broken shells. This innkeeper was a peculiarity to behold as well. Wearing a greyish cloak and a bowyer's uniform beneath, all of the garments appeared much too baggy for him.

Just then his eyes flicked over to regard Anargen. Ocher orbs, unlike anything Anargen had ever seen before. The innkeeper flashed a grin at Anargen, bearing an abundance of oversized teeth, teeth so large they scarce seemed to fit in the man's gaunt mouth. Though the longer Anargen stared, the more the man's whole face looked abnormally long, a fact accentuated by his sharp nose.

"Thank . . ." Sir Cinaed began, but stopped until the innkeeper finally looked away from Anargen. "Thank you for the welcome," Sir Cinaed continued. "We are on a journey and were driven here by the rain. We would like to rent two of your rooms tonight. If you have vacancies, of course."

"Vacancies?" Bertinand whispered in a conspiratorial tone from behind Anargen. "I think it would be wishful thinking if anyone actually stayed here a night. I was right, this place is dead."

"I think you might be right," Anargen murmured, too low for even Bertinand to hear. Every moment they stood there, Anargen shivered more with cold than when he was outside. Not to mention the dark here felt viscous, as though it had a weight and texture of its own, one that worked at him, as though trying to submerge him.

The rain's pounding intensified, punctuating Sir Cinaed's request. If this had any impact on the innkeeper's consideration, it was not evident. The man's grotesquely long face twitched a bit, the way a mouse's might, and he sucked in a light breath. "This is an hour of darkness and storm. It would be cruelty not to find you a place of rest." His words slurred.

Anargen's brow furrowed. Was the man drunk to slur his words so? It would certainly make him seem a good bit less strange.

Glancing over the desk, Anargen saw the man run his finger along the ledger. He had a palm thick like an ape, but long, bony fingers. The spindly digit stopped, and he tapped a line invisible to all the others. "Yes, yes, there is a place for you." He raised his arm, thick as a beech tree sapling. He kept it bent and scrunched as though it would break for brittleness. It took Anargen a moment to realize he was pointing to the right. "Down this hall. Do you require a guide?"

Sir Cinaed didn't answer at first. He stared hard and long on the man, till any trace of the strange pleasure creeping into the innkeeper's tone faded from his features. In its absence was an agitation, not quite nervousness, but some form of anxiety. "No, we will not," Sir Cinaed said at last and stepped towards the hall. "I'm quite familiar with this inn."

In a single, smooth motion Cinaed drew his Spiritsword and held it aloft like a torch. The sword's flames traced up the blade with a crackle and then a whoosh. Its light consumed a sizable swathe of the shadows, which eased some pressure from Anargen's chest he hadn't realized was building since coming inside.

"Argh!" the innkeeper exclaimed and leapt deeper into the corridor to his back. Wrapped once more in the garb of deeper shadows, he shuddered for several seconds before biting out, "What sort of fiend would draw a sword on his host and set a fire?"

Eye brows raised, Sir Cinaed answered, with an ingratiating ring to his words, "My apologies. My sword casts off light to help navigate the passage."

"Have you no manners, Knight? I will not give you a room till your sword is sheathed."

"If I sheath it, then I won't be able to see as well," Sir Cinaed protested with a touch of bewilderment.

An audible sigh of frustration, almost a growl, issued from the dark where the innkeeper had stepped still further back, and his slur was sharply cut. "Away with it or no room."

Everyone looked to Sir Cinaed who pursed his lips for a moment. "Very well, I suppose." He sheathed his Spiritsword. Darkness enclosed them again, its pressure this time a noticeable addition.

The innkeeper strode back to his desk and snapped, "I've never seen such a lout, drawing a sword on his host. Have you even the gold for your stay?"

"Of course," Sir Cinaed answered, plunking down a small pouch of gold coins, which made a muffled clinking sound on the counter's aged wood.

"Very good," the innkeeper replied, weighing it in his hand before pocketing it. Darting like a black streak into the back corridor, he returned with equal speed bearing a ring of jingling iron keys. No one spoke, or had time to do so, though Anargen's mouth felt as though it could loll open in confusion at the transformation witnessed.

Had the brittle man really just dashed back and forth fleet as a falcon?

Sir Cinaed offered a tight smile as he took the keys. "Thank you, Mister . . ."

"My name is of no significance, traveler. If you must have names for everyone and everything, you may call me Mr. Keeper."

"Names relate something of the bearer. For instance, I am Sir Cinaed, Knight of Light. As such I bear the name of the High King upon all I do."

Cinaed paused for the other to mull his words. From the look of Mr. Keeper, they were not savory in the least.

"Well, we shall take our leave, goodnight. We do not wish to be disturbed if you can help it."

"All shall be silent as the grave this eve, Sir Knight," Mr. Keeper answered. "Your rooms are the last doors at hall's end."

Cinaed turned and drew his Spiritsword again, this time facing away from Mr. Keeper, who shrank into the shadows with a snarl. Not bothering to respond, Cinaed marched down the hall.

All the younger Knights fell in tow, with somehow Anargen being the unfortunate last. By the time he passed the desk, Mr. Keeper treated him to a baleful glare. Anargen was struck, too, by the oppressive stench of wet dog.

16

DREAMS AND DREAD

"There is a terror that only those who have felt trapped within a nightmare know. Greater still to discover on waking reality is far worse."

- ANARGEN'S JOURNEY JOURNAL, 1605 M.E.

CINAED STEPPED into the room he'd acquired and whirled around motioning wordlessly for the others to file in as well. Once all in, he pushed past the teens and locked the door behind them. It was a surprisingly easy feat, for the room was much larger than the average inn's room. At least such as Anargen had sampled on the journey thus far.

For a few seconds after everyone was circled around him, Sir Cinaed stood there, thoughtful and distant. Sudden as the first peal of thunder in a storm, he began. "Something is very wrong, lads. The innkeeper has been the same for thirty years, an affable little man named Edward Goodby. I have suspicions foul happenings have beset Bracken, and I need to investigate, alone."

Caeserus opened his mouth to protest, but Sir Cinaed held up a hand to cut him off. "This is not a discussion. As your elder

I am ordering all of you to stay here. Lock the door after me, and do not allow anyone in apart from me." He hesitated a moment and added with some heaviness, "If I haven't returned by morning, ride north and make for the country of the Dag-Vogtere."

"The who?" Bertinand asked, a bit louder than he should have. He was sternly shushed by the rest of the Knights.

Shaking his head, Sir Cinaed amended, "Never mind that, just make for Estonbury. It should be a ride of several days from here. You must speak with Sir Orwald."

Before any additional questions could be asked, Sir Cinaed strode to the door, unlocked it and crept into the hall. Before he pulled shut the door, he whispered, "May our Great King, Lord of all the realms, be with you, lads." Then he was gone, the door shut with some creaks of protest.

In his absence it took the teens some time to gather their thoughts. After a minute or two had passed, Terrillian stepped forward and locked the door. There was no bolt, though scoring from where one had once been could be seen upon close inspection.

"This could all be another elaborate test," Caeserus stated as Terrillian turned back to face the other Knights. "His version of the spooky rhyme to see if we have the bravery to weather a place like this alone."

"He did go on and on about how well he knew this place and seems to be in tight with everyone including, 'Mr. Goodby', aka 'Mr. Keeper', mayhaps?" Bertinand offered.

"What do you propose we do?" Terrillian asked, crossing the room to peer futilely out a window.

"We show him we aren't cowards," Caeserus asserted. "We go out there and find him. Stand up to his test."

"What if this isn't a test of bravery but obedience?" Terrillian countered. "Then to leave would be to fail."

Caeserus rolled his eyes at Terrillian. "Oh please, we are not his slaves. We're servants of the High King as much as he, so how can he order us to do anything?"

"He is our elder and a good deal more experienced than you," Terrillian retorted.

Anargen stepped back from the ensuing argument. Already it was growing too loud and too heated for such a precarious situation as theirs. Unlike the others, he did not see this as a test at all. Cinaed's behavior in the foyer with Mr. Keeper was like a show but one meant to be obvious to everyone, even Mr. Keeper. Whatever Cinaed had realized sincerely vexed him and if anything could so trouble Sir Cinaed, it did not bode well for any of them.

Standing beside the door, Anargen heard the creaking of the floor boards before the others and stepped back just as a heavy knock shook the room's door through its hinges and frame. All trace of the argument from moments before disappeared into the long silence which ensued.

At length, when each of their hearts had only just begun to slow their pounding, a caterwauling voice called out to them, "Hello, Sir Knight, are you there?"

All of the teens looked at one another, eyes wide and uncertain what to do.

Once more the innkeeper called to them, "Hello, Sir Knight, are you there?"

This time Caeserus strode forward and answered through the door in a firm voice, "No he isn't, he has stepped out. What troubles you, Mr. Keeper?"

"Nothing troubles me, Young Squire. Nothing of this world. But my guests, my other guests, find your bickering a nuisance. Might you three quiet down?"

"The four of us are quite in control of ourselves," Bertinand answered back with a snippiness. "Thank you and good night, Mr. Keeper."

There was no answer.

"Mr. Keeper?"

No answer, not even as many long minutes stretched on. Eventually Anargen crept to the door and leaned against it. He could hear nothing in the hall. They were alone again it seemed.

"Right, so . . ." Caeserus began.

"You shouldn't have told him Sir Cinaed isn't here," Terrillian admonished.

"Well, he would've guessed when 'Sir Knight' never answered," Caeserus deflected. "Besides, Bertinand is the one who blabbed how many of us are in here. Basically told him Sir Cinaed is alone."

"Hey! I thought we were brave, this is a test, and all that brilliance," Bertinand said, giving Caeserus a shove.

"Enough of this, all of you," Anargen spoke up, finally annoyed and unsettled enough to weigh in as well. "This isn't helping. We need to plan what to do now, not prattle like children."

Terrillian and Caeserus each looked at Anargen with a combination of shock and indignation. Fortunately, Bertinand was only surprised and the first to speak, blurting out, "So what's your plan then, wise one?"

Taking in a deep breath, Anargen looked around the room. A bed, rather modest, was situated in the room's middle and braced perpendicular to the left wall. There was also a sort of desk, with no chair, opposite it. The room's lone window was directly facing the door on the far wall. Through it, Anargen couldn't make out much apart from storm-stirred tree limbs swaying, illuminated when a flash of lightning took place.

Otherwise there was nothing outside or inside the room of note. Anargen began slowly. "I think it best if we stay here and get some rest. One of us can act as lookout and watch for Sir Cinaed. We could each do shifts till morning. If by then Sir Cinaed hasn't returned, we look for him, no matter what he commanded us. I would rather fail for compassion than cowardice or trite disobedience."

There were a couple nods from the others, even if they didn't totally agree. "We could move the bed and desk so they are flush lengthwise against the walls and then take a corner each," Anargen added.

"Put two walls behind our backs and have a better view of all directions," Caeserus surmised. "I can live with that."

Bertinand trotted to the far right corner, grabbing a pillow off the bed as he went, and dropped to the floor. "Not it for first watch."

"Not it," Terrillian reciprocated. Parroted by Caeserus. Looking at the other three and shrugging, Anargen said, "What is the harm in having first watch?"

"In this storm? There's no good way to track time," Bertinand answered, already settling down with his pillow to a more comfortable position. "First watch is probably *the* watch."

Anargen groaned. "Well, why don't I stand guard until I get drowsy and then wake one of you?"

"You can, but you better make sure you're ready to collapse when you do," Caeserus answered. "No wimping out twenty minutes in."

"Fine," Anargen said, rolling his eyes. "Will any of you be helping me with the bed and desk?"

"Sure," Terrillian and Caeserus answered together. Bertinand looked as though he was already close to sleep and didn't stir as they rearranged the room.

Everyone took a position thereafter. Anargen had the pleasure of watching each of his friends fall asleep. First Terrillian in the far left corner opposite Anargen. Then Caeserus slumped under sleep's weight, at Anargen's right.

For the first several minutes, Anargen just listened to the sounds of the room. Aberrant creaking, the rain on the roof and window, and sounds of breathing with the occasional snore. He thought about the day, about home, about Seren.

The latter left such a strong pang of longing, he tried to distract himself. Drawing his Spiritsword, he examined the luminous blade, letting its faint whisper fill his ears as he worked to understand the words engraved on it.

After two hours had passed, he found drowsiness creeping up on him. In all the stillness and banality of the past hours, Anargen found himself feeling silly. Silly to worry after Sir Cinaed in a town where he had old acquaintances. Silly to set up a guard and hide from a peculiar but harmless innkeeper. Most of all, silly for worrying after dark and storms and the poems of idle children.

Anargen wasn't sure, but he felt he had waited up long enough. Sleep pressed down on him heavily, its allure stronger than desserts to a man dying of hunger. Looking over the others for his replacement—Bertinand was out cold and probably willing to fight to keep it that way. Terrillian would at least be willing, was further away, and deserved a rest.

Caeserus beside him would have to do for now. "Caeserus," Anargen whispered.

No response.

"Caeserus," he said louder, waving at the other Knight.

At last, Anargen reached over and tapped Caeserus on the shoulder. An immediate grumble came forth, and Caeserus swatted without aiming at his irritant. "Hey, it's your shift. I need some rest."

Another shake and run through of his narrative was required before Caeserus mumbled an, "All right, all right."

Stretching out in his corner, Anargen closed his eyes, took a few shallow breaths, ignoring the minor discomforts without much difficulty. Seconds later, Anargen was asleep.

◈————————————◈

ANARGEN'S EYES SNAPPED OPEN. *He had been asleep, but something was wrong. He did not hear Bertinand's noisy breathing any longer. Nor could he hear any of the others. The room was totally absorbed in a nebulous mist, lightless except Anargen's own* armor, and he had to strain to see a strange yellow beacon in the room's midst.

The beacon's station in the room was not fixed as a candle's, but instead roved nearer to Anargen, becoming more distinct with every bouncing move. Then he was able to hear the low snarl and make out the pronounced muzzle and teeth, glistening with moisture illuminated by his armor's shine. The yellow beacon narrowed into an angry sliver, and Anargen could feel a thrill of terror chilling him to the core. From somewhere beyond the approaching glower of the massive wolf's baleful eyes, he could hear faintly the words Bertinand had spoken earlier.

> "Doors locked tight,
> Fear at its height,
> Glimmering white,
> Dread fangs in the night,
> New Moon's bane,
> Full Moon's gain . . ."

As Anargen's eyes opened, it took some time to focus his thoughts after the vivid dream and reorient himself to the real world. There was still the faint light offered by the lantern several feet away. Much of the room was garbed in shadows all the same, but it was enough.

Though it took several seconds to get his bearings, whether leftover from his dream or something more, Anargen had an immediate sense of dread. Something was amiss. Still wearing his armor, he didn't want to move much and make any noise that would unduly wake the others. It was Caeserus's watch now, but Anargen could give him a few moments, particularly given how he had dozed some of the time himself.

The nagging sensation of something being off still gripped him. Glancing around the room opposite him, he could not see anything amiss. Bertinand had slumped to the floor and was sprawled across it, and Terrillian, though more difficult to see for the room's bed, appeared to still be dozing soundly.

Anargen turned his head slightly towards Caeserus. The door to the room was ajar. Not totally open, but enough that someone could slip through it. The locks they had used were undone but not broken.

Tracing from the opened door to where Caeserus was propped up in his corner of the room, Anargen's eyes widened. A startled cry of terror rose in his throat and hung there. Hovering inches from Caeserus's face was a creature all too similar to the dream Anargen had just woken from.

He blinked several times, trying to rid the room of the monster or convince himself to wake up, but the sound of the steady rain on the roof above, the musty odor of wet animal fur emanating from the creature, and, most pronounced of all, the pressure of his heart pounding in his chest told Anargen he was very much awake.

Across the room, the creature's long canine-like muzzle split to reveal wicked teeth that caught the light of the lantern. But it was the eyes, those evil eyes that seemed pupil-less and regarded Caeserus less like prey and more like an object of contempt, that sent chills through Anargen's frame.

What could he do?

Nothing in his life seemed a sensible preparation for a confrontation of this sort. Nor was there time to sort it out. This was not the time to evaluate. He had to act. Quickly! The creature was leaning in to snap at his friend's throat.

Help me, Great King!

Anargen sprang to his feet, sidestepped the door, and leapt at the creature. He didn't have time or room to draw his sword, so he swung out his shield as he crashed into the beast's side.

His haste had proved valuable. The creature didn't realize what was happening till the shield bashed against its misshapen and mange-tufted head. It staggered from the blow but gave more resistance than Anargen expected.

Young Anargen sorely underestimated the beast's speed as well. The thing bobbed to the side, clutching its skull between two hands with unreasonably long, claw-tipped fingers. It stopped beside the lantern, and as Anargen looked at it, he realized it wasn't like the werewolf of his dream. This was something in between a man and a wolf, as if caught in the transformation and incapable of completing it. More sickening than its bizarre lankiness and unnatural movements was the tattered remnants of an outfit Anargen identified as those the innkeeper had worn. Whether Mr. Keeper was the victim or somehow the vicious monster in front of him, Anargen could only guess.

He had spent too long contemplating. The creature leapt with startling speed and swung a long, lithe limb. Anargen just managed to get his shield up to catch the blow and guard his face from the claws which raked with a screech across the shield's surface.

Behind Anargen, Caeserus stirred. "Watch out!" Anargen shouted just as he caught a second blow in his exposed torso. His cuirass protected him from the lacerations, but the impact sent him flying into the door which slammed shut.

Aches filled Anargen's body and spots floated in his vision. Too slow his shield came around to ward off the monster, which leapt over and landed with the crushing weight of a creature far more substantial than it looked. It pinned his arms to the floor and those jaws that had born down on Caeserus moved in for the kill.

Summoning all his strength, Anargen twisted to try to throw the monster off its perch, but he may as well have been lifting a mountain. Out of the corner of his eye he caught movement and lay flat just in time to have Caeserus's sword slice through the air where the beast had just been.

It, too, must have seen the sneak attack and gotten out of the way. Anargen looked up to see his friend move to a guard stance Sir Cinaed had taught them. One of the more aggressive styles.

Around the room, the other two teens had woken as well and now gaped at the fiend before them.

"What the—" Bertinand began before Caeserus made a swipe at the creature, causing it to leap onto the bed, bounce up to the ceiling, and then as if its spine were a rope, bend and flip down to the desk by the time Caeserus finished cutting nothing but air.

"Question later. Spiritswords!" Anargen bellowed, struggling to his feet and grabbing his sword's hilt.

The monster must have understood Anargen's words. Its head snapped around and it let out a furious snarl that was part growl, part shout, and wholly beyond the worst nightmares Anargen had ever dreamed.

It kicked the desk towards Bertinand with a long, oddly jointed hind leg, revealing a whip-like tail that seemed to grow even as the thing battled. Before Bertinand could get out of the desk's way, the monster leapt beside Caeserus and shouldered a leg out from under him.

Caeserus went down hard. It had been the same one hurt before. Before anyone could react, save Caeserus to raise his shield, the creature was snapping at him and battering his defenses.

Terrillian crossed the space in two quick strides, raised his sword, and struck. Some hairs got singed off the creature as Terrillian's sword began to burn.

This new light in the room enraged the beast, and it hoisted the bed completely overhead and tossed it at Terrillian, who ducked just in time to only be clipped on the pauldron by the bed's passage.

Shattering against the room's wall, the impact broke a hole that let the pouring rain run inside. The monster took one meaningful step towards Terrillian a furious roar building in its throat.

By now Anargen had seized his courage. This was his moment to step forward, and as he did, he heard a whisper and felt a rush of warmth. The Spiritsword in his hand glowed white hot, and flames began to encircle it.

Whatever the monster was, it feared the flames. When its eyes locked on them, it grabbed at its chest as if nursing a wound and barked vaguely human words at the sword. Fixation on the fiery sword blinded it to an unsteady Bertinand bringing his sword around till it was too late to escape.

Though the monster did try to dodge, the sword caught it broadly over one arm, gashing its strange hide.

A screech as piercing as a bell with a morning star for a clapper erupted from its mouth. The creature leapt away, into the wall, through the wall, and out into the rain-soaked night.

Too stunned to speak, Anargen stood there staring into the darkness beyond. In his hand, the Spiritsword's flame burned lower and the faint whisper he had been aware of quieted.

Nursing his side, which must have been struck by the desk, Bertinand sheathed his sword. Seldom at a loss for words, he quipped, "So, like I was trying to say, what was that?"

If anyone ventured to answer, Anargen could not hear it. In the back of his mind he had a name for the creature. They had all joked about it hours earlier. Those jokes no longer felt amusing. What they had experienced felt too fantastical to discuss now that it was only the rain assaulting them and the night's stillness pressing down upon them.

"We should find Sir Cinaed," Terrillian said, having to clear his throat just to be heard.

Rather than go back through the darkened and suddenly suspicious halls, the Knights climbed out of the wound left in the inn's exterior, the only remaining physical evidence of what they had witnessed. Droplets plinking off their armor offered a steady cadence to their march. Slow, stiff, no one ventured too far from the center of their little party.

Almost as suddenly as the creature had come upon them, they saw the flame of a Spiritsword blaze to brilliance and come swinging around. There was a startled bestial cry and the sound of heavy footfalls on the moistened ground. Then stillness again.

The fiery glow found its way to the four youths and did not fade. Coming to a halt several paces away from them, Sir Cinaed called out over the din of the downpour, "I told you to wait for me."

17

BY THE HEARTHSIDE

"If only the warmth of the fire could undo the awful chill of guilt."

- ANARGEN'S JOURNEY JOURNAL, 1605 M.E.

"WE HAD an encounter of our own. What was that thing?" Terrillian asked, reiterating Bertinand's earlier question.

"You already know," Sir Cinaed replied with a grimace. There was an edge to his voice. Not sharp, as though his anger had been worn down to weariness. "It was no mere chance you were all discussing their kind as we first stopped in at the inn."

"What you're talking about is impossible," Caeserus asserted, his arms crossed. "Werewolves don't exist."

"Tell that to the big, furry figment of our imaginations that almost killed us," Bertinand countered dryly.

Before an argument could ensue, Sir Cinaed spoke up. "Much of what you know as legend has long been hidden reality. Tales are not often told where there are no survivors. We were not meant to pass on what we've seen, I'm sure."

"Why were they here?" Anargen asked, his voice sounding hollow even to himself.

Sir Cinaed's large pauldrons accentuated his shrug. "Good question. There are none left from Bracken to tell us, if they ever knew."

This forced Anargen back a few paces. It was Bertinand who asked rather bluntly, "They're all dead?"

"Yes," Sir Cinaed answered, rubbing the bridge of his nose. Hints of tears gleamed in his eyes but never fell. "I suspected something was amiss when we arrived. Bracken never showed such inhospitality before, raining or not. There is one more house to visit, but all the others were . . ."

No one offered to finish for him. After several seconds, however, Caeserus did speak up. "Did you know that thing was after us?"

Anargen kept his eyes on the ground, no one answered for a very long time. A cool breeze gusted amongst them, and he couldn't help shivering with the rain and horror of what had happened around them.

"We should get inside, start a fire," Sir Cinaed stated.

As the imposing Knight began to trudge in that direction, Caeserus all but shouted, "We aren't going anywhere with you until you stop playing games with us and give us the whole truth!"

Perhaps it was because Anargen still carried the guilt of not sharing what happened outside Abarros, but this struck him as harsh and hypocritical. Not that he dared speak up now to tell either side of their mutual failings to be forthright. He bore his inward war in silence.

"Inside," Sir Cinaed replied but with a greater gravity to his words, as if he could simply pull them along by his tone.

Caeserus was going to challenge Sir Cinaed again. Anargen could tell by the way he tensed. Anargen reached out and grabbed his friend by the shoulder and held onto the other's pauldron till they locked eyes. He nodded in Sir Cinaed's direction and gave a pleading look. Whether or not Caeserus could see it for the dark and rain and distance with only the light afforded by Sir Cinaed's burning sword, the young man let a rush of air flare his nostrils and shook off Anargen's hand. "Fine. But we deserve to know everything."

"Don't we all," Sir Cinaed muttered, or so Anargen thought he heard the Knight Errant say.

◇━━━━━━━━◇

ONCE INSIDE, a fire was started from the smashed furniture of the inn. Sir Cinaed insisted on its use after the real innkeeper was found mangled deeper within the tavern built onto the inn. No one wanted to venture how long he had been dead, but the blood had not fully dried everywhere yet.

With a crackling fire in the tavern's modest hearth, the familiar smell of burning pine helped to displace the less welcome odors that Anargen hadn't been able to shake since encountering the monster. Till he settled by the crackling flames, he hadn't realized he was tired. Or how much he craved the warmth. Even with his armor keeping him dry, the chill after the rain was undeniable.

A few feet from Anargen, Sir Cinaed dropped another shard of a smashed stool onto the fire and collapsed into a nearby chair. He sat there for a moment pinching the bridge of his nose and drew in a sharp breath. Suddenly he leaned forward, steepling his fingers, and looked at the four young Knights in a loose semicircle around him and the fire. "Okay. Here is what I know. The creature you faced tonight was not here by chance. Several nights ago, while staying in Bonus Mare, I grew suspicious that we were being followed. It must have been pursuing us since then.

"I discussed my suspicions with the elders of Bonus Mare and was told legends about a terror, some called a werewolf, others swore was a goblin. For the past two hundred years, all have known it as the Grey Scourge. These are not the first tales of the Scourge I've encountered. Till tonight, however, I had never had them confirmed, but one of the victims bore the mark of the Scourge."

Sir Cinaed produced a grey scrap of cloth with a circle of black ink and tossed it to Caeserus before continuing. "I knew we would face opposition in this journey, but in all my travels, I have not felt so targeted by the forces of darkness in this world. There is some eminence about events now. Beyond what I foresaw."

"But not beyond what I foresaw," Caeserus commented, tossing the scrap of cloth to Terrillian.

Arching a brow with no amusement that Anargen could discern, Sir Cinaed responded evenly, "Your dream and this task may not be so implicitly intertwined as we first believed." Bobbing his head in a half bow, Sir Cinaed held a hand out like he was offering Caeserus a gift. "Or, they may be a thousand times over. Nothing is clear right now."

"We agree on that," Caeserus sniped. His blue eyes, hard, roved over to the other teens for support, and Terrillian merely averted his gaze and tossed the scrap of cloth on to Bertinand. Anargen was close enough to lean over and get a peek at the cloth.

Before he could get a long enough look to elucidate anything, Bertinand coughed as if choking and exclaimed, "There's no way! I've seen this before!"

All eyes immediately fell on Bertinand. Now that he could, Anargen looked at the rag and suddenly found his throat feeling dry. He had seen it before as well. Though a bit muddled, the memory of the fabric used to bind the wound on the bandit Caeserus stabbed had been of the same color and had carried the same simplistic circle design. At the time it meant nothing, but now . . .

"Where did you see this?" Sir Cinaed asked, rising from where he sat with greater speed than a man his size would be expected to.

"On the bandits . . ." Bertinand realized too late what he was saying and ended out wavering only a few seconds before completing, "we met on the way to Abarros."

If Sir Cinaed could ever be said to look stunned, now was that moment. Anargen watched as surprise faded into thoughtfulness and then darkened to something else. Anger certainly simmered just beneath the cooler exterior, not unlike a dormant volcano. "When you were injured," Sir Cinaed began and didn't bother finishing.

When none of the others had the courage or will to speak up, Anargen found he had to answer. "Yes." It was as much as he could manage before his throat felt like it had closed off entirely.

Sir Cinaed's eyes roved to each of them, resting last on Anargen. The emotion on Sir Cinaed's face Anargen couldn't place before had sharpened in focus and was now plain. Disgust.

"You four should get to bed. We ride early on the morrow," Sir Cinaed dictated and then turned to leave without further word.

"Where are you going?" Caeserus called after him, a challenge in his tone.

Whirling around, Sir Cinaed's countenance and bearing evoked the image of a provoked bear. "The rain has stopped, and I will have plenty of work before dawn. I will not see you till morning comes."

Whatever boldness possessed Caeserus, it was snuffed out like a wick by a sharp wind. He did not even offer comment as Sir Cinaed disappeared into the shadows outside.

In the tension holding sway over them thereafter, Anargen was stricken by a horrible realization. "What happened here is our fault," he announced, growing in volume and surety as he said it. "The bandits we encountered, they are the Grey Scourge. We brought death on these people."

18

WHAT LIES AHEAD AND WHAT CAME BEHIND

"What lay slain was more than those strangers. Any notions of our world as a simple place, a good place, is perished forever and leaves us with just this: A place, a purpose, heretofore unknown to us."

-ANARGEN'S JOURNEY JOURNAL, FALL 1605
M.E.

WITH THE PALE autumn morning barely daring to peer between the tangled limbs of Bracken's copse, Anargen and the other Knights prepared to leave. Each horse wore its packs and all four teens were ready to ride when Sir Cinaed approached. Wet dirt still clung to him from the grisly task of burying the townspeople. He had insisted on doing it alone. It may have only been Anargen's well-wishing, but Sir Cinaed looked less angry than the night before.

"Everyone ready to leave?" he asked, sounding ragged, his eyes half shut from fatigue.

"Yes, sir," Terrillian replied smartly.

"Good. On the road to Estonbury, I need to discuss what

lies ahead. There are things about our quest you need to understand."

This received no objections whatsoever. Now that their secret had been exposed, it felt all the more pressing to have the whole truth from their mentor as well. Most important, it gave them something to focus on rather than the fresh mounds of damp earth and waking nightmares that would forever imbue this place.

As the Knights rode away, Anargen spared a glance back at Bracken. Even the spindly trees were sullied, rent apart by the storm. Branches, a few whole trunks, lay askew. He resolved to someday return, when he could forge new memories not draped in the dark garb of fear and death and sorrow.

TEN MILES or more from Bracken's ruin, Sir Cinaed found his voice again. "Have any of you heard of the histories of the 'Painted Warriors' or the 'Northern Dwarfs'?"

Anargen glanced at the others. With a quiet ride till then, they too seemed surprised by Sir Cinaed's sudden question. Terrillian spoke up in demure tone. "No, sir."

"There is so much to tell," Cinaed concluded glumly. "It will take some time to examine all the pieces. We have been traveling north to the country of Ordumair, populated by a race of dwarves known by such names and as the Ords. Ords being short for Orderers, because for many centuries, the Ords were fervent servants of the High King."

This made nothing clearer for Anargen and from Sir Cinaed's frustrated expression, it bore no significance to the others either. "Let me tell you all a story. Long ago, a Knight Errant from Ecthelowall was able to interpret the dream of the Ords' first ruler, Thane Ordumair I. The very Thane who is said to have built a Knight Hall in the heart of a great mountain with dual springs."

Caeserus, seemingly trying not to sound irritated, and failing, interrupted, "Sir Cinaed, what does any of this have to do with what just happened in Bracken?"

"Shh. You want an answer, but to have an answer you must know the question." Cinaed eyed Caeserus for a few seconds as though weighing out something. "I suppose the full histories of the Ords hold more meaning to me. I will try to be brief.

"Ordumair and Ecthelowall began their war when a usurping noble from Ecthelowall killed his cousin who had been the bride of Ordumair I's grandchild Ordumair II. Both countries were ravaged by the start of the war and fell into a tenuous peace once the noble was overthrown. Centuries of flares in fighting ensued. A series of setbacks and deranged rulers led the Ords to build a massive fortress in the mountainside around Ordumair I's Knight Hall." Sir Cinaed paused and glanced at Caeserus, clearly wanting to give more details but resolving not to broker a greater dispute.

"An impenetrable bastion was added known as the Great Bulwark. Its construction marked a turning point in the war. At the cost of every acre of land apart from the Valley of Ords encircling the fortress, the Ords completed it. But they never again suffered a loss at the hand of the Ecthels.

"Each side lost something in this war," Sir Cinaed said, his voice faint. "Ecthelowall incurred tremendous costs during the struggle and lost their legendary grove of golden trees said to bear leaves and fruit for healing any sickness. The Ords became reclusive, hiding in their mountain, eschewing all foreigners, especially Knights of Light, for it is on our shoulders they rest the blame for the entire war."

"What? That's absurd," Terrillian broke in. "How could they possibly blame us?"

Sir Cinaed swallowed with some difficulty and winced, some bitter memory choking him. "That can wait till later. For now, you need only understand that we are meeting with an envoy of Ordumair in Estonbury. There we will discuss our role in brokering lasting peace between the Ords and the Ecthels."

"You still didn't answer what the Grey Scourge has to do with us or these Ords," Caeserus noted, but without malignance. None of the Knights could look on the hollowness in Sir Cinaed's usually cheerful face without pause.

"True. I did not," the Knight Errant answered with a nod. "I cannot tell you what I do not know. Creatures like the Grey Scourge rage against all who carry the banner of the High King. The lands we passed through hadn't known the High King's light for many years, and the country we ride to has been without it for decades more. Anything threatening those shadows will draw them to battle. What form and what time and why this foe, I cannot say."

"Would it help to know the full history of the Ords?" Anargen asked, feeling as if everywhere he looked he might spot something wicked.

"Like why they're called 'dwarfs'?" Bertinand quipped.

Caeserus rolled his eyes and rejoined, "Because they're short?"

"On average, taller Ords are a foot shorter or less than other peoples," Sir Cinaed corrected. "I will impart more about them when I can. At Estonbury, my contact might uncover a greater cache of insight."

"Whatever happens, whatever we face, you all must stick together. The High King has summoned us to something beyond anything you have ever known. He does not summon his servants into battles he believes to be lost."

Conversation amongst the group ceased again. Were it to have picked up, Anargen would not have been able to participate. He was already withdrawing into the haven of his own thoughts because Sir Cinaed's last statement, while comforting, left him with a potent question. This journey was beyond anything he and the other teens had ever known, but Sir Cinaed had not included himself. Was the mysterious past what vexed the Knight Errant or the unknown path ahead?

19

A GRIM MEETING

"What I had seen in travels in no way enticed me. Home still held my heart. But then I saw it, or rather perceived it. Everything I've longed for without ever knowing."

—ANARGEN'S JOURNEY JOURNAL, FALL 1605
M.E.

APPROACHING THE HIGH, cracked walls and weathered gates surrounding Estonbury, Anargen had to wonder if there was even a living soul within. Then they passed through the gates and his eyes widened. Within the walls was the largest city he'd ever seen.

"There's almost nothing left of the original Ord village. They called it Estona then," Sir Cinaed informed the group.

"In the hundreds of years since, the village passed from the hands of Ords to Ecthels and then to a race of war-like and fearsome raiders, the Dag-Votere."

"They've updated it some since then," Caeserus observed tartly.

Pristine white stucco buildings with dark wood half

timbering and prominent gables rose up all around. As did throngs of people unlike any Anargen had ever seen. Mostly because the diversity of the people was so obvious. Estonbury was clearly a trade city that attracted peoples from all across the western Lowlands.

"Much has changed since the early days," Cinaed confirmed, without slowing his pace. "The raiders settled and became more respectable governors of the realm. Ferderic III, duke of the region, is in fact a Knight himself, far from the savage and brutal ancestors who first laid waste to the region. Dag-Vogtere, Guardians of the Day."

"Which ones are they?" Terrillian asked in as low a voice as he could. The choral of thousands of voices in the symphony of daily life made it difficult to hear. Even so, Anargen could understand if he felt strange for asking. After all, they were talking about the place as though the Dag-Votere weren't all around them.

"They tend to be tall, with solid builds. Flaxen hair, kept long. Most of the men will be dressed the way you'd see anyone in this era. Vests, capes, breeches and the like. Women here tend to be more practical than elsewhere. Their dresses aren't as voluminous, and corsets are rarely worn."

Glancing back at his charges, Cinaed frowned as he looked at their puzzlement. "Of course. You've not seen anything but Walhonde. It tends to be older in its styles."

"You mean backwards?" Caeserus amended. "There's nothing like this there."

Sir Cinaed picked up again as though he hadn't heard the comment. "Many of the older men wear armor in public. There is still warrior pride in them. Not unlike the Ords."

Anargen dodged around a cart stacked with furs for trading. "Is that a good thing?"

"Heritage playing a vital role in identity is roughly where the similarities end," Sir Cinaed replied, before abruptly stopping.

They had reached a wide plaza with a fountain in the middle and a multitude of shops and carts all around. "Let me get my bearings, lads. It's been some years since I was last here."

Terrillian jabbed Caeserus in the arm and pointed to the shop nearest them. There three golden-haired girls about their age smiled back at them. Drifting to join the pair, Bertinand called out, "No, hurry."

One of the girls carried a porcelain pot with some dark liquid she kept pouring. Her eyes, blue like a clear sky, stayed on Anargen. When he realized she was watching him, she smiled at him and beckoned him to come. A lump formed in his throat and he offered a tight smile in return.

"Of course the prettiest one would be interested in him," Bertinand complained.

Anargen found his hand roving to his satchel. Seren's letter was still there, still weighing him down like a stone. This other girl was pretty. But Anargen would sooner be dragged to the depths in false hope of Seren's love than to chance betraying it.

"Like it matters," Caeserus asserted, rolling his eyes. "We're on a quest, remember."

"Hey, haven't you read the courtly romances?" Bertinand challenged.

Not interested in hearing another argument or being the object of interest for the Dag-Votere girl, Anargen stepped away. He couldn't go far, there were too many people moving through the town square like an eddy in a great river.

Standing about three yards away, he looked around the square. Not too far on his left there was a quartet of minstrels playing some lively tune for those willing to stop and listen. On the right was a row of shops for silver, furniture, textiles, candles, and every other imaginable good. Neither did the trick of taking his mind away from the letter in his bag. The fountain in the middle of the square, however, was something to behold.

At least a score yards away, and partially obscured by people moving about, it was still imposing. Atop a pedestal rose a stern figure of a warrior. His braided beard was caught in the air, as his whole body twisted in contrapposto. The slack arm held a short, broadsword, and his flexed leg was bent as if he were climbing a hillside. On all sides, streams of water shot up from the mouths of what looked like bears.

Anargen headed toward the statue. He had to see its face. There was something there, in the warrior's expression. Yearning, intensity, a determination. Finding himself only a few feet away, Anargen stared up at the massive statue. He felt compelled to mumur, "Speak to me."

That's when he followed the flow of the statue. Its flexed arm was stretched out, terminating in a huge opal finger which pointed away to somewhere. At first Anargen thought he'd find the city's keep there. He'd noticed Estonbury had one on the walk to the square. But that wasn't the case. It didn't seem to point to any major gate or street or other building in the city Anargen could see.

Shaking his head, Anargen glanced down at the base of the statue. There engraved onto a smoothed portion of the sculpture was a title: "Thane Ornand of the Order, Greatest Among Knights." The teen's eyes widened, and he looked up again. Following the finger he strained to peer beyond what he could see in the near distance. Nothing came into focus, at least not so long as he tried, but he understood now.

"You're pointing to the Highlands. To the City of Light, aren't you?"

Of course, the statue did not respond, but Anargen knew now. That look of fervent pining was for the Kingdom of the High King. His most sacred realm. Though he couldn't quite frame it in simple terms, Anargen felt a shift in himself. "Thank you," he whispered.

Turning around, Anargen was back in the moment again. "Oh, no." He'd wandered away and there were at least a thousand people passing in and out of the area.

Anargen tried to sieve back through to where he last remembered standing. Somehow it was harder now. People pushed and shoved to get anywhere. He noticed now raucous laughter of those enjoying a sport or spectacle somewhere nearby. This bustle was almost like a game, a kind of challenge to those meet for the task.

Trying to skirt the edge of the square, he passed a bakery and wished he hadn't. Rich aromas of freshly baked breads and pastries rushed out in warm gusts as doors opened and closed.

His stomach ached. If he had any coins of his own, he might have risked going to buy one of the steaming loaves he could spy. Keeping to his task, he had worked back about three quarters of the way to where he'd begun, when he caught sight of Terrillian ducking into a building.

Pushing through the crowds like a current, Anargen reached the door a minute later.

Nondescript for the city, it had the tresses around its latticed bay windows and a pungent aroma of malted drinks and tobacco coming from within. The sign above the door, which hung from an ornate wrought iron arm, read "Arbear's Inn and Tavern."

Another inn? A chill raced through Anargen's body, as every feature of Bracken forced itself over this place and then receded like the tide rushing in and retreating. Looking around, Anargen suddenly felt very exposed in spite of the crowd. He dashed into the tavern.

Inside, the smell of various tobaccos being burned struck him harder. Some of the odors were mild, almost pleasant, and reminiscent of other things. Wood burning in the hearth at home or the smell that floats on the breeze in late autumn. The majority were of a cheaper, more offensive nature to his nose.

One thing helped distinguish Arbear's from Bracken. People. Even in here there were more people than all of Black River. Hazy rooms filled with boisterous laughter and people of all levels of society interacting with others of their station. Anargen was sure he didn't fit any of the groups he was encountering.

Which should have made finding his fellow Knights easy. It wasn't.

He had almost resigned himself to asking for help from the next person he met, when he saw Sir Cinaed standing under an archway staring straight at him. It was hard to say, but Anargen thought his face had a disapproving cast.

Once more weaving through the crowds, Sir Cinaed greeted him with, "It's good of you to join us. Please, don't get lost on the way to the table, Anargen."

Sir Cinaed led Anargen, who kept his head down, to stand alongside the other teens. There were only a couple tables in this part of the establishment and it was very clear which one was theirs. Seated alone and taking slow sips from a tankard was an Ord.

An older Ord, if not elderly, at that. He had pronounced hairy brows and a large pointed nose. Anargen marveled at his long, coarse beard, which was white hair with an almost violet sheen to it. Though that may have been due to the lighting. Or even the regal tunic of a deep blue he wore over silver plate armor. His bulky frame added size to his diminutive stature. Though in all fairness he was taller than the myths of dwarfs.

He wore no helmet, so his crown of extremely long, but full, white hair ran down his back and fanned out in curling tendrils on his plush cape. Most defining of all his features was how the old dwarf was already so on edge. His thick, age-spotted hands fidgeted with anxious energy. They clenched and unclenched a beige napkin while each of the Knights took a seat.

Sir Cinaed greeted him formally. "Sir Orwald, it is a pleasure to see you once more. I'm surprised you were able to leave Ordumair to be the one to greet us here."

Anargen's eyes darted between his mentor and the messenger. This Ord was a Knight?

There were many reasons Sir Cinaed had enumerated recently to make this an anomaly. Indeed, the Ord seemed further unnerved by the enunciation of his title. "Speak softly, young friend. And call me Elder," the dwarf's voice rumbled and cracked, evocative of an ancient volcano still afire, but only deep within. "You do well to remember the difficult position I am in. The Knight Order is not well respected these days within Ordumair's walls. Nor am I well respected in these lands."

His expression tight, Sir Cinaed assessed the other man. "Very well," he replied, his voice softer. "Your courier did not say to expect you. This is a welcome surprise, I assure you."

The aged dwarf glanced inquisitively at the assemblage of younger onlookers to their meeting. Evaluating, it seemed, each of those in attendance. His expression betrayed only faint interest, but within his dark blue eyes there was a hint of something more. "Ordumair is in capable hands these days. I find myself o' lesser influence with each year." Then, as if unable to avoid the formality of asking, he added, "Who are these lads?" The previous carefully attenuated brogue of the Ords broke through.

Nodding, Sir Cinaed answered, "These are four young Knights from the village of Black River in Libertias. I served as Knight Errant there for some years, and I felt led to bring them along with me on the mission implied by your courier."

For some reason, Elder Orwald lifted his bushy brows in response to Sir Cinaed's words. A stern look from Sir Cinaed neatly curtailed the potential for an explanation. Instead, Sir Cinaed pointed to each youth in turn. "This zealous one is Sir Caeserus. The stoic one is Sir Terrillian. Our joker is Sir Bertinand. And then Sir Anargen. Each of them are promising young Knights, as I'm sure you will find out for yourself soon."

"I should hope not, lad. There has been enough turmoil for me already in my lifetime. But, I shall take you at yarr word." He paused to draw in a breath and let it out heavily. "Please, excuse my accent. I was better at controlling it before . . ." Orwald eyed Sir Cinaed and seemed to see in his expression something that kept him from finishing the thought. "The messenger spoke with you at length about our troubles?"

"He mentioned enough for me to get the gist of the matter.

Ecthelowall is suing for peace. They are sending a delegation to meet with Thane Duncoin on Fylleth 28th. The anniversary of the Three Hundred Year War's start?" Sir Cinaed sounded casual mentioning such a highly auspicious occurrence, given the history of the long running conflict. This may have been to deflect the interests of any eavesdroppers nearby or the occasional over-nosey barmaid.

Elder Orwald's brow furrowed in consternation. Softer still he grumbled through clenched teeth, "That would be the simplest version. Still more vexing is the nature of the ambassadorial party approaching our Thane. Viceroy Ecthelion is expected to be coming to negotiate the terms personally. None of the Elders are comforted by this notion."

The Ord took a hefty swig from his mug as though to drink away the foul taste the news left in his mouth. Sir Cinaed's eyebrow raised in curiosity. Hesitantly he began, "The Viceroy himself is coming? That seems unnecessary. Recent attempts at negotiations have always been handled by diplomats from either side."

There was a slight shrug of the Orwald's shoulders, but he continued to drink from his mug. For several seconds, Cinaed hesitated, eyeing Elder Orwald in a thoughtful manner. Almost rueful he asked, "Could it be the Viceroy wishes to ensure genuine, lasting peace?"

The old Ord waved his hand dismissively. "No' likely. Our scouts report the Ecthel army's camps haven't yet broken. Not a single division has marched from the borderlands back to Ecthelowall. Even a cautious soul would be tempted to remove at minimum three such groups to alleviate the tensions. The younger nobles amongst our people, of course, do not see it that way. They think we can leverage this to our gain."

Anargen cringed a little at the derisive sneer which accompanied the Ord's words. It was clear he thought little of the next generation's wisdom. Under his breath, Anargen whispered to

Caeserus, "Orwald's being overly cautious to the point of injuring his position. He would not be the first."

The other teen nodded. "You think?"

"That is why the Thane summoned me, isn't it?" Sir Cinaed inquired spreading his hands palms up. "He wants to hear my take on the matter. Observe the discussions and consult the High King? The Thane should know I object to his rationale for my visit. If he wishes to consult the Great King of All on this matter, he may himself. He does not need me to do so for him."

The Ord huffed out a sigh of resignation. "I thought you might be so opined. You may bring it to his attention. I wish you well in that endeavor, but my task is to bring you and your Knight lads 'ere to the Thane as swiftly as possible. Will you follow me to Ordumair or should I report to the Thane you 'ave reconsidered your assistance?"

Now it was the relatively younger Knight Errant who sighed. "I cannot refuse him. He was like my brother in youth, and he remains my brother now. Even if he denies it. The youths and I will accompany you back to Ordumair and offer whatever aid you need of us. I only warn that the Thane may not enjoy all the words I have to offer him."

Sir Orwald snorted out a mirthless laugh. "I'd wager not. All the same, I'm pleased to have you with us. We should set out quickly now. Time is short, and you were slow in getting here."

With that, the old dwarf jumped down from his seat, stretching so that his armor creaked and scratched its plates against one another. Orwald plowed forward, parting the line of young Knights. Each of them looked with questioning eyes to their leader.

Sir Cinaed stood slowly and shook his head with a sort of melancholy humor hanging over him. Watching the Ord's retreating form, he motioned for them to follow.

Each of the Knights fell into line and filed out of the tavern after Elder Orwald. Anargen had so many questions he wanted to ask but knew they would have to wait till a private moment outside Orwald's earshot. Perhaps even Sir Cinaed's.

Surprisingly spry, Elder Orwald kept a pace that forced Anargen to focus on the present and keep tight to the pathway he carved through the tavern. For all his grizzled appearance Sir Orwald possessed remarkable physicality. Yet another curiosity which begged itself be asked after, later.

20

FORDING TROUBLED WATERS

"There is so much to this world I do not know. So many legends which hold more truth than most seem willing to admit. What dangers lie therein?"

—ANARGEN'S JOURNEY JOURNAL,
AURIGIDS 1605 M.E.

EVERYONE WAITED on Sir Cinaed to finish acquiring needed supplies from a trade caravan on its way to Estonbury. The Knights had traveled some days from there and were camped near a stand of evergreens, untouched by the deepening passage into fall. While waiting Anargen wrote in his journal about Ord history. When Orwald strode over, he hurried to stow it away in his satchel, next to Seren's letter.

A look of determination was firmly cast in the old Ord's demeanor. It made Anargen a little uncomfortable. The regal Ord seemed so stern and remote. Unapproachable by the commoners from a tiny village such as Black River. Yet, the heir of hundreds of years of Orderer tradition and noble blood chose to converse with peasants of Libertias.

Orwald's nostrils flared in a huff. There was a severity undergirding his tone as he addressed them. "You lads have traveled far on behalf of my people. For that I thank you. However, this will not be for the weak willed. Your Captain, Sir Cinaed, told me I should warn you now of the dangers you shall face within Ordumair. Though my people have been called Orderers for centuries, it has been some years since Knights of Light have been amongst us. In fact, it is said our woes began with our alliance with the High King."

"That is sheer ignorance. None of your people's 'woes' are from service to the King," Caeserus interrupted, disdain hardening his demeanor. Anargen could not believe his friend's impertinence, but Elder Orwald seemed undaunted by the sudden accusation.

"Ignorant though it may be, it is what the people believe. As such, you will find little welcome within Ordumair's walls. Some may even dare to strike out against you. If you continue on, you must accept the dangers that await. Do you all understand? You have lived in Black River, with those who love Knights. In Ordumair, you will find nothing but hate."

The wizened sapphire eyes of the Ord roved over each of the four young men. No doubt they appeared green to him, unprepared for the ardors ahead. It occurred to Anargen to wonder if he was in fact truly up to the task.

"How could they hate us? They have never seen us," Bertinand challenged.

"That is Cinaed's tale to tell. He knows it better than anyone," Elder Orwald said, rueful. "I know he hasn't shared it with you yet. Perhaps that is for the best."

Terrillian cleared his throat. "I might be speaking just for myself." He paused to look around at the other teens. "But after everything we've been through already on this journey, how could some spiteful dwarfs scare us?"

Darkening like the clouds before a storm, Orwald's expression showed no amusement over the bravado. "I do not believe you fully grasp what you will face. You will be in danger of losing your lives if you are not careful." Quiet ensued again, but it was the dwarf noble who was thoughtful now.

Some flash of remembrance crossed his features and deepened into intrigue. He quipped in a bemused tone, "Sir Cinaed mentioned there are dark forces at work. What dangers have you faced already?"

Caeserus spoke up, rather acidly. "Well, werewolves for one!"

"Yeah," Bertinand piped in. "And not just any werewolf, the Grey Scourge!"

Orwald's mouth hung open in a wordless cry. If possible, the deep blue circlets of his aged eyes darkened further. "Werewolves?" For once he did not appear so spry but more the elderly little man that he was. His jaw was tensed, and his voice strained as he lost his hold on his accent. "Where did ya encounter these beasts? How many were there?"

"We ran afoul of them at Bracken. They killed everyone in the village and turned their teeth on us," Terrillian answered with a bitter edge. Then looking thoughtful, he added, "I'm not sure how many there were in all. Sir Cinaed did battle with most of the pack while we fought off one."

"When did you do battle with these creatures? How long ago?"

"About two weeks ago, I think," Bertinand answered.

"It was a new moon that night," Anargen added darkly. "Nightmares are nothing compared to waking to find those menacing eyes and glistening teeth in such darkness."

A low moan escaped Orwald's mouth. "You will see far worse than that this night, young Anargen. Werewolves are far more dangerous during the full moon." Wringing his hands, Orwald stopped suddenly. "You say Sir Cinaed battled the rest of the pack alone?"

"Yeah," Caeserus intoned. "If stories are true, though, they were only 'puplings,' new to lycanthropy and all that." Caeserus's words seemed almost dismissive. As though the nature of the werewolves lent to or detracted anything from the feat of holding off several of the supernatural creatures at once.

"Ack! This is worse than I thought! Do you know what happens when mongrel 'puplings' you speak of see their first Full Moon?" Without so much as a breath's pause to allow the Knights to consider this, he continued. "They transform into their full werewolf-self like all the others! Creatures with blinding speed and near impenetrable hides! Teeth so sharp and hard you could sharpen an axe on them! That is what happens on Full Moons."

"So?" Bertinand queried as though all the horrible imagery was evocative of nothing more than the distant legends of youth. "It's not like anyone here got bitten."

"Argh! Lad! Do none of you realize you encountered an entire pack of werewolves? You bested them and vexed one of the eldest such beasts before his new pack. We are only a handful of nights before the next full moon! If they have followed you then we are all doomed to a grisly fate—shredded to bits by their claws and teeth!"

Bertinand's usually smiling and rosy face was ashen, and Caeserus scowled as his eyes scoured the lands around them for some sign of the menace. "Cursed full moon," Caeserus growled.

"Cursed?" Sir Cinaed enquired as he rejoined the group. "How can you say the light in the night is cursed?"

Caeserus looked around at the other Knights, his brows furrowed and eyes wide. "Because, you know. 'Full moon's bane, new moon's gain,' and all that."

"You have it backwards," Bertinand muttered under his breath.

Caeserus shot him a withering look.

"What exactly do you think that poem means?" Sir Cinaed levelled a hard stare at both Caeserus and Bertinand. Both shrank under his gaze as though reprimanded.

Caeserus was bold enough to point out, "The wolves spread

their curse on new moon nights and reach their worst by full moon."

"That's what all the legends say," Bertinand added in support, his eyes flicking to Elder Orwald who gave a nod.

"All the legends you say?" Cinaed shook his head. "All the frivolous fear-tales told children. But the true stories, those that mean something, say something very different.

"The curse is spread on nights of the new moon, because it is the darkest, their prey is disadvantaged. The beasts are equally wicked then as any day. It is merely moonlight that reveals their truest nature and gives no cover for what they are. So, no, the full moon is not cursed. It is a gift to see in the dark what would otherwise take us unawares."

There was a protracted silence as even Anargen, who had not questioned or cursed, felt abashed. Orwald, drawing himself up, finally broke the stillness. "So why do they not show up in the sun?"

Cinaed shrugged. "I do not know. Perhaps they hide in the day. Seek shade, wear coverings, but I suppose the greatest reason is they are creatures born of night. In his benevolence the Great King gives them the chance daily to seek from him the cure of their poisoning. Something any real creature of the night will regard as anathema."

Glowering at the ground, Elder Orwald muttered something in a language Anargen didn't recognize. When he looked up at Cinaed, he snapped, "Then what do you suggest we do, my young friend? We have little time to decide and cannot afford to not prepare."

As soon as he said it, Orwald gestured around. "They may yet be in hearing distance now."

"Agreed," Sir Cinaed conceded. "We should pack up the supplies and move on, try and reach Glastonae before nightfall. If we do, we should be safer and have a better vantage point on the landscape if they are still pursuing us."

"Glastonae?" Orwald choked out. "That city has been in

ruins since before I was born into this world! How can we find shelter there?"

Cinaed put his hand on his old friend's back. "It was a fortress city in days past. Besides, we have precious few options. We can't stay here. Even if we retreat straightway to the nearest city, we'll be ambushed before we get within a dozen miles of doing so. But, the choice is yours, Elder."

A rumble of resignation shook loose from Sir Orwald's throat. "I suppose you have a point, lad. But we should make haste. I do not wish to be caught like a fool unprepared. I'm not certain if this be the night, but if not tonight then soon there will be a full moon and we both know what sort of horror awaits us on that fell night."

Whatever his former assertions, it was evident from the set of Sir Cinaed's jaw he did know precisely what it was they would face. In the span of a few minutes' time, the possible dangers to be faced from Ordumair were eclipsed by the distant rising moon.

SECOND INTERLOGUE

THE OLD MAN PAUSED, his eyes clearly looking past his audience. A honey-haired man in a suit stood at the opposite end of the room. Stoic and stiff, his cool, azure eyes locked on the storyteller.

Taking in a breath and stretching his limbs, the old man groaned out, "Mm, I hope you all can forgive me, but I must take a break. Please, feel free to enjoy our fine rolls as a courtesy. I shall rejoin you shortly." As he stood, he winced a little and then called out, "Aria, please bring our guests some rolls."

After this, he walked with slow but steady strides straightway to the man in the suit. As soon as he was an acceptable distance away, whispers began. "That's Councilman Erickson. This is the third time he has been sent here."

"If that old bat isn't careful, they will shutter his doors or take him off to the asylum."

"Serve him right for telling these crazy stories and dressing the way he does. Bet he fancies himself a knight."

Jason's brows furrowed as he watched the exchange between the old man and Councilman Erickson. What could he have done meriting confinement to the asylums? The old storyteller certainly didn't seem insane as he conversed with the councilman who, by now, looked mildly agitated.

The chatter around Jason died away as suddenly as the sea drawing back for a tidal wave. Between him and the scene unfolding at the opposite end of the room stepped someone in a maroon dress. Jason's eyes traced the dress' lines from where it swirled near the wearer's ankles upward. Up to where it hugged her waist, up all the way to the hot emeralds of Aria's eyes. He felt as though he had been caught committing espionage, even if it was only idle curiosity. Aria's scowl reinforced the sensation of the former. "Roll, sir?" she snapped.

Jason looked at the nicely browned roll and suddenly became aware of its rich scent. Finely toasted wheat and creamy butter. "Oh, yes, miss." He snagged one of the larger offerings and took a bite. The warmth of the roll spilled through him, and he found himself taking two more bites in quick succession. From the amused twinkle taking up residence in Aria's eyes, he must have looked starved. It had been a day and a half since his last warm meal.

"Thank you," he managed to get out as he forced down the last of the bread faster than he was ready. "Did you make them yourself?" he asked, wanting to distract from his behavior.

A flicker of pride crossed her features, and Aria drew up a bit. "As it happens, I did. I do all of the baking for grandfather's inn."

"Well, these are excellent," Jason said, taking another bite with a bit of exaggerated relish. It felt a bit silly, even to him, but there was something about this Aria that induced it in him and made it feel accepted.

A knowing smirk was Jason's reward. "You have good taste then. You will have to try some of my other treats later."

Part of Jason was stirred by that offer and was more than willing to stick around to find out about those other treats. An equal share of him was more focused, however, holding to his purpose for being there. Without intending to, he scowled.

"Or not," Aria said, her tone somewhere between disappointment and dismissal.

"No, no. I'm sorry, I would be delighted to stay and try them. But, I'm here on business."

"Really? What kind? You look awfully young to be an oil baron."

He chuckled in spite of himself. "You have me there. My fortune is in coal." Much to his surprise, he found himself noting the girl's long, curling tresses were dark as a vein of the mineral.

A tight smile of amusement played on Aria's lips and Jason realized he was staring at her. He cleared his throat. "I'm here on family business," he amended, less the earlier sarcasm. "There is a debt my family owes, and I came to Brackenburgh to resolve it."

"I see—" she began but was soon cut off.

The old innkeeper had come up beside them and was hovering just to her right. When her eyes flicked to him, he said, "Aria, will you see to this gentleman's needs?" He gestured to Councilman Erickson who looked calmer, but no more pleased than when he entered. "He will be staying for the remainder of my story, and I must get back to its telling or the guests will grow restless."

She nodded and set off to tend to her grandfather's request. As soon as she was about it, the old man turned toward Jason, eyeing him up and down. His heavy, slate-tufted brows furrowed in the examination, and he clapped Jason on the arm with surprising force. "Come now, lad. You won't wish to miss this next part."

21

A DESPERATE STAND

"I haven't ventured into the former shops and homes beneath the castle lest I find the remnants of the battles. Worse yet, remains of normal lives interrupted, laid bare for the viewing. Mausoleums for lives lost to ceaseless war. If one ever wondered where the terms gloom and ruination came from, Glastonae gave rise to both."

—ANARGEN'S JOURNEY JOURNAL,
AURIGIDS 1605 M.E.

NIGHT WAS FALLING over the sundered timbers and shattered stone edifices of Glastonae. Surging up the final flight of stone stairs, Anargen reached the tower he and Caeserus would be holed up in for the night. Sir Cinaed had divided the group up by twos and staggered their positions within the ruins of the city so that it would be more difficult for the werewolves to find and corner more than one group.

Closest to the point of entrance by which the wolves were expected to come was a broad and tall bastion. Much of it had been destroyed in the siege that laid waste to the city centuries ago. Centrally located on the outer wall of the castle, huge portions of its length now lay exposed to the open air of the night. A help and hindrance to their cause. Sir Cinaed and Terrillian were positioned there. The plan was to light a torch to mark the wolves' approach. However, clarity of sight meant equal exposure to the enemy's keen senses as well. Not to mention the burden of being the first to face the snapping jaws of their adversaries.

Anargen and Caeserus were located in a tower on the inner wall of the old castle, the midway point one could say. The donjon had been reserved for the elderly Orwald and Sir Bertinand. It was the fall back point for everyone and the sturdiest structure remaining in the city.

There was a dry amusement to glean, considering they would be facing the onslaught of these fiendish creatures on the site of the first battle in the centuries long war between Ords and Ecthels. The Battle of Broken Bridges had taken place atop the grounds the sprawling castle stood over. A network of causeways and battlements spanned the gaps, where far below the dark waters of the rock strewn and angry River Glaston churned. It, along with three other tributaries, Rivers Bradden, Ermar, and Orthall crisscrossed the area. They made it treacherous to settle and navigate, but also an incredible, resilient point of defense.

If the worst should happen, all had been instructed to flee through the tunnel to the rivers and away from the city. The convergence of rushing rivers would confound the wolves' senses and keeping any pursuit at bay till daylight. From that point on, it would be a sprint to reach the walls of Ordumair, hundreds of miles north. Their horses were tethered somewhere out beyond the city to help make such a dash more plausible.

A robust full moon overhead offered Anargen's eyes the luminance needed to see that Caeserus was crouched behind the arrowslit. He seemed to be gazing thoughtfully at the glowing inscriptions on the blade of his Spiritsword.

Not willing to disturb him, Anargen dropped to the ground on the opposite side of the hole and closed his eyes. He took in several shallow breaths to calm his unruly nerves. Already drowsiness was settling in. This was certainly not the time to be turning in early, or at all. A deep sleep tonight would mean death for more than just the slumberer. Thus when a less than subtle clearing of Caeserus's throat echoed through the chamber, Anargen's eyes snapped open without a grudge.

"Don't drift off to sleep on me, Anargen," Caeserus jibed. "We've both seen what sleep can earn."

"No worries. I was just trying to relax some. This waiting business feels as if it could be worse than the actual thing."

The other Knight shrugged at the sarcasm. "I wouldn't mind having this ordeal over with. We have better things to do than mess with a bunch of deranged mutts."

Anargen chuckled. It was good to be joking with his friend for a change.

"It would've been nice to have found a better spot to make this stand against them though," Caeserus noted. "As much as the rivers will hinder them, I think it will be worse for us. All the wall walks and battlements make this place look like a giant spider-web. Only we aren't spiders and I don't know how we're expected to thread our way through this accursed place." He snorted before Anargen could reply and added, "Eh, maybe those clumsy scoundrels will be too baffled by this place to even find us."

A weak smile was all Anargen could offer. Beneath the sarcasm there was a bitter edge. He suspected Caeserus was ignoring the role their deception with the bandits had in getting them to this moment.

At worst the location was as beneficial as it was detrimental. Each of the three concentric walls to the structure towered at least forty feet over the water and town below. Each had battlement bridges connecting, at various junctures, to other points on the castle. Tiers tended to rise in elevation to the next level, except for the bridges which diverged and skewed off to meet random oddities in the construction. Like lone towers affixed in the middle of what should have been the ward of the castle if it were built on more reasonable terrain. In the peak of conditions, it would have been a ponderous task to navigate but offered numerous defensive options. As things stood now, the integrity of some bridges was dubious. In truth, the stability of the whole thing was far from being above suspicion.

Cool air gusted through the tower, nippy but not frigid. Blustery huffs of the sort had been coming intermittently. Almost no natural sounds could be heard in this hollow shell of Ord pride. It was unsettling to have no noises. It felt too reminiscent of barrows or vaults where even the living keep to somber stillness as they pass by. What was worse, even with the moon's light, the dark grey stones of the castle all but disappeared in the dark of night.

"At least it's not storming tonight," Anargen offered.

A piercing howl cut through the night air and instantly traced icy fingers of dread down the nape of Anargen's neck. The teens looked at one another and peered out their hole.

A collection of softer, less potent yowls followed in the wake of the first. No doubt the werewolves were scouring the streets of the desolate town beneath.

Small but undeniable, a yellow-orange light flared into existence in the tower Anargen and Caeserus were watching. Soon after, the surprisingly intense glows of Sir Cinaed's and Sir Terrillian's Spiritswords joined it.

Seconds slipped away as the lights behaved curiously. They never moved to give a signal at all, holding fixed as if in indecision.

Anargen spared a glance at Caeserus, who was looking around them, vexed. He appeared to be concentrating on something other than the eminently important fight that must have begun below. "What are you doing?" Anargen whispered.

"Shh!" Caeserus urged. "Do you hear that?"

Listening now, Anargen could hear the faint pattering of footsteps. Caught up as he was in the sudden onset of the night's battle, it could very well be the pounding of his own heart.

Unwilling to listen to whispers in the wind, Anargen turned his attention back to the tower below. To his horror, no lights remained in the tower at all. They had vanished or worse, been snuffed out.

"Anargen! Did you hear that?" Caeserus asked emphatically, this time not caring how loudly he spoke.

"Hear what?" Anargen asked. And then, he did. The grunts and growls beneath them. Peering directly downward, towards one of the battlements on the inner wall, Anargen could see three enormous forms. Their shapes, etched in moonlight, stalked along the wall walks with startling dexterity.

The trio was following the bridges towards the donjon. Anargen stifled a gasp with his hand. Little wonder the others had appeared riddled with conflict over what to do. The whole pack was descending in unison on one spot. Distracting them would invite a devastating assault upon themselves, but to do nothing meant condemning Orwald and Bertinand. Now the burden of this decision was on Anargen and Caeserus's young shoulders.

Looking over at Caeserus, Anargen whispered, "What should we do? They're moving on the keep. We had the Great King's favor that they did not hear us when you yelled at me."

"How many are there?" Caeserus whispered back.

"All of them. Well, I saw three definitely, but the shadows of the others were not far behind. If we don't do something they'll slaughter Sir Bertinand and Elder Orwald!"

For a moment, Anargen was distracted from the current crisis by his own words. The reverberations of his own speech seemed peculiar to him. It felt odd to refer to his longtime friend now as Sir Bertinand. To perceive him for what he was, a Knight of an ancient and noble order.

The distraction was short-lived as Caeserus shot back, "What about Sir Cinaed and Terrillian? Where are they?"

Anargen shook his head dismally. "I don't know. Their lights are no longer in the central bastion."

Louder than he should have, Caeserus snapped, "Those verminous, overstuffed hounds of darkness! They will pay for this!"

From the winding stairwell behind the teens came a rumbling sound completely unfamiliar to them. Spinning about they found at the doorway to their tower's chamber the gargantuan form of a wolf staring at them. Its great shoulders heaved up and down as the sound they'd heard issued from its open jaws.

It was laughing at them.

Anargen's grip on his blade's hilt tightened as the bark of macabre humor persisted. Crouching into a battle stance they'd learned, Anargen readied himself without question for what was to come. Fear, anger, pity, disgust, uncertainty —all had to be swept away. In their place resolve, determination, and trust in the High King was needed. Drawing his Spiritsword, Anargen heard the crackle and whoosh as the flames leapt up the blade, consuming it in a blaze more potent than any he'd seen on it yet.

Caeserus mirrored Anargen's move and the werewolf shrank back. The cackle died in its throat as its fiendish eyes fixed on the flames emanating from each Knight's blade. Each sword burned still brighter, more intensely. It was as if they were stirred to readiness by the appearance of a creature whose existence defied the rule of the One True King.

The beast hesitated for an instant. In the cramped space, the fires' light vexed it sorely. Anargen and Caeserus did not, however, hesitate in kind. With a glance of assurance to one another, each gave a shout and rushed forward at the same time from either side.

As they did, the werewolf, eyes wide with terror, let out a shrill bark of fright. It reared back into a crouch and sprang forward. The huge missile of fur and muscle split the difference between the two Knights. Both teens were battered aside as it landed in the chamber's center.

Skittering to a stop, it whirled around. A second ago, it

might have been attempting to flee. Seeing each Knight so unsteadied, its arrogance returned. A low growl grew wicked.

Readying himself, Anargen was wary. Looking to Caeserus, he tried to move in tandem. However fast, the creature couldn't defend both sides at once.

Cocky, the lycanthrope allowed them to get on either side without opposition. It eyed each Knight in turn, snapping at whomever moved for a strike. With such a large beast between them, Anargen couldn't see Caeserus to coordinate an attack. Two-to-one and they were struggling. They had to do something drastic before others of its kind arrived.

Another snap was ventured by the wolf at Caeserus's latest sortie towards him. Sensing the opportunity, Anargen shouted, "Now!" He charged forward, Spiritsword raised overhead.

The werewolf whipped its head around. With blinding speed it shifted to avoid the attack. But Anargen wasn't so unwise.

The werewolf found the burning gleam of Anargen's shield coming into its desired route of attack. Stopping short of mauling the crackling shield, its eyes narrowed into slits against the brush of the flames. Blinded, it never saw Caeserus coming.

Seizing the opportunity, Caeserus brought his Spiritsword down on the beast's back with a furious stroke. The blade sank in deep.

An ear-piercing screech of pain and disbelief followed and Caeserus staggered back. If he'd continued, the blade might well have sliced completely through the creature.

The wound sizzled with little tendrils of smoke curling off it. Thrashing about, the creature began snapping wildly. A wounded animal, it was more dangerous now than before!

Over the whines and snarls, Anargen shouted, "Have a plan over—" Before he could finish he was forced to duck the claws swiping at him. He missed being battered aside like a rag doll by inches.

"Nope! Thought I'd play it by ear!" At that moment, he ran forward and jumped at the beast, going for a quick kill.

Even in agony, the creature was not caught off guard by such an obvious advance. The beast's shoulder connected with Caeserus's abdomen. Anargen was frozen watching his friend's lanky form fly backwards into a wall.

Stone from the wall crumbled away and dropped into the churning waters below. Caeserus groaned as he slumped to the ground. The beast seemed torn between finishing Caeserus off and battling Anargen.

They stared at each other for what seemed like an endless expanse of time. Within Anargen's heart he felt the subtle push from that familiar voice to strike. Now.

Without hesitation, he leapt forward, drew back his arm, and plunged it for the creature's heart. At the same instant, the creature turned on Caeserus to finish him off. The strike from Anargen was perfectly timed so that the wolf's head was facing away.

Anargen's Spiritsword plunged deep into the werewolf's side, slicing through its sinews and hide with equal ease to Caeserus's. This time, the blade-bearer did not relent till he was sure he'd inflicted a debilitating wound.

As Anargen removed his sword, the creature cried out, pain in its voice beyond understanding. It writhed, too injured to fight. Soon its screeches faded to whimpers, and Anargen was left staring at his friend over the colossal mound of its body. By this point, Caeserus had reached his feet and looked back. Before Anargen could offer an alternative, Caeserus silenced the creature for good.

Still caught in the rush of battle's unyielding tide, Anargen shouted, "We have to help the others."

22

IN KEEP IN CLOSE

"You think when you first go under swimming—as water creeps into your nose and eyes—that is the worst. But then the burning starts, and you thrash to the surface. The next time you go down you only pray you'll have the strength to make it up again."

—ANARGEN'S JOURNEY JOURNAL,
AURIGIDS 1605 M.E.

EACH KNIGHT MADE his way onto the connective bridge between the battlement nearest their tower and the keep. They bounded with a swiftness they had never known. Ahead the keep's great poplar door was flung off the hinges and lying on the ground. There were deep scratches marring the carvings of Ord warriors on the paneling.

The dark maw of the keep's massive entryway towered before them. Gazing into its darkness, Anargen felt a pressure upon his heart and thought he heard a faint whisper. The voice instructed, "Drop to the ground." Already rushing at a sprint, Anargen determined not to question the High King's command. He dropped into a roll on his side. The momentum carried him into the keep. From the ground, he saw a flicker of motion.

As he regained his footing, there was a crash. Anargen saw a werewolf shaking its head as though dizzied and then collapsing with a shudder.

Anargen looked at Caeserus, grey eyes wild with surprise. The other Knight took in two deep, shaking breaths of his own and nodded toward his Spiritsword.

The words inscribed on the blade were suffused with still more vibrancy than usual. It was as if the blade was glowering at something. Then Anargen caught it. A faint odor of burning hair and a little curl of smoke rising from the werewolf's motionless form.

Caeserus spoke soft, "I heard the Great King tell me to raise my Spiritsword. About that time you went into a roll and that werewolf leapt right over where you would have entered. I think he was trying to maul you . . ."

"And your blade cut into him as he passed by," Anargen finished, his voiced filled with wonder. "If I had questioned the Great King's instruction for one moment, then I would be no more."

Wonder and terror mixed to form a potent tonic keeping Anargen from moving. Just one moment of doubt would have been death.

Caeserus grabbed Anargen by the shoulder. "Come on. We have to get to the others."

"Right," Anargen replied, sounding hollow even to himself.

The grasp of Caeserus had tightened, and he gave Anargen a shake. "Hey, snap out of it. That's two down and four more to go. We have the advantage now."

It was true. The battle suddenly seemed in their favor. Or was it that way all along?

Shaking his head to clear it, Anargen forced his frozen limbs to move. He wrenched free of Caeserus's grasp and gave him a light jab on the shoulder in kind. "Let's go."

As they sprinted forward, the fire of their swords helped to navigate the passages to the keep's feasting hall. A hidden rear gate was there as well as the last line of the night's defense.

Coming around the final turn a chilling howl sounded off the stony walls. Another of the werewolves had met with the fury of the Spiritsword. Comfort was short-lived. Two uninjured wolves snarled at Anargen and Caeserus on entering. One wolf lay downed nearby. The other two had Orwald and Bertinand cornered.

"Oh, you've come to join the festivities," Bertinand called out. "Was there good fun out there as well?"

"More than I care to say," Caeserus replied, keeping a wary eye on the monsters.

"You are all insufferable. Keep your mouths shut and your minds open," Orwald snapped.

"Right," Anargen answered. He took one step towards the fray and heard the voice from earlier. Louder and clearer. "Take a path along the right wall." The voice stopped short of telling him what to do thereafter. Remembering the peril he'd just avoided, Anargen dashed off in obedience.

Caeserus stayed to the room's center, approaching with cautious steps. Once in the position he felt guided towards, it became agonizing to watch Caeserus's slow creeping. What was he supposed to do?

Elder Orwald held both an axe and his Spiritsword at ready, his back against Bertinand's. Gripping tighter the shield he held, Anargen wondered at such a decision, given the sturdiness of the shield. The Voice spoke once more to him. "Give no worry to that, the Ord's decisions are his own." Though he was given nothing explicit, Anargen believed he saw the whole picture now.

Inches from where he was to run, Anargen heard Caeserus give a shout. The loudest and most menacing of his life, which echoed in the enclosure. Startled, the monsters spun to face their threat. Yet even as they did, the one on the right had only a moment's chance to catch the glimpse of Anargen barreling towards him, before Anargen's shield came smashing into the beast's ribs.

With a squealing whimper, the creature went down on its side and scrambled to get up. It bumped into its fellow monster, which had been tensed to jump at Caeserus.

"Nice work," Caeserus called to Anargen as he squared himself to face his beast. This left the dazed werewolf to Bertinand, Orwald, and Anargen.

Seeing the three Knights advancing on it in unison, the monster growled, its huge head swishing back and forth trying to track its foes.

Orwald made a move to get close, a yip and a snap. Taking his opportunity, Caeserus charged it from behind, aiming to tackle it.

No more expecting this action than the other Knights, the werewolf saw the attack a second before it happened and whipped its head about to snap at Caeserus. By then Bertinand was on its flank. A swift slash across its right shoulder brought the creature to the floor.

Raising his sword to deliver a killing blow, Caeserus overestimated his speed. At his back the other monster crouched to pounce.

"Watch out!" Anargen yelled and jumped forward, pushing Caeserus out of the way even as the werewolf reached him.

In the ensuing tumble, the jaws of the creature grated against the indomitable will of Anargen's shield. Growling, it snapped to either side, hunting for a place to sink its fangs into Anargen's flesh.

Matching each snap with narrow dodges, Anargen realized his sword was out of reach. He was trapped and could only delay the inevitable so long. Another snap and somehow his left arm got pinned beneath a massive, clawed-paw.

The creature crinkled its nose. Faint burn marks from where it had bit at his shield still smoked. It opened its mouth and leaned down, slow. Life and death were only inches away from each other.

Suddenly, the beast yelped. Fumbling to the side, it turned around to see what had struck it. The agent of Anargen's timely aid was a double-sided battle axe of ornate and skillful design. "Bless you and your axe, Elder Orwald!" Anargen mumbled as he rolled towards his sword and made it back to his feet.

The impressive axe was sadly ineffective against the beast. Good only for a distraction. Scanning the situation, Anargen called out, "Where's the other one?"

"It fled," Bertinand called back. "Sorry to cut things close there."

"I'm not going to complain. Do you have a plan for this one as well?"

"We end it," Caeserus replied, advancing on the last beast.

Outmatched, the beast arched its back as though prepared to spring for an attack. At the last second, it let loose a resounding howl and rushed out the doorway of the room, disappearing into the winding corridors.

Anargen sucked in a sharp breath and let it out slowly as tensed muscles could finally relax. He would have dropped to the ground again if the faint memory of at least one more wolf being outside had not come to him.

A shriek echoed down the passageways, followed by the most fearsome howls Anargen had ever heard. Startled, he immediately looked to the wounded werewolf, which merely raised its head and barked out a shrill moan before collapsing again.

"The Grey Scourge. Brace yourself lads, he's coming this way!" Elder Orwald called out.

Around the chamber, the defenders tensed. The silence broken only by a hurried tapping sound from beyond the room. Metal or razor claws, clacking off the stones, it was impossible to tell. Anargen had a guess and raised his sword to the ready.

Moments later, both Sir Cinaed and Terrillian came

bounding into the room. "It's all right, the night is ours!" Terrillian called out.

Anargen all but dropped his sword rushing to them. "Sir Cinaed, Sir Terrillian! You're all right!"

Terrillian sucked in a deft cut allotment of precious air and choked out, "Ha! Barely. I don't know about you guys, but from now on I'm carrying a crossbow loaded with silver bolts."

From across the room, Orwald responded with a low whistle. "Good you didn't try that sort o' nonsense tonight. You would've made yourself an easy kill. Silver is an old wives' tale. Better to have some hardy steel if you want to avoid becoming a meal."

Ignoring the somber note, Anargen helped Sir Cinaed find a good place to rest his weight against the wall as he recovered. "What happened to you both?" Anargen asked. "Your torch and swords went dark. We thought the werewolves . . . you know."

"Hmph," Sir Cinaed answered, grimacing. "We saw the creatures were splitting up. They must have caught our scents from the moment they entered the city. The pack divided themselves and headed after each of us in turn. So, Sir Terrillian and I set out to flank them. We assumed it would alert you without revealing we were on to them."

Sir Terrillian picked up, his hands keeping pace with his exuberance. "We found ourselves at the disadvantage of facing the Grey Scourge himself. Worse than all the rest of the pack combined. Had you and Caeserus not dispatched a werewolf in such short order, he might have been more determined to end us. As it was, he was slightly distracted trying to listen to the battle's progress, I guess. With every yowl, he flinched and drew further back to launch his attacks. Caution cost him a victory against us.

"We chased him up towards the keep, but he leapt to somewhere along the battlements. Another wolf was already waiting for him. There was some banter and he gave his order to withdraw. We caught that last one on our way in!"

"So, we did it," Caeserus mumbled, sounding awed. He clapped his hands together and shouted, "We took out a whole pack of werewolves!"

Before the cheers and shouts of victory could catch with everyone in the room, Sir Cinaed amended, heavily, "This has been an evil night. I do not relish what has transpired here. The deaths of these creatures, even if foul-natured, is something to lament. They were men at one time and as such, were deserving as we of the High King's favor. That we have found it and they chose to spurn it is not something to revel in."

It was then Sir Cinaed noticed the wounded werewolf on the ground still breathing deeply. A brief look of surprise lit his countenance before a more discerning expression set in. "This one survived the battle?"

Bertinand answered off-handedly, "Oh, yeah. I guess he did. I got him pretty good, and he squalled out in an awful way. Ever since he's been lying there. He didn't seem as ferocious as the others. If he'd been paying more attention when we started to fight, I doubt I would've gotten him so easily.

"Hmph, might've made the whole fight go poorly for us."

Elder Orwald spoke up from where he leaned over the werewolf, examining it. "Lads, we best be on our way at first light. These creatures aren't werewolves as we believed."

"Uh, I'm pretty sure that thing over there isn't a normal wolf," Bertinand said, nudging the prone creature with his boot tip.

Orwald rolled his eyes. "Then perhaps you should listen twice as much as you talk.

"These monsters are werebeasts, not werewolves."

Even Sir Cinaed raised an eyebrow at this. "What exactly does that mean?"

"It means trouble if we stick around here too long. My people long recorded tales of this kind. Werewolves are creatures of instinct and prowess, but no real cunning. They kill out of rage and mindless animal fury. The werebeast, however, is every bit as cunning as any man. These fiends kill by choice and with all the ferocity and power of their lupine cousins."

"Hmm, well, we still bested the whole pack," Caeserus commented after a breath's silence.

Shaking his head, Orwald countered, "Yes, but if the legends be true, these beasts have not yet reached their apex. They are said to have the bodies of bears, the backs of bison, the heads of wolves, and the minds of men. I would say this was only a taste of what is ahead."

"So we're doomed then?" Terrillian piped up, arms folded over his chest as he braced himself against a wall. Anargen marveled at the blasé way they tossed about the topic of their death and the subject of mythical monsters. Then again, he also knew all too well how exhausted they were. Fatigue can drive one mad.

"No," Orwald said, with surprising cheer. "Soon we shall be with my people and no beasts of legend, no matter how old and mighty, would dare come within the walls of Ordumair. I simply wished to make sure none of us gets the fool idea to linger here unnecessarily."

From the way Orwald looked at Sir Cinaed, it was clear he was aiming the comment at the Knight Errant. Anargen noticed their mentor let the verbal blow glance off him. He was staring at the downed werebeast. "Fine," he muttered. "We ride for Ordumair at dawn."

After some time, everyone set about the more practical aspects of the night ahead: building a fire in the keep's hearth, determining watches, and planning their route when dawn arrived. It was difficult for Anargen not to notice that after Elder Orwald's comments, Sir Cinaed was only partially present the remainder of the night. Though he spoke with warmth and a portion of his usual humor, some part of him was elsewhere.

What menace did he seek to vanquish within the walls of his mind? From the tightness around Sir Cinaed's eyes it could spell portends of great import to the futures of all present. On that, Anargen's certainty was unshakable.

After everyone else was asleep, Sir Cinaed came to Anargen and woke him. He whispered a request to Anargen. "I need to write a letter. You have a quill and parchment?"

The teen nodded, sleepiness muddling his thoughts.

"Good," Cinaed replied. "Then you can pen the letter I dictate for you. Our captive friend over there isn't quite what Orwald thinks either."

23

TO THE WALLS OF ORDUMAIR

"And so the Ord warriors gave iron for iron. The howls of the felled echoing in the night air as the mighty timbers of Ecthelan burned. But Thane Ordumair, the Great Bear, wept."

HISTORY OF ORDS, VOLUME 1

SUNSET WAS ONLY an hour or so away when Anargen's eyes, at last, beheld a faint glimmer. In the distance was their destination. The tiny flickers of auburn sky turned to a dull, yellow glow, cooling to darker hues with every step. Each step allowed the wan light to reveal a little more of Ordumair's gates.

Already it looked at least thirty feet high but could have been taller. Anargen's only frames of reference were the colossal outcroppings of rock to either side of it. Everything beyond in all compass directions was mountains cloaked in the haze of twilight.

A chill surged through Anargen, but not of fear. They were so very near to the completion of their task. Before they were done, he had an important piece of business to attend. The letter requested days ago by Sir Cinaed.

Riding at the back of the column, Anargen's keen eyes

discerned the contours of a formidable keep, with high towers having only the narrowest of arrowslits for windows. Sitting still higher, even for its great distance, Anargen could make out the dark and deeply ominous form Fior-sruthain, Ordumair's mountain. A weathered peak stretching for miles to either side in its gradual ascent to zenith. It loomed at least two thousand feet above the valley floor, likely far more than that compared to sea level. The whole area was rough and mountainous.

The valley was much obscured by other lesser crags, staggered on either side of the Fior-sruthain, which had a central location on the horizon. These mountains were Ringwald, to the right and nearest, and Thane's Peak, to the left and slightly more distant. The foot of each rested near enough for the Ords to build the ring wall to their great fortress in the gap. Any invaders wishing to enter the Valley of Ords would have to overtake the massive wall. Or attempt the treacherous climb over the granite sentinels the High King himself had affixed there.

On the approach, Anargen studied the castle. He was near enough now to see in sharper relief its parapets and walkways connecting its defensive array. Given the time to consider it, the fortress of Ordumair paled in comparison to the description offered him by Sir Cinaed. This castle seemed no more formidable than the one at Glastonae. Indeed, it was far less impressive in both scale and defensive ingenuity.

Try as he might, Anargen couldn't assuage a feeling of disappointment at the sight. A grander sight than anything in Black River, but hardly the source for the regaling epic tales of heroic defenses.

Ahead the column slowed to a trot as a cadre of riders hastened to meet them from the direction of the Ord stronghold. Their horses were smaller than normal, but thick, impressive. They looked to be capable of doing well the work of a Clydesdale at only half the height. They moved fleetly for their bulk as well. These steeds were fitting complements to the Ords, who were known for fast and ferocious combat.

Shortly they were upon Anargen and his companions, forming a "W" shaped blockade to the Knights' progress. The rider at point traipsed a few more paces before reining in his horse and raising a gauntleted hand. "Halt!" he boomed.

The speaker was only a dozen paces away from Anargen. In the failing light of day, his features seemed rigid and gloomy as a statue. The eyes beneath the prominent browband and nasal of his helm were certainly as hard.

All but Elder Orwald halted their horses as directed. The Ord proceeded with slow, deliberate steps. No longer masking his accent, Orwald raised his arm in greeting. "Hail, Seumas Arno, valiant master of the castle guard! Greetings to you on this eve."

Arno nodded to the men flanking him. All but two dispersed in tight, choreographed moves. Meanwhile, Orwald glanced back, and Sir Cinaed spurred his horse, coming alongside the aged Ord. This earned a scowl from Captain Arno.

Impossibly, Arno's accent seemed even heavier when he spoke. "Your honor, I see the journey met its goals. The Thane is in the fortress. I will escort you to him personally. Your companions must stay here." As he said this, he eyed Cinaed with particular distaste and added, "You know the laws of our people."

Elder Orwald did not seem in the least deflated.

"Nobles keep impassive," Anargen noted in a whisper to Caeserus. The other didn't acknowledge him. Even if his friend didn't see the value, Anargen knew they needed to learn quick to keep from shaming themselves at court.

Old Orwald answered benignly, "That I do. I will see the Thane tonight. There are urgent matters for us to discuss. You will see to it that my companions are shown the fullness of our benevolence?"

The subordinate Ord eyed the Knights with blatant annoyance. "These hungermen—"

Orwald cut him off, a low burn in his tone. "None of that.

They are guests of the Thane. By the Thane's order, Sir Cinaed's every request must be filled."

Arno nodded curtly and made way for his elder. Elder Orwald spoke a few words to Cinaed, too soft for Anargen to hear. Then the elderly Ord was off to the main gate.

At first, no one spoke. Captain Arno merely continued to glare at them, seemingly content to do nothing. Giving a reasonable amount of time, Sir Cinaed spoke up, his voice echoing off the mountainsides with authority. "Captain Arno, it is a pleasure to meet you. I have need of your assistance. Matters have arisen in our travels, which necessitate delivering a message. I need your swiftest rider to carry a letter to Estonbury. It is imperative the letter reach the Knight Hall there."

"No," the bulky Ord replied. Though a good foot shorter than Anargen, the little warrior wielded tremendous force of presence. Perhaps it was his bulky frame and even thicker armor, or simply his unflinching mannerisms. Whatever the case, Anargen felt like a scolded pup rather than a scorned guest.

"No?" Cinaed questioned.

"No. There cannot possibly be such need as to divert my best rider from the castle's defense with the Ecthels arriving soon. You would not diminish the security of our lands, would you?" A faint smile turned up the corner of his mouth.

"Do all Ords conceal daggers in their smiles?" Caeserus muttered to Anargen. Arno's eyes were hard on them, as if in confirmation. Apparently they were not so discreet with their whispers as they thought.

Cinaed countered, "Did not one of your own come to me in Black River? That is much further than Estonbury. Send Erreth, he is the one who visited me and is certainly capable of handling a much shorter journey."

"I cannot spare my men to go chasing some fancy of your Order. We need all the men available to keep watch over the security of our lands with the Ecthel emissaries en route."

Glowering at the Ord, the tension in Sir Cinaed's jaw was

noticeable. "Your people would be better served by relinquishing one man to save many than to keep all present for disaster. Elder Orwald was clear—"

"That your requests are like an order from the Thane? But I have literal orders from him to defend this castle.

"Now, if there's nothing else, you will follow me to your quarters."

There was no question in his words, and Sir Cinaed gave a dismissive wave, acquiescing. As Arno led the way, Bertinand asked, "Hungermen?"

Under his breath, Sir Cinaed grumbled, "A slur the Ords use for us Knights. When Duncoin's father Denhard was Thane, the war with Ecthelowall got worse. Some unfortunate circumstances led to hunger among the citizenry. Our Order was blamed and banished."

The soldier ahead let out a sigh. "Quicken your pace, hungermen. We haven't all night."

Thereafter, the ride to the colossal gates was spent in a forced silence. This fact bothered Anargen less once they were near enough to view the carved oaken doors. They were polished and coated in a dark lacquer. Sentries bearing torches at regular intervals leading to the gate provided enough luminance to see the images adorning the entryway's paneling. The torchlight cast shadows in the depressions and highlighted each ridge, revealing there to be sixteen squares. Each contained a scene involving a different looking dwarf. One of them was on his knees, face stricken with grief, as a fire raged behind him.

Gnawing on his lip, Anargen debated asking Sir Cinaed if the heartbroken man was Ordumair II. Cinaed had told them that Thane was ruined after he lost his beloved bride, Alessia. The fire would then be the Ecthel's Forest of Golden Leaves burned in retribution. Anargen realized the better question was how would the Ecthels feel on seeing these?

One thing did loose Anargen's tongue. "Where is the Great Bulwark of Ord legends?"

No one answered him.

Indeed, this castle was formidable. It would take great effort for any army to overcome it. Yet its structuring was wrong. The famed central rampart was missing completely. The keep, which should have set atop it was nestled behind a second massive wall, curved to deflect projectiles. Around it stood numerous imposing towers. It was reminiscent of a forest in a way. An architectural detail almost certainly, and ironically, taken from the men of Ecthelowall.

Causeways crisscrossed the structure much the way they had at Glastonae. Anargen couldn't shake his observation. This is not the resplendent bastion described in legends. Did Sir Cinaed know this was not Ordumair?

24

DWARF COURTESY

"Months of hard travel and leaving at my back everything I held dear. Yet here I am, at the culmination of the endeavor, wondering if we are welcome at all."

—ANARGEN'S JOURNEY JOURNAL,
FYELLTH 1605 M.E.

THE INTERIOR of the keep was less a display of dwarf ingenuity in defense and more a strange kind of prison. Several rooms formed a block, several blocks a corridor. Those in turn were a sample of many more.

Every passageway was stark, bare except for regularly spaced torches and stern looking guards. Each sentry stood rigid, but their eyes followed the teens. Baleful, Anargen could tell those guards would spring to attack if given permission.

Coming to a door with a double guard, Captain Arno shoved open the door and gestured to the darkened room beyond. "In you go. You will not be permitted leave of this room, apart from the will of the Thane."

All four teens waited, expecting something more to be said,

but no further details were produced. "What about meals? Or at least a candle for our room?" Bertinand asked, incredulous.

"In you go," Captain Arno replied without an ounce of compassion.

The teens complied and as soon as they were in, the door slammed shut behind them. Anargen drew his Spiritsword, allowing its flames to light the room. On a pine chest at the room's back, Terrillian found an oil lantern, which Anargen lit with his sword.

It was dim in the room, but it looked as if the Ords offered them an unused portion of their barracks. Not long ago, a standing army would have been an oddity. It was likely the Ords had a standing army long before the rest of the Lowlands adopted such a strategy.

Such superficial observations only served to underscore the tense silence hanging over all of them. Caeserus noted dryly, "What a warm welcome we've received."

"Not an ill word to be heard the whole way here," Bertinand added lightly. Looking around with cursory interest, he gestured to the rest of the room. "I wonder if all their guests are so well received."

"It could have been worse," Anargen pointed out. "I think to say that our presence here is unwanted would be a gross skewing of the truth. I have never felt so utterly loathed by strangers."

"That's not the half of it," Terrillian said. "Did you see how that captain looked at us? If Elder Orwald had not been nearby, I doubt our welcome would have ended so amicably. Maybe we should speak with—"

From near the doorway the sounds of strained groans broke into Terrillian's words and overshadowed them. Anargen, Caeserus, and Terrillian turned their attention to the door. Bertinand was yanking and pushing in alternation on its brass handle. The oak barrier did not budge, not even a conciliatory creak.

Seeing his work futile and the others watching him now, Bertinand said, "I think they've barred the door from the outside!" His tone, filled with shock and disgust echoed in the small room.

"Dwarf courtesy," Caeserus summarized.

25

VISION OF DESPAIR

"Sitting in that room, it was so like a prison. But worse, for we were guests. Supposed advisors. So rather than all of us bearing our verbal daggers against our captor-hosts, we found them turning on each other."

—ANARGEN'S JOURNEY JOURNAL,
FYLLETH 1605 M.E.

DAYS PASSED. A few quick trips out to the castle's garderobe and a larder to receive rations were permitted, but nothing more. The room felt ever smaller, stuffy, and tepid during the day. At night, bitter cold through the threadbare sheets they were given as bedding. There was precious little else in the room. Their pine chest containing lanterns had nothing else inside, not even dust motes.

None but Elder Orwald ventured by. He visited only once to assure the teens he was seeing to it the Thane knew they weren't being treated as guests. He tempered his championing with a reminder. "This is a barracks after all, not a dungeon, lads. Fresh recruits for our army dwell in the same." Perhaps from their time together before, he thought to add, "As does Sir Cinaed." It didn't help.

Anargen's day was filled with sketches and writing a letter to Seren. He did his best to explain the Three Hundred Year's War. Painting the tragic history to underscore how momentous these peace negotiations were for each side.

"What are you doing?" Caeserus suddenly asked, wandering over to Anargen.

"I'm doing some writing."

At this Caeserus's face softened a little, though his voice was still gruff from poor sleep. "Oh, what is it? Another letter to Seren?"

The song that was her name sent Anargen's heart racing off like a wild horse. Reining in his thoughts and emotions, Anargen tried to cover the parchments. "Yeah. I'm trying to explain the Ords' history to her. Help her understand all this."

"Ha," Caeserus huffed, his mood darkening. "There's not much to understand here. They hate us. Never mind what happened a hundred years ago or twenty or whatever. These dwarfs choose to hate Knights. I doubt they'll accept us being here much longer and certainly not allow Sir Cinaed to sit in on their negotiations. Invited or not, we are not welcome."

Anargen offered a rueful smile and paged away from the letter. The damage was done, however, as Caeserus began railing about the "ruin of the quest." "Wretched little mountain gnomes" and "their petty fight." "It's their fault."

After a while Anargen tried to pay the ravings no mind. Focusing on drawing what the ruins of Glastonae looked like in the moonlight was much more soothing. Into Anargen's sketch-therapy, Terrillian blurted out, "You know, Caeserus, for all your complaints about Sir Cinaed not telling us anything, you've never spoken one word of your vision to us. All I know is 'terrible evil will befall Libertias' and 'those wretched mountain gnomes will ruin it all.'"

"I withheld telling of it at Sir Cinaed's request," Caeserus bit out and shot a surprised Anargen a withering look.

"Then don't let a thing like honoring your word stop you now," Anargen snapped back.

"I didn't pledge my fealty to Cinaed of Black River," Caeserus spat in reply, coming to loom over Anargen.

On his feet in an instant, Anargen glared back at his friend. There were so many things he wanted to say. Anything to knock the knowing smirk off Caeserus's face.

"None of us did," Terrillian spoke up, moving between Anargen and Caeserus. He waited there a few seconds more for Anargen to let fists he hadn't known he had been balling go slack. Whirling to face Caeserus, Terrillian posed a simple question. "Since it doesn't mean anything to you, out with it. What's your great vision?"

Caeserus pursed his lips in thought. Of a sudden he shrugged. "Sure, fine.

"Everything was dark, black like a moonless night. After a few minutes, I saw a fire catch in the distance and from its light, I could see I was in Black River. Slowly beneath the fire rose a tower. It allowed the light from the fire to touch everything. It was so warm, like the sun at noon.

"Then came another darkness. A deeper one. First shadows, flitting on the edges. It crept towards the tower's base, making the tower sink into the ground. The darkness grew and surrounded the tower. Wicked things began to dance within the deepest depths of shadow. They wanted to tear down the tower.

"That's when I saw them. Saw us, I mean. We ran out from Black River as it was swallowed and surged forward to support the tower. Keep it aright. We struck down the beasts that tried to tear it down. That kept the tower from falling and the dark from overtaking everything. Then I woke."

"And that's it?" Terrillian asked.

"Yeah," Caeserus confirmed.

"So, what happens if we don't keep the tower up?"

"I don't know," Caeserus admitted, rubbing the backs of his arms. "There haven't been any more visions."

"How'd you know it was us?" Bertinand asked. "Did you like see our faces? Did you see future us?"

Anargen rolled his eyes at what sounded like boyish enthusiasm from Bertinand. He thought about dropping back to his pallet and finishing his drawing when Caeserus's answer struck him like a sucker punch. "I didn't see faces. Just four teens leaving Black River and saving the tower."

Anargen's mouth dropped open. "What?"

"Wait?" Terrillian gaped, looking as shocked as Anargen must have. "You didn't see the four? How did you even know it was us doing this? Or you for that matter?"

"Well, I just knew I was one, because it was my vision. When the rest of you came along, it confirmed my vision."

"But there were five of us who left Black River," Anargen mouthed, feeling a tingling in his limbs and a bit dizzy, as though he hadn't eaten in days. "Five set out. Not four."

"Sir Cinaed doesn't count," Caeserus retorted.

"Doesn't he?" Terrillian spoke up, sounding like he'd woken from a dream. "You said you couldn't see faces. Any one of us could be that unneeded fifth. Or your vision could just have been a silly dream!"

Caeserus shoved Terrillian and pointed a finger up in his face as he all but shouted, "I didn't dream anything. It came to me in the Knight Hall. It is a vision and I think I can tell the difference between the shape of Sir Cinaed from one of us. I may not have seen a face, but I remember what I saw."

Everyone grew quiet then. The sound of their breathing the only noise in the room. At some point, Anargen did sink to his pallet, the dizziness overwhelming him. This whole thing could be a farce. He left his home and Seren, everything, for Caeserus's guessing.

Minutes passed, and Bertinand suddenly spoke up. "Has

anyone else noticed these Ords have a massive chip on their tiny shoulders?"

"Yeah," Terrillian muttered. "I might have noticed."

"Well," Bertinand quickly picked up, "why?"

A series of dull thuds echoed in quick succession. Though the others may have looked, Anargen kept his eyes firmly on the floor. His thoughts were still a jumbled maelstrom, and his heart felt like the storm's first victim.

The door to the chamber swung open and crashed against the wall as Arno strode in. "Hungermen. It's time. Gather your most stately effects and come forward. The Thane demands your attendance for the historic accord to take place this hour."

Glancing at the Spiritsword and scabbard already strapped to Caeserus's belt, Arno's dark eyes narrowed. "Your weapons will not be needed nor tolerated. Leave them."

"This is happening now?" Bertinand asked blankly.

Arno's eyes flicked to the ceiling and back to them in disgust. "I said so, didn't I, hungerman? Now, out with you!"

Everyone staggered at a turtle's gait to comply. Anargen overheard Caeserus whisper to Terrillian, "This has to be a trick. I've counted. Ecthelowall's emissaries shouldn't be here for days."

The Ord captain must have caught the comment as well because he replied to Caeserus, though not in his usual heated tone of disdain. "Ecthelowall's nobles come in their own time. It is not ours to question the noble born of any people." Snapping out of his mildness, Arno added in a grumble, "Now, stop dawdling!"

After what transpired in the room moments ago, the walk to anywhere would have been surreal for Anargen. His faintness continued, as though he had been drained of all his will with those words, "Your vision could just have been a silly dream!" With the added importance of the occasion, Anargen felt he was drifting on choppy seas and could not recover. Every few feet it seemed the retinue of Ord soldiers and sentries increased, till a small host was walking with them. At a gesture from Arno an enormous pair of doors, at least twelve feet tall, were opened. Inside awaited a great feasting hall.

Seated along one side of a long rectangular table was an array of the most impressive looking men—no, dwarfs—Anargen had ever seen. Their steely armor gleamed in the light of a thousand candles, throwing into contrast the deep indigo hues of their tunics, capes, and the tapestries of the room.

Anargen's thoughts shifted, betraying him. They shouldn't be there. They were commoners. Children. This was a hall of the mighty.

The group was ushered deeper into the room and made to align perpendicular to the table and its seated nobility. Backing up flush to the room's right wall, Anargen saw seated at the focal point, one particularly impressive Ord who looked like a younger Orwald. The Thane, he guessed. Beside him there was a familiar face.

Sir Cinaed! Things came into focus. Though Anargen wasn't sure why. He didn't have time to elucidate the mysterious sensation of cure either, because at that moment horns were sounded. Not like the deep bellowing sounds Anargen had occasionally heard blown by the Ords since arriving. This was a lighter sound. Notes airier with a touch of a melody. Three more trills sounded, and Ecthelowall's ambassadors entered the room.

But villainous noble's plot did overturn,
And hope's sweet blessings share burn.
With golden forest leaves long lost,
Ordumair's heart turned to frost.
In this hour, much good is to gain,
As wrongs be righted to eternal fame."

The minstrel took a step back, and the Thane gave an approving nod, beckoning another round of applause. At the end of the ovation, the Thane gestured to the Ecthels. "Honored Viceroy, welcome. Please, let history's annals bear record to the cause for which you come to our gates."

The Grey Scourge steepled his fingers and drew in a breath. A broad smile spread over his thin, angular face. When he spoke, his voice was smooth and even, elegant in its crisp language and resonance: "I, Ecthelion of Halifax, Viceroy of the Commonwealth of Ecthelowall accept your kind welcome, exalted Thane."

More applause followed. Anargen looked over at Sir Cinaed again. His mentor was engaged in a reluctant clap.

Looking away from Cinaed, Anargen knew he couldn't get his most pressing questions answered tonight. Is the Grey Scourge really the Viceroy of Ecthelowall? How did no one realize this?

"Indeed, our two peoples have been locked in the most dreadful conflict either nation has ever known for years so long our grandfathers' fathers told tales of it as though it were some mythic struggle. Yet, in Ecthelowall, as in Ordumair, I'm certain none has forgotten how this sorrowful battle began. Nor the treachery and the indomitable stubbornness costing thousands their lives and the prosperity of generations."

There was some stirring amongst those gathered as the oration continued. It seemed each side's envoys had their own take on who the villains and traitors were in the narrative. From the fidgeting and glares across the table, it was a wonder to Anargen this meeting was taking place at all. Worse still, he had

26

SYNCOPATION

"In all the turmoil that ensued, it never struck me. The irony that once again our Order was being blamed for a tragedy we did not create."

—ANARGEN'S JOURNEY JOURNAL,
FYLLETH 1605 M.E.

TWO PARALLEL LINES of tall men filed into the room. Each had on armor unlike any Anargen had ever seen. It was sleeker and seemed to fit tighter to the wearer. There were many plates for less restriction of movement. Compared to the heavy armor of the Ords, this seemed to sacrifice defense for dexterity. Unless the well-polished armor were of a sturdier composition. Working in the smithy, Anargen knew size could be deceptive in terms of protection.

Over the armor, they wore dark green sashes wrapped at the waist, and white cuffs terminated the vambraces. Each man, fifteen in all, had a short cape with coloring that reminded Anargen of fir leaves. All of them had swords, rapiers of a kind, strapped to their hips. Of greater interest were the large, angular implements cocked against the right shoulders of both lines. A term came to him. Arquebus. He had only heard it once, but it stirred memories of rumors and accounts of battles far from Black River. The envoys of Ecthelowall toted guns, the weapon said to be slowly reshaping how wars were fought. Seeing the weapons prompted the teen to do a quick scan of the Ords. Not one of them held any sort of gun or powder-using weapon.

Two more horn blasts echoed into the hall and a final trio entered the room. On the left and right were the most fell looking warriors among the Ecthels. At center was a man wearing an extra green sash, with intricate ivy patterns adorning his armor. This almost certainly meant the man in the middle was the Viceroy of Ecthelowall.

Ecthelowall's envoys arrayed themselves at the table before their Ord counterparts. Just before taking his seat, the Viceroy shot a glance towards Anargen. A flicker of a grin touched his face ever so briefly before he set his eyes unwaveringly on the Thane.

If before these events felt surreal, the dream-like quality had taken the turn for nightmare. Impossibly, seated as the leader of Ecthelowall was the grey bandit—the Grey Scourge.

Eyes wide with shock, Anargen's gaze shifted to Sir Cinaed, who managed to keep a neutral face. When their eyes met, his betrayed anxiety. A faint gesture that looked to mean "stay put" was given. He hoped the others saw too. Ill though the portents may have become, the Knights could not interrupt the proceedings now.

At the Thane's gesture, everyone around the table took their seats. A cold chill swept down Anargen's back and traversed every inch of his frame. The frigid sensation never left thereafter. Whether this was because the evil presence in the room carried with it the cool of death or because the thought of the beast worked the same effect in Anargen's mind, he couldn't be certain. It was immaterial, because now none of these proceedings mattered. At least not in the manner they were intended.

Anargen wanted to speak up, to cry out in warning. One

look at the regalia of those gathered and the ceremon which everything was being done, and his tongue sudden immovably heavy. Who was he to tell these nobles any Besides, Sir Cinaed was advisor to the Thane. If anyone speak up, it was him.

But Sir Cinaed did not speak up, not even after the f heraldic readings announced each party's representative their honorific rights to attendance. Notably Sir Cinaed wa out. A few more ceremonial activities took place and the began in earnest. Thane Duncoin raised a hand to have sil He spoke in a fittingly deep and commanding voice. "Welco distinguished guests, to Ordumair's halls. Your presence at auspicious gathering is most welcome. Too long has this hou peace eluded our peoples."

Pausing for a moment to beam a great smile, the Th boomed, "Can you feel the glory of this day? It is our generat which takes the reins of history and makes right that which wrong.

"Mark this day. Let all history remember it! And let th proceedings which reshape our world commence."

There was some formal applause, some genuine intersper to be sure, but undeniably there was begrudging approval. Mc sickening to Anargen was seeing the Grey Scourge offering hearty effort at enthusiasm.

No, worse. His was genuine, but to what was he assenting?

An Ord strode forward from his place along the back wal He was dressed in stately attire and immediately began to recit in a commanding voice,

"Strike the lyre, pound the drum,
Tell of the glory that has come.
Was ever a warrior bold as Ordumair,
Or love so tragic as his with Alessia fair?
From their union, joyous sweet,
Two peoples in peace dared meet,

to wonder if he and his friends were meant to be here. Perhaps just by being here they had skewed events to the ill.

"This is rubbish," Caeserus whispered to Anargen.

Anargen swallowed back the nausea building within him, realizing he was drifting into his own thoughts and replied, "Why do you say that?"

"Haven't you been listening? The Viceroy has been going on and on recounting the whole history of the war between each group. How is that at all beneficial to these proceedings? I mean the Ord minstrel was tacky. But if anything, it's as though he's goading the Ords."

Anargen realized Caeserus didn't recognize the Grey Scourge. Maybe it was for the best. Giving his full attention back to the verbose feints of phrase, he recognized in them less pomp and protocol. The Viceroy was building up to something.

Of a sudden, the speech stopped, though the Viceroy clearly wasn't finished. The Thane had held up his hand to silence his guest and now stood once more. Leaning towards the Viceroy he spoke in a gruff tone. "This is not necessary. We are all aware of the events past. We gather now to speak o' something new. Have you no manner of speech or is soliloquy all you prepared for this day?"

The Viceroy seemed unabashed by the stern Ord's rebuke. Waving his hand dismissively, he spoke in sheer condescension. "There is no need for such harsh words. I merely seek to bring to clarity the importance of our proceedings. We are on the cusp of history. See past it to a tremendous future filled with such promise! It is, in fact, imperative we make plain the transgressions of the past, so the promise of the future may be understood for what it is."

Duncoin's blue eyes had become more solidly cast than the armor he wore. Any amusement or pleasure over the sudden arrival of this long hoped after day was gone from him. The expressionless mass of Ord nobles about him seemed equally disenchanted with the peculiar manner of their guest, which bordered upon rudeness.

"Speak plainly or be gone from our hall! We have waited these many years for peace to finally run rich through our lands like the fountains of the Fior-sruthain."

A scathing glare from the cool eyes of Duncoin lanced through the speaker, who was one of the older looking members of the Council of Elders. After the bold dwarf, shamed by his outburst, claimed again his seat, the Thane spoke wearily. "My brethren speak out o' turn, but the message is a fair one. We would 'ave you to bring the words o' peace you have travelled so far to give."

Once more the Viceroy, the Scourge, leveled a brief gaze and wicked smirk at Anargen. "As you wish, good Thane. Let the matter be known in plain terms. The Commonwealth of Ecthelowall has grown tired of the senseless and futile fighting that ravaged our people. Thus, it is my burden to present you with our demands."

"Demands?" an assorted group from the Council of Elders choked out. Anargen swallowed uncomfortably against the palpable storm of malcontent brewing in the room.

Nonchalant, the Viceroy continued. "Ecthelowall demands two things. The first is full reparation for losses incurred by the aggressions of Ordumair over the years in this struggle. Its full amount is not to be less than the sum of monies required to build the fortress of Ordumair. This seems a fair duty given it is this fortress which has been the bane and barbarous obstacle to this conflict's resolution for so long.

"The second are the seeds of the Golden Forest stolen by your ancestry. It is known that your Thanes have long held them in secret, and the people of Ecthelowall can no longer tolerate their loss whilst you enjoy the benefits of the theft of their birthright.

"If you comply, the people of Ecthelowall can promise you no further encroachments upon your lands will occur preemptively. Know, of course, the Ecthel people will defend their own borders against any encroachments by your people."

The storm of disquiet in the room became a furious squall, peals of which rang out in clear cries of contempt and roars of fury demanding justice for the Viceroy's impudence. Guards around Anargen and the others dropped into a loose defensive formation and began to close the distance to the Ecthels. This only seemed to please the Viceroy further, who smiled as his guard rose around him in defense.

Into the clamorous debacle interjected a loud and forceful command, stilling the room for a moment. "Be still!"

Ruddy from anger, Thane Duncoin pointed a finger at the Viceroy. "You 'ave insulted all of us. Your terms are a mockery of peace. What alternative do we have but to expel you from our lands forever? What could renewing old hatreds with fresh vigor possibly serve any o' us?"

The Ecthel party edged toward the doors to the hall, being regarded by each Ord sentry as a wild animal might a predator threatening its young. Viceroy Ecthelion put his hands together and gave a half bow. "This was an offer to allow you a choice in your people's destiny. One I'm sure your advisors will adjure you to pursue." A fiendish glint was in his eye as he looked at Sir Cinaed and then the younger Knights before regarding the Thane again with dark intensity. "This conflict is over, so you must choose whether you will peaceably comply or be forced to, Thane. The Commonwealth of Ecthelowall is not without compassion. Its people do not wish to overturn you, but it will do so if necessary.

"Shortly this fortress will be leveled and all who defend it swept aside. The treasures of your people will be claimed with or without your permission. Consider carefully your next course of action. You have a respite to determine your people's fate. If for good, then send your emissaries. If not, then my fury shall descend upon you. These are the fullness of Ecthelowall's words for your people. Heed them or not, the discourse of this day, indeed glorious, is at an end."

Anargen's breath caught in his chest as he and the other Knights were shoved aside as all the Ord soldiers at the ready rushed the Ecthels. In turn, the band of fair-skinned, dark-haired men fled as a few of them brandished weapons. Clearly escape was anticipated as the inevitable end to the dialogue.

Pursuing them till out of sight, the clomp of heavily armored steps mixed with boisterous shouts and sharp, quick clang of steely implements echoed from the corridors outside the hall. The tumult took far less time than it felt, and at its end the room was left all but empty.

The trappings of the hall, its banners, decorative lamp stands, and the long table's chairs, were in disarray. Whatever manner of peaceful existence between these two peoples was much like the room. Months of travel rendered useless in minutes.

Some time passed and Anargen took stock of those left in the room. The Thane, Sir Orwald, Sir Cinaed, five nobles, and two guards. Whispers drifted amongst them, too faint to over-hear. Surprisingly they seemed sober. Perhaps shock kept discussions from turning heated.

The first sure voice to sound off the hall's sturdy stones was the recently returned Captain Arno's. Breathing heavily, he gave report. "They 'ave fled, great Thane! The cowards retreated to an awaiting band o' their own. Five of their number fell in the escape. We await your order to give chase."

Every eye in the room now turned to the ruler of the Ords. Thane Duncoin stood as still as the decorative reliefs carved into the gates of the castle. His fists were clenched, and his lips tightly pursed as his mien turned to blatant disgust and anger.

Before the Thane could speak, however, Sir Cinaed cleared his throat and spoke in a gentle, soothing tone. "Dear Thane, I would speak with you in private. There is more to this than is immediately evident."

Captain Arno spoke up. "Your honor, let me remove these hungerman. Their counsel is suspect if it must be in secret."

Scowling, Sir Cinaed held his hands wide. "What would you do if you catch the Viceroy? Kill him? Ransom him? That ensures a war you could not be ready for if you came to the table of peace in honor. True, the Ecthels are perverse, but following now is imprudent. They must have known speaking such words would mean immediate retribution. Something more is transpiring now. Caution might preserve the lives of your people more than a rash retaliation."

One of the Council of Elders snorted and shook his head, sending the huge tangle of auburn braids in his beard into motion. "Again, the Knights offer only forbearance? How many more o' our people need perish before their words be counted for their worth?"

Sir Cinaed's brows lowered over his intense hazel eyes. He responded with more verve. "You speak about matters you can't possibly understand."

"What I understand," the Elder countered, hotly, "is our people died for your Order's foolishness! Thane, why do we suffer such ineffectual advisors?"

"How dare you!" Caeserus erupted, his hands quivering at his sides. "You lavish your impertinence on allies to your injury. You summoned us here only to waste our time with mindless insults. Little wonder your people's great realm is just a speck now."

Whether his gaze was fiery or icy, the Ord's stare was fixed on Caeserus as a huff flared his wide nostrils. "Who is this whelp that he speaks so? Guards! Take this upstart and his pack to the dungeon till they can learn manners in the presence of their betters."

Before he could react to this final disintegration of matters, a guard struck Anargen from the side, crashing him into Caeserus. The guards and two nobles advanced on the teens. Captain Arno hung back, his eyes on Sir Cinaed. Anargen also turned his eyes to his mentor, searching for some sign of what to do.

Cinaed's great shoulders sank. He held a hand up, mouthing, "Don't resist." Ruefulness briefly scrunched the Knight Errant's face before he whirled to face the Thane, speaking words too quick and soft for Anargen to discern.

More guards descended on the teens. As the four were led out into the halls beyond the chamber, Caeserus snapped off a string of insults until a soldier shoved him to the ground and kicked him in the side.

Though it was doubtful the blow hurt Caeserus, with his armor protecting him, the utter lack of restraint kept him quiet. Thereafter none of them fought back, not even as they were led beneath the earth into dark depths. Orwald had warned they would be unwelcome guests. Only now did they understand, they were looked upon as enemies equal to the Ecthels. Save the Knights had not had the foresight to flee.

27

DESTITUTION

"Where they placed us . . . I couldn't imagine a filthier hole in all the world. It is a place deserving only of every nightmare and murderous fiend."

—ANARGEN'S JOURNEY JOURNAL,
FYLLETH 1605 M.E.

UNINTERESTING AND SPARSE as the barracks the Knights stayed in was, their quarters now made those seem fit for nobility. The dungeons of Ordumair were utterly devoid of light apart from dim, smoldering torches at long intervals along the damp, incongruous corridor. At its end was a precarious descent down unfinished stairs carved out of the stone of a cavern. At the stair's end a cage waited.

A few ornate carvings lined the passage into the dungeon as though it had been meant to be something of greater prestige and was abandoned during construction. Left to erode, mold, and become the frigid place of destitution only a heinous few should witness. Most disconcerting, Anargen couldn't help noticing that none of the flowing script on his or the other teen's armor burned quite so bright anymore. They all seemed only as the final embers of a spent fire, a heavy orange, in a stubborn fight against extinguishment.

"Well, things can't get much worse," Terrillian said with a sigh as he dropped down to the sleek stones beneath him. Their escort had long since disappeared into the shadowy chambers above and slammed a heavy oak door shut behind them.

Can't it?" Caeserus replied with a snort.

Bertinand coughed in response, clearly not appreciating the musty aroma of the dank air. "I dunno, this place has . . . character?"

Rolling his eyes Caeserus plopped onto the ground. There was more resignation than malice about him. "The Grey Scourge is the ruler of Ecthelowall! Those Ords may not know it, but sooner than later they'll be massacred and here we'll be locked in."

Anargen raised his brows. Caeserus had noticed after all.

Letting out a long whistle, Bertinand summarized, "That is worse."

"Yeah," Terrillian added, sounding hollow.

Anargen did not bother speaking up. A deep gnawing void was spreading in his chest. This entire quest was built on pretense. Caeserus's vision. The treaty Sir Cinaed was to mediate. Even the Ords' desire for them to be present for it. He had walked away from everything dear to be kept in prison till a monster found it convenient to come and end him. If he could see to write it, he would have written his farewell letter opening with, "Oh, Seren, I was wrong. This wasn't my quest. I can only hope you did not wait for me."

Closing his eyes Anargen tried to focus on his breathing to slow his erratic heartbeat. With so much sorrow strangling him, he had to fix his thoughts on someplace else. Someplace far from the abysmal maw of darkness and the continual dripping of fetid waters. Someplace free of failure and regret.

Only one place suited him. A place feted and glorious, where the Magnificent King's light cast away all shadow and tore away the veil of sorrows shrouding his life. There was peace, joy, and safety ever after where the Knights joined the High King in his great land.

Some hours passed before the distraction succeeded in giving Anargen enough peace of mind to drift off to sleep. A fitful, pain-filled sleep on the rough, slick stones. Dreams and memories swirled into a torturous canvas he could never seem to cover over.

"Now isn't the time to rest, lads."

Anargen jerked awake. Melancholy as the voice sounded it must have been born of a dream. Then he heard it calling out again from the darkness. "There'll be enough of that when in safer quarters."

A flickering flame approached. The bearer was still several feet away when his identity became clear. In his hand, Sir Cinaed's Spiritsword exuded a brilliance that sliced through the gloom far more effectively than the younger Knights' armor.

From somewhere within the chamber, Caeserus stumbled with halting, ungainly strides to where the rusted iron bars insisted he stop. Anargen heard his friend crash against the bars, the tinny cry of shock from impact drowned out by Caeserus shouting, "Why are you down here? Did they not carry you off as well?"

Coming closer, Sir Cinaed's large jaw was noticeably taut, the effect emphasized all the more by the deep shadows clinging to the contours of his face as his blade's flames danced. "Though a poor host, the Thane respects me enough not to send me here. He has no personal dislike for you, only the sentiments of his nobles to worry after. Removing you was his attempt to spare you an attack from—"

"This is a courtesy?" Caeserus asked, incredulity the nicest word for what his tone held.

Sighing, Sir Cinaed looked around the bleak cavern and said, "This has more to do with bitterness over the past than anything. Their first inclination, and easiest means of coping, is to blame us for the unfortunate turn of events earlier."

Caeserus huffed, hardly appeased by the explanation. "Did you still the madness of the agitator among the elders? The whole lot of these stone-hearted savages is likely as not rushing to their destruction."

Sir Cinaed scowled at Caeserus. "Not completely. The Thane is holding off following the Ecthels for the night. Tomorrow he will send an advance party to scout out their path and determine whether there is a larger force waiting to meet the Viceroy. If not, then they are to capture or kill them all.

"Ulryl Tengrath is the name of the noble you have issue with, by the by. He was young during the siege years ago that birthed their ill-will towards our Order. Such experiences become painfully burned into one's memory." Cinaed's words turned wistful, before he seemed to shore himself up. "Divisions exist among their ranks, but on the whole, we are hated. I had not anticipated such a full disintegration of our Order amongst their people in so short a time."

Terrillian offered a question that seemed to be of pressing concern to him for some time. Wandering to the edge of the Spiritsword's aura, he leaned toward Cinaed from between the bars. "Will it be possible for us to help the dwarfs then? That is our quest, isn't it?"

"Being prisoners aside?" Bertinand asked with ironical amusement.

Undeterred by Bertinand's sarcasm, Cinaed replied, "I've spent most of the hours since your imprisonment in discussions with those counted to be their astronomers. They confirmed some nagging fears.

"You can't know it for having been confined so long, but in a few days, there will be another full moon, the Harvest Moon."

None of the teens seemed to respond as Sir Cinaed hoped, and he rubbed his free hand over his jaw, as if unsure how to word things. He dropped his hand with a huff and must have chosen to be blunt. "Our foe, the Grey Scourge, must be planning to assail the castle on the night of the Harvest Moon. With the honor guard and his pack, he'll have numbers enough to attempt a raid. It will be so much worse for the peculiarity of this year's Harvest."

"What do you mean by that?" Sir Bertinand said as he staggered to his feet and stumbled over to stand beside Caeserus and Sir Terrillian.

"The astronomers tell me this will be the most impressive such moon in nearly four hundred years. I cannot claim to understand all the significance of what is transpiring now, but I fear the Ords are not prepared for what will come." Sir Cinaed's voice trailed off, choked by some emotion.

Cold as stone, Caeserus accused, "I thought you chided us for thinking the moon means anything to how those beasts behave?"

"I only said the moon does not change their nature," Cinaed countered. "Not that it doesn't point to darker conjunctions, which do."

Turning his head away towards the dark, he took a few seconds and then faced his charges. "You asked me if aiding the dwarfs is our quest. Now I see the answer. The Great King led us to this place at this hour. I did not think to see such gathering dark in my lifetime. We are witnessing the days of the Ords' last stand.

"If they would seek the King's favor, they should not stumble. For their hardness I can only see peril looming before them. We will have to stand beside them in this struggle, even if they don't understand their own need."

Anargen got up and made his way over to join the Caeserus and Terrillian. Something had stirred inside him. If Sir Cinaed told the truth, then regardless of deceptions to get them all to Ordumair, there might yet be a purpose for their journey. It was a faint hope, but one to which he clung fiercely. Over and over to himself he repeated, "This is our quest. This is our quest. This is our quest."

Dimly, Anargen registered Caeserus posing a terse question. It was the answer given by Sir Cinaed that drew Anargen back from stoking the fire. "No, I wasn't able to explain the Grey Scourge's involvement to the Ords. I suspect most would have dismissed it."

"Either way, I don't think they'll free us. And if they did, I can't imagine them listening to us," Terrillian pointed out.

"They will have no choice. I'm going to release you from this dungeon tomorrow night. I need you to be ready to assist the Ords in their inevitable retreat to the safety of Ordumair's walls. When death's breath chills their spines, they will listen to you."

Of all the questions to pose with the sudden turn of things, Terrillian asked, "Will the Ords tolerate our release? Even if we are defending their precious fortress?"

Sir Cinaed made a peculiar face and replied, "This is not the fortress of Ordumair."

"It isn't?" Bertinand asked, only half-interested as he stood up and knocked loose gravel off his armor.

"No," Cinaed answered, glancing back towards the door of the cavern, probably in concern for how long he'd been there already. "This castle is something of a gatehouse. No foreigners have been permitted within the city or fortress of Ordumair since Duncoin became Thane. Construction was completed sometime after the Ecthels were expelled, and it serves as a mustering house for their most capable warriors. The first line of defense against any incursions."

Taking in a deep breath, Sir Cinaed added, almost as an afterthought, "If this castle falls, though it is not in the nature of Ords to retreat, you must convince them they can better serve their people alive than slain before the real defense of their lands begins."

"What if they do not 'need' our assistance?" Caeserus asked, his tone devoid of concern for the Ords or himself. "These do seem to be a stubborn lot."

The elder Knight's eyes took on a fierce look of disapproval. "You will have to convince them of their need. I did not come to release you so you can make an easy escape. We have a task ahead of us, so we'd best make use of the time accorded us."

A presumable counter from Caeserus was stifled by a meaningful look from Cinaed. Whether from fatigue or something more profound, there was no disagreement to be found this night. Not to say Caeserus gladly took the order. The young Knight stepped back from the bars to lean, arms crossed, against a rock wall. There he seethed while Anargen and the others milled on in a silence.

When the absence of response from the others persisted longer than he could stand, Anargen moved alongside the cell's bars. "Sir, do you really believe this was our quest all along? We haven't already failed?"

Sir Cinaed braced his forearm against the cell bars and leaned forward, his voice matter-of-fact. "I don't claim to know the Grey Scourge's involvement in full. Legends of our Order warn against wicked nights. That and my heart's unease suffice to tell me we must be ready for something more awful than we've ever seen. You lads do your part, and I will fulfill mine.

"Now I have to be off. There are a few loose ends I need to tie before I'm able to rest peacefully tonight. Sleep well, young ones. In the morning, I will return to speak with you further." As he spoke, he backed away and strode back to the makeshift stairs, the light he brought with him fading from its service to the teens.

Anargen's heart hammered in his chest. "But, Sir! The quest?"

From almost halfway across the cavern, Sir Cinaed replied, and though difficult to make out, Anargen thought he said, "I can't tell you anything more than you already know."

Then he was gone, and the shadows engulfed them all once again.

28

SOMETHING WICKED THIS WAY COMES

"In an instant. One second's space, the world went utterly mad."

—ANARGEN'S JOURNEY JOURNAL,
FYLLETH 1605 M.E.

AN HOUR or more must have passed, because Anargen found himself being startled awake by the sound of iron against iron. Anticipation and dread struck with polar punches to his chest.

A brief glimpse of the noise's origin merged the two into simple surprise. Sir Cinaed was giving a final, measured hoist of the gate, lifting it off its hinges. Letting it clang to rest against the side of the cell, he breathed out in satisfaction.

Without a word of invitation, Terrillian shot out of the cell, followed by Caeserus. Anargen struggled to his feet to follow and skidded to halt. Rougher than he may have needed, he gave Bertinand a shake.

Clearing his throat, Sir Cinaed undid a cloak he wore, revealing four long shapes, two on each side of the spread garment. They clinked lightly against one another. "Take them," the Knight Errant instructed.

Reaching into the cloak, Anargen grasped one of the four

objects and smiled. Pulling it free from the straps holding it in place, he reclaimed his Spiritsword. His grasp on the blade brought a sudden vibrancy and warmth to the chamber and himself.

"I don't care how or when you got these," Bertinand said, enthusiasm melting his lethargy away. "You're the best."

One of Sir Cinaed's old smiles passed over his features briefly, like the rising and setting sun. "You lads look quite like Knights of Light. May the High King grant you to behave as such in the coming days."

"You've gotten us early?" Caeserus asked with notable appreciation as he regarded his fiery blade.

"Plans have changed. You'll need to make an escape tonight. The guards are not at their posts for the moment. They received secret orders to report to their Elder's mustering hall at once. All the guards have been likewise called. I was not privy to the particulars, but it's not hard to guess. The Ecthels are already on the march."

The four teens exchanged glances, but Sir Cinaed continued, not giving them full time to process the news. "We will take these stairs and then make a left. From there we must take two rights and then I will open a special passageway. You are to make use of this passage only tonight. When the siege on the castle begins, do not return to use the route I show you, no matter what. Do you understand?"

The ferocity with which he demanded this led the four young men to an uncertain, but quick, reply of compliance. Seemingly appeased, Sir Cinaed took a deep breath and added, "Thank you.

"Now, there is one other thing I must ask of you. Once in the passage I show you, take a left, right, and then run straight on until you have passed another corridor and then go right, right, and up the stairs. You will be in the valley stretching before the Fortress of Ordumair. Keep to the shadows and find cover till the evening on the morrow. I have here some food and water for you. It should be far superior to what they've brought you over the course of our stay."

"Thank goodness," Bertinand said as he and the others reached into a sack Sir Cinaed handed over. Sure enough, some warm bread and hard cheese was inside along with skins of water. Given the meals they'd had were virtually non-existent, each teen gobbled down his portion in a matter of minutes. A second sack was produced containing their shields. Anargen eyed Cinaed with wonder as he strapped it to his back. The how was once again of lesser importance to the feeling of being whole again.

Waiting till they all finished, Sir Cinaed added, "You will not see me till after a few days have passed. It is imperative you find Sir Orwald and have an audience with the Thane. Duncoin will be distraught, and though you will not be permitted to meet him in formal manner, look to the Knight Hall within the city not long after your arrival. He may appear stern and absorbed by his people's resentment for the Order, but at heart he is a Knight and will come there at length. You must instruct him to barricade every entrance to the Fortress, no offensives, understand?"

Terrillian started to speak for the group, clearing his throat after having choked down his food. "Uh, but why won't you—"

"When you speak with him, tell him I will be coming shortly, if the King wills it, and I won't be alone," Sir Cinaed interrupted. "Encourage him to stand firm and convince him not to do anything rash till I have arrived."

Surveying his pupils, Sir Cinaed asked, "Is this clear?"

"Clear." Terrillian was first to speak, though it was also plain he did so with reluctance. After each of the others voiced assent, Terrillian tried again. "But Sir, why won't you be with us? I'm sure we could gather more of the Ords and present a more persuasive front for the Thane if you were there."

Cinaed was careful in composing his reply. "I have other matters that need attention. Do not fear, the Great King will be with you and he is far more capable of guiding you to success than me. And I will try not to keep you worried for me long.

"Now," he added emphatically, "follow me!"

Suddenly the shine of the great man's form was in motion heading towards the precarious stairs leading out of the dungeon. All the Knights had to fall quickly in line to keep up and work doubly so not to slip on the uneven stones of each step. The stairs led much higher than Anargen remembered from their descent into the room, and he did his best not to consider what a fall would mean.

Ahead, Sir Cinaed incautiously flung open the door to the dungeon and rushed ahead into a corridor with sporadic cells that seemed amiable by contrast to the dank dungeon. The stones here were a light umber and even cut, allowing Anargen to find surer footing and to pay closer attention to the sudden sharp turns their leader took. The little column was like a whip, snapping at each turn through the narrow halls forming the guard house of the castle.

Too soon Anargen and the others could see Sir Cinaed skid to a halt in front of an unassuming stretch of wall. The moment of parting was already at hand? Their early experiences in this quest seemed trivial now compared with the gravity of their new task.

A small tremor shot through the floor beneath them. Just subtle enough to seem inconsequential, but enough to notice.

Looking at the floor and then to the others, Anargen's eyebrow arched in an unspoken question to Caeserus, who was nearest him. His friend shrugged and opened his mouth to ask Sir Cinaed, but never got the chance.

Another tremor, much greater in magnitude, rippled through the corridor. It ripped the footing from under Anargen, sending him crashing into the wall at his back. Caeserus tripped into Bertinand and both went down hard. A terrible groan of wounded stone tore through the passage. Dust exploded into the hall to their back, rushing through the midst of the bewildered Knights.

Coughing, Anargen, steadied himself against the wall and offered a hand to Caeserus. Terrillian and Sir Cinaed hoisted Bertinand up. Dust and then smoke began to fill the tight space. Amidst the drifting haze it was hard to tell where to go.

From behind came the shouted remedy of their fuzzy incomprehension: "Get out now! The castle is under attack!"

29

FORETASTE OF THE HARVEST

"I thought I knew the worst of things. The worst of pain. The worst of sorrow. In truth, it seems I know far less than there is to learn."

—ANARGEN'S JOURNEY JOURNAL,
FYLLETH 1605 M.E.

LOOKING AT SIR CINAED, Anargen could not move. His mentor's brow furrowed, and he grabbed Anargen by the arm and slung him the direction he needed to go. One by one he moved down to each teen forcing them on their way, bellowing, "Go! You cannot take this passage now.

"Get to the guard house. Take the central causeway to the keep's outer wall. Follow the stairs and hall to the end."

Sir Cinaed started to turn to run the opposite way, and hesitated. Gnawing his lip, he added, "The postern gate will be heavily guarded. You must convince each of those guards to come with you. They are amongst the most noble of the Ord warriors and will be greatly needed. If you see Sir Orwald, tell him to follow you, but don't delay.

"Be well, my young friends. Let the Great King of our Order give you his guidance!"

With that, Sir Cinaed dashed through the billows of crushed stone still wafting into the passage. He spared a glance back. Looking at Anargen with hazel eyes hard and bright, like the sunrise on a meadow, he mouthed, "Go."

Anargen turned and realized Caeserus and Bertinand were already several yards down the hall ahead of him. Terrillian nodded to follow them. "Let's go!" Once more the stones under him shuddered. Catching himself against the wall, Anargen nodded.

He was faster than Terrillian and caught up to Caeserus and Bertinand after a few seconds. Everything of the world became the next step. The next breath. He was sure the stones shifted under him on occasion, but it didn't throw him.

Anargen almost didn't notice a pair of Ord soldiers in his path till he was on them. Barely slowing in time, he had to jump up and kick off the side of the passageway to avoid barreling into them. He landed hard and rolled. Before he got up, another tremor rocked his narrow world. Shards of stone from the hall buckled on one side and the pair of Ords he'd just passed tried to escape.

The dust swirled and before it cleared he heard one of the Ords crying out in pain. Drawing his Spiritsword for better light, Anargen found the soldier, a man in his forties, pinned under a cascade of block fragments that had claimed his companion.

Caeserus, Terrillian, and Bertinand leapt past at that moment. Caeserus skidded to a stop. "Come on. We have to get out of here!"

The Ord groaned again.

"I can't, we have to help him," Anargen pleaded as he tried to divert enough chunks of stone to free the man's legs.

"Sir Cinaed said we have to get out of here now. Leave him."

"Since when do you care what Sir Cinaed says?" Anargen shouted, more acerbic than he intended.

For a few seconds Caeserus stood there, looking to where the others were hesitating further down the corridor. Shaking his head, he slammed a fist against a wall and said, "Fine."

Bending down, the pair of teens gave a sharp tug and got the Ord unpinned. The little man uttered some curses and looked like he'd rather have been left, but muttered, "Thanks."

Moving as fast as he could with the extra weight, Anargen found at least Caeserus kept pace. The Ord was able to hobble a bit. Catching up to the others, they burst out into the night seconds later.

Anargen expected a rush of cool, clean air from night, but found only a smoky haze. The gates were burning. Overhead a projectile whooshed through the air and crashed into a wall turret in the distance, smashing it to rubble.

"Ordumair's ghost!" the Ord with them muttered, his jaw slack.

Awaiting them was chaos on the web of causeways that traversed the castle's structure. Ord soldiers marched across the stone spokes, carried by the urgency of sudden-war.

Some, bearing bows, headed to parapets and towers. A few launched volleys from where they stood. Overhead, the moon was already out and loomed ominous over the flurry of activities oddly accompanied by few if any stars.

"Just keep moving," Caeserus advised.

Anargen swallowed hard but complied with Caeserus's advice. Terrillian and Bertinand hung back but ran about a dozen yards ahead. Somehow, they made it across the bridges to the first inner wall. As soon as they did, Anargen glanced back over his shoulder.

A sound like thunder echoed in the night. There was no flash of lightning, but the walls shook. Catching Caeserus's eyes wide as well, Anargen repositioned his hold on the Ord with them and grunted out, "Let's not look back."

They only made it halfway to where the outer wall intersected the next causeway when twenty or more Ord soldiers clomped towards them. Terrillian nearly didn't stop in time to avoid being skewered on a halberd held out in the path.

Over the maelstrom of collapsing stone, the whistle of arrows, and roar of some terrible siege machines Anargen could not even see, the wiry Ord demanded, "Halt! You canno' pass!" Then as if examining the odd collection closer he exclaimed, "Aren't you the prisoners who ruined our negotiations with the Ecthels?"

"Out of our way, dwarf!" Caeserus shouted. The little warrior quieted but seemed unabashed in his defense of the path onward.

"NO! You are responsible for this!" Pointing to the injured Ord with them he motioned his men forward. "You betrayed us to the Ecthels!"

"You ridiculous little gnome!" If Caeserus had his arms free he would probably have unsheathed his sword and charged the soldier. Fortunately, Terrillian stepped between them, speaking in a more even and imperative tone. "You need to move. We were rescuing your fellow soldier from this attack. Our leader told us to pass the orders on to your men that you need to retreat for the Fortress of Ordumair, with all haste. Your Thane and his defense must be made there."

"What?" The young Ord squinted at them, his head shaking slowly.

As Anargen watched, nerves building, he noticed this Ord had only a faint downy beard and by his relative size, he couldn't be more than thirteen. Maybe fourteen.

One amongst the others at the young Ord's back called, "Bawrnig Iaegon! Should we not press on?"

Whatever a bawrnig was, it must have meant he was in charge. The young Ord bit at his bottom lip. Some of his men fidgeted with their weapons, all too eager to rush into this fight —trampling over the Knights undoubtedly preferred.

Terrillian looked at him imploringly. "The Fortress lies beyond. If you can get us to Elder Orwald and the postern gate, this can all be explained."

A giant stone sailed through the air from somewhere below. It arced over the gatehouse and crashed close to the mountainside.

"Soldier," Bawrnig Iaegon called out. "Do they speak the truth?"

Heretofore silent, the injured man looked from Caeserus to Anargen, clearly torn. Almost rueful, he got out on a groan, "I was pinned under some stones that killed Viktor. They pulled me out."

Nodding slowly, the young Ord's eyes narrowed marginally. With an emphatic flourish to his men, he gestured to their injured brother. "You two, help him. You Knights . . . follow us. Tulles and Jurin, flank them." As he passed through the ranks of his men towards the bridge some grumbled soft curses or complaints. To Anargen's awe, they all charged off after the young commander all the same.

As soon as he could, Caeserus slugged Anargen in the pauldron and pointed a stern finger at him. The look he gave clearly meant not to pull something like that again.

Anargen fought an over-innocent grin as they marched off after their escort.

Midway across the bridge to the inner wall, the cacophony of the siege was compounded by a new sound. Piercing and so preternatural it set Anargen's hairs on end, even though he recognized it.

"The Grey Scourge!" he blurted out.

Beside him, Bertinand's eyes went wide and he pointed to their back. Whether he said, "Look" or not, Anargen could not really tell. Any words were lost to terror.

On the highest terrace of the guardhouse leaped three, massive forms, one a grisly grey and larger than the others.

Immediately, it leapt down into the deeper defense works below the Knights. Screams and shouts sounded after him.

The two remaining werebeasts leapt towards other points on the castle. One towards a crenelated tower, from which flew a volley of arrows. The other made for the bridge leading to the outer wall of the keep. Nimbly, more so than even Anargen remembered, the werebeasts bounded off to do their dark deeds.

A few Ords who had just mounted the outer wall rushed towards the werebeast. In a blinding flurry of motion the monster struck each dwarf down.

From nearby Anargen heard a strangled cry. Young Iaegon and his band watched, dumbstruck by the unfolding horror. One of his men pushed past the Knights, dropped to a knee, and loaded his crossbow. Taking aim at the fell creature, he loosened the bolt.

The shot found its mark. Even so, the werebeast just tore free the missile from its shoulder blade, shook it, and slung it aside. Its gleaming yellow eyes locked on its attacker, wicked jaws hanging open hungrily. A long tongue lolled out from the side of its jaw, creating an unnervingly canine sense to the sight, though the Knights knew it had the cunning of a man.

The hands of the thing looked more like paws, with long, sharp claws terminating the ends. These tools of maiming and laceration were even now clenched tight to display the litheness of forelimbs and arms akin to a great ape's. Anargen imagined they could rend stone itself if desired. The crossbow bearer stumbled back a few paces as the werebeast charged towards him.

Anargen and the other Knights unsheathed their fiery swords, but they were hemmed in. The causeway wasn't very wide and the Ords around them had been like statues since the bolt failed.

As the werebeast reached the bridge, the Ords suddenly came to and dashed to the inner wall, fanning out. The targeted Ord made it back into the grouping of soldiers. With shaky hands, he tried to reload his weapon.

Before Anargen and the other Knights could step forward, Iaegon rushed to the front of the formation. The beast wasn't far now, and he jabbed his halberd toward the creature in warning. Loping to a halt a few feet away, the monster barked at Iaegon, snapping its jaws for show. It seemed pleased to make sport of the youth.

Standing firm, he struck, managing to clip the overconfident beast across one of his thickly muscled forelimbs. With a yelp, the monster swatted the Ord aside, sending him crashing into the inner wall's back parapet.

The halberd hung loose at Iaegon's side. Moaning, he slumped to the ground holding a buckler that had been meant to bear the brunt of the blow. Instead it had shattered his bone and left his good arm useless.

Huge and menacing, the werebeast's dark-furred back raised a little as it approached him snarling, again the confident conqueror. The ease of Iaegon's defeat renewed the other Ords' inability to do more than stare numbly.

Before it could sink its sharp teeth into the shaking Ord leader, Caeserus and Bertinand pushed through and each took a swipe.

The beast managed to react in time to be grazed by Caeserus's burning blade. A serious cut was delivered by Bertinand's an instant later. Slinking back, it wailed in misery over its fresh injuries.

Terrillian began routing the other Ords to the inner wall's stairs. Meanwhile, Anargen positioned himself as rearguard to the Ord retreat.

Pressing the attack, Caeserus and Bertinand followed the creature in its slow retreat. Anargen hoped they weren't being foolish. The monster could launch another vicious attack at any moment.

Mustering its strength, the monster leapt from the bridge it had backed to onto the inner wall. It made straightway for the Ords.

Anargen charged forward to meet the beast and caught it in the side as it tried to roll around and snap at him. If the wound slowed him, Anargen couldn't tell. The creature pushed on, battering aside one Ord, who had almost gotten away, before facing down Terrillian. A short, punctuated dance of combatants began. The bite and feint pattern were broken by Terrillian burying his Spiritsword into the monster's hide.

Now only concerned with escape the werebeast crawled away. Bertinand stepped in and delivered a final strike to its back. The thing lay whimpering and shaking as Anargen helped Iaegon to his feet.

Another howl brought fresh worries. The other werebeast was free from its task. It was only a guess, but from shattered merlons, Anargen felt sure the tower and all on it had fallen.

Stalking them, wary, the beast was sandy blonde, with highlights of white in the moonlight. Milky eyes like the first looked over the group, but in a much more calculating manner.

Terrillian retrieved his Spiritsword with a crackle and sizzle and brought it to a guard. Bertinand rushed up to help Anargen move Iaegon to safety. As he helped hoist up the Ord, Bertinand said, too loud, "I've got him."

The beast's attention jerked to him. As if a lever was pulled to lower the gate of its humanity, the monster charged.

Without hesitation, Caeserus jumped in its path and struck. Caught by surprise, the beast pulled back further on the bridge.

Bertinand felt safe enough to charge past, mostly dragging Iaegon towards the inner wall's stairs. Any remaining Ord soldiers closed ranks and followed, with Terrillian acting as their rearguard.

Anargen spared a glance at Caeserus. His arms were tensed for violence equal to any werebeast's.

Cold blue eyes roved to Anargen, and Caeserus's brows furrowed for an instant. Nodding to the bridge, Anargen said, "Let me repay you for earlier."

Smirking, Caeserus backed off the bridge onto the inner wall to allow for a staggered attack, though he kept the monster in his peripheral vision.

Their plans were instantly ruined, as the beast jumped to land at their backs. At least twice the distance they'd imagined it capable of making. In a breath's space, it bore down on the two friends.

Anargen spun and brought his sword around too slow to clip its side. The beast wobbled from its intended trajectory and half-crashed into Caeserus, sending the teen tumbling over the wall to dangle above the castle's courtyard far below.

"Caeserus!"

30

TAKING FLIGHT

"There is no shame in retreat. But some foes are better to die before than to flee and thereafter live with such a guilt."

—ANARGEN'S JOURNEY JOURNAL,

FYLLETH 1605 M.E.

CALLING out to his friend earned Anargen the monster's attention. A moment later, he had to duck a swipe and rolled past the monster. Sprinting to the parapet, he grabbed his friend by the forearms and began hauling him up. Somewhere in the back of his mind he realized the creature was turning on him.

A second later the monster was on him and leveled a swipe such that all Anargen could do was tense for the impact. Sent sailing through the air, he landed hard on the bridge and rolled, stopping just shy of plummeting over one side. Before his breath returned to him, still dizzy from the impact and pain, Anargen staggered to his feet. He waved his blade defensively in a gamble that teetering off the bridge by accident was of less concern than being made a werebeast's snack.

To Anargen's surprise, the monster hesitated. What it saw in him, he could only guess. Gritting his teeth against his pain,

Anargen dashed back onto the inner wall and lunged forward. Narrowly he landed a lightning hit on the creature's side. Yowling in pain, it put several dozens of yards between it and Anargen's sword.

From somewhere near, a ruinous sound, more akin to a roar, ensnared Anargen's attention. The Grey Scourge leapt onto the outer wall in the distance. Beyond him another clap of what sounded like thunder shook the castle. The whole world seemed to heave as thousands of pounds of stone suddenly took to the air and rained down. Anargen leapt and grabbed Caeserus's arms. "Hang on!" he demanded.

Though every muscle in his arms ached, and the seconds stretched for seeming hours, the tremors subsided. Anargen exhausted the last of his strength hauling Caeserus back over the edge onto the inner wall. A cloud of dust swept past, choking them. When it cleared, Anargen dropped to his knees.

The guardhouse beyond the Grey Scourge was gone. Fire licked the ruined edges, revealing still more missiles pelting the silhouette of remaining strong points on the castle.

Sir Cinaed. Anargen's hands shook. He had never tasted loss like this. Never felt the sting of death's claim on someone he cared about.

A gleeful chortle rumbled from within the ashen chest of the Grey Scourge. His wicked doggish grin revealed jaws stained red. Suddenly Anargen's arms forgot their weariness and his fingers fumbled on the stone till they found his Spiritsword's hilt.

Before he had given it another thought, he was up, moving toward the bridge. He ignored the other werebeast. It was nothing. Just another minion.

Unconcerned by Anargen's approach, the Grey Scourge swished his tail with pleasure as a little stream of drool dripped from the corners of his ravenous maw.

"You'll answer for this, you filth!" Anargen snarled.

Before he could make it onto the bridge, he was grabbed

from behind. For a moment, he struggled, realizing that ignoring the other monster had been brash.

"Stop struggling or you'll get us both killed," Caeserus snapped, dragging Anargen backwards. "We have to get to the others."

In something of a daze, Anargen did not resist. He let his friend pull him back a few more steps and then joined him in a sprint towards the stairs.

The Grey Scourge was much swifter than its younger kind. Out of the corner of his eyes, Anargen saw the master werebeast was already crossing to the inner wall.

They made it to the stairs but heard the beast's claws scratching on the stone not far behind. Taking two and three steps at a time, down they careened. Down towards the guardhouse at a headlong tumble. Tiny shards of stone were torn free by claws digging into the walkway at their backs, and the horrid odor of the Scourge's hot breath was in the air.

Leaping the last steps into the lower guardhouse's entry, Caeserus and Anargen tumbled across the stones and looked up to see the door slammed shut and a bar thrown across it by the awaiting Ord soldiers and Terrillian. From without, a howl echoed, the bitter melody of their shame. Though stalwart, the doors shuddered. Anargen stared at them for a second, still haunted by what he'd seen.

Another shudder. He turned and joined the others, already moving down the passage. Dimly he registered Caeserus explaining what had happened. No one seemed to speak after that.

Inside the lower guardhouse, the corridors were more brightly lit. The stones seemed tighter fitted and sturdier than the fallen forward guardhouse. Even so, no one slowed as shudders began to seize the structure. Anargen guessed none could bear turning to find the Grey Scourge following.

Along the passages, Bertinand needed a break from helping Iaegon and traded out with Caeserus. Iaegon winced over the switch off and spoke up. "The secret of the Fortress of Ordumair is only for those entrusted it by our elders. Your courage on our behalf makes you seem rightly trusted. Thank you for your service."

"No problem," Bertinand answered easily as he stretched his worn arm. "Just don't pick fights with huge, hulking creatures of lore any more, all right?"

Gritting his teeth, Iaegon looked up at Caeserus questioningly. Caeserus answered, "Ignore him. He has a bad sense of timing about jokes. And terrible jokes for that matter."

Bertinand rolled his eyes and muttered something intentionally vague. Then louder, "How far is it to the postern gate?"

"Not far," Iaegon answered. "Though I do not know if they will let us pass."

"Why not?" Caeserus demanded

"You are foreigners, and our castle is under attack. They will not let any pass without the orders to retreat from an elder council member."

"Can't we persuade them?" Caeserus gaped. Pointing back the way they'd come, he groused. "This place is never going to stop what's coming. There have to be more werebeasts out there. Not to mention, if those siege engines managed to chew through your gate house that quickly, they must be something worse than I've ever heard of."

The Ord remained quiet for a moment, sullen-faced. He was only a boy, not the man or soldier he was expected to be in such a dark time as this. Nor of a rank sufficient to persuade the guards at the gate.

"Great," Caeserus said with a huff.

"Just great?" Bertinand quipped.

"Leave him be, guys," Anargen asked remotely of them, rather than demanded. "The Great King will give us what we need to get out of here." To himself he insisted, "Just as he did so for Sir Cinaed. I know he delivered him."

Caeserus's tone softened. "We might as well keep moving.

Maybe we'll be fortunate, and the guards will listen to reason, or be pliable enough to move aside."

"Yes, you might reason with them," a voice echoed from within the corridor ahead. "But I think you will find them a little harder to push aside than the average Ord."

The Knights' heads craned in the voice's direction. The figure had not yet rounded the crucial corner for identification. From their shaky defensive stances, it was obvious the other Ords, silent till now, weren't put at ease by the speaker's kindly timbre.

For Anargen, a moment's thought was enough to discern what his eyes could not see. "Elder Orwald?"

"Aye, Anargen," the aged Ord replied as he at last came into full view. Some amongst the Ord soldiers stood at attention. Others bowed their heads in respect. Iaegon struggled to stand against the aches of his injuries.

Orwald waved dismissively at the displays of veneration. In a quick, pointed cadence he noted, "There are only four o' you. Where is Sir Cinaed?"

At this Caeserus and Anargen looked remorsefully to one another. Before either could find the words, Terrillian crisply answered, "Sir Cinaed stayed behind in the forward guardhouse. He said he had matters to attend to apart from our own and told us to find you. We need you to accompany us to the Fortress."

"This is no' good. I was told to meet you elsewhere hours from now. Cinaed may find himself in greater trouble than he bargained for." The Ord's blue eyes disappeared under white tufted brows as he drew in a great breath. When they reappeared, they seemed more vibrant and determined than those of the younger Ords. "We must move along then. He had counsel greater than ours.

"Follow me. I will convince the guards to move. I warn you, lads, Ordumair will be nigh as painful for you to enter as for those Ecthel scum."

THIRD INTERLOGUE

"A WORD WITH YOU, SIR," Councilman Erickson interrupted. From somewhere at the back of the group he stood adjusting his collar as though it chaffed him.

"As you like it, honorable Councilman," the innkeeper replied and stood with a groan of the age-worn. "We shall reconvene soon, friends," he added, this time directed to his audience.

Finding himself free to move about, Jason's eyes gravitated to where Aria stood by a table taking an order. Her deep green eyes lifted from the customer and met Jason's. Immediately a pleasant crinkling around them formed.

Jason jumped to his feet. As he passed by, he half-ignored the hushed conversations of those around him. Some about the wacky old man and his wild story, others speculating over the nature of the councilman's interruption.

A table about halfway between where Aria was now and the storytelling area was open. Jason meandered over to it, the whole time holding Aria's gaze. When he reached it, he smirked, then pulled out the chair facing opposite her and swung around into the seat in a smooth movement. It was as much practical as it was flirtatious. Now he could keep an eye on the old storyteller as well.

While Jason had no interest in the others' pointless hypotheses, he was highly intrigued by the man around whom they circled. No one told stories like this anymore, at least not as though they were true. It was an effective tactic to keep an audience, but Jason couldn't shake the sense that the storyteller was deeply convinced of his story's reality. That was fascinating.

Aria's arrival brought along that faint scent of cinnamon that seemed to cling to her. "Enjoying your stay, sir?" she asked with just enough edge that he knew she was teasing him. Was she so playful with every patron? He hoped not.

"Very well, thank you, miss." Then suddenly remembering them, he added, "Though I have heard the baker at this establishment is excellent. I think I should like to sample the best she has to offer."

"Coming right up," Aria replied, fighting a laugh that let Jason know he overdid the mock formality.

A few minutes later, she was back with a pair of scones on a stone platter and two ceramic cups. "Wow," was all Jason managed to say, before she had sat herself across from him. She placed the large stone between them to make it clear who was to take what.

"My required work break just started," she informed him with a thin smile.

"I am honored," he replied, repressing a grin with all he could muster.

"Not yet, try the scone," she instructed, picking at hers. From the brown swirls on it, Jason guessed the cinnamon aroma on her was a byproduct of baking rather than an attempt at being alluring. He preferred it that way.

His scone wasn't swirled with brown, though it did have a light glaze of sugary icing just as hers did. The scone before him was speckled with dark spots. Blueberry. His favorite. Jason glanced up and cocked his head to the side as he asked, "How did you know this is my favorite?"

"A guess, but now I know," she said and took another bite of her scone, looking very smug.

Jason shook his head. "Fair enough. What about you, is cinnamon your favorite?"

Aria shrugged. "Not really, we had some in the back so I didn't have to make anything fresh like yours." She eyed the scone Jason was already greedily biting into. "Chocolate is my favorite, but it is rarer so I don't often get it."

"That's a shame," Jason commented, sincerely disheartened that she wasn't in danger of devouring her scone the way he was. "Is it frustrating having to make other people delicious food and serve them every day?"

"It doesn't feel frustrating, though I don't always plan to be in that kitchen," she mused and picked at her scone further. "It should be a clear sky tonight."

Jason raised an eyebrow. "Looking forward to an evening out?" Beyond her, the discussion between her grandfather and the councilman was going strong.

"Oh, yes. I love nights in the summer. The sun burning late and low on the horizon so that it feels warm while being cool. Things just linger that way in a dreamy twilight as if the sky and land cannot bear for the day to end."

"It sounds like a wonderful way to spend an evening," Jason remarked.

"You're welcome to join me," she said without missing a beat.

Jason was more in tumult. "I would like that. Is that another courtesy of the inn?"

Ugh, dumb question.

She just shook her head and smirked. "No, though if you want to come with me, it will cost you something. One carnation."

"Those are a tad rare in these parts," he pointed out and then brushed aside the pragmatic banter he had in mind and simply said, "But I think I can find one. Red is best?"

Her smile was approving. "How did you know my favorite?"

"A guess, but now I know," he answered and laughed. She joined in, and they sat like that sending one another into a new fit of laughs with just the right look.

Jason felt good. Better than he had in a long time. And it was so strange how it came to be. The more cynical side of him, the practical side he thought it, was growing agitated by how easily he was being swept up by this whole thing. He had important business to tend to, and he was being rather indulgent. But how could he break away from Aria? Or from the story before it was all told?

Out of the corner of his eye, Jason saw her grandfather get up from his discussion with the councilman. The old man's head was shaking, sending the wispy, gray and white strands of his beard swaying, wild. A few more words were exchanged, and he stalked off.

Aria did not notice nor acknowledge his distraction. She simply continued, perhaps testing if he were truly giving her any attention. "I'm even studying astronomy, when the upkeep of this inn allows me time."

Turning his focus fully on her, Jason found himself still wearing a goofy grin and fought to suppress it. He suddenly blurted out, "And what do you think of your grandfather's tales?"

Almost immediately he regretted saying anything of the sort. After all the snide comments and jests at her grandfather's expense because of the stories, it had to be a sore spot. But to his surprise, Aria didn't seem thrown at all. "Well, I've been hearing them since I was very young. I suppose they are as much a part of me as my hands or my eyes or my heart."

"So, you like summer sunsets, carnations, are quite the baker…" He held up the blueberry scone he had been enjoying and nodded with approval. "You do the work of an innkeeper while studying astronomy, trifles. Oh, and the stories of wonderful deeds and unflagging hope are woven into the very fabric of who you are. Do I have a fair portrait of you now?" he concluded.

Aria grinned and looked down at her hands, which she splayed open. She looked up again. "It is a start."

Jason just grinned and raised his remaining bite of scone. "To a wonderful start."

"Here, here." Aria giggled.

As Jason put the last of his scone in his mouth, he couldn't help noticing that Aria's grandfather had drifted back over to his story-telling seat. Some of the other listeners were already waiting. Unlike past occasions, he did not seem inclined to wait on Jason though.

"And what of you, Jason? You've told precious little of yourself," she pointed out.

For his distraction over the old man's continuing the story, Jason failed to mask the displeasure that descended on his expression. He hadn't needed to tell her any of his preferences, though nothing truly telling anyway. It was vexing and enticing that she was such a reader of souls. In other circumstances, he was sure it would only be alluring, but at this moment, he felt more agitated than not. He looked down at the table. "There isn't much to tell," he ground out.

To his surprise, he felt her fingers on his face lifting it so his eyes once again held hers. "I doubt that very much," she replied so gently her voice reminded him of a lullaby's melody.

A sigh escaped the doors of his lips. Aria was a stranger, a welcome one, but far from his closest confidante. All the same, those eyes, large and gleaming like gems, were undeniable. He found himself forming the words. "I have to pay someone's debt. I'm here to . . ." He struggled to tell of his greatest shame.

Aria let her hand drop away and glanced towards her grandfather as if beckoned. Jason turned and saw the old man was indeed giving her a meaningful look, though he was also engaged in a conversation of sorts with someone in his audience. "You should get back to hear the end of my grandfather's tale. You won't want to miss it," she said with a muted enthusiasm.

"Yeah, I suppose not," Jason replied, once more unsure of himself and the beguiling girl he lingered to speak with. Or was he here for her grandfather's story now? Both? If ever he believed in spells, Jason felt now he had some proof.

As he stood to walk over and join the other listeners, Aria grabbed his hand and whispered, "When it is over, come back to me. Yours is the story I wish to hear."

A shiver ran through Jason. Once again, whether of pleasure or paranoia, he couldn't quite say. Particularly as he found himself seated before the girl's grandfather and listening to the story before he even realized he had crossed the room.

"Where was I?" the old storyteller enquired.

No one else answered, so Jason offered, "The Ord castle was overrun, and the Knights were fleeing to the Ordumair Fortress after Sir Cinaed died."

Pleasure radiated from his face as the old man replied, "A sharp one you are, Jason Landsby. Now, I think I shall let Anargen tell us some things of that great fortress from his initial impressions.

Feyllth 22nd –Fortress of Ordumair

Dear Seren,

Would that I could send you any news of good tidings. But I cannot. We fled across the valley to the gates of Ordumair's Fortress. Behind us the ruined castle soon after flew the emerald of Ecthelowall.

How the guards knew to open for us I do not know. I only recall the colossal doors swung open with a rush of air that forced me back a step. They are marble and at least a foot thick!

Beyond it was a second set of doors, formed from oak reinforced with steel and inlaid with bronze ivy patterns. After us came a steady stream of weary, wounded, and battered Ords for nearly an hour.

We've been here now for a day with no further news of the Ecthels' aggression, the Thane's intentions for us, or the fate of Sir Cinaed. Elder Orwald has us stowed in his personal quarters and since has disappeared.

From the little of the fortress we've seen, there's a stark contrast. That first castle was a lump of rock, and this a sculptor's masterwork. The Fortress of Ordumair's passages burn brightly with oil lights in ornate lanterns, hung from columns with exquisite carvings in granite and limestone. Tapestries done in rich blues and deep grays hang at regular intervals. They depict the emblems of each company of Ords within their army.

Sir Orwald's lavish quarters are comprised of three rooms and are said to be nothing by comparison to the Thane's. One room serves solely as his bed chamber!

Plush furniture, marble floors polished to catch light and throw it back like stone mirrors, bronze candelabras. Do people live like this elsewhere? Is Stormridge as resplendent?

Hanging upon the back wall of the room is an axe overlaid in gold filigree with the language of the Ords inscribed on the head. The prominence of its placement and the heraldic tapestries hanging on either side suggest it belonged to an ancestor of some importance. Maybe to Ordumair himself?

It may sound foolish, but I can't help wondering what you are doing right now. Are you well? Have my repairs to the plough held up? I may never get to give you this letter, but you are always on my mind. Were I to see you again . . ."

Stopping abruptly, the innkeeper looked up at his audience and shrugged. "The entry ends there. My assumption has always been the young man was interrupted at that moment by something. So, I shall pick up from there."

31

HARD DAYS AHEAD

"Till we take that step out of what we understand into the unknown, we do not know whether our fears are right or wrongly founded."

—ANARGEN'S JOURNEY JOURNAL,
FYLLETH 1605 M.E.

"THAT'S IT. Anargen. You, Bertinand, and I will discover the location of the Knight Hall even if Terrillian refuses," Caeserus said, his voice full of determination and ire. He clasped Anargen tightly by the shoulder as though claiming him for the cause.

"I'm in," Bertinand said, contentment bearing a broad smile on his face as he jumped up from the polished hickory chair he had been reclining in. His grin turned mischievous as he added, "I'll take a peek outside, see if there are any guards to our room this time."

While Bertinand rushed to the door, Terrillian voiced his anxieties. "We can't just do as we please! We are guests of the Thane during a time of war! Getting ourselves captured in the streets of Ordumair can't possibly benefit us. Elder Orwald will never get us an audience with the Thane after that."

"There is a war raging. That is precisely why we can't stay holed up in some princely estate while the work we were given to prevent this Fortress's fall remains unfinished! Sir Cinaed did not give us orders to obey the whims of the Ords who, I might add, are completely opposed to their own rescue."

Terrillian crossed his arms over his chest and looked away. Examining his Spiritsword's inscriptions, Anargen sent up a silent plea to gain the guidance from the Great King. No fear of capture or failure remained in the moments after.

Across the room the door was open. Bertinand had already slipped through.

Anargen looked out into the hall. As soon as he did, he saw Bertinand come back around a corner and wave to him encouragingly. Nodding, Anargen ducked back in and said, "Shh, both of you. Calm down. There are no guards. We should hurry while we can still go. Terrillian, you can stay behind if you like. If Elder Orwald returns before we complete our task, then you can explain our absence and come to our aid."

Shaking his head, Terrillian gestured to the door with a sweep of his arm. "This is a mistake." He watched long enough to see Caeserus trot across the room, a smirk on his face. After Caeserus was down the corridor, Anargen gave a rueful nod to Terrillian. The other teen was already pretending to busy himself.

Even without the presence of guards, Anargen crept down the corridor with the controlled steps of one who had walked without sound in the woods. It was impossible for him to avoid thinking of home. And wondering if he would ever see another forest.

<hr />

REACHING the entry to the city was uneventful. So much so, Anargen and the others almost walked brazenly out into the great open area in front of this level's city gate. The sounds of clomping hooves on the stone brought them up just short of exposing themselves. Caeserus peered out from their cover in the fortress passage and whispered, "It's okay. Just more farmers being evacuated from the valley." Anargen shuffled forward to get a look. This was the first of Ord citizenry he really got to see.

This group wore clothes markedly similar to the people of Black River. Practical garments from tough, if uncomfortable fabrics. All in shades of brown. Hair was kept short and wasn't styled. Their skin was much darker as well. They were taller and sinewier than their counterparts in the fortress.

Ahead a pair of soldiers were halting a group of farmers and their livestock. As wide as the corridor was here, it could scarce accommodate them all. Over the din of the animals lowing, the soldiers ordered, "Halt! No one passes without inspection."

"Great, now what do we do?" Bertinand asked.

Anargen shot Caeserus an uncertain look. His friend shrugged and said, "We sneak in among them."

"Right, because we totally look like them." Bertinand rolled his eyes. "I think I'll hang back and see how that plan plays out."

This didn't make sense. Earlier he had felt certain the High King was leading them to this course of action. As Anargen watched, a scuffle broke out between the farmers and the two soldiers keeping the gate. No one was watching the wagons nearest them. Dashing over on his stealthiest feet, he crouched down. The wagons sat low, but he thought there was enough clearance there to slip along the underside. Climbing under, he braced himself. Not the most comfortable, but it could work.

Seconds later, he saw Bertinand and Caeserus emulating him. Shouts from the Ords on both sides were getting heated and a flurry of curses in their old tongue flew between them. From under his wagon, Bertinand hissed, "Worst idea ever." Anargen just put a finger to his lips and grinned.

When the sounds of quarreling died down, he heard a guard say, "You will proceed to level fifteen, dirt pusher. Now get out of my sight."

A minute later, the wagon jerked, and they were rolling towards the entrance. "This is going to work," Anargen murmured to himself.

Hanging on was a challenge. The wagons were likely loaded with everything of value to the farmers. From the way the carts lurched over the fortress stones, Anargen got the sense they weren't made for a trip like this. This might have been the only time Ords from the valley were permitted to leave their farms and come inside.

Remembering the other night, Anargen thought he saw other Ords dressed in finer garments among those pouring in. Perhaps those were merchants. Go-betweens from city to valley Ords. Did the Ords really divide themselves that way?

Anargen knew they must. Even from under the wagon and in foreign words, the animosity between the guards and farmers was palpable.

"You there! Halt!" one of the soldiers bellowed. Anargen's heart leapt inside him. The cart stopped a few feet from passing into the city. "Let me have a look at that cart."

Boots shod in polished steel clomped over and stopped in front of him. Though his chest burned from holding his breath, he dare not utter the faintest sound. He couldn't even look at his friends, though he could hear the other guard standing among their carts now as well. This wasn't going to go well.

"What do we have here?" The soldier knocked the cart and Anargen's muscles screamed as he fought to hang on. Then he heard it. Above him were quiet whimpers. "You have children in these carts. That makes your party twice as large!"

The other soldier spoke up. "You sorry liars are going to round thirteen, Barrow District."

Anargen almost sighed in relief. But he fought to hold on a little longer. The farmers bickered again, and he fervently hoped they would quiet soon. He couldn't hang on this way much longer.

The soldier nearest him cut off the farmers. In a voice colder than the fortress stone he growled, "Get moving to where you belong, or we'll escort you back outside. See if the Ecthels care about your complaints when the siege army arrives."

That did it. No one else said a word. Even the animals hushed. "Good. Now, move." The carts bumped along into the city and Anargen waited a few seconds before drawing in the quick breaths he so badly needed.

His arms still ached from strain, but he could endure however long it took. It was hard to see much. What he could was astounding. At the city round they entered, twenty-four he believed, everything was alit with lanterns hanging from stone ceilings above. The streets were a smooth creamy stone. Shops and homes of the same composition lined space carved from the mountain. Huge round pillars rose up to help support what must be round twenty-five, just three levels below the very top of the city and fortress.

Ords moved about on the level with a brisk pace and barely seemed to note the farmers passing through at the periphery. These city Ords were stiff and proud in bearing. They wore bright colored linen garments. Variations of blue, grey, and white were favored with the occasional flourishes of reds and yellows. No green of any kind could be seen. Well-kempt, many citizens sported bangles, rings, or necklaces. A few even wore bedecked armor.

After a minute or so, Anargen could tell the group was entering some separate structure. Suddenly tilted on an incline, he clenched his teeth and locked his grip. He hadn't been able to see it coming. A faint groan reached him from what he thought was Bertinand's cart. "Hang on," he murmured too low for anyone but him to hear.

Painfully, the farmers followed the soldier's command without rest. Down the spiraling stone ramps till they reached round thirteen. Once there they exited the column between the levels and moved through a much less opulent portion of the city. Here lights were lower and the Ords moving about less impressive in their garb. They didn't strut like the haughty Ords at the top rounds. But neither did they acknowledge the farmers who must still be less than dirt in their estimation.

About five minutes later, they came to a stop. It felt colder here, and the stones were more uneven. They lost their creamy hues to dinginess and stains from years of refuse deposit. Certainly, their stench still hung on the air.

Anargen waited till he heard the farmers moving away from their carts with their children to ease down from his hiding spot. He drew in a much-needed breath. He almost didn't care the air tasted of rotted vegetables and sweaty animals.

Then his eyes caught hold of Bertinand. Visibly shaking, his grip on the cart was going to give out. "No, no—" Anargen's whispered words were cut off by the loud clunk Bertinand's body made as he hit the ground.

Around them, the animals spooked, crying out and attempting to scatter.

Not waiting to see if anyone came to check on the commotion, Anargen rolled away from his cart and made a crouched sprint for the deepest shadows he could find. At his back came his fellow Knights.

A few seconds after reaching their cover they heard the farmers with a couple soldiers inspecting the livestock. Apparently they had been corralled in a makeshift stable. The quick constructed pin was strained as the agitated animals tried to get away. After some time, they calmed and the Ords, unable to find the cause, dispersed.

Anargen wasn't at ease. He motioned to the others to follow. Together they wove between cracked buildings, all dark and still as death. Some lacked doors and none appeared to be in use. About three such blocks away, Anargen collapsed against a building and muttered. "That was close."

Caeserus shoved Bertinand into the wall. "No thanks to this lout."

"Hey, it was Anargen's plan. Besides, how was I supposed to know it would spook the animals?"

Putting his hands behind his head, Caeserus just stalked a few steps away grumbling. If he was like Anargen, as much as he wanted to pummel Bertinand, he was just too tired.

"Where are we?" Bertinand finally asked. Anargen looked around and snorted, "The 'Barrow' District, I guess."

"Barrow as in place for the dead?" Bertinand asked, uneasy.

"That is one way of looking at it," another voice answered.

Anargen jumped to his feet as Caeserus charged back to his side. Both reached for the hilts of their Spiritswords.

As the speaker strode forward, Anargen relaxed. "Bawrnig Iaegon?"

"Not any more I'm afraid," the little Ord replied as he drew closer. In full view Anargen could see he wore a sling over his injured arm. It was his face that looked worst though, wearing utter dejection on it. "After I helped you to the fortress I was stripped of honors. I'm only a sergeant-at-arms under the Stone's Edge banner now."

"My condolences," Caeserus replied in a snarky tone.

Rolling his eyes at his friend, Anargen was gentler. "Why are you down here?"

Glowering at Caeserus, Iaegon answered, "Part of my punishment is to oversee these valley-dwellers' quartering in this abandoned district." Eyeing the Knights thoughtfully, he added, "Though I got off easier than Droc, I suppose."

"Droc?" Bertinand asked as he peered around the little Ord. Watching for other soldiers, Anargen guessed.

"He was the soldier you 'rescued.' Droc received sixteen lashes for treasonous behavior. Normally it's sixty-four, but with his injuries they didn't want to kill him." In a surprisingly dry tone for one his age, Iaegon said, "It blunts the lesson if the pain ends too soon."

"So, he got beaten half to death and you got demoted."

Caeserus let out a low whistle. "How'd you work out those terms?"

Iaegon hesitated answering. "He did not belong to as prestigious a banner. And his house is more common than mine."

Before anyone could comment, Iaegon shifted the conversation. "Now you must tell me. Why are you here?"

"We are following the last command of our mentor, Sir Cinaed. He ordered us to find the Knight Hall of Ordumair. There we are to speak with the Thane about the fortress's defense."

A sharp blow to Anargen's right pauldron alerted him to Caeserus's disapproval. Speaking with the young Ord soldier, who could easily report them to the other guards, wasn't the wisest course for the moment.

Iaegon laughed, a low forced sound. His eyes darted around. "As though the Thane would venture to one of your halls. You Knights are not so well-loved here as you believe."

"That's pretty plain," Caeserus struck back while he peered about to make sure the conversation would not be noticed or overheard by others. His posture eased when no additional Ords appeared. "Regardless, we have our orders."

"Then you should be quick about it. You don't want to be found skulking about the City."

"Maybe you can help us then?" Bertinand asked with impertinence. "We have no idea where the Knight Hall is and can't exactly ask directions of the other locals."

Rubbing his injured arm in its sling, Iaegon said, "I think I may know the way to the old Knight Hall. It is a blot on the City. From childhood we are told not to tread near it."

Caeserus smiled with feigned cordiality. "Then we will happily follow you there. Lead the way, with haste, my good Ord."

Breathing in and out once, his little face sagged. "I owe you as much for my life."

Heading past them, deeper into the shadowy back streets,

Iaegon waved them to follow. "This way. It starts on round twelve and goes to fourteen. There should be an entrance on this level."

Without another word, he was off, jogging past twists and turns. Whole blocks of buildings rushed past in a matter of minutes. Forewarned or not, Iaegon was familiar with these districts of the city.

Their hurried pace persisted until Iaegon halted at the edge of another alleyway. Evidence of looting was present, and it was dark enough here they needed to draw their Spiritswords. Each teen did so. Their Ord guide looked disquieted and searched them for some sign of release from his kindness.

Caeserus gave a stern nod to proceed.

Sighing, Iaegon continued, this time slower, holding to the facades of buildings as he went. Anargen made no attempt to do the same. In the faint light their armors' flames produced, the deep recessed dark of the windows and splintering doors of each empty building were too evocative of skulls. As though they were among the skeletal remains of some great beast's prey.

After a few dozen paces, Iaegon stopped. Even swathed in the dark shadows, the displeasure on his face was unmistakable.

"Keep going?" Caeserus whispered, his words rushing out as a snarl.

Before the young Ord could answer Anargen spoke up. "He can't see the light from our swords' fire! Remember, Sir Cinaed once told us those at opposition to the King's Light cannot see it. It must be totally dark here for him."

Bertinand added, "You're right. But I don't think he has to show us any further. Look at the building ahead. Doesn't the symbol there remind you of those in Black River's Hall?"

Caeserus ran to the door. "It is! All manner of stories from Knight histories are carved into the door's face." He paused and cast a baleful glance toward Iaegon. "It looks scarred from vandals."

Iaegon hung his head. Apparently the Ords had forsaken the

Knight Hall only after expressing their distaste in a violent manner. Bertinand rushed over as Caeserus began to tug at the door's rusted ring. It seemed unwilling to budge.

Halfway down the street to assist his friends, Anargen was grabbed from behind by Iaegon, who whispered, "Why can I not see, yet you do?"

"Uh, well," Anargen started to answer and realized it would only birth other questions. Ones for which he had never thought to prepare answers. Swallowing against the mustiness choking him, he tried to weave together the simplest answer he could. "It is because our King, the High King of All Realms, is the King of Light. All we who are his servants carry with us his fire to help drive away the dark. A reminder to us of his presence with and protection of us."

The answer did not seem eloquent enough to do justice to the splendor of the Great King, but whatever lack of loveliness to his speech or depth of the description, it seemed Anargen's words resonated with the young Ord. Iaegon's lips were pursed as he mulled quietly.

Caeserus suddenly let out a huff of exertion, and the sound of the door's hinges breaking could be heard echoing down the path. Anargen looked just in time to see his friends staggering under the tremendous weight of the Knight Hall's door. The huge thing looked as though it would crush them.

Without time to consider what to do, Anargen sprinted to them and got under one side. Even with their efforts already applied, Anargen could feel its weight pressing down on him as well. His already tired muscles ached and strained as he tried to help bear up the massive thing.

"To. The. Left." Caeserus ground out through clenched teeth.

Mustering all he had left, Anargen heaved. The other two teens did the same and the door flipped off their sagging shoulders. It came crashing down on the stony street with a clamor that echoed down the alley like a cannon's shot.

Worse than the noise, the door's impact shook loose a layer of dust and soot covering the floor all around them. The taste of the powdery fog was acrid and burned Anargen's throat and eyes.

Shaking his head to clear away the foul fumes, Anargen doubled over, hacking and retching. Desperate, he struggled to find someplace to turn for escape.

Through the billowing haze, he saw a faint glimmer in the Knight Hall move to one side of the room and then vanish. Dazed and still unable to breathe, Anargen stumbled back the way they came, with Bertinand and Caeserus already following Iaegon in that direction.

As soon as Iaegon found sufficient light, he began to rush down this and that unused street without further words. Once sufficiently convinced they would not be found, he skidded to a halt and braced himself against the column of an old pottery kiln's portico.

Chest heaving, Anargen collapsed to the ground. His lungs felt they could not draw deep enough on the cleaner air.

Bertinand took a few hefty gulps in before asking, "We are supposed to meet the Thane there? I don't think anyone has visited that place since before our parents were born!"

"That's an exaggeration," Caeserus replied, though even he must have noticed the thin layer of dust adhering to all of them.

"I warned you," Iaegon spoke wistfully. "We should not return till some time has passed. There is no guarantee there won't be others following the sound of the crash."

Caeserus nodded. "That might be wise. We'll make our way up to higher levels for an hour then —"

"No!" Anargen interjected. "We should go back right away. I think I saw someone in there. A fellow Knight."

"What?" Caeserus and Bertinand replied at the same time, incredulity traceable within the dusty lines on their faces.

"How? When?" Caeserus pressed.

"I saw someone just before the dust became too thick and forced us away. They wore the *Panoplia tou Theos* and its fire was faint, but I saw it moving within the chamber you had just opened."

Perplexed, Iaegon asked, "Might that have been your Sir Cinaed?"

Anargen winced and looked to the others. His friends all shared his grim reluctance to admit what had happened. A few seconds elapsed before Caeserus coughed and said, "Uh, no. It couldn't be him."

"Elder Orwald then?" Bertinand offered.

The distress and puzzlement on Iaegon's face was double that of earlier.

"I doubt it. Why would he run from us?" Anargen countered.

"Well, it's worth going back at the very least to see the Hall Sir Cinaed asked us to find," Caeserus said with a shrug as he began walking back the way they'd just come.

"Why would any of our people be Knights?" Iaegon struggled to say. "Your Order betrayed us! Caused the deaths of thousands!"

Caeserus noticeably stiffened and whirled on the Ord. "Hardly! Some among us sought to guide your people away from the last conflict with the Ecthels. If you had listened you wouldn't be facing the destruction of your civilization!"

"What?" Iaegon asked, less vexed than utterly terrified by the vehemence and condemnation in Caeserus's words.

"Caeserus," Anargen scolded, "Iaegon isn't to blame for the lessons of his people!"

"Our histories do not record your Order having offered counsel in the last war with the Ecthels. It is said the Knights tricked our leaders into an ambush many years ago. We lost our Thane and many noble warriors to that treachery. We hid starving in our Fortress till our bravest warriors drove off the Knights and Ecthels!"

There was a war of conviction in Iaegon's expression. Truth, precious commodity it is, seemed to hover just out of his firm hold.

"No," Anargen countered quietly. He had never encountered blatant lies like this. It was unsettling. "That sounds as though two events in your history have been merged and twisted to blame our Order of crimes it would never commit."

Iaegon eyed Anargen with apparent suspicion. He looked from Knight to Knight but said nothing.

Squaring himself, Anargen continued. "Ecthels have ambushed and killed many of your nobles, even thanes. In fact, Thane Duncoin's father perished in an attack.

"The Knights among your people tried to sway your remaining leaders away from a costly battle with the Ecthels and pursue a reasonable peace. If such a thing could be obtained with such a grievous injury. Never would any true Knight in service to the Great King of Light act in such heinous a manner as your historians suggest!"

Iaegon's expression betrayed a struggle between suspicion and ethnic pride. "If you were never treacherous, why do my people hate you?"

"Suffering came to all when the Ecthels trapped your people in the Fortress. It cost many warriors their lives to expel the Ecthels after the Thane rejected the Knights' counsel," Caeserus stated, his cheeks no longer flushed and his tone somber.

"But why would they lie?" Iaegon struggled.

"They need someone to blame," Bertinand filled in. "We're shiny targets."

Young Iaegon shook his head and could no longer look up at the Knights. "If what you say is true, tell me one thing. How may I have light to see this matter clearly?"

"Yield to the High King of All as your true King. Swear your allegiance to him alone," Anargen answered.

"I swear?" Iaegon said with a shrug.

"Not flippantly," Caeserus chastised. "The King isn't a fool. Pledge yourself in sincerity or not at all."

The Ord closed his eyes and mouthed the words. There

seemed to be a rush of warmth through the passage. This time it was several moments before Iaegon spoke again. When he did, his eyes were wide and his mouth slack. "I saw him!"

Iageon looked up at Anargen and his eyes finally refocused. Suddenly he began trembling. "Your armor! It's on fire!"

32

GHOSTS OF BYGONE YEARS

"This rhyme has been passed down for generations by those of Ordumair:
  'Haint in walls of sure stone, Hidden doors for Thanes alone. Watching o'er little Ords asleep, Passing through walls without a peep. Ordumair's care for subjects shown, Never wavering after grown.'"

—HISTORY OF ORDS, VOLUME 1

"ARE you certain someone was here, Anargen?" Caeserus asked with a dubious edge to his voice. "I don't even see another way out of this place."

The evidence was hard to dispute. The chamber the Knights opened was enormous, boasting ceilings so high they were lost in darkness even with every Knight bearing his Spiritsword. The columns supporting the ceiling were at least four feet in diameter. There was room to seat at least a thousand and dozens of offshooting rooms on this level. On the other rounds were a library, a huge kitchen, and a training room with a handful of discarded Spiritswords. Eager to take one up, Iaegon grinned at its sudden blaze.

"You did not tell me these burn as well!" the young Ord chided. "Do you use it as a normal sword?"

"You saw us fight the werebeasts with them," Caeserus answered, blunt. "Come on, we have to keep investigating."

The dismay on Iaegon's face was plain to Anargen. He could remember those first hours after swearing fealty to the High King as well, being caught in the wonder of discovery. For once Iaegon also appeared his true age.

"I'll stay with him," Bertinand suddenly offered. "I could use some practice myself anyway. Never know when a ghoulish fiend may pop up in these lands and put you on your guard."

Anargen smiled but stopped just as suddenly as he started. This place, for all its impressive size and décor, was hollow. It was as if they had climbed into a crypt.

While Bertinand stayed with the boy, Anargen and Caeserus continued looking around. Some signs of pillaging were evident, though much remained untouched. Over all the rooms a thick pall of grey dust had settled. Even a chandelier hanging from the ceiling, cast in brass, was completely shaded by grimy signs of disuse.

"I know what I saw," Anargen insisted. "The figure stood at the center of the room and rushed over towards that side and vanished."

"That's the training room. I doubt he could have hidden in there, and I don't see any prints leading to or from there save our own," Caeserus countered.

Taking in a breath, Anargen took careful steps towards where the figure initially might have stood. Looking about, he could see a pair of footprints, but the dust around that area was too disheveled by the Knights' movements and the collapse of the door to know for certain whose they could be.

Turning about, Anargen stopped, facing the entrance to the room. Suddenly curious, he shuffled to the left. Then a little bit more, and a little more, till he could not see outside the entrance. He knew he wouldn't have been able to see that point from outside. Looking to his side, he saw only a wall standing before him.

He sighed and shook his head. About to turn in defeat, something caught his eye. Facing the wall, Anargen stared intently at a patch of discoloration. "This wall looks a little strange but is the Thane a specter that he moved through solid stone?" he muttered to himself.

Suddenly Anargen's eyes grew bright. He remembered something Cinaed had mentioned about Ord history. A tiny atoll in the sea of other facts he'd shared.

"So, ready to leave?" Caeserus asked with a resigned shrug.

"No! Caeserus, come here! I know where the Thane went. Here, into the wall!"

Caeserus eyed his friend with concern now. At least until his own eyes fell on a pair of footprints, smaller than Anargen's, near the wall.

"He went through the tunnels known only to Thanes. Secret Tunnels of Ordumair!"

A smile formed at the corners of Caeserus's mouth. More genuine than for some time now. "Now this is more like my vision."

"Only if your vision ended in a pummeling!" a hard voice chided from the back of the room.

Anargen's heart leapt to a frantic pace. He winced and took his time turning around. As he feared, Elder Orwald's reproving old eyes were hard on him. At his side was Terrillian, who looked down at the floor and banged a clenched fist against his leg.

"We had to see this," Caeserus protested and stepped forward. "Cinaed's last orders . . ."

"I do not care what Sir Cinaed thought you should do. Venturing out into Ordumair is dangerous for our Order. You will come back with me immediately!"

At that moment, Bertinand and Iaegon cautiously entered the room. Orwald's reproachful voice must have echoed throughout the abandoned chambers. As soon as Iaegon entered the room, Sir Orwald sucked in a sharp breath.

Puzzled and concerned, Anargen looked from the old Ord to the new arrivals and understood the shock. Iaegon was carrying a fiery Spiritsword he'd found.

More amusing, there seemed an almost comical symmetry to Orwald and Iaegon's expressions. Before they were looking one another in the eyes and had the same expression it had been difficult to tell, but now it was obvious. To Caeserus, Anargen whispered, "It's like looking into a mirror and instead of seeing one's reflection, it's a future self."

Caeserus's face lit up like a flash of light in the summer sky. "Iaegon and Sir Orwald are family! No wonder he got off easier on the punishment."

"Nephew?" Sir Orwald said with awe, confirming the suspicions.

"Uncle, it is good to see you. What brings you so far from the Fortress?" The young Ord answered stiffly. His uncle did not seem either full of anger or joy, but a strange amalgamation.

"I am here to reclaim my wayward charges. These young Knights, they had you bring them to this place?"

"They did. While here they caught sight of someone walking within this room. They are searching for the mysterious figure."

There was a bleariness about Orwald's eyes and quaver in his voice. "It seems you found more than just evidence of shadows, lad."

Young Iaegon looked puzzled for a second and then nodded. "I have, sir. The Knights told me of the High King and of how grandfather truly died." The boy paused, his eyes roving to a distant point of introspection before hardening. "Why didn't you tell me you are a Knight, Uncle? Why did no one tell me the truth of grandfather's day?"

Licking his lips, the old dwarf winced. "For your protection, lad. Some of the Elders took advantage of your cousin Duncoin's newness to rule. They took matters in their hands for a time and re-wrote the accounts of what transpired. By the time Duncoin was established, we had to accept we would be the last generation of Knights to live within Ordumair."

Unabashed, Iaegon cried out, "But why? Why would the nobles do such a thing? The Knights did not attack us! Nor did they force us to war with the Ecthels. Shouldn't we have some measure of freedom within the walls of our own Fortress?"

As the blood rushed to Iaegon's face, a few tears collected at the corners of his eyes. "The King warned me his light won't hold back the shadows when the doors are closed to it. Your generation may have been the last of Ord Knights, but mine might be the very last altogether!"

Orwald's face fell under the admonishing gaze of the boy. Shame was something new to weigh his worn brow.

Looking to the Knights assembled around him, including his own flesh and blood, Orwald appeared to gather himself. "I will take you to the Thane. We will make sure the past's failures are not repeated this day. Come, all of you. Especially you, Sir Iaegon."

33

CRUMBLING FROM THE TOP

"Great things are expected of those born to great families. The only greatness I have ever imagined came through books. Till the High King spoke to me."

—ANARGEN'S JOURNAL JOURNAL,

FYLLETH 1605 M.E.

THE TRIP from the forsaken Knight Hall to the very top of Ordumair's Great Bulwark was long and quiet. Elder Orwald saved his whispered words for his nephew. They led the procession, a bold jaunt, through the streets of the City garnering stares of disbelief and disgust. Several guards joined the procession, only keeping back because of Elder Orwald.

In the silence, Anargen noticed the pallor of the buildings in higher rounds of the City had changed. There must have been more outlets to the surface than he'd imagined. Whereas the buildings earlier bore casts of gold and cream, now they appeared amber and terra cotta. Shadows loomed around corners and pooled at the feet of the still crowded streets. The whole sight gave him the feeling of something unnatural. As though the city were caught in a slow burning fire.

The final ascent to the top of Ordumair brought with it the chill of the night's air. Starless for gathering clouds, the valley below stretched gloomy and foreboding like the depths of the sea. Anargen sucked in a deep breath. It was oddly clear atop the bulwark. In the midst of the sky, gray with cloud-armor, was the tremendous Harvest Moon. Every bit as full and foreboding as predicted. The familiar envoy of night looked cruel, a perversion of its true self. It was ablaze with deep oranges and even a tinge of red, like the menacing, spectral eye of some phantasm too hideous to speak of.

Anargen averted his eyes, focusing on the marble and granite façade of the Thane's Hall and the rest of the mountain's vast height above. These were fixed and, though foreign, had a familiar touch to their form.

The nearer Anargen and the others drew to Ordumair's keep, the more intricate the sculptor's work was revealed to be. In the marble columns lining it, the surface appeared a singularly smooth cylinder of grey and black swirls, save for the caps that were done to resemble the same exotic ivy Anargen had seen inlaid in the gold filigree of Sir Orwald's ancestral axe.

A relief on the facing of the structure was the largest scene of Ord history Anargen had yet observed. Life size figures depicted via collage the most critical events in Ordumair's history. From the first Thane to Duncoin's victory over the Ecthels, each was exquisitely exacted into the granite of the foremost wall.

Oak doors, heavy and sure, were atop a set of stairs, also formed from the same polished marble as the columns. At either side, a cadre of guards stood watch. They eyed Elder Orwald with respect and curiosity. Even after he explained the Knights' purpose for being there, the guards looked ready to spit.

Sir Orwald and Iaegon strode forward, reservation and veneration evident in their bearing. Anargen and the others tried to follow, but the guards slid back into their placements and barred the way.

"Only one may enter. The rest of you will have to remain here."

The harsh expression on the face of the Ord who spoke offered little in way of bargaining room. Being still mindful of his humble birth and station, Anargen turned and stepped back first. The four teens formed a huddle.

"I should go," Caeserus asserted. "We need to be firm with the Thane and make certain he perceives the peril his people are facing."

Terrillian's face contorted, revealing his discomfort. "I disagree. The Thane will need someone who will be respectful and courteous as well. Someone who won't reach for his sword when things appear to go poorly."

"Send Anargen," Bertinand offered benignly. "He seems to keep records well enough. At least we'll get a good report on the Thane's response."

Before Anargen could protest, Terrillian nodded in assent, and Caeserus shrugged. The guards watching the debate must have been listening to the conversation, because they parted their halberds in anticipation of Anargen's entry.

"This is insane," Anargen protested.

"Yeah, so go make some sense of it," Caeserus replied and gestured to the keep.

Driven by the need of the hour, Anargen scowled at his friends and stalked up the steps and through the entry. He only hesitated as he passed the guards, who each brought his weapon to bear so fast, he felt the air off their steel.

Hurrying down a corridor of solid, polished marble, he found himself in an enormous chamber similar in design and decoration to the first castle. Except for the most exquisite of increase in the worth of the items adorning the room.

Bronze was replaced here by gold, wool with silk, and the table was carved from a single, enormous oak tree. Indeed, the table's forebearer may have been revered, as an ornate pattern of rings and swirls formed a tree on a huge ultramarine banner hanging behind the Thane. The tree was all silver, and at its base were swirls that Anargen could not quite figure out.

Still more impressive than any of it was the Thane, seated at the head of the table in the full regalia of his nobility. One fist rested below his thickly bearded chin, and his eyes were fixed on a point unseen as those around him were in a heated debate. It sounded to be over the proper response to the attack on the castle.

Picking apart individual petitions amongst the squalor was difficult, but Anargen thought there were three competing sides. One was backed by an Elder with auburn hair. His side had the most supporters. Another was headed by Elder Orwald, who having just arrived already vehemently opposed what the majority willed. The remainder seemed to be offering still another plan neither of the two primary sides wished to consider. Behind them, a massive fire within a cream-hued hearth snapped and crackled as it threw wild shadows all about and gave an eerie aura to the proceedings.

It was all a bit much for Anargen, who stood fixed at the far end of the long table unable to bring himself closer to the mass of furious figures. He had to speak on behalf of the Knights, on behalf of the King, yet the very thought of interrupting the tumult sickened him.

"Hungerman!" shouted an Ord while Anargen still dithered. He spotted the red-haired noble pointing at him. The Ord's face was growing as red as his hair. "How dare you enter this hall after you so vilely betrayed us! Should you not be with the Ecthels? Do you think us so feeble minded that we would hear more of your deceit?"

The chief guard, Arno, was already striding towards Anargen, along with a complement of soldiers. Anargen took a step backward and fumbled to find the words to turn back his accusers. "No! We . . . I'm here to speak to the Thane! The Great King sent us here to warn you of what is coming!"

In another second the guards were upon Anargen and with brusque deftness grabbed him, pinning his arms behind him. Arno scowled at Anargen and motioned to haul him off. The teen could only hope they didn't just toss him off the Great Bulwark at this point.

Before the eager guards could haul him away, another voice thundered over the remaining squabblers not distracted by the scene at the hall's back.

"Halt! Leave off him. He shall speak. I have heard the counsel of many today, why not hear it from one who claims to know just what has befallen us?"

The Thane's voice was firm. His great authority and station in life afforded him control of this moment alone. Outside his people were being swept away, but in here, for now, he reigned.

Sir Orwald appeared both pleased by this and concerned. Had he hoped to be the one to persuade his nephew of the benefit of following the High King's wishes? Perhaps in penance for not speaking up years sooner.

Beside him, Iaegon was fidgeting with the hilt of his newly acquired sword. Locking gazes with Anargen, there was pleading in those azure orbs for Anargen to succeed, to show Iaegon his fealty was rightly placed.

Anargen's throat suddenly felt tight and his mouth dry. Swallowing against fear's constriction, he looked about the regal audience. With as much intentional sincerity in his demeanor as he could intimate he said, "Good Ords. My name is Anargen of Black River. I am a Knight in service of the High King of All Realms. My fellow Knights and I were chosen by the King to accompany Sir Cinaed in his journey to your grand Hall. We now feel certain it is to deliver a message of warning."

"Who is this whelp from this 'Black River' to give us counsel?" The red-bearded Ord noble bellowed, a sneer on his lips. "He is to give warning of what? That the Ecthels are treacherous?"

"Be still, Tengrath," the Thane ordered, rising to his feet and pounding his fist against the table. "I have heard your pitiful plans to oust the Ecthels from Castle Valesgard and found it no more sound than the sands by the sea. Sir Cinaed chose him as a companion and in Cinaed's memory I will hear him speak!"

There was a perceptible tensing around Tengrath's eyes, a twitch at one cheek's corner. A common hush fell over the assembly all the same. The fiery noble still watched, venomous daggers waiting to slip from eyes to lips. One misstep would bring this one chance for deliverance to an end.

"The High King sent us to warn you of the Grey Scourge. I have seen him with my own eyes as have some amongst those present here on the night of the attack on Castle Valesgard . . ." Anargen uncertainly presumed the name and saw only exasperation from those in attendance at his inadequate knowledge. "He is more than a myth. He is a real monster capable of wreaking terrible devastation upon your people."

"It was the Ecthel siege machines that tore through Valesgard, hungerman," Arno coolly informed Anargen. "We all witnessed their fury, heard their roar sound off the mountain's slopes. We need strategy, not fables."

A general rumble of consensus over the words rose around the room. The siege weapons they spoke of had never been in Anargen's sight, and so he could only guess at what manner of advance in the art of war had startled the Ords. He had only heard stories of things like gunpowder, how then did these Ords, sequestered for over a century, perceive such things?

The clamor continued to rise till each side again insisted it offered the only means of deliverance. A few cried out in support of completely fleeing their realm in search of safety amongst the Albarons further north and west of Ordumair. "Our oldest allies they were!" one Ord cried out and was immediately challenged by three others.

Terror over losing their outermost defenses was driving the most noble of the Ords into folly's embrace. Anargen felt a sudden swell of pity and compassion within him. They must never have imagined their defenses penetrable, much less so easily thwarted. But if the Ecthels could so easily thwart the Ord guards, why did they need the Grey Scourge?

"Good Orderers!" Anargen shouted, swept up by a sudden burst of bravery beyond himself. "You need not fear! I hear some of you speak of retreat. It hurts to know that such a noble people as yourselves could be shaken by the Ecthel terror. Stand strong and remember who you once were!

"The Great King of Light sent us here to your Thane and your people to remind you that he is a faithful King and will not soon forget oaths of loyalty even long past. He will stand with you in the fight to come, but you must not shut out his words. The High King's counsel can rescue you from this hour."

The room was quiet, perhaps stunned by Anargen's sudden outburst after being so timid. Elder Tengrath, however, seethed, rising from his seat, building himself for a retort no doubt intended to pummel Anargen to bits.

A terrible, shrill sound sliced through the night and sounded all throughout the Thane's Hall. A howl. The clarion call of villainy itself.

Dozens of similar sounds followed and became a malevolent choral. The Ords within the hall spun about as though searching for the source.

On the nape of his neck, Anargen's hairs stood on end. He could not be certain, but he felt the room, once warm and bright with the fire's blaze, grow cool and dim.

The boy, Iaegon, was the first to rush towards the Great Bulwark. A moment later, Anargen had a terrible thought.

Shirking the guards, Anargen charged after Iageon. He burst out of the keep and looked towards the ruins of Valesgard. Though it was beyond the reach of his sight, he could easily imagine the whipping of tails and snapping of menacing teeth as hideous wolfen eyes roved in the dark looking for men to devour. Behind him the remainder of those assembled in the Thane's Hall flowed out from the safer confines and into the bitter dark, hearing with bewilderment the bellows of feral fury.

A rush of frigid air swirled around the mountain, forcing Anargen to steel himself. Looking up, Anargen saw the huge and sinister gleam of the Harvest Moon.

34

THE STORM

"I know well the sensation of cold running down the neck to the extremities. It is the soul whispering to the body, 'Beware. Fly now!'"

—ANARGEN'S JOURNEY JOURNAL,
FYLLETH 1605 M.E.

"WHAT MANNER O' wickedness is this?" the Thane snarled as soon as he emerged from the keep. The wind outside tugged at his beard and fur-trimmed cloak.

Over the distant din, Anargen replied, "What you hear is the Grey Scourge and his brigands. As I warned you, they are every bit the menace of myth and tale. Their bite is truly fatal, and their hunger is for your people's ruin."

A hushed grumble broke out from the midst of the Ord leadership shivering alongside the Thane. Duncoin seemed to ignore it. "If what you say is true, nothing of its like has ever transpired in all our history."

"No, nothing of its like has ever happened. The Great King sent us to warn you of this danger, but you caged us like villains!" Caeserus snapped as he shattered the imaginary closure of the previous meeting. "Now it is upon you, and you must act quickly to preserve your people."

"And what would you have us to do, young one?" Duncoin asked.

"Make ready for the most desperate fight for survival the Ords have ever experienced. Bar all entrances to the Fortress of Ordumair, station all those able and fit for the defense there. The beasts can't fight as effectively in closed quarters."

After a pause, Anargen added, "Most needful is for your people to turn from the errors of the past and follow the Great King once more. Be the dwarfs, the people, so dedicated to the Kingdom of Light that you are honored with the mantle of Orderers once more."

"And how will serving the mythic King lead to rescue for Ordumair, young hungerman?" Tengrath retorted as he shouldered his way nearer the Thane. "Can you even explain the nature of this purported Grey Scourge's presence here?"

Cheeks warmed by the challenge, Anargen replied, "It is to destroy your people. That much is clear. We need not know the motives fully. Maybe the Ecthels promised him plunder from the alleged Treasures of Ordumair. Regardless, darkness is enveloping this realm, and the only cure is to embrace the Light offered by the King.

"In pledging fealty to him, the way to proceed will become clear, as though the sun has broken through the depths of foulest night. The High King never abandoned you, though you forsook him, and even now he awaits your return to his number of servants."

"What of the Ecthels then?" another amongst them spoke up. "Their swords and arrows pierce us easily as the fangs of any fairytale-beast."

"Hatred and violence beleaguered both your peoples over the centuries and built to this most dire of days. Listen. Hear the monsters coming, hungry, merciless in their quest to destroy you. Whatever the evils of the past, they pale in comparison to this. Let the King of Light bring clarity to this matter. He is worthy of your allegiance."

Some flicker of pseudo-motion cut across Anargen's peripheral vision at that moment. A faint blur of bleakest grey against the ebon night. It may have been a trick of his mind, mischief of the hour. Save this was no ordinary eve, and the ethereal flights of fantastic fear, which so plagued men in the dark, might certainly be stalking them this moment.

"Did you hear that?" Caeserus spoke up, edgy.

"What are you about now, hungerman?" Arno chided.

Then Anargen did hear something. It was as the sound of flint striking against stone in order to ignite a fire. The sound happened for several seconds and then ceased. By now everyone heard. Several guards, along with Caeserus, rushed to get a look at the valley below.

Waiting for a report, Anargen's whole body tensed, ready for battle. Just then something flew right in front of his face. He leapt back, startled. A round of cruel laughter started from some of the Ords to his back. Looking down, he understood why. His source of alarm had been a simple snowflake.

Falling light as a leaf on a breeze, lackadaisically searching out a path to the ground, another landed before him. In a minute's time, there were a dozen compatriots to the scout and more arriving at a swifter pace. It was then that the scratching sounds echoed through the stillness once more.

But the sounds no longer drifted in and out of his hearing nor sounded to be coming from the valley below. Anargen's eyes roved to the side, fixing on the mountainside to his back and then from the keep. There he glimpsed it, masked by the shadowy recesses of the rock face.

Seeing the size of the form, Anargen gritted his teeth and by instinct unsheathed his Spiritsword. A welcome warmth rolled off the dance of its flames and the crisp sheen engulfed a wide swath of the Bulwark. Snow was beginning to stick to stones around him.

Nearby, the guards moved to intercept him again, but a low growl carried along on a fresh bluster of icy air stopped them. Abandoning their stealth, the creatures leapt upon the Great Bulwark nimbly as no ordinary man could. They had ascended the very heights of Ordumair's Fortress without hindrance. The beast Anargen could see most clearly wasted little time in falling with gleefulness of the most vicious sort on the Fortress top's posted crossbowman, who only then began to turn and face death's arrival.

One Ord gave out a cry of terror cut short. Sprinting towards them, Anargen moved faster than he thought possible. He crashed into the beast with his shield before it could sink a painful riposte into its next victim.

The blow sent the muzzle of the beast wide of its target, and the creature found itself feeding on stone instead of soft flesh. It let out a low whimper, and in the fiery aura of his Spiritsword, Anargen could see this beast was not like those he'd seen before. Larger than the others by a slight degree, it was also ganglier, as though a pup instead of full-grown.

Perplexing as the monster looked, it was of secondary concern. All around, blurs of motion suddenly came racing across Anargen's peripheral vision. A howl preceded the sounds of scores of things scrambling up the rocky face of the mountain. An attack order.

Looking on in shock, Anargen made out many more were-beasts descending on the Great Bulwark from the mountain's side.

Arno gave a cry to, "Fire bolts!" A dozen or so crossbow bolts clattered against the mountain's thick hide. More blurs came rushing from their perches, having obtained the highground without their opponents ever being aware it was contested.

Seeing the furor only dimly, through the haze of falling snow, Anargen hesitated and gave his foe time enough to shake its huge head and reassess the plan of attack.

Eyes the color of rust regarded Anargen. The cursed orbs

shied away from the light of Anargen's weapon, as from something extremely unpleasant. The creature's whole body strained away the longer it stared at the marvelous implements of defense afforded to the Knights by the Great King.

"The King's light never fails to strike deep into the heart of those wrapped in darkness. You are no different," Anargen informed the monster.

The paralyzed beast need not find its own will to counter. Even as it gazed in awe and agony on the light vexing it, another creature came up on its flank and snapped at Anargen's exposed arm, forcing him to spin and bring his shield around to block.

Coming out of its daze, the initial beast looked to its comrade as a soldier to his commander. Unimaginably, the second monster was even bigger than the first and more muscular in its build. The lead beast was much less uncertain in its movements with respect to the Knight's burning guards. Even as it circled more to the right of Anargen, a handful of bolts lanced out from the nearby Ords and distracted the monster.

Dodging them deftly, the creature snapped its teeth at the Ords. Thinking it distracted, Anargen struck and managed only to catch it across one shoulder with a shallow slice. Anargen gaped. This new beast's agility vastly overshadowed those he'd encountered before. It was faster and by the looks stronger than any he had yet seen.

The first beast held back, awaiting the barked order of the second before advancing. The larger monster then stepped back and lunged towards the crossbowmen reloading their weapons as disbelief slowed their efforts.

Anargen's brows knitted as he was forced to dodge right. Claws scoured the stone of the Great Bulwark's wall inches from him, taking with it a scattering of shards from the stone. Unwillingly, Anargen gave up some of his positioning with respect to the bigger monster in order to better face this threat. Feinting a blow from his shield to bludgeon the thing's skull, he instead brought round his Spiritsword in a midlevel swipe that cut only air.

"Great, even the weaker one is fast!" he called out to his friends. He didn't expect an answer but hoped it might warn them.

Anargen dodged just in time to avoid being pounced on and brought down his sword with as much force as he could, being off balance as he was. A loud sizzle and plume of smoke indicated a dire wound on the creature's flank.

Almost immediately, it sent the creature into a tantrum of squeals and yelps as it nipped and pawed in fright. "Watch out!" Anargen wanted to cry out, as horribly, the thing stumbled and writhed till it fell off the edge of the Great Bulwark to the valley below.

A snarl tore free from the larger beast's throat. Inspite of its canine alienness, Anargen could read annoyance in its face. No heartbreak over the loss came through. The creature turned its huge, shaggy head and let out three short barks.

More blurs on the mountainside joined the fray, but Anargen wasn't the target. The young Knight had been too distracted with his struggle to notice other werebeasts had been busying the guards and his fellow Knights as well. Now the newest arrivals moved on the Ord nobles and their Thane, who all stood in a loose circle. Anargen tried not to begrudge any of the Ords who shook with visible fright.

"Get the Thane and nobles inside!" Anargen shouted over the whipping winds and snaps and snarls. The snow fell so much faster now, finding his way to the Thane was becoming guesswork.

Through the building blizzard, Anargen could see Arno shake his head. The other guards were far fewer in number now for the werebeasts devastating their ranks. He bellowed back a disagreeable retort seconds before a beast battered him aside like a child taken up by a tantrum.

Another voice just managed to cut through the frigid air.

"Heed the boy. Get inside now or we all perish here!" It was Sir Orwald, his burning blade making him a beacon for his fellow Knights. He swung his slightly curved sword around in a brilliant display to keep back a pair of advancing creatures.

Terrillian must have recognized their need at the same time as Anargen and called out, "Get to the nobles! We have to hold off the creatures."

Bertinand and Caeserus immediately obliged and charged off towards the circle of dwarf leaders and their monstrous antagonists.

Anargen took one step in that direction and felt the overwhelming imperative to throw himself onto the stones at his left. A second later, as the cool stone rushed to meet him in a rougher impact than he intended, he caught glimpse of the huge were-beast directing the attack sail past where he just stood. It just narrowly avoided overshooting and falling off the Bulwark altogether.

Rolling to his feet, Anargen heard a whisper to block. The teen hesitated for just a second, wondering if he really heard the voice or if he'd been tricked by the wind. His shield was a second too slow to totally deflect the creature's next strike. Anargen had to roll with the blow to keep from getting pinned down. As he staggered to his feet, he resolved to let the voice guide his actions.

A little flaring of intensity in his blade, now at guard, set the creature rearing back. Anargen heard the voice command him forward. Obeying, he battered the creature with his shield. The faint fire of the shield sizzled as it made contact with the beast's exposed underbelly. Little tendrils of steam escaped where the fire flash evaporated the snow building on the beast's fur coat.

Once more the creature reeled, and though Anargen wanted to move quickly for a finishing blow, the voice told him to stop and pivot right. Anargen spun in response.

Another massive paw with unreasonably wicked claws landed where he just stood, scraping up a bit of stony chunks from the Bulwark. Anargen jabbed the new arrival in the ribs with his elbow couter.

"Pivot," he heard again. Anargen spun all the way around behind his new foe in time for the first beast to drive a hard swipe of its claws across the flank of its compatriot. Anargen backed away. The second beast, furious over the miss-strike, leapt on the back of the first werebeast. An awful tussle out of some nightmarish realm where horror is plentiful as air began.

Having neither the stomach nor time for such bloody sport, Anargen felt himself being drawn to his initial goal. Right away he noticed the standoff had degenerated into open fighting and costly fighting at that. Some of the nobles lay still on the stones where they had moments ago stood. Others were locked in combat with what remained of their guard and Anargen's fellow Knights. If anything positive might be said, it was that only three werebeasts remained to battle, and they seemed increasingly guarded.

Anargen leapt to the side of Tengrath and brought his Spiritsword round to graze the shoulder of one of the creatures. By now a guard was opening the passageway back into the Fortress and the Thane, Sir Orwald, and at least a dozen other nobles lined up to dash through.

Tengrath gave Anargen a shove and snapped, "Keep your distance, hungerman."

Gritting his teeth, Anargen held his tongue. His eyes were on the beast in front of him, which nursed its wound and backed away. It seemed the perimeter would hold, and all was well till Anargen caught sight of an aberrant flash of fire on the far side of the defensive perimeter. A few nobles had made a dash for the keep rather than the interior of the Fortress and a Knight followed them. Even in the snowy maelstrom, Anargen knew it was Iaegon.

The beast to Anargen's front noticed as well. Its bright crimson tongue licked it chops. With a low growl, it broke off from the others.

Anargen gasped, "Iaegon!" Without looking, he tried to follow after and crashed into Tengrath, who had moved ahead of him to maintain the perimeter.

This time Tengrath took a swing with his short sword, a kindness as his axe in the other hand could have made contact, and bellowed, "Fool! Hold your place or do me the courtesy of feeding yourself to those beasts farther away."

There was no time to bicker. Anargen side-stepped the little fire spit of an Ord and plunged his Spiritsword forward. This forced the beast ahead of him to shift out of the way.

Anargen was a blur. The teen felt himself move faster than he understood possible. He made the distance seemingly in three strides where scores were required. Reaching the keep just in time, he grabbed Iaegon by the arm and spun the young Ord back and away from the door. "No," he ordered.

Iaegon looked bewildered more than anything and couldn't quite form a response. A howl from all too close wrenched Anargen's attention elsewhere. His original foe, flanked by two newly arrived beasts, was stalking towards them. At his back, Anargen also heard the doors to the keep swing shut, and a loud thump indicated the door had been barred from inside.

"Cowards," Iaegon muttered. "I tried to tell —"

"Run, now," Anargen cut him off and shoved the Ord away. He had just enough time to leap off the keep's dais himself as one monster crashed head first into the doors and almost battered them down.

Grasping the lad's wrist, Anargen sprinted for the entry to the Fortress. Once more he ran faster than any time in his life but not nearly as fast as he had alone. Whether because of Iaegon's added weight or something else, he knew he was only just keeping ahead of the werebeasts.

Caeserus and Terrillian were the last of the rearguard and already at the bottom of the stairs leading to the doors of the Fortress. They waved and shouted something Anargen couldn't hear.

Three steps from the top stair, Anargen heard a whisper, more like a shout. He slung Iaegon forward to the stairs, spun and jabbed his Spiritsword forward. The werebeast crashed into Anargen like a boulder coming down the mountainside, and Anargen for a brief second was flying off his feet, his whole world formed of the beast's fur and snow and the fire burning away at both. Then he crashed to the ground, and he felt the weight of the thing smashing him harder into the stones than he thought possible. Briefly the world lost focus. He bounced once, twice, and then skittered to a stop, pinned under the monster.

Lying there, only half-conscious, Anargen blinked, trying to see around him. To keep alert. His life depended on it and though he knew it, he didn't think he could get up. Pain radiated all over. Holding on to consciousness felt like he was trying to wade through neck-deep mud. How long would it be till the monsters were on him?

Before he let his eyes shut, an arm reached out and grabbed one of his pauldrons, then the other. He felt himself being dragged. Looking up, he saw Caeserus pulling him towards the Fortress gate. "This would be easier if you could help," he grunted. "By the way, this makes two you owe me."

Somehow Anargen struggled to his feet and with an arm draped around Caeserus, the pair stumbled back to the stairs. Ahead, Terrillian stood waving his sword in warning to all their enemies. Most were more interested in the keep at the moment. It looked like they were fighting over who would break its doors down.

Anargen stumbled down the stairs, falling down the last three, and ended up hobble-crawling to safety. Behind him Caeserus and Terrillian entered and the doors slammed shut, muffling the raucous cackles of the monsters outside.

35

WOES WITHIN, WITHOUT

"We barely survived. Now we wait for orders that we may not have the strength to fill.

Will anyone ever even read this?"

—ANARGEN'S JOURNEY JOURNAL,

FÓMHAR 1605 M.E.

ANARGEN TAPPED his quill against the desk he was using. Sir Orwald was out speaking with the Thane about plans of defense, leaving the young Knights to sit idle. A rest before the counteroffensive to take back the Great Bulwark.

Terrillian paced around the room anxiously whilst Caeserus watched him in a feline fashion from where he lounged, arms crossed, against the room's rear wall. None of the Knights had been soldiers before accepting the High King's call to fealty and joining his number. Only Terrillian had expressed interest in joining Libertias's armies. They had not wintered in a war camp or worried over provisions in a siege. Anargen found it to be so ethereal, dream-like in a nightmarish way. Holed up in this gargantuan bastion thousands of miles from home, battling a foe some in Ordumair still insisted was only legend, it was crazy.

Hadn't his biggest worries once been whether he would work in the mines and if Seren would return his affections?

Terrillian suddenly spoke up. "It's good we haven't fought any Ecthels yet."

Bertinand was lying down and sat upright. "Oh, do tell."

"Well, it's just," Terrillian began and then huffed, shrugging. "The werebeasts are different. Vile. Cruel beyond the tales. The soldiers of Ecthelowall may well be in the battle by compulsion or necessity. Maybe some fight to feed their families."

"And maybe some fight for spoils and renown," Caeserus almost spat.

"No, this entire conflict is cloaked in darkness," Anargen spoke up. "It was easy to miss what the world has become when we were in Black River. Narrow streets, homely shop, smiling familiar faces. Sorcery and science are no longer so far apart now."

"Thank you, bard," Bertinand said, sardonic.

"He's right," Terrillian reproved. "That castle's destruction gave us proof. Worse, men who once bowed in allegiance to the King of Light now no longer honor their ancestors' oaths of loyalty. It seems your vision was all too right, Caeserus."

Anargen looked away. The sudden discussion continued, but it did so without him. Things were all wrong now. A hard day's work, an evening spent in the flights of his imagination. The comfort of his father and mother's home, the enclave of an idyllic meadow, the humble Knight Hall, the warmth of Seren's hand in his. All of it so distant now, nearly fables. Like a dream within a dream, too sweet to find sound passage to morning's light. While nightmares filled the waking world.

Dimly it occurred to Anargen his parents might even now be back in Black River. He wondered if they would be proud to hear he'd followed the Great King's calling or worry after him. Would they ever know what had befallen him if the High King did not deliver them from this bleak fate?

What of Seren? Had any of the letters reached her? Did she

long for his return as he longed to be able to see her once more? Anargen reached for the letter from her.

From across the room came a creaking. The hinges of the room's door protested as it opened slowly, seemingly to avoid disturbing those within. Once Sir Orwald had entered, however, he could plainly see he had long been awaited. His sullen countenance did not brighten.

Closing the door, he treaded to his couch. Pushing Bertinand's legs off of one end, he dropped heavily onto it. A rare instance of him seeming his age.

No one spoke. As the silence grew more and more protracted, Bertinand blurted out, "Well? What of it?"

Sir Orwald leveled a dark stare back at Bertinand and his face scrunched in distaste. "The Thane believes we should mount a counterattack at dusk. As many of our army as can be spared will follow us into battle."

"Us? As in we're going to lead the battle formation against a ton of eager-to-eat-us werebeasts?" Bertinand's incredulity was far from thin-masked.

"It's an honor to lead a charge, even a desperate one," Caeserus informed Bertinand. "But what more is there to the plan? Are we to just ride out there and hope there are enough of us to batter them away? Is there no secret passage or solid tactics to give us an advantage?"

Terrillian shook his head. "I don't think we can scale the mountain face from lower down. I watched the werebeasts. They see well enough even in the pitch blackness out there. Climbing that far up with them on the prowl would just get us all massacred."

"What about secret passages?" Caeserus insisted. "Surely the tunnels of Ordumair can't all be legends. Didn't we see proof in the Knight Hall?"

"The Thane's Hall is our keep and was built with only one entrance. No one ever imagined Ordumair could be attacked from the top downward or that the fortress could fail."

"What about —"

From above, the coarse, canine laughter of the werebeasts could be heard faintly. Sir Orwald's residence was not so far from the pinnacle of the Great Bulwark that their raucous celebrations could not be overheard at times. This, however, seemed particularly spirited in its torturous pleasure.

"What are they on about now?"

"Mangy . . ." Caeserus's words were left to trail off. A faint tremor rippled across the room as though a small stone was skipping across a pond and they were floating on the water's surface nearby. "What?" Caeserus asked of no one in the room. Another stronger vibration could be felt.

Then there was dread silence and stillness for what felt to Anargen like hours but really could only have been ten or fifteen minutes. At the time's end, from without the door to Sir Orwald's quarters came an insistent knock.

"Enter," Sir Orwald announced. His eyes still searched the walls to his room and beyond their stone for the source of the tiny quakes.

"Sir!" Iaegon managed to sputter in between ragged gasps for breath. The boy shook some as he spoke. In the corridor beyond him, soldiers could be seen rushing about, headed differing directions along the corridor in great haste.

"Easy, lad," Orwald said. "Gather your breath."

"They are attacking the Great Bulwark from the valley!" the young Ord finally managed.

"So, what of it?" Orwald replied. "The beasts atop it are a more pressing concern."

"No!" Iaegon said shaking his head emphatically. "They're damaging it. The Ecthels have moved their siege engines nearer the fortress and are sieging it directly! The Thane has ordered you all down to the main gate. You must ride out and attack the Ecthels immediately!"

Grabbing the boy's shoulders in his heavy old hands, Sir

Orwald asked, "What of the defenses atop the fortress? Those werebeasts are still up there!"

"He said nothing about it to me, sir. Only to insist you hurry forth!"

"You can't abandon that entrance! That might be their plan. Lure our forces away and let loose their hounds within the innards of the fortress itself!" Caeserus shouted back.

"Silence," Sir Orwald grumbled. "I know that, and my nephew does as well. Sir Terrillian, Sir Bertinand, Sir Iaegon, and I will see to it that those guarding the Great Bulwark do not leave their places. Sir Anargen, Sir Caeserus, you must join those riding out against the Ecthels."

"Wait —" Someone was preparing to protest, but the plaintive words were cut off before Anargen could discover who tried to speak. A curt wave of Sir Orwald's hand stopped any further conversation on the matter. From somewhere without, a thunderous rumble accentuated the Ord's position.

"May the King of Light be with us all," he pronounced.

36

ALL THE THANE'S HORSES AND ALL THE THANE'S MEN

"When all the journey is done, where shall we be? Heroes or villains? Victors or vanquished? Only the Great King knows."

—ANARGEN'S JOURNEY JOURNAL,
FÓMHAR 1605 M.E.

"ONE THING CAN BE SAID for these Ords, they can certainly muster their volunteers," Anargen noted, looking around the chamber between the outer and inner gates of Ordumair and seeing thousands more than he imagined. Hundreds more still defended passages within the fortress. Even the old and infirm appeared eager for the "glory" of this battle.

Caeserus, to whom Anargen had addressed the observation, did not even seem to notice Anargen had spoken. It was unsurprising. Conversations, shouting chants, singing songs of victory and conquest, and even the playing of small lutes and drums filled the space. Anargen hadn't noticed how vast this entry area was the night they were ushered in as Valesgard fell.

A familiar flare of pain over Sir Cinaed's loss hit him. Anargen had the awful suspicion Cinaed would not have approved of the Ord battle plan. Mounted soldiers at the front of the amassed army were to ride out, break the enemy lines, and take out whatever horrid machines were sending shudders through the stones of the fortress. Even with the chorus of boasts and general revelry from many thousands of Ords, the song of the siege engines battering the Great Bulwark echoed over it all. Whatever sorcery and science had been brought against Ordumair, it would not be soon enough removed.

After the cataphracts moved out, the regular infantry must charge and engage the enemy until the mounted Ords finished their task. If the bawrnig did not believe they had a strong advantage, which he seemed absolutely confident they would possess soon, they were to draw back into this very room. Ballistae would launch attacks until such a time as the defenders needed to pull back deeper into the tight passages of the fortress, where ambushes lay in wait.

Whatever their deficiencies, the Ords had long prepared for such a day as this. It almost gave Anargen hope this battle could be won. But try as they might, none of the Ords would listen when he warned of the Grey Scourge. Even after the testimony of the survivors from the attack atop the Great Bulwark. Those commanding this army would not allow for such a thing as werewolves to be real.

Beneath Anargen, Patch stirred, huffing with growing unease. His large cream and sorrel dotted head turned this way and that as some movement amongst the ranks nearby took place.

Anargen patted his faithful mount with a gentle hand and soothed, "Shh. Hold it together, boy. We'll see this through." Or so Anargen hoped. His horse had been confiscated and taken away to Ordumair soon after the Knights had arrived. Caeserus was likewise seated on his horse, just to Anargen's right. Both steeds had not been the same since arriving in the fortress's stables.

It did not help that all around them in a massive staging chamber were thousands of Ord foot soldiers, armed with swords, axes, pikes, halberds, and on occasion a crossbow. With their blue tunics, the dwarf soldiers milling around the room were like a living sea with islands of iron dotting it.

Something caught Anargen's eye. Ahead, closest to the gate outside was the leader of this grand army, Elder Samohan and his mounted troops. He seemed to be stirring, readying himself to give the order to open the gates. To begin the first real battle of Anargen's life.

At Anargen's back were archers, apothecaries, and ballistae with their crews. Ever since being ordered into the middle of the array rather than with the mounted Ords, Anargen had been trying to figure out the purpose behind it. Thinking on it gave a respite to his frayed nerves.

"Good of them to place us here where we're good and safe, huh? Maybe they're warming up to us?" It was more an attempt to get Caeserus's attention to discuss their strategy than actually discuss his musings.

There was only partial success, though, as Caeserus half-turned toward him, as if he heard something but couldn't be sure of it. Anargen sighed and noticed an older Ord at his right with a great round belly was chuckling. This annoyed Anargen for some reason. "What's so funny?"

The Ord looked up, a twinkle in his hazel eyes, and he stroked the curling plumes of his brown beard. "You, hunger-man. You were not placed here for protection. It is a mark of shame. Only we who are old or unfit and the cowards, traitors, prisoners — those with no honor — are placed in the center of the formation. When the battle starts, we are trapped. We have no choice but press forward until pushed right into the midst of the enemy. That way, none of us can flee, and the fate of the most noble and the most despicable will be the same."

Anargen's cheeks reddened as the hefty Ord indulged in a more boisterous laugh. The young Knight tried to not let that laugh, a bit like an old dog's yowling, bother him. Deep down, the old Ord must have been retching inside. After all, he was a shamed one too. At least Anargen could push it off on being an outsider. This man had to live with a very personal disdain.

The point was moot. Echoing through the enclosure was a horn blow to call for silence. Soon they would open the main gate, and it would begin. Though he recognized this was a pivotal moment in the history of the Ords, Anargen did not feel any more alert or sense time's passage in some momentous way, only seconds passing into minutes and minutes into the looming hour where all would be decided. Win or lose, Anargen would be facing it in a manner not so different from every other day or event of his life.

What might he be doing now if he hadn't left? What was Seren doing?

Shaking his head, Anargen pushed such things aside for another time. The horn had ended and orders to open the door had been issued. A sound, the low growl of heavy timbers on stone, signaled the closure of the inner gates to the fortress and the outer gate opening to the battle ahead.

The inner gate was closed much sooner than the outer, and just before the massive stones ahead parted, Caeserus smacked Anargen's arm. His expression was ominous as the thunder before a storm. "Stay on my flank. We'll cut across the line of siege engines till we draw the . . ."

His words were lost as what could only be termed as a roar went up from the Ords around them. A single chant carrying all the bitter fury of generations wronged. The centuries of war and privation spoke through the freshest entrants in the struggle. It was as magnificent as it was awful. Death waited beyond those doors, but no Ord standing there let fear soften the cry.

Hope crested and crashed down over Anargen, swelling in his chest. They weren't doomed. After all, weren't there accounts of the Great King leading his people to victory with longer odds?

Then the doors parted, and the wind from outside burst in through the gap. Defying reason, it seemed to throw open the doors wider. If the Ords roared, it bellowed and screamed, sending a swirling volley of snow hurtling into Anargen's helm's faceplate just as he closed it.

Anargen felt his breath catch as the icy wind slammed into his chest, threatening to unseat him. It felt as if a thousand tiny hands all pushed against him in unison. All working to find a weak spot in his armor and hooking their frigid fingers into his flesh, freezing him to the core.

Several seconds passed before the bluster of the storm relented, and Anargen could see more than a white haze of snowflakes. Several Ords had been blown down off their mounts and were righting themselves slowly. The hefty Ord beside Anargen wasn't down, but neither was he laughing anymore. His full concentration was devoted to rubbing his arms.

He wasn't the only Ord quaking from the new cold descending on the room. Horses shrieked, and there was some commotion about closing the doors. If the commander heard this, he was too stalwart and well-disciplined to turn back.

Moments later the horn sounded, and soldiers obeyed. Marching into a grey and white void beyond. Whatever courage, whatever confidence, seemed muffled already. No more boasts, no more shouts. Only grim obedience.

Somehow Anargen knew it was not chance this storm had beset Ordumair and sapped the defenders of their resolve. Something dark indeed was making its bid to annihilate Ordumair, and it awoke an indignation Anargen had not known was within him. By instinct he reached for his Spiritsword and drew it from its scabbard, raising it overhead. The sword caught fire and burned bright in the gloom.

Ords nearby, including his heckler, seemed to strain toward the flame, as though they felt its warmth. Anargen certainly felt no cold now. When the moment came to spur his horse on, he found himself shouting in defiance of all of the evil brought against this place, "For Ordumair and the glory of the Great King!"

Then he was in motion galloping out into the darkness and

drifts of snow higher than expected. It had piled on so quickly. Had the storm really only begun a few days before? Beyond the icy drifts, Anargen heard crackles and pops. Little flickers of fire preceded screams of terror.

Still he rode on, not remembering to keep on his friend's flank. As if caught by a magnet he hurtled on horseback towards the growing sounds of terror and turmoil, where he was certain he would be needed most.

A bellow from cannons ripped through the air so very near Anargen that Patch almost threw him off. Anargen tightened his hold on the reins and altered course towards the source of the sound. In the next moments, the cannon snarled again, followed by a cadre of tiny cracks. Through the blizzard he perceived a few Ords clutching at various parts of their bodies. These broke off their charge as if hit by an invisible arrow.

As Anargen passed them, he saw tiny streams of red pouring from beneath disfigured plates of armor. There was nothing on the air now. Only the smell that comes with a winter snow. All the same, Anargen knew the Ecthels were using guns. Unfamiliar with them as he was, these guns seemed to have remarkable accuracy and devastating effect.

Another cry of determination that could only be Caeserus cut through the dimness. Anargen spurred his horse on once more to close that remaining distance. Momentum in a battle seemed like a morning mist, present one moment and gone the next. He had to do his part to ensure it didn't slip completely from the Ords' grasp.

Charging up and over a snowy hillock, Anargen gained speed on the downside. At its base, Anargen saw Caeserus pressing on to face a menacing feature of the field. A great black barrel supported by a wooden framework with huge spoked wheels was positioned to face down the Fortress of Ordumair. A cannon!

It loosed another fiery volley that shot through the air in a blur and whose only sign of effect was the stony cry of a wound in the mountainside and a brief ringing in Anargen's ears.

Behind the cannon was gathered a number of forms obscured by the dark and storm. They raised their weapons, and it was clear they were archers, yet instead of the whoosh of an arrow or the snap of a crossbow came a tiny rumble like that of the cannon. Arquebusiers.

A warning rose within Anargen's throat and rang from his lips a second before the guns sounded their hateful call once more. Only a trio of Ords remained uninjured of a small band Caeserus had brought with him, a precious few. A second round of cracks sounded, and Anargen saw Caeserus drop from his horse.

Numbness overtook Anargen as he watched his friend rolling in the snow. Patch continued carrying him towards those who had struck Caeserus down. Fury choked Anargen, and he bore down on the Ecthels, his sword's flames crackling against an upraised rifle as he did. Coming back around, he found two of the six or so Ecthels scrambling away.

Dropping down off his horse, Anargen charged for the cannon, slogging through the snow as fast as he could. Not everyone had abandoned the siege weapon, however, and one of the remaining four charged him, a rapier drawn and swishing through the air.

When the distance between them closed, Anargen watched as the other man pulled back to stab with his blade, and Anargen easily sidestepped him, battering down the other man's sword. The teen brought forward his shield and slammed it into the Ecthel's side, sending him tumbling forward into the deep snow drift.

A flurry of curses were launched at Anargen as the man spun awkwardly to his feet and tried to whip his sword back around again to catch Anargen's upper arm.

Anargen was able to sidestep, parry, and hammer with his shield.

Another of the cannon crew was emboldened by Anargen's distraction and charged forward, a halberd held overhead. Before the halberd made half its wide cut through the air, Anargen deflected with his shield and came back around to also slap aside another strike from the first man, this time shattering his rapier.

Swordless, the Ecthel gave a startled cry. Anargen stepped forward to deliver a blow from his sword's pommel, sending the man unconscious to the snow. With only a whisper's guide, Anargen whirled around. Dodging, he caught the halberd being brought against him like a lance at mid-shaft. The Ecthel wielding it blinked dumbly at how fast the movement had been.

Anargen, too, marveled at how effortless fighting the Ecthels was proving. It was then he remembered Sir Cinaed telling them about the supernatural blessings bestowed by the armor the High King gifted them. Maybe that was how the Knights also could battle the werebeasts whereas the Ords were so easily overcome.

Twisting the shaft and rending it from the bearer's fear-loosened grasp, Anargen tossed down the halberd and stepped forward to slam his gauntleted fist in a right hook to the man's jaw. The Ecthel crumpled, and Anargen was left with two foes.

He ran at them with a shout. Both men manning the cannons had only short swords to defend them. Three well placed blows from his Spiritsword bested each of them, and Anargen was left with the huge cannon.

Anargen drew a few deep breaths. "Okay, so what now?"

Marvelous as it was, he wondered if the Spiritsword could pierce the cannon's thick iron hide. Even if possible, he didn't know enough about the manner they worked to be sure that would totally cripple it. Observing how it rested on a wooden frame for mobility, he slashed at the wheels and cart. After a few moments the whole thing was a mess of burning, shattered wood. The heavy cannon collapsed and sank into the snow's embrace, seething as the fire met the snow.

It was at that moment, encircled in a haze of mist from his work's completion, Anargen heard a howl.

There was no way to tell exactly where it came from, but Anargen did hear Patch neigh in fright. When the mist cleared, he could see the hulking form of one of the beasts sauntering towards him some distance away.

Anargen slogged a few feet forward to face the monster, before deciding against it. Being on Patch's back would be a vital advantage in these conditions.

Turning and sprinting for the horse, he heard the half chuckle-half bark of the werebeast and knew the thing was picking up speed. It must have relished the chase, thinking Anargen fled in terror.

When he was a foot away from grabbing Patch's reins, the horse spooked and dashed to the side, leaving Anargen to lunge for empty air and tumble over the back side of a high mound of snow. The beast's howl of pleasure was lost in the sound of snow being crushed under him, then silence.

Anargen didn't have a second to spare. Trying to turn back over, he felt an awkward helplessness as if he was swimming through syrup.

He got to his feet, shaking off the snow, just in time to fling up his shield as the monster crashed into him. The beast's jaws were held back by his shield, snapping at him from inches away. Hot breath off the mongrel's maw reeked of death and decay and blinded him in a thick haze of vapor.

Pushing off against the creature with all his might, Anargen brandished his Spiritsword, the blade's flames swelling and growing brightening in indignation at the abomination.

The monster buried its eyes and muzzle in the snow as it swiped with one huge, clawed paw. This was Anargen's chance, and the youth took it. Dashing back to his horse, he climbed up into the saddle and directed Patch on toward his foe.

The creature faced him again, its hackles rising with an evil glee. Anargen's horse neighed and started at the sight of the thing. Hanging tight to the reins, it was all Anargen could do to keep the animal from throwing him off and fleeing.

"Patch, no! We mustn't fear," Anargen encouraged while he worked the rigging to force the cooperation of his mount. It was only a few seconds, but already the werebeast bounded with inconceivable speed round the Knight and leapt from the same direction as before.

Once more the Great King spared Anargen, and the young Knight narrowly warded off the dreadfully sharp fangs of the wolf-like monster. A terrible thought struck Anargen as he watched the thing again leaping and bounding around him with such fleetness.

These beasts are faster than any we've encountered before. They were only encumbered before by the limits of the Great Bulwark's space. Here they are free to unleash the fullness of their deadly prowess!

How can I face such speed and ferocity alone?

As if to further discourage Anargen before destroying him, the werebeast rushed to Anargen's left, stopped short of the Knight's position, rose up on its haunches, and swiped at him. Claws raked over Anargen's shield, nearly unseating him.

A contented rumble came from within the monster's chest as it resumed its offensive. Frowning, Anargen fought with growing desperation to keep his eyes trained on the thing. In the swirling white blur of snow falling and high drifts, the beast, a light grey, was a blur. A streak that might be imagined as much as perceived. This beast was only toying with him. Having a bit of fun before finishing him off.

Even if by some miracle he survived this encounter, he had many more such beasts to face with diminishing numbers of others to aid in the struggle. Anargen was alone on a battlefield fighting for the losing side.

The beast charged again, succeeding in battering Anargen off his horse to come crashing into the snow. Disoriented and breathing in ragged gasps, Anargen whirled and brought up his shield to discourage a snap from the monster that might have been his end.

Slashing after the creature's retreating form, Anargen slipped and rolled down a snowy mound. From its bottom he looked up into the bleakness, the weight of the dark and despair numbing his limbs as much as the icy crystals breathing frigid fire into his flesh.

In the midst of harsh and unforgiving sky, Anargen thought he could perceive something. A single place of luminance masked by the grey and ebony swirls. Beyond all the storm's fury there was still light in this world, hope. Looking down from the veiled sun, Anargen saw etched into the blade of his Spiritsword some words he'd read once before.

Tilting the blade to better examine them, he heard a whisper, sweet like honey for the hungry and cool as mountain's streams for the thirsty. *This storm won't last forever, and I am not alone. Thousands of years ago the King ordained he would never abandon even one of his servants and inscribed such on the blades of all Spiritswords. I am his servant. So what is this wolf that he should try and make a lie of the Great King's word?*

From above, standing on the top of the snowy mound, the werebeast sounded a cruel howl as if in victory. Anargen gritted his teeth. "You're celebrating your end," he mumbled. Even if Anargen fell on this battlefield and was carried by the Great King to the Kingdom of Light in slumber, it would not be by the craft of this werebeast or any other.

Maybe hearing him, the monster incautiously leapt at him.

Dropping to the snow, Anargen spun and brought his Spiritsword up. Finding its mark, the blade slashed the creature along its length. A squeal of agony and steam filled the air as the flames from Anargen's sword crackled with the impact.

With punctuated crunch, the creature landed in the same low place that so nearly became Anargen's grave and lay still. There was fear and anguish in the creature's eyes. A measure of pity welled up inside Anargen, but he could lose no time in concern over felled enemies.

Once more at the crest of the hill, Anargen heard something approaching and turned to face the new antagonist. Instead, he found his friend Caeserus, armor caked with snow, perched atop his horse and holding the reins to Patch as well. His friend shouted to him, "Hurry! More of them are coming! We have to get to the center of Ord's attack and make sure it holds!"

Irresistible, a smile worked its way on Anargen's lips. He looked at the burning blade in his hand. "Thank you, my King, may I not fear again. Your might and magnificence will be known, no matter the foe we face."

Scrambling to reach Patch as fast as the slippery snow allowed, Anargen stopped in front of his horse and examined his friend. The other Knight did not appear gravely injured, only intensely serious.

Each horse was spurred on without further delay. Both teens charged into the midst of Ords and Ecthels, beasts and engines of destruction alike as the desperate defense of Ordumair raged on.

37

BEST REGARDS

ANARGEN REINED BACK his horse Patch. Beside him, Caeserus surveyed the state of the dwarf effort. Lifting his helm's faceplate, Anargen coughed and rubbed his face. He hoped he was mistaken in what he saw.

There was no coordination, only chaos. The legendary tenacity and gallantry of the Ords in battle seemed only so many braggarts' tales. Even now the mounted troops were turning back and scattering as the disarrayed foremost lines of foot soldiers ignored the horn's sounding to press on.

Little wonder. Those who pushed forward were rushing to their deaths. Support from the Ord's riders was non-existent. Any archers and crossbowmen in place to offer aid were being devastated without ever engaging their foe. Not that the archers would be of great use. This weather hampered the Ord bowmen more than the riflemen on the opposing side. Worst, by far, were the aberrations on the landscape, blurs executing merciless injury on the unsuspecting Ords.

"More werebeasts," Caeserus grumbled. "Where did these cursed things come from? Weren't there only four or so before?"

Anargen managed to pry his gaze away from the unfolding

defeat of the Ords. "There weren't many, no. And we've felled a fair number since then."

"Where are they coming from then?" Caeserus snapped with incredulity. "It's not as though you can fabricate the things like a sword or shield on a forge."

"They're spreading their curse!" Anargen understood the reason for Ecthels' delay. He waited a few moments to see if Caeserus would arrive at the same conclusion.

Caeserus sounded out the logic, "Anyone bitten on the night of a new moon and without the will to resist the poison is transformed by the light of the full moon. The Harvest Moon was only a few nights ago?"

The face of Anargen's friend took on a frustrated look of incomprehension as he pondered how to fit together the pieces to this riddle. His expression dissolved into one of distress as realization gripped him. "No. There could be hundreds, thousands of them by now!"

Already wearied, Anargen sighed. "We can't let the Ords keep fighting in this wretched storm with an entire army of those things lurking in the darkness."

"We have to rally them and take care of those cannons," Caeserus pointed out. "Otherwise they might break through and open the way for the werebeasts to enter at will."

"Any idea of how to go about it?"

"We'll have to gather at least one company of the Ord horsemen and bring them round behind the riflemen in the center. If we can get a fraction of momentum for them, perhaps we'll have time to take down those manning the siege engines."

Caeserus saw Anargen's grimace. "Admittedly not the most probable plan to succeed, and I'm sure these Ords will be skeptical, but what choice is there?"

"None I can find," Anargen said, spurring Patch on. "So, let's be about it!"

Around them the explosive envoys of the cannon crashed in a bombastic melody, waylaying any man who stood in their path. Patch was indeed a fine horse or aided in his efforts by the High King Himself to find a safe course. A bolt, weaving through the crumbling counterattack to where the Ord cataphracts' retreat was slowing. Coming upon them, the two teens swung wide around to intercept a withdrawing commander.

"You there! Stay where you are, Ord!" Caeserus snapped, time and mood for courtesy spent. The captain, startled by the Knights' arrival, turned his horse to the side as if to make ready for combat with Caeserus. The rest of the men halted and thankfully recognized the Knights.

"You cataphracts! Follow us! We have to take out the cannons," Caeserus bellowed.

"Are you daft? Those cannons are why we fall back," the lead cataphract spat in retort.

"It doesn't matter that others have fallen," Caeserus replied. "Their work on behalf of your people's legacy is finished. But you must forge your own. We have a plan to stop them."

"A plan you say?" from his tone it was hard to tell if his interest was genuine or ironic.

Anargen spoke up. "If you help us flank those riflemen, we'll have a chance at reaching the cannons. Without the cannons, you should be able to hold formations again. Moreover, you can rescue your honor."

"Flank them, hmm?" the commander stroked his brown beard, twisting a bead on one of its braids.

"Follow us into the fray," Caeserus enjoined. "We will come around behind the rifle lines of their assault's center and break them up. You and Anargen lead half of your men left, while I take the rest right. We have to hurry though!"

Something changed suddenly in the Ord's sour expression. He whispered a few words to each of his nearest subordinates and then said, "Very well, lead the way."

38

RUINATION

POUNDING FURIOUSLY against the shifting slopes of slush and snow, the riders raced towards the riflemen formations. As Anargen came upon the first unwitting rifle bearer, he brought round his Spiritsword. Splitting the rifle at the middle, the force of it sent the arquebusier to the ground. Then he crashed down another and two more. For just a moment, Anargen dared to imagine triumph. What these Ords did now would become the valors of legends, engraved in stone and steel in Ord halls and upon their armor.

Anargen's group had broken at least three rows of the Ecthels' front line before those assembled responded. The storm had become detrimental to all. While Anargen's horse slowed and he struggled to batter aside a gunner, the Ord commander blew his horn. A long somber cry echoing off the mountainside with a deep crescendo.

Turning each way in his saddle, Anargen saw all around him the Ords were breaking off the attack and moving away from the arquebusiers. "What are you doing?" he shouted at the captain as he, too, turned to ride off.

"We have our own plans, hungerman! Thank you for providing a worthy distraction!"

As the soldier spurred his horse on, he continued blowing the horn in short blasts. Anargen realized the commander had decided to abandon his and Caeserus's plan in favor of attacking the Ecthel's mounted units further back. The cavaliers employed by the Ecthels had not even had to move from their position yet.

Gritting his teeth, Anargen wondered if dying in combat against the cavaliers carried more honor to them than the teens' plan. A whisper of warning stirred Anargen to turn Patch at an angle as a shot from a rifleman hammered his shield.

They abandoned me here to draw all the fire!

There was no time to let bitterness or anger settle in. He had to ride!

"Patch!" Anargen shouted and drove his heels into the horse. Patch reared and took off, pushing through the snow at an angle, taking Anargen away from the center. All around him a hail of lead balls rained. He half turned in the saddle to hold his shield up, catching a dozen shots before Patch could put enough distance between them and Ecthel lines to offer any safety.

Once out of rifle range, Anargen spared a glance toward where the Ord cataphracts had met their Ecthel counterparts. He could not spot them and the horn calls from the commander had gone silent.

Yanking hard on the reins, Anargen got Patch stopped. Horse and rider waited there taking in unsteady breaths of the icy air. "They betrayed us, Patch," Anargen moaned. Patch just huffed through his nostrils, little vapor clouds billowing to each side.

It struck Anargen, with all the chaos of the battle, they could escape. If they skirted the edge of the valley and were careful, he and Patch could get away from all this. From treacherous Ords who only hated him. From a war he had no stake in beyond being pulled in at the worst hour. From losing any hope of seeing his home, his family, his Seren.

Anargen looked up into the dark, unforgiving sky. He no longer saw that little spot of light. Closing his eyes, he cried out.

It was a garbled wail. When he opened his eyes, he looked at the burning sword in his hand. "I can't do it, Patch," he said. "I can't run. Victory today or not. I know my oaths. Whatever Caeserus's vision meant, somehow, I know this is my fight as well."

Drawing in a deep breath, Anargen heard Patch neigh softly under him. "We have to do something soon though, boy, or the fight is sure to be a lost one."

Bringing Patch around a little further, in the near distance, Anargen could just make out another battery of siege engines. Not as impressive on first sight as the towering trebuchets and cruel cannons he had intended to dispatch, but anything now was better than running.

Only after Anargen had committed to his new course did he hear the indistinct siege machines loose a bellow that shook the ground. Still riding on, Anargen saw the projectile it fired strike the face of the Great Bulwark like a mace batters a shield. A smoking blemish on the battlement was left from the impact, and Anargen thought he saw fragments of stone falling away.

Protecting the weapon, Anargen soon discovered, was a formidable assortment of pike-bearing Ecthels and riflemen. By the time Anargen reached them, the soldiers had noticed his approach.

Bearing down at a gallop, Anargen swung low and clipped off the tip of the nearest pikeman's weapon. As he did so, Patch spun around. His reins had been yanked hard by an unseen hand. A blast from a rifle barrel hit Anargen's shield, hard. Unsettled in his seat, Anargen tried to gain control of his mount. As the horse swung round, he took a swipe with his sword and disarmed the attacking rifleman.

The crew working around it looked up in disbelief as Anargen's sword battered aside the two other pikemen's sorties. Shivering and disarmed, they drew back. Now Anargen could move on their squat weapon. Smoke still drifted from its broad opening. It reeked of burned gunpowder, though Anargen was more fixated on a building ringing in his ears.

Not wasting the opportunity, Anargen leaned down and struck at the wooden frame as he had before. Each blow to it brought a little touch of fire that soon caught and was licking up the wood with a righteous joy.

By now the gunners manning the thing had fled. Anargen looked up just in time to see that it wasn't for fear of him. Raising his shield and tugging at the reins, he just managed to ward off a strike from a ruddy-colored werebeast.

The blow put him off balance, forcing him to turn his steed to stay seated. Behind him the werebeast had already hopped lightly to Anargen's right and then in a bound leapt into the air to sink its fangs into the teen's shoulder and neck.

Anargen let the momentum of the turn sling him off the back of the horse, and he landed with a roll. The werebeast soared over the horse and snapped at its prey. A low growl issued from its quivering canine lips. Charging towards Anargen, the beast instinctually went once more for the young Knight's throat.

Rolling to his feet, Anargen spun to bring his shield up and block its grisly maw from clamping on him.

Pragmatic, the thing took a couple ginger swipes at Anargen. Wispy puffs of mist drifted from its ravenous jaws which dripped with frenzied saliva. Finding no point of attack, its fur raised, the beast slapped some snow at Anargen's face, missing wide.

Back and forth the gentle game of reflex continued until the werebeast feinted a strike from the left and instead reached out with its right paw to batter Anargen to the ground. Falling for the move, Anargen struggled to bring up his sword and caught the beast's paw as it struck his right pauldron. Though he was sent tumbling through the snow, Anargen's Spiritsword seared deeply into the soft padding of its enormous paw. While the beast roiled in pain, Anargen shook his head and looked up from where he'd landed. His muscles ached. Sucking in a painful breath, he fought back to his feet.

His opponent glared at him, as if to destroy him with a thought. Unable to will Anargen's death, the monster charged forward.

The injured paw refused to be pressed into the bitter-cold snow covering the field and forced the creature to pitch to the side at the last moment. Anargen leapt deftly aside and spun to batter the beast's huge head with his shield.

Landing in a crumpled heap, the werebeast was disoriented. It was too far for Anargen to reach for a finishing blow. Clever as it was, the monster tried its trick of tossing the snow to blind Anargen. This time as Anargen rolled he felt a gentle whisper guiding him to the right.

As he came to his feet, his Spiritsword at the ready, Anargen found he wasn't facing the werebeast at all. He was looking at the Great Bulwark, nearer it than he imagined. The battlement loomed high above in a blinding veil of snow fall.

Even with the storm's mask, Anargen could see the once mighty structure looked grievously injured. His eyes wide, the young Knight realized the colossal element of the bastion was on the brink of collapse.

The familiar whisper warned him, "Flee!" Ignoring the werebeast who watched him as it favored its injured front leg, Anargen dashed past the thing, which was too puzzled by the teen's behavior to commit to an attack.

Before Anargen could reach his horse, the monster overcame its stupor and leapt to bar his path. Arching its back with fur bristling, it let out a serious bark, challenging him.

Slipping and leaping aside before he ran straight into its waiting jaws, Anargen rolled back to his feet and circled around the werebeast trying to reach his horse before Patch galloped off in terror.

Anargen realized this was futile as the wolf-like creature wheeled to keep itself facing him and shouldered aside the horse, who whinnied in fright as it was sent sliding down the hillside. Tentatively watching the horse, Anargen saw Patch get back up, but rather than flee, he stood snorting in wait. *I love that horse.*

The sounds of a cracking, like a thousand oaks snapped in half at once, shouted over the sounds of all else in the valley. For the moment, even the werebeast had to suspend its bloodlust and heed the sounds.

Seizing the opportunity, Anargen ran and jumped from the relatively higher point, sideways to Patch, and in desperation swung round his Spiritsword as he did so. Such a move landed him hard against his horse and instantly sent painful waves of regret through his torso.

A howl of pain told him the werebeast had been struck by the swing of abandon. What became of the blow was lost to Anargen. As soon as he crashed into Patch, the paint horse whinnied in fright and took off at remarkable speed. Anargen's right arm got looped through the reins by accident, and he found himself being drug, facing away from whatever lay ahead.

Snow rushed past him in a cool, ivory blur, forcing him to work to take in breaths as clumps of snow crashed over him like the foaming billows of a stormy sea. Bouncing and twisting, he had to fight not to allow his burning blade to slice Patch or himself. Had the blade not been so dear, he would have let it go. Instead, he sorely hoped that soon his arm, now in excruciating pain and keeping his mind well-informed of such, would slip loose from the reins and this agony would pass.

The relief he so dearly longed for came sooner than he expected. Behind the horse and rider's flight, the Great Bulwark was hit by another hammering ball from a cannon and with a deafening groan, a tremendous chunk of the proud battlement tore free and plummeted to the valley floor below, followed by a dozen smaller shards.

A series of tremors raced through the ground and ripped away Patch's footing. Knight and steed each landed in a sprawl several feet apart.

Dislodged snow covered Anargen, and through bleary eyes he could see a cloud of dust issuing from the ruined portions of the fortress. The cloud blanketed the area as it rushed away from its source, a grim messenger of ill news.

All was silent, or the cacophony had deafened him. Anargen tried to move and pain raced through his limbs. The miasma of grainy debris approached him. Forcing himself to one knee, his head throbbed, and the world spun. Collapsing back to the snowy ground, he felt the snow welcome him with a chilly embrace. His eyes closed.

Not a single fiber of him was willing to stand against the pains and aches besetting him. At the pain's edge was the fatigue. At the fatigue's edge was the icy chill of the ground, numbing and biting at him in one. Already tiny fragments of stone and ash began covering him as if in burial. It would be so very easy to stay there, to embrace the surrender of that rest.

How long he lay that way, resigned to his fate, he couldn't say. He might have lost consciousness, even been dreaming. Or so he believed, because he heard a voice with a fatherly voice saying, "Anargen, get up!"

Though he wasn't sure if he was loud enough to be heard, because he did not try very hard, Anargen mumbled back, "I can't. Didn't you see? The Bulwark is fallen. Everything is undone."

"Anargen, lad, I did see. But nothing is decided. We have to get you back to the fortress!"

The voice was coming from so close now. But why be concerned about a defeated bastion in death or dreams? Especially since the voice sounded so very like . . . Anargen's eyes snapped open.

"You need to get up or I'll have to pull you up. There's work to be done," the voice chided him once more.

A coolness touched Anargen that licked at him like tongues of fire. He beheld death time and again this day, yet nothing struck such fear into him as this specter.

Lifting the faceplate on his helmet, as if to dispel the apparition before him, Anargen drew in a breath and couldn't quite exhale at first. Even with the dismal swirl of icy flakes and oppressive grey all around, there could be no denying it. Sir Cinaed's burning form stood before him.

Struggling to his feet, a storm of emotions to rival the blizzard rose up within Anargen. Joy, anger, confusion, anxiety, hopefulness. All billowed within, battering his already wearied mind with their disparate surges. On the heels of the real storm's latest peal of thunder or cannons — Anargen couldn't be sure which — he closed the distance and wrapped his arms around the great man in a tight embrace. Over the din of the wind and siege he shouted, "My captain! How are you here?"

Sir Cinaed had to be careful with his footing in the snowdrifts and pulled back from Anargen, placing a hand on his shoulder. "I escaped Valesgard's demise to seek aid for us."

Hearing no further explanation, Anargen looked past him to see several dark, hunched forms nearby, crumpled in on themselves to fight off the cold. Though lacking a regal posture, Anargen could make out the distinctive garb of high ranking Ecthels, probably members of the honor guard to the Viceroy.

Anargen almost cried out in warning, but the alarm died in his throat. These men wouldn't have been here, so near to Sir Cinaed, by chance. Shirking the older Knight's grip and taking a step backward, Anargen gazed up at Sir Cinaed. The teen's brow furrowed with a dozen freshly crafted questions. All were melted down and cast in a single heated accusation, "You are with them?"

"They are with us," Sir Cinaed corrected with ease.

Taking another step back, Anargen wobbled a bit as he sank, off balance, on the slope and slammed shut his faceplate. "You can't keep speaking in riddles," Anargen protested. "We thought we lost you and now you're standing with murderers!"

"Murderers? No. Those who would have been murdered were it not for me. All will be made plain. I need only your trust for a few hours more. Have I ever behaved in such a way as to discourage that trust?"

"Yes," Anargen blurted out.

"Truly?" Sir Cinaed replied, not sounding defensive, only like a disappointed parent.

"You never told us everything," was ready at the doors of Anargen's lips, but all that escaped was a little cloud of vapor. In all his friends' bickering and suspicion, he had never once pointed out that their right to know all was only perceived, not mandated. Sir Cinaed was their mentor, sharing counsel as needed, not by compulsion.

Again, Anargen's eyes flicked over to take in the grouping of Ecthel officials. There were only three. Could Sir Cinaed be trusted now, when things seemed so bleak and puzzling?

Anargen looked back to the fortress. Steam drifted lackadaisical, as if in sorrow, from where the warmth of Ordumair now leaked piteously out into the frigid air of the battlefield. Somewhere in the distance a howl rang out and soon became the familiar wretched choral.

Slowly, Anargen's gaze made its way back to hold to Sir Cinaed's worn face. There was a hard set to his jaw, and his eyes were locked to the distance where he must have known the monsters would be amassing for an assault on the gash in the bastion's outer wall.

All around them, the wind gusted and whistled. Looking once more on the fortress, Anargen could see only the thick driving snow from the storm and the massive wreckage of the fortress's most formidable battlement. A shiver ran through him. Closing his eyes, he could feel the tension in his body as well as his Spiritsword's weight in his hand. He breathed in, listening for the whispered voice that had guided him before.

When his eyes opened again, Anargen answered, "I confess, I don't understand, but you haven't broken faith yet. What do you need of me?"

An approving father's smile overtook Sir Cinaed's reserved

expression. "Find one of the commanders. Have him sound the horn for a strategic retreat to the far west portion of the fortress. Once all the Ords and your fellow Knights arrive, wait there till I come. Can you do this?"

"I suppose I can try," Anargen replied, remembering the cataphracts' betrayal with a dull ache. "But it isn't a stretch to say they'd rather die than listen to me . . ."

Cinaed looked at his wistful charge for a few seconds before saying, "Tell the commander you know the secret passages of Ordumair. Tell him, 'Fire and ice may never meet, but joined at once produce springs of water doubly sweet.'"

Anargen raised an eyebrow and stared back at Sir Cinaed. "Okay," he managed to say.

"It is an old Ord proverb, only shared during the accession of a new Thane." He paused, assessing Anargen's bewildered expression. "The commander will trust you."

The corner of Anargen's mouth twitched up in an attempt at a smile, as he tried to fathom how Cinaed could know such an obscure Ord phrase. He looked past Cinaed at the Ecthels and frowned. *What to do with them? Have to think fast.*

Fast or not, a thought did occur to him. Pointing to the Ecthels, Anargen said, "We should bind them. The moment they are revealed, no one will care to listen. If we present them as prisoners, at least they might blink first."

Cinaed scowled but didn't speak right away. After a moment, he replied, "We do have the chains I freed them from. If they agree to it. Otherwise leave that matter to me." Almost as an afterthought, he added, "All will be well."

"I sincerely hope so," Anargen said, more to himself than anything.

As if struck from behind, Sir Cinaed stopped and looked back. "Have you no confidence in the High King, lad?"

Wincing, Anargen blurted out, "I do, but the enemy has taken the fortress top, shattered the Great Bulwark, and massacred the defenders sent out in combat. Sir, I don't know if this is a battle the Great King wills us to win."

In all their travels thus far, Sir Cinaed did not seem so out of step as this moment. His head dropped, and he said in a tone as hard as Ordumair's stone, "It is the Great King's to decide. But do not give up hope yet, Sir Anargen. We may yet see better days come swiftly to us."

39

RALLYING THE TROOPS

IT TOOK LONGER than Anargen had hoped to find a commander of the Ords still alive. When he did, the greying Ord eyed him with some suspicion, particularly given the hesitant way Anargen dismounted and approached the Ord, as though the commander were a rabid beast ready to tear him to bits.

"Are you injured, hungerman, or do you wish now to retreat?" Two other Ords trotted up and began to give a report on the casualties and positions of the Ecthels' divisions.

Anargen tried to wait out the report. In particular, he needed to compose himself. The accusation in the commander's voice when he said, "retreat," made Anargen's message from Sir Cinaed feel too ironic.

Soon he found the Ords' reports dragging on, becoming a dialogue on the greater battlefield, suggesting the Ord Anargen had stumbled onto might have been the most senior ranking soldier left in the fray. He'd best not foul this up then. "Excuse me, commander?" Anargen projected, louder than expected.

The Ord turned a pair of annoyed eyes on Anargen. "We

have no 'commanders' in our armies. I am Feingohl, Barwnig under the Ironhold banner. I have no time for your ignorance, hungerman," the Ord said and turned back to his subordinates.

The frustrating possibility Sir Cinaed wasn't so well versed in Ord culture as he implied occurred to Anargen. There was no point in wringing his hands. "'Fire and ice may never meet, but in each other's presence, produce springs of water sweet,'" Anargen bellowed over the running dialogue.

This time there was shock and anger etched onto the dwarf's face. "How do you know those words?"

"A better question," Anargen replied, taking in a breath to shore up his courage, "is how much of our precious little time and the lives of other Ords are you going to waste before hearing a plan to save us?"

"You dare speak so to me?" the barwnig snapped. His subordinates looked at one another and started to draw their weapons.

"I do so because we need to fall back to the western side of the fortress," Anargen replied with a more ingratiating tone.

"Withdraw and do what? Climb the mountain, wait there until surrounded and die?"

Weathering the acerbic rain of Feingohl's words, Anargen countered, "No, we'll return to the fortress and mount the defense from within, which we advised as the most prudent course in the first place."

A low growl, almost feral, ripped through the Ord's clenched teeth. "Foolish then, foolish now, hungerman. We are trapped out here now. The bulwark's collapse has blocked the fortress gates. There is no retreat for any of us."

Toward the end Feingohl had softened some, enough for pity to unsettle Anargen's burgeoning chagrin. "Then we will use the entrances not blocked."

"There are none," one of the subordinate Ords piped in, his round cheeks burning and his eyes like steel. "Stupid, cursed hungerman!"

The barwnig, however, tugged at his silver streaked beard

with a gauntleted hand. "Don't taunt me, boy," he commanded. "The only other gates are to legendary tunnels. You would not presume to claim knowledge of those tunnels. Tunnels we do not even waste time teaching our children of any longer," he added with a gesture to the flustered subordinate.

"No, I do not," Anargen began and held up a hand to prevent a ready string of curses from the younger Ord soldiers. "But my captain, Sir Cinaed, does. He taught me your rhyme and he will show you the entrance. If you will trust me?"

"Trust is earned," the barwnig countered with narrowed eyes.

"Then test me on this," Anargen countered, feeling a surge of hope well up within. "You have nothing to lose from it."

Feingohl huffed through his wide nostrils and looked around at the storm already burying the four of them to the ankles and higher. "Very well," he answered. "We will give you this one chance." He cocked his head to the feisty subordinate and said, "Blow the carynx. We gather at the western reaches of the mountain." To the other Ord soldier, he said, "Orn, you spread the word best you can to any stragglers."

Both younger Ords stood there unmoving. Orn raised his hand as if about to plea against his orders. The hand dropped under Feingohl's withering glare. "At once, sir," they both answered. Taking off through the snow, Orn plowed through, bounding over it, faster than Anargen would have thought an Ord capable. The other Ord remaining produced a long, curved horn with a sculpture like a bear's head atop it. After one last glance at Feingohl, the dwarf drew in a great breath and began to blow.

The sound of it was akin to a dirge. Low melancholy notes punctuated by brief staccato wails in alternation.

"There, they will meet us, as you requested," Feingohl stated. As he turned to mount his small horse, he said over his shoulder, "Know this, if you mislead us, it will be my blade which kills you, long before any Ecthel steel can, hungerman."

"Fantastic," Anargen replied as he climbed atop his horse

and spurred it on past the dwarf and through the sheeting snow towards the western half of the mountain. In the distance, to his far right, Anargen could see, even through the falling snow, the smoldering ruins of the Great Bulwark.

40

THE WILL AND THE WAY

ANARGEN WAS cold and growing tired. As he rubbed his arms, fighting to work warmth to them, he could only imagine what the Ords felt. Many leaned against the mountain or sat in mounds of snow they had gathered up.

Eventually, Anargen found himself dropping to a crouch several dozen yards away from the camped mass of Ords. Waiting as a sentry, he found himself examining the luminous letters engraved on his Spiritsword to pass the time. The blade's fiery dance was the closest thing to a source of warmth and comfort as could be found in this icy vortex. It was a wonder to him how any of the Ords coped without such hope as he had. His lot for the time may be no different than theirs, but ultimately, the Great King would not leave him forever to a quiet repose and disgrace.

Carried off in his thoughts, he was startled when an Ord ran up beside him and struck him on the back. Bracing himself with one hand in the snow, he glanced up at the Ord. The dwarf was an older one of their number, or perhaps it was simply the abundance of snow and darkness around them that made him appear grizzled. Ignoring Anargen's chagrin and bewilderment, the Ord pointed out into the distance at a lone traveler, too tall to be his kinsman and in gleaming armor. Then three other darker forms appeared, following in tow.

Anargen leapt to his feet and sheathed his sword, waving to Sir Cinaed. The elder Knight offered a much calmer gesture in kind and maintained his steady gait. The teen could hear the Ord spit loudly and grumble, "They are bold, aren't they? Coming at us like this?"

He turned and ran back towards his fellow dwarfs, yelling, "Ready, men! They've found us. This is our last stand!"

Shaking his head, Anargen pursued the dwarf, overtaking him and yelling louder than he knew he could. "No! No! Stand down. It is not the enemy. Sir Cinaed, my captain, approaches! Do not be afraid!"

The Ord skidded to a halt beside Anargen, kicking up a pile of snow with him. Looking up at Anargen, he appeared to want to contradict him, his dark eyes searching for something. Weakness? Insincerity? Doubt?

Drawing in a quiet breath, Anargen faced the Ord and arched his eyebrow. He tensed his jaw and after a long silence glanced towards the rest of the Ords and then back at the overeager sentry. From somewhere near the back of the assembled mass of Ords, Caeserus roused from his allotted station and rushed to join Anargen.

Sir Cinaed was already upon the group by the time the lookout shuffled back to his brethren. There were whispers amongst the group, most of them idle wondering over the encounter.

The commotion intensified as Cinaed came near enough for the chain held in one hand to be spotted. Tracing its links brought dozens of Ord eyes to the haggard forms of the Ecthel honor guardsman, each shackled as planned. Whether truly wallowing in dejection or simply good actors, the Ecthels did not even raise their eyes from the ground before them.

If Sir Cinaed was aware of muted gossip, he did not oblige it. Instead, he wasted no time in striding forward and gripping

Anargen's arm in greeting. Caeserus arrived at their sides a moment later and exchanged the same cordial welcome. Barwnig Feingohl strode up and though he eyed the Ecthels, he only said, "You are these hungerman pups' master?"

"I'm their elder," Sir Cinaed answered with a steady bearing. Cocking his head to the side, he added, "Thank you for your willingness to hear us out. I know the very proposition of this retreat could cost you your title."

Feingohl swallowed loud and seemed to be fighting to bring moisture to his lips. He turned his head to the side and looking away answered, "Yes, well, be quick about this. What rescue do you offer, hungerman?"

With a nod, Sir Cinaed stepped around the barwnig and bellowed in his most stern voice, "I will be brief. As you might have guessed, the battle for the valley is lost. We have all suffered a sound defeat. It will only be a matter of time before the fortress is breeched, though not before each one of us has been picked off and struck down. Your enemies have the luxury of standing back and demolishing Ordumair stone by stone. The people inside, however, will not last that long."

"Did you come here to torture us with ill news we already know?" one of the Ords asked, throwing his hands up in despair.

"Who are those three with you?" a young sentry enquired, gesturing to the Viceroy and guard. "What're they doing in chains?"

Feingohl rolled his eyes and looked ready to backhand the oblivious little dwarf. Anargen had to fight a similar response. It never occurred to him Ords might fail to recognize the Ecthels. Three hundred years of war with a people they don't even know for looking at them.

"These three are Ecthel prisoners. We will need them if we are to come in before the Thane without yet attaining victory," Sir Cinaed pointed out.

"And who are you to speak of 'we' and 'us?' I have never seen you before," the older, sentry Ord piped up, his voice high and his lightly bearded face stained with bitterness.

"But I know you, Harrar, and you, Thornwell. My name is Cinaed, but when I was a boy, living in Ordumair, my name was Meredoch. I'm the only living son of Sir Augustine MacCowell, the last Defender of the Northern Realm, not the least member of which was and is Ordumair."

There was a faint murmur from some of the older Ords present. Meredoch was a half-forgotten memory that had nearly passed into the realm of dreams for them. If Cinaed was Meredoch, the son of Sir Augustine, then that would have meant his father had been the Knight leader expelled from Ordumair in that last war with the Ecthels. It was his father who was betrayed all those years ago. His family had suffered much at the hands of the Ords.

Looking on Sir Cinaed now, the bond between Thane Duncoin and Cinaed made so much more sense. Growing up, they knew one another, but more than that, because Cinaed's, or rather, Meredoch's, father had been the most influential and elevated Knight in all of the northern realm, they could have interacted as equals. The Ords, the Dag Votere, the Albarons, and the five duchies of the Knors were all under the Northern protectorate, making Sir Augustine a very prominent Knight. Before his disgraced expulsion, at least.

The son of such an important Knight, and he walked away from all of it to be in the speck that is Black River.

"What proof do you possess to show you are who you say?" another Ord answered, shuffling to the front.

"What does it matter what proof he has?" the horn-blower from earlier complained. "He's a hungerman. We do not need him."

"I beg your pardon," Cinaed cut through the chatter, his voice sounding off the mountainside. "But I thought you wanted to save your fortress."

"Are you daft?" Thornwell responded on behalf of his fellow

countryman. "Of course we want to save our fortress. But we cannot enter it again. The gates are blocked by the fallen stones. No one can get in."

Grumbles sounding spiteful, verging on mutinous, rose up among the soldiers. Sir Cinaed's confidence never seemed to waiver. Anargen's was a fragile, fraying thread.

"That may be true, but what if I told you that not only do I know from experience your legendary tunnels of Ordumair are real, but I can navigate you through them such that you will be back with your families and fellow Ords before the hour is past?"

It was the barwnig, Feingohl, who spoke for all. "Before we take one step with you and your hungerman henchmen, I will be requiring a token of good faith."

"Aye, how can you prove you are Meredoch, son of Augustine, and you have returned to 'rescue' us?" Thornwell demanded, his voice cracking as he spoke. It was clear he remembered those days of the last war well. Perhaps he also remembered Sir Cinaed well enough to be sincere in his plea.

To Anargen's surprise, Sir Cinaed not only was not frustrated by this but clapped his hands together and nodded. "I do have just that," he replied as he reached within his cuirass and produced a large, golden ring.

The design inlaid on the ring seemed oddly familiar to Anargen, though he couldn't quite say why at first. There were gold ringlets interlaced around a silver pillar in the middle and some ancient lettering. Realization struck him like a slap to the back of his head. He had seen it before, just not in this color palette. It was the same insignia as adorned the massive tapestries of Ordumair's Keep.

Slipping the ring onto his right hand, Cinaed stated, "This is the signet ring of Ordumair II, the mighty Thane of Ords. It was given to my father before he was kidnapped by the Ecthels and expelled from Ordumair for life. Come. Come close, see the seal of your Thanes! I welcome your inquiries, but I urge you do not delay, because the hour is late, and we have much work to do, should you accord me your trust."

Harrar spoke up. "Fool, hungerman, the Thane's signet is on his hand even now. And it is silver over sapphire, not your two-tone forgery!"

"Hush, Harrar!" Feingohl snapped, staring hard at the signet but saying nothing more. The Ords were all quiet with the oldest Ords taking on pensive expressions. Those younger dwarfs amongst the group only looked confused. They had never known their people as the once obedient and loyal Orderers. All of this had to be befuddling. Between weariness and cold, they had to be longing for the rest this stranger offered them.

At last Feingohl spoke for them all. "We will confer on this matter."

"Do what you must," Sir Cinaed replied with his hands up in deferral.

Feingohl barked out something to the group, and another pair of Ords, with armor and mannerisms indicating them to be the officers, strode to Feingohl's side. Along with Thornwell, the two other Ords joined Feingohl in a small circle to discuss the matter.

While the Ords held their impromptu moot, Anargen glanced at Cinaed and whispered, "Cinaed, er, Sir Meredoch, is this wise?"

Meredoch shrugged and replied, "It is the truth, lad. The truth may not always be easy, but it is wise. And Harrar is the foolish one. Feingohl knows as I do, the ancient signet of Ordumair is two toned in memory of the golden orchard long lost."

Again, Anargen was abashed. *How had I not seen it before?*

Mentally shirking the self-castigations, Anargen quipped, "What of the Ecthels? The Ords will never let them come. They barely tolerate us, even now."

Shaking his head, Sir Meredoch replied, "They must. We were brought to arbitrate a peace agreement and their penance is the best chance for succeeding in our task." Meredoch looked meaningfully over at Caeserus, who seemed to chafe under the gaze but said nothing.

Caeserus had said precious little to Anargen when he joined Anargen's group by the western stretch Meredoch proposed. One need not be a sage to guess Caeserus did not trust the Ecthels anymore than he could lift the Great Bulwark's debris aside with his bare hands.

"What if we lead them, still chained?" Anargen looked over at Caeserus who at last feigned interest. "Present them as prisoners to the Thane as well?"

A low muttering issued from Sir Meredoch's lips, and his face looked like he'd tasted something foul. "I can't imagine the Ecthels would accept that. And we risk their actual imprisonment if our bluff is called."

"What bluff?" Caeserus piped in. "If they are genuinely repentant then let them accept whatever judgment is assigned them," he stated and crossed his arms over his chest.

Meredoch's eyes narrowed marginally, and he pursed his lips. "Well spoken, Sir Caeserus. They will remain secured with the irons. Just maybe these dwarfs will truly listen."

Caeserus snorted. "Even if those stone-headed, mountain gnomes listen to us, what good does it do us?"

Then, like the sun shattering the cool clouds at dawn, a grin broke out on Sir Meredoch's face, one reminiscent of earlier days. Of Black River. "All the good that we can do, lad." He stepped away from Anargen and Caeserus. Wandering over to the mountainside he said, "I'm going to get us back into the fortress."

"Yes?" Anargen said, his heart suddenly stirred to thrumming after a relative calm. He looked to the group of Ord commanders, nonplussed and wondering how he had overlooked the delivery of their verdict.

None of the Ords had spoken yet. They were still conferring with one another.

All the same, Meredoch reached behind a rocky outcrop and

produced a long pole made from some sort of gnarled tree limb. Stepping to the side, he wedged it behind the rocky outcropping and, with a grunt, began pushing aside the stone of the mountain itself. The sound of stone screeching as it ground against its fellow stone filled the air.

Everyone immediately quieted and watched in wonder as a passageway, dark and deep, opened more and more to their view. The opening was large enough for a single, broad-shouldered man to fit through. Holding back the great rock, Sir Meredoch, through clenched teeth, instructed Anargen, "Get inside. Set the counterweight. Hurry."

Blindly obeying, Anargen ran inside the passage and immediately covered his nose as it was bombarded with the smell of dank stone and stale air. Looking about in the faint light his armor afforded, Anargen drew his sword and was at length able to see a series of weights and ropes. One loop of thick rope was hanging free, and one peg of wood, thick as Anargen's arm, was untethered, being joined to a great round stone. Tugging on the rope with all his might, he managed to loop the rope over the peg. Finished, he called out, "I think I've got it?"

With a cry of relief, Sir Meredoch released his hold. The peg and stone tried to roll forward, but the rope held. He walked over to the quartet of leaders who wore looks of disbelief. "What is your decision?"

41

A PENITENT'S PLEA

IN THE PASSAGES was a collection of oil lamps and torches to light. Even with them, the passage was an eerie one. The tunnels were dim at best and the heavy, musty odor of disuse and ancientness never lifted, though it became tolerable. Shadows leapt and danced around the torches positioned every dozen or so yards apart, and the way the light played off the faces of those passing through, their concentration on the route made them appear entranced. Spectral echoes of long forgotten forebears filled the narrow-walled confines of the tunnel system.

Fortunately, the tunnels were tall enough that Anargen didn't have to pass through a cloud of smoke from the low torches. Though he and everyone else may well have been pleased to walk through fire itself to escape the battle outside.

Ahead, Sir Meredoch was lighting the torches in advance of the Ord barwnig. Anargen was in the middle of the company and to his immediate back were the Ecthels, followed by Caeserus. Beyond them was the remainder of the Ord army.

Suddenly, Caeserus grabbed Anargen's arm and whispered, "I don't trust Sir Cinaed or Meredoch or whoever he is any more than these Ecthel slime. His story of rescuing them and his escape from the castle seem too convenient."

Anargen didn't argue the point. Truth be told, he questioned Sir Meredoch as well. There were still secrets to the man, and all of it seemed too much hope to cling to in such a dismal hour. For his doubts, guilt was tighter in Anargen's chest than the iron shackles on the Ecthel's wrists. After all, couldn't such a marvelous rescue come from the Great King?

Wanting to say something, Anargen quipped, "Why are you coming, Caeserus?"

Caeserus rolled his eyes, barely keeping his tone low enough for the Ords not to hear. "Anything is better than dying out there in that icy torment. If I fall, it will be within this fortress, not yielding an inch to the Ecthel fiends."

"I thought you hated the Ords," Anargen whispered, eyeing the Ords nearest them for any sign they overheard him. If they did, there was no reaction to indicate it.

"Don't you?" Caeserus countered.

"How can I? Knowing their history, can you blame them for being so jaded?"

"Everyone has a past, Anargen. It never justifies cruelty in the present."

Anargen had mulled over Caeserus's words. He was so unsettled, he just managed to step around a sharp turn he was about to walk straight into. Fatigue from the battle and light-headedness from the smoke were affecting him more than he realized.

Doubt, distrust, those were the currency of defeat. Defeat now meant death, not just for him but scores of others, and he couldn't accept that, especially not with the letter from Seren resting warmly in its pocket on his chest.

"So why do you fight at all?" Anargen murmured, half to himself.

Caeserus heard. "We are Knights. I defend the honor of that title if nothing else."

Even if Anargen had something meaningful to counter with, he knew there was no point to it. They were close to their destination. How he knew it, he couldn't say, maybe a shift in Sir Meredoch's gait?

Ahead the column had slowed and in proportional inverse, Anargen's heart picked up its pace. Some of the Ords were even now whispering stories of the cruel punishments inflicted on cowards and deserters. None of them knew to add towing along enemy leaders with a message of peace. More than once Anargen wondered whether it would be by the steel of Ord halberd rather than Ecthel gunpowder or werebeast's fangs he would be felled.

A figure from ahead filtered through the ranks and stopped before Anargen. In the low light, Anargen could only guess, but he thought it was Harrar. "Your captain orders you to the front."

Harrar coughed, a dry throaty sound, waving his hand to dispel some of the oil lamp smoke issuing next to him and added, "Be quick about it."

Threading through the Ords with their baleful little eyes glinting in the dark was about as fun a prospect as using his bare hands to extinguish the oil lamps. At least in his quick jaunt through the gauntlet, he only suffered a few grumbles and one Ord spitting on him.

Everyone must be too exhausted or dazed from the fumes to be bothered by his passage. Which was just as worrisome as the belligerence he had expected. Worn-out warriors would not make for a good defense, and by now the Ecthels had to know the remainders of the Ord offensive had somehow withdrawn. Time, prowess, numbers. All cast their favor on the Ecthels' side. Hope grew pale but continued to flicker in Anargen's heart that One greater than these still favored the defenders.

Coming alongside Sir Meredoch, Anargen overheard him instructing in hushed tones for one of the Ords to keep the column in wait. Once the Thane had accepted their counsel, then he would return and help usher the defenders out of the tunnels into varying outlets of the City of Ordumair.

Some minutes passed before Sir Meredoch's attention turned to Anargen. "Just beyond this door is the inner council chamber of the Ords." He paused, his eyes flicking towards where another passage, more deeply swathed in shadows, emptied out at the same level. Anargen thought he saw a flicker of motion in the dark but cast it off as a play of fire and shadows.

Meredoch quickly regained his composure and began again, this time addressing Feingohl. "Speak the truth, as will I."

"Even if the Thane rejects your proposed withdrawal?" Feingohl countered. "Or your rights as the hungermen's defender of the realm?"

"On my honor, even if he rejects all my counsel, I will not interfere with his edicts," Meredoch stated, ignoring the insult.

Another surge of dread ran through Anargen, this time over how the Ecthels, in hearing distance, would react. Sir Meredoch's words made it sound as if he would not protect the Ecthels if the Thane demanded their surrender and capture. Anargen only just resisted stepping to guard from attack in their direction when Meredoch added, "But the Thane is wise and will heed my words." Meredoch pushed open the last door and stepped inside.

"Wisdom is proven of her children," Feingohl stated as he joined Meredoch in entering the open doorway.

"True words. Just as they were more than a thousand years ago when a servant of the High King first spoke them," Sir Meredoch replied without looking back at the dwarf.

If the battle of wits persisted, Anargen missed it. His attention was on the room they entered. This chamber looked something like a cook's larder. Brown stone lined the simple room, and from the abundance of smoked venison and game fowls, it appeared this was part of the quarters for an Ord of great importance. Perhaps one of the nobility had sacrificed his personal palace on behalf of the Thane and Council's meetings, but more likely this was a residential complex for the Thane.

The room stretched long before them and, though presently empty of persons, had a busy feeling imbued in it from the number of wooden tables and bounty of breads baked some hours before. Anargen's mouth watered as the earthy scents of toasted harvest grains reached his smoke-wearied nose. An abundance of fruits dotted baskets around the room. Likely these were collected weeks earlier and kept in the cooler portions of the mountain in order to present the nobles' pallets with primly preserved pastries and other delights.

Sir Bertinand would have snorted and cracked a joke about how the Thanes would, of course, have a secret passage leading to such an amply-stocked kitchen.

The thought made Anargen wince. With the jagged wound carved into the face of Ordumair's Fortress, only the King of Light could know how Bertinand would fare in this fight.

"Anargen, Caeserus," Sir Meredoch murmured, forcing Anargen from his melancholy wonderings. "When we enter, you'll need to bookend the Ecthels as well. But first, I need each of you to stand at either side of the doors ahead and rip them open, full as you might."

"Won't that startle everyone?" Caeserus asked, though his body was already oriented towards the side he was assigned.

"They know we are out here if their guards are worth their salt," Meredoch deflected.

"The lads in there most certainly are," Feingohl grumbled, his voice low. "But I see your aim. Better they see us immediately than to be passive and have them crash down on us at their own timing." Feingohl motioned to his two comrades, and the trio of Ords stood at a rigid attention a few paces back from the door way.

With Ords ready, the great Knight raised his thick arm and brought it down. A moment later, Anargen and Caeserus yanked hard, forcing the hefty doors apart.

As the doors swung open, faster than anticipated, a group of four halberd bearing Ords formed up and started to charge out when they saw their kinsmen standing in wait and halted. The moment the four saw Sir Meredoch standing off to the side, however, they tensed again and called out, "None have been summoned before the Council of Elders. State your purpose."

Anargen gripped his Spiritsword's hilt readying himself to draw it. He imagined Caeserus was doing the same, though he couldn't see Caeserus, or the hostile Ords for that matter. A fight was imminent even without the Ecthels' appearance.

"Peace," Feingohl said, though his tone and words weren't overly generous. "We are here to see the Thane and give report on the battle for this fortress's defense." The barwnig swallowed hard. "And present to the Thane prisoners of war."

"Moreover, the good Thane should know that Sir Cinaed seeks an audience with your Thane to deliver grave and great news," Meredoch chimed in, drawing a disapproving scowl from Feingohl.

Utter disgust twisted the guard's face, but from behind boomed the Thane, "Let them pass and deliver their report."

The quartet of sentries kept their opinions to themselves and backed away, forming pairs and standing at attention on either side directly at the room's entry.

Gesturing to the Ords, Sir Meredoch waited until Feingohl and his compatriots had entered and then followed after, tapping on Anargen's door to signal to Caeserus and Anargen to come as well.

Once the first of the Ords entered, Anargen stepped out and waited till he saw the Ecthels form up behind him. He could also see Caeserus shaking his head at the back of the column. He seemed to be mouthing, "This is a bad idea."

Anargen didn't respond. He was a half-step behind and had to get in before too many questions were raised. Though it was only two rows of guards, it felt like running a gauntlet.

Soon the whole party was flush against a back wall of the room, arrayed so that those seated at the few long tables of the room could see them all. A bevy of oil lamps gave plenty of light for the task. Expressions on those arrayed at the tables were far from warm. Shackled and heads down in shame, the Ecthels there drew every eye.

Lining the left, right, and far sides of three tables sat about eight Ords of varying age, size, and splendor. Sir Orwald was notably absent. The most magnificent seated at the head of the middle table was, of course, Thane Duncoin. In spite of his welcome to approach, there was a shrewdness about his demeanor, particularly as he eyed his old friend so near his enemies.

Once the group was in position, Feingohl shuffled forward, giving a gesture of respect and humility before the rulers of his people. Thane Duncoin spoke first. "You may speak."

There was a faint but perceptible tension in Feingohl's bearing, undoubtedly due to the harsh stares from around the room. Eight of the former twenty-eight-member body of Ord elders now looked at him much like they might a traitor.

"I am Feingohl, son of Finlay, Barwnig under the banner of Elder Ironhold," Feingohl began, his voice strained. He gave a gesture to one of the older council members, who in turn gave a slight nod of acknowledgment, though his expression was far from approving.

"What have you to say, Feingohl, son of Finlay? Your herald," the Thane said. His sharp eyes shifting to Meredoch for the briefest possible span before landing harder on the Ord again, "has informed our assembly you have word of the defense?"

"Yes, honorable Thane," he answered with another bow of respect. "Our forces have been crushed."

From the left of the room a, "Harrumph," could be heard, and Anargen managed to turn his head in time to see a dark-eyed Ord with a bawdy fur robe slam his fist on the table as he rose. "Crushed or abandoned by those of a coward's convictions?"

Anargen expected Ironhold to say something on behalf of Feingohl, but he just steepled his fingers and seemed more interested in how the charge would be answered.

Feingohl hesitated, keeping composure with noticeable

effort. He drew himself up. "Perhaps, my honor, the Thane, would like to hear the full matter of our, um, setbacks?"

Rather than voice his answer, the Thane just gave a half nod.

"After the gates opened, we charged out. The storm had grown worse, so much so we could scarce see. Elder Samohan led us. He felt it wise to form small groups and use the storm as cover.

"Ecthelowall's regulars were waiting with their weapons of fire and smoke."

Feingohl paused to collect himself. "The weapons were so loud and vicious, many fell at the gates, but we were steadfast and broke their line. Elder Samohan's plan was followed, to great loss."

There was some murmuring at this. Anargen looked at the scowls and consternation worn by many, and in particular the shame on Elder Ironhold's face. The words and will of the Ord nobility seemed to be above question.

Holding up his hand, anticipating some form of rebuke, Feingohl pressed on. "He could not have known of their fiery weapons nor the terrible power of the fell creatures under their employ. We were overwhelmed, scattered, broken. The storm, by fortune, managed to hide the shattered remnants of our army. Thereafter we inflicted marginal losses. Had Sir Cinaed not allowed us entry to the fortress through the legendary tunnels, we would all have perished. I bear witness, having seen the enemy, and witnessed legend made real, the words of Sir Cinaed of the Knight Order may well be worthy to heed."

"And whose advice should we give ear to, hmm?" Elder Ironhold spoke up with brusque verve. The greying dwarf looked questionable himself, his beard done in a series of braids with expensive jeweled clasps, and beneath hair in wild disarray. His small eyes flicked around the room like a hare leading a fox on a chase. Then his gaze fell on Feingohl again. "Perhaps you are right. The hungerman you've allowed to dishonor you and your family by cowardice is the one we should listen to."

"He is no common Knight," began Feingohl in protest, raising both hands as if to deflect an impending storm of criticism from all sides.

Another among them called out, "They are all debased meddlers. I say we have the lot of them . . ."

"Silence!" roared the Thane, who rose from his chair to glower down at all of his assembled nobility. The entire cohort looked like a bunch of scolded pups. Seeing it let Anargen breathe a little easier, though he hadn't realized till then he'd been unable to do so.

"It's about time the Thane stood up on our behalf. We are here at his summons, have they all forgotten that?" Caeserus muttered just loud enough for Anargen to hear.

Unable to resolve the question for himself, Anargen watched as the Thane nodded to Feingohl, who drew himself up straighter. "The Knight, Cinaed, revealed to myself and my subordinates," he gestured to either side, sparing the men the disgrace of being named before the council should things go poorly, "his identity as Sir Meredoch of Ordumair. This man is the rightful Defender of the Northern Realm in his Order, succeeding his father in that role."

Feingohl hesitated as the Thane pressed, "Go on."

"We found on Sir Meredoch's person the Signet of Thanes."

The murmurs of before picked up again with increased potency. While there was debate, in one smooth step, Sir Meredoch was at the forefront, which set the guards, caught up as any in the barwnig's account, back on edge and stepping closer to intercept him as needed.

If the great man noticed, it scarce made an impact on his bearing. He seemed even larger, more imposing than ever before. "Friends, I am Meredoch, son of Sir Augustine MacCowell, as the honorable Barwnig Feingohl has informed you. In my hand is the signet of Thanes, given to my father by Thane Denhard and passed to me at the due time. A sign of my honor and right to offer counsel to you in just such an hour as this."

"Dare you claim such a thing?" Tengrath enquired, his ruddy hair swaying as he whipped his head back and forth looking on everyone in turn. His face twitched with the tides of his incredulity and sent the large beads braiding his beard tails to clacking against one another. "No Thane would give a hungerman such a precious relic. If you have the real thing, it is by theft or worse!"

Anargen could see Meredoch's jaw muscles tighten and the fire in his eyes. Somehow Tengrath's implication meant more to Meredoch than Anargen understood.

Thane Duncoin spoke up. "Quiet yourself, Tengrath. My father was not a fool and there were many Ords at his side to the end. I had feared the Ecthels somehow claimed it years ago, but it seems we are indebted to Sir Meredoch for returning it to its rightful home." The Thane then held out his hand toward Meredoch in wait of the impressive ring.

"Surely you jest," cried Tengrath. "Indebted to him? Why he —"

"Surely you jest!" Thane Duncoin roared back. "Is your Thane's judgment to be so questioned?"

"When it turns to madness and folly, the Elders must question," Ironhold spoke up. Out of the corner of his eye, Anargen saw Feingohl cringe.

"Bite your tongue!" a dark-haired Ord, at the room's right exclaimed. "He is your rightful ruler, be you an Elder or a yeoman. His word is law."

"By our authority it is law," challenged Tengrath, his voice the icy drifts from without the fortress walls.

"When did our people abandon the wisdom of eras past and make such a fool pronouncement?" demanded another older Ord on Duncoin's side of the room.

It was at this moment Anargen realized why the room was laid out as it was. To the left of the Thane was a party of Elders in favor of the council superseding the Thane, to the right loyalists to the Thane. In the middle, he guessed, were those willing to sway either way. Ordumair's rule was a house divided.

"Maybe when your kind began to be nanny-goaded by these hungermen!" shouted Tengrath, rising from his seat again so fast he had to clear his red locks from his face.

This pushed both sides over the edge with each faction rising to join in the verbal fray. The Thane sat in the midst looking vexed but helpless to act. For all his bluster and fire, Thane Duncoin walked a very thin line as master of Ordumair. The tumult increased, till it was so boisterous and cacophonic it could turn into a chaotic bedlam of blows. A loud clap, like near thunder, echoed in the hall. All eyes turned at once toward the source, which turned out to be Sir Meredoch.

The Defender of the Realm let his great hands part and boomed bigger than himself, "Quiet, the lot of you. You sound like children prattling. Is this the splendor of Ordumair? Are you sincere in your claims to rule your people justly? Because as I see it, you are bickering like a bunch of blind mice while your house burns all around you."

"How dare you speak so to us!" Elder Ironhold chided, though he was not so firm as before.

"By the authority of the High King, you will be silent till this hour of danger is through!" Sir Meredoch pronounced.

Ironhold grabbed at his throat, and his eyes went wide. No matter how he strained, no words came.

"Sorcery!" cried one Elder. "Treachery!" another.

"Be still," Duncoin finally spoke up. "I would hear what he has to say."

Anyone interested in challenging the Thane's authority then had only to look at Elder Ironhold's mute mouth and gaze at the now splendid, yet terrifying, countenance of Sir Meredoch to find his peace. Seeing no competition, Thane Duncoin said, "Speak, friend of Ordumair."

"I had hoped reason might yet prevail among this noble body, but that hope grows faint," Meredoch began. "I see now I was wrong to begin by stating my heritage. It is not by my birthright I have authority to counsel you. It is by the will of the High King I speak to you.

"You must rid yourselves of all fool notion your pride and ancestors' prowess will save you. Listen to the words of your own barwnig. The armies of Ordumair are devastated, your fortress is crumbling, and your people will all be slaughtered, to the last child, if you do not heed the words I bring you now."

"Dear Thane," Tengrath spoke up, his voice silk, though Anargen suspected it was the comforting tone of the spider speaking to the fly. "I was rash in my pronouncements earlier, but can we take this . . ." He eyed Sir Meredoch warily. "Knight's words for truth? He has wholly given himself over to exaggeration."

Duncoin's thick brows raised, and he looked over at Sir Meredoch. "Oh? Have you an answer?"

"I do, dear Thane, if you will accord me freedom to make my case as I see fit, without restraint or interference from dissenting parties." Meredoch turned his hard gaze to Tengrath. "I remember you were not much older than I when your father fell to the Ecthels. As such, I bear you no ill will." Tengrath fidgeted some in his seat but said nothing.

A grumble issued from the Thane's chest. "I suppose accommodation can be granted. But be quick about it. If all said be true, we haven't long to waste on discussion and 'dissent.'"

"Very good," Sir Meredoch said. Then, he turned around to Caeserus and Anargen and said, "Lads, bring forward the last witnesses."

A thrill of terror rushed through Anargen. This was it. The end was at hand. While a newfound respect had clearly befallen all in attendance, this thing would undoubtedly overthrow all of it.

All the same, Anargen and Caeserus heeded their orders and escorted the cadre of Ecthels forward. Once halted, each Ecthel stood tall and lean, like cedars in their dark green cloaks. And just as exposed.

Previously the Ecthels' presence, while noted, had not caused a stir. Perhaps the Ord nobles had fancied them a sort of offering, a blood sacrifice as to goblins that were performed in the darker realms of the Lowlands. Whatever the case, their attention was now squarely on the Ecthels and the reaction instant. "This is folly! Why listen to the counsel of enemies?" "They bring the very fiends into the heart of our fortress!" "They mean to slay us where we sit!" "Not if my blade drinks of their blood first!"

"Be still, all of you," bellowed Sir Meredoch, as swords, daggers, axes, and glaives were at once produced across the room. The guards were already surrounding Anargen, Caeserus, and the Ecthels, their halberd's spear tips pointing at them from a diamond formation. Anargen noted with some awe no one had dared to raise a weapon against Sir Meredoch.

"Be still?" Thane Duncoin mewled. "Do you think us daft to react so? You have brought our enemies into the very heart of our stronghold to guide us in its defense? I think it is you who shall be required to enjoy the silence of the grave if you do not give good reason for this affront with all haste!"

A slow, measured nod was Sir Meredoch's initial response. After a painful heartbeat's space, he spoke. "Very well. I understand your trepidation, but these men of Ecthelowall were placed in irons and strung from the Castle Valesgard's shattered battlements to rot. They can tell you the nature of the plan at work against Ordumair."

"Haven't we heard enough nonsense?" Tengrath said, looking around the room and finding empathetic faces. "Guards, why do you restrain yourselves? The law is clear, death to all traitors and enemies!"

"Hold yourselves," Duncoin called, though he clearly seethed as well as any other Ord. "What say you to these charges, Meredoch of Ordumair?"

Without missing a beat for the insult of ignoring his true title, Sir Meredoch replied, "I say you have no right to withdraw clemency from these men or myself. I bear the Signet of Thanes. By the very laws you claim condemn me, I claim my right to speak in full without challenge or to grant such to whom I deem worthy. These men must speak, for the good of your people, dear Thane. Heed them or not, by the laws governing all of you, they will be heard."

The gentleness in Meredoch's bearing and demeanor was intriguing. The gale was now a breeze, though somehow just as firm. Willing, it seemed, the body of obstinate Ords to agree with his proposition.

As Duncoin hesitated to respond, Tengrath looked from Sir Meredoch to the Thane and back and said, "Surely we do not entertain such mockery. He has brought our oldest enemy into our deepest counsel. He should be —"

Duncoin woke then from his stony slumber. "He and his ilk are free to speak by the honor of our ancestors and the authority of the Thane." Eyeing all those around him, the Thane added, "Now, if one of you dishonors our people by violating the law and the will of your Thane, it is you who will be carried off in irons." Before anyone could properly react, the Thane's baleful glare rested on Sir Meredoch and he said, "These may speak, as you wish, but know it is on your life and honor their actions rest. Any deception, and I will skewer you myself, old friend."

Stoic, Meredoch held up his hands at either side. "Most gracious Thane, by my life, I promise these men have no mischief planned, only needed insight." Turning to face the Ecthels, he said, "Viceroy Ecthelion, stand forth and speak."

Whispers abounded, whatever the Thane's threat. The Thane himself gripped the table as if he were going to rend chunks of the heavy wood from it and toss at them.

The middle Ecthel strode forward, the halberds of the guards trained on him with glistening tips hovering dangerously close to his throat. Sir Meredoch pulled back Ecthelion's hood for him.

Ecthelion's face was a contused and lacerated mess. One eye was swollen shut, and a long scar traced his right cheek to jaw. It looked only partially healed.

Giving Ecthelion's arm a pat, Meredoch instructed the Viceroy, "Tell all you know."

42

TREMBLING IN THE CORE

ANARGEN COULD NOT HELP GAPING. He had suspected the maligned Ecthel defectors were high ranking, but was this man really Ecthelion? Looking him over, he seemed vaguely like the Grey Scourge in features but clearly not a twin. All Anargen could do was listen rapt with the rest of the room in hopes of hearing some truth.

Gaunt and pale, Ecthelion was still composed, his bearing not rigid but fixed, untouched by the danger he now stood in. A boldness which begged many questions, questions Ecthelion seemed hungry to answer, as he began straightaway into a speech in a raspy, strained voice, bereft of its expected powerful lilt. "Ecthelion of Halifax, son of Andros, a man far nobler than I, once Viceroy of Ecthelowall, now her exile."

A surge in whispers rose to a dull roar and overflowed into speaking tones. Anargen heard one of the Ords joking about the "man far nobler than I" bit. Such conversations were slain by a sharp look from the Thane, which Anargen took a silent pleasure in. Whoever this Ecthelion was, he bore only token resemblance to the pompous and proud monster Anargen had seen at the false peace talks.

Ecthelion continued without need of direction, speaking

swiftly as his hoarse throat could manage, verbally careening from thought-to-thought like a spooked horse through the woods. "To say I and my brethren with me are sorry would be a poor apology, and you need not suffer such pitiable entreaties from our likes. However, what we can give you of value in restitution is the truth of what you face.

"Ecthelowall has been in tight financial straits. Ever since losing the colonies of Libertias, her empire has been unwieldy, fragile. Prone to internal discord requiring expensive countermeasures and at odds with the nations around her borders. Add in a poor harvest in Ecthelowall itself and the winds of change left the land scorched by desperation. Our nobles saw we were in decline and began looking for any means of correcting our course. My son was among them and brought to us one Baron Thomas Swifton. He offered us new weapons from the most advanced foundries in Libertias. When he delivered us seeds of the cannons, mangonels, and all manner of weaponry brought to bear against you now, he had our nobles' ears. To my shame, he had mine as well.

"We took what he gave us and made improvements. Over the course of five years, the Baron convinced us that in our world, only through continual conquest can any empire long endure. The nobles and I agreed with him. It wasn't he but another of the nobility who put forward the suggestion of bringing arms against Ordumair again. In hindsight, I can almost hear him speaking the words for the other man."

A wistfulness seemed to overtake the Viceroy momentarily. "The allure of treasures all still believed to be in your vaults was temptation enough. Though we faced a serious problem in the form of the Dag-Votere. Their lands buffer yours and ours, and we did not wish to incur a conflict with them.

"To get around the retaliation of marching our armies across their land, it was decided we must take the path of a peace treaty first. We knew you would never leave your land for arbitration. Thus, we had an excuse to transport a large retinue across the

Vogteremark in peace. We had our hidden weapons, but we found no opposition. Our history of distrust and mutual hatred made even two thousand soldiers seem a reasonable force to secure the negotiations.

"We estimated you outnumbered us five to one, but our weapons were a strong force to even those odds. Moreover, Baron Swifton promised the aid of his personal guard and new armaments more potent than any we'd yet seen.

"You must believe me when I say we had no knowledge of his true plans. Of his loathsome nature or his identity as the Grey Scourge. In Ecthelowall, such things are considered fanciful nonsense."

Ecthelion swallowed with some difficulty, and his timbre took on a darker tone. "Before arriving, I insisted we actually follow through on the peace talks and merely use our forces as a bargaining chip. It was then that Baron Swifton revealed himself. He began turning my own guard and best soldiers into his wicked minions. I was held prisoner while he departed to handle the 'negotiations.'

"In his absence I managed to rally some men. During the attack on your guardhouse, I staged my attack, which was crushed. Holstein and Gandermond here are the only men loyal to me still living. Once bested, fear and promise of reward wrested the remainder. We were held in bond, tortured, and left to die. We were so near it when Sir Meredoch, most noble Knight, rescued us. He showed us a new road."

Ecthelion glanced at Sir Cinaed. "Though it is a pittance, we are here now, new men, devoted to the High King and to defending you to our dying breath. Do with us as you will, but I urge you, do not underestimate our common foe."

After his words were at an end, a deep silence followed. Most were ready to speak but feared the Thane's retribution. Tengrath was not among them. "What utter drivel. Even if we take your free pack of lies, do you think us fools enough to let you live even one hour longer?"

"Quiet, I said, or you'll enter the fray without as lone defender." Thane Duncoin barked. There was sincere menace in the way he eyed his fellow Ord.

Instead of looking chastened, Tengrath showed only surprise. Duncoin wasted no further time on him. "Say we spare you Ecthels, what have you three to offer my thousands of Ords do not?"

"Knowledge of the enemy. Weaknesses of strategy, armor, weapons. Most of all we know much of the fiend's plans and how wise Sir Meredoch was to pull back your defenders. The plan was to destroy your battlements with the cannons and block off the exit. Originally it was to starve you out, but with his wolves, the Grey Scourge may now pick apart what remains within. Lacking the added defenders returned to stave off a breach of the fortress, you may have lasted only another twelve hours. And know this, he means to have not only the treasures of Ordumair, but the blood of every last Ord present. He will erase your people from the very annals of history."

Thane Duncoin rapped his fingers on his table and stood. "You lie. Why would any people pursue such a thing?"

"Because of what you have in your vaults," Sir Meredoch answered for Ecthelion. "My father told me the vaults of Ordumair hold tomes and tokens of enormous importance to all of the Lowlands. The Grey Scourge cannot leave alive any who may tell of what transpired or yet possess memory of the vaults' contents."

"I know of no such treasure," growled Duncoin. "Strange your father would have known of it but mine did not."

"But he did know, dear Thane," a shriveled old Ord on the Thane's side of the room spoke up. This Ord had gone unnoticed, withered and curled in on himself from time's unyielding pressures. He raised a shaking hand. "We all know of a sealed treasure, passed down by the ancients to us, which no man was to open till the 'proper hour.'"

"'The proper hour' and when is that exactly?" Duncoin asked, rolling his eyes.

"Aye, aye," assented Tengrath who received a stern look from the Thane.

"We did not know then or now. It was told in older days, when the hour arrives, the treasure will be revealed."

"How convenient," Tengrath assessed, his words dripping with dubiousness.

"Be still or I will make good on my earlier threats." Duncoin kept an eye on Tengrath for what seemed like minutes before turning to face the elderly Ord. The elder only smiled back at his Thane, and at length Duncoin sighed. "We shall investigate these claims."

"Lovely," another elder spoke up from the central table. "But what of the defense? Are we to leave it to falter?"

Though the noble's inflection made it clear he did not mean to sound sarcastic, Duncoin snapped, "Guards, away with Elder Norling. Let him remain on the front lines of the defense a few hours and ask him then his opinion on the matter."

The guards hesitated. "Now!" Duncoin thundered.

Grabbing the man, they hauled him out. Anargen could tell he was too stunned to even fight his sentence.

No sooner than a blink after the guards were out of earshot, Tengrath spoke up. "Are we ferrying off to judgment our own before the enemies in our midst?"

This time when eyed with displeasure, Tengrath did not shrink back. In the absence of the intensely loyal guards, he could make his challenge plain.

"Perhaps we should reconsider our choice of Thane if friends be foes and foes friends with this one," he said, gesturing to Duncoin, open disgust on his face.

The room grew very quiet. Both sides of the room looked as though they were sizing the other up. On the left there were younger Ords and greater numbers, something they seemed to determine as well. Anargen found his hand drifting to his Spiritsword's pommel. Duncoin had to tread carefully or a civil war would be what finished his people off.

"If I may be so bold," Ecthelion spoke up. "Though I am an outsider and have no business to say such, I cannot help but plea, remain calm. Now is not the time for overturning your anointed ones. It is the hour to dig in, shoulder to shoulder, and make ready to defend your city as one people."

"As though we should listen to you," said Tengrath taking a step towards Ecthelion and gripping a nasty looking dirk. "Every word you speak is poison to my people. If I have a say, you won't utter a single word further in this life!"

"Forebear it!" shouted the old Ord, his snowy white locks shaking in sheets like a banner in a gale. "We have no right to challenge our Thane's rule or those accorded his protection!"

"Stand down, Thornek. Who is to say Duncoin is rightful Thane, besides us elders?" replied another cooler tempered Ord on Tengrath's side.

"The High King," interposed Sir Meredoch, striding to Duncoin's side. "I bear the Signet of Thanes on his behalf, and on his behalf, I grant to Duncoin son of Denhard, the signet as proof of Duncoin's authority and worth as Thane of all Ord peoples everywhere."

There was a lull in speech and motion and, for Anargen, understanding. When Sir Meredoch had stepped forward and made his pronouncement, Anargen had expected it to be viewed as of no importance, less if possible. Yet, even Tengrath stood, his brow furrowed, and jaw clenched tight. "Could the ring mean that much to them?"

"It must," Caeserus answered on a breathy whisper. Anargen's cheeks rushed to red as he realized he had spoken his thought aloud. Caeserus continued, "Tradition is important to them, to say the least."

"Nay," replied a nearby Ord who heard them. "Our ancestors' legacy is everything. I will not undo what many hands have wrought. I'm for you, Thane Duncoin!"

"And I." "I, too, pledge loyalty to you." "Valens will follow Duncoin, Thane of Ords."

Around the room it went, gaining a sort of irresistible force with each new pledge, till only Tengrath and Ironhold had yet to speak their assent.

"You're choosing to follow a friend of hungermen on the authority of dead men and the hungermen's mythic lord?" Tengrath gaped.

Beside him, Ironhold stirred. He walked in front of Tengrath, gripped his shoulders, and nodded. The silent old Ord took a place on the room's opposite side.

Tengrath spat after Ironhold. He raised his dirk and pointed it towards Duncoin. "You are going to destroy us on the word of this illegitimate son of a hungerman's wench!"

About that time, two of the four guards returned and to their surprise, found the room in arms. At first they glared at the Knights but soon noted it was to Tengrath the room's collective animosity was directed and observed the dirk pointed towards the Thane. The guards repositioned themselves in an instant and moved to block Tengrath.

Before the guards got in halberd range of him, Tengrath dropped his dirk to the floor with a clang. "Fine," he said. "If that be the will of the council. I, too, will support Duncoin as Thane."

"Support him? Ha, you should be locked away, you scoundrel," Thornek called out.

"No, no more fighting amongst our own," Duncoin announced. "Not with one another, not with the Knights of Light, and not with the Ecthels who offer their lives to us. Our quarry is at our gates and we shall stand ready to meet them."

Perhaps over-estimating the extent of his fortunes, Tengrath protested, "But if the barwnig's words are true, then we can't overcome the foe. And if the hungerman's words are true, then we are all doomed to die horrible deaths."

"If they want every Ord dead, then let them not take an inch till every last drop of our blood be shed in the defense," Duncoin replied. "They wish to erase us, but they will never be able to forget what we do here this day. Though they die here or a thousand years hence, let us fight such that their last breath carries with it a shudder of what they faced in us!"

Reaching into the folds of his robes, the Thane produced a small, clay bottle of unknown contents. At its revealing, many in the room began to chant something in an older variant of Ord language, similar to that uttered in the field earlier.

Others produced similar vials. Opening them, the elders drew streaks of brazen blue on their faces. Anargen recalled before they were known as Ords and Orderers, they were the *Bogiáboreia*, Painted Warriors of the North.

While shouts of assent arose from many in the room, Anargen felt a chill run through him. Not of fear, but of fire. A coolness which gave way to a burning everywhere it touched. He imagined it might feel so to a forge blade dunked in the water as all the steel came to find its fiery cast coming to resolute form. Anargen knew better than most that even steel can be broken, but he took solace in it does not do so quietly nor without great effort.

43

BELEAGUERED

"The hour is dire. We wait for the enemy to breach the fortress. It is only a matter of time. Men are starved and parched, cold as ice, and exhausted. All my fortitude is spent in simply writing this; to the end, I fight."

—ANARGEN'S JOURNEY JOURNAL,
FÓMHAR 1605 M.E.

"KEEP GOING," Anargen told himself, under his breath.

More bloodshed and carnage had been witnessed than any tales had prepared them for. The Ord warriors returning from the valley arrived in time to bolster the faltering lines around the enormous gash in the fortress left by the Great Bulwark's partial collapse. Even so, by gradual degrees the defensive positions were being pushed back into the fortress.

Anargen winced as he had to step over a large stone. Every muscle ached for rest. Stones like the one he just encountered were strewn throughout the passages. Anything considered expendable, including furniture, crates of textiles, etc. were used to blockade passages. With each retreat, the dead were left as obstacles for the invaders, as if any place could have been found for them otherwise.

Passing by a pair of wounded Ords, he heard one grumble, "These hungermen promised deliverance not a delay of death."

Anargen kept walking. Huddled behind the makeshift defenses for an hour or two at a time, the Ords only had time enough to become aware of the cold and weariness of their bodies before another onslaught began. Initially kept a secret, word of Sir Meredoch's aid spread to keep hope's flame burning in their hearts. Clearly for some even that fire burned low.

Finding a good spot near the front line, he collapsed against a wall. A tremor rolled through the passageway sending dust and tiny fragments of stone raining down on him and the other defenders. He held his breath, hoping the passageway wouldn't collapse.

A little plume of dust kicked up. Anargen waved it away and let his head sink back against the passage wall. Exhausted. Worn to fraying, he didn't know if there was strength left in Ordumair to repulse another attack. The fortress would fall and everyone would die.

Eyes shut, he let that realization sink in. He would be among the slain. Here thousands of leagues from home. From his family. From Seren. A twinge of pain struck his chest. Familiar, reaching to his bones. Hiraeth.

> *"Summer's here, there's wheat to tend,*
> *Over our eyes, we sun rays defend,*
> *Missing word from any—Did you send?*
> *Will you be home again?"*

As he sang, he noticed the pain began to morph, as though shaped by his song and this place. It was no longer despair, but still an earnest longing. He would never come home to Black River, but he would die for his King without regrets.

"When all our journeys'ways mend,
Will you be home again?
Will you be home again?"

"That has to be the saddest song I ever heard, young one."

Anargen looked to the speaker. He was an Ord grizzled and well beyond years justifying his involvement in this battle. "The saddest Walhonde's hills ever produced," Anargen affirmed.

The aged Ord asked, "You would follow the King's call here again, wouldn't you, lad? There is something more to our plight than just bad blood betwixt old enemies?"

"I have come where the High King sent me," Anargen responded with conviction. "I do not know why the Grey Scourge is here, only how. Where there is no light, things of the dark need not skulk. They are free to be brazen and cruel. Your land has been without light for a long time."

"You came to die then, hungerman?" another Ord asked, his voice cracking.

Anargen worked some moisture to his mouth. Why had he and his friends been drawn into this if the outcome was death? For a panicked moment, he had no idea what to tell the Ord. The whole passage rested on the knife's edge of despair. If he incensed the Ord, it could slip into a self-destructive quarrel. Anargen's heartbeat became erratic. One compromised passage and thousands would die.

Taking a steadying breath, he started with what he knew was not the answer. Unlike the Ords, he certainly wasn't fighting for his glory and honor.

He drew in another breath. It wasn't for his friends' deliverance. He had no more power over that than to command the sun to shine.

When he tried to take in another breath, it caught in his throat, and a tear worked its way to the corner of his eye. It wasn't even for the chance to return home to his parents and Seren.

Ords around him were stirring, having heard no answer. They looked tired, dirty. Some had wounds still bleeding. They needed something, a stronger reason to hope.

Anargen forced himself to draw a steadier breath and found the answer.

"Sometimes we are called to make a stand, even if it ends in sorrow. Sometimes it is the stand which is the most powerful implement for the High King to cast off darkness. If I die, it will be for those who hate me, at the hands of horrific evil, and ultimately for the Great King's honor. Live or die, the light I carried here with me will shine the brighter for what I do now."

Silence pressed in from all sides, heavier than the stones of the fortress. Beside Anargen, the old Ord stirred. All the good humor drained from the aged dwarf's face. "After the last battle with the Ecthels, our Elders cursed your — nay, our, King's name, and forbade us to speak it."

Anargen's brow furrowed. What was formerly history, words inscribed upon a page, was breathed to life by this Ord. Pains and passions accompanying mistakes made by the "great" and "wise" were woven into his fabric.

"Lad! Do you know today is nearly the forty-eighth year since that battle with the Ecthelish? Here we sit, myself and a young Knight, defending the fortress again from the Ecthels. Save now we face darker foes and our end."

The old Ord's lip quivered. "No. There is still light to be found within our borders. We are Orderers!"

Standing as fast as his age-ravaged body would allow him, the Ord reached his feet and faced his people. Many had looks of complete exhaustion etched into every contour of their faces. A scattering looked on in curiosity over the outburst.

The feisty old Ord spoke in the voice of a commander to them all. "My fellow Ords! I have a song for you:

"From the mountain's hold march,
From the valley's embrace they race,

Young and old, all of them bold,
Foes to vanquish, evil to slay,
By aid of our burning blades.
Tomorrow a whisper, nothing more,
Honor flees with passing of the day,
We warriors shall not miss it,
Glory is serving our King and his Thane."

"That is the song of our ancestors. Our heritage. Our blood. If these beasts want to spill it, then may it ring so loud their ears will never escape it till all realms end!"

A few nodded and one even stood. The old Ord began his song again, this time as a chant. An infectious one that began to spread through the passage.

Watching the spectacle in wonder, Anargen wasn't certain what to think. Before Anargen could speak, a sentry stumbled over and in a fit exclaimed, "The beasts are upon us! Brace yourselves!"

The hall went silent. Dozens tensed for the attack. Stones and crates shook and toppled to the floor, one splintering on impact. No familiar sounds of yips, barks, or howls could be heard. Just faint scratching and the shifting of the debris that held the enemy at bay.

Caeserus, came to the front of the group, his Spiritsword bared, knuckles ruddy. "Come on then, you mongrels," he demanded, as stony as the fortress around him.

No sooner had Caeserus uttered his taunt than the barricade gave way. A hairy, wicked face bearing a monster's grin smashed through. Barking and snapping its jaws, it seemed to savor the dismay in the air.

Caeserus's face twisted with rage. "Ahh!" he rushed forward, stepped to the side, kicked off the wall, slamming his shield on top of the beast's head. Its startled cry echoed in the corridor. Drawing a cheer from the Ords watching.

Pulling back, the creature staggered from the front of the

assault. A moment later, a second beast bashed through. Looming tall and malevolent, it let loose a howl and leapt past Caeserus, charging the Ords.

Another broke through and landed in the wake of the first. This one, however, caught a glimpse of Caeserus's fiery blade and turned to snarl at him. Anargen caught a glimpse of his friend smiling as he dodged right, again pushing off the opposite wall. A swing of his sword just narrowly missed the monster as it leapt further into the passage.

Volleys of arrows pelted the monster, earning only a ghastly sound of fury. Two more beasts entered the breach and rushed towards the awaiting Ord lines.

One beast crashed into the lines with horrible force, the brunt of which Anargen bore. Holding their ground, the Ords forced back the second with an array of pikes. Caeserus charged forward and jammed his sword into the side of the distracted monster. His hand gripped the scruff of its neck as he hammered the blade in deep.

Craftier monsters leapt off the walls in a blurred streak of ash and brown hues. A pair of Ecthel riflemen entered the passage and dropped to a knee, letting loose volleys that startled those within more than anything. These were the first of the Ecthel regulars to enter Ordumair. Their uniforms still appeared crisp under their light armor, wearing a slushy glaze of snow that had not yet released the smoothly contoured steel. Behind them came a trio of soldiers bearing rapiers and verve for battle.

Anargen's shield blocked the first of their strikes aimed to slay the Ords around him. Advancing, with a quick parry, an attacker was sent reeling into one of his gunners. More men pushed through the hole in waves. Too many for him to handle.

Suddenly Anargen found himself flanked by Ords as they pushed forward to meet their longtime adversaries. When two more waves failed to break the Ords' resistance another were-beast entered battering aside all threatening to slow the Ecthel advance.

Anargen swung at the creature but found no purchase on the blow. Rather, it nimbly skirted away. Its next leap landed it in the seething sea of combatants far from Anargen's reach.

Glowering and turning to block a rifle's report with his shield, Anargen felt his heart thudding in his chest. Down the passage he saw one final figure enter, more fell and loathsome than any of the others combined. "The Grey Scourge," Anargen called to Caeserus.

The Scourge paused to survey the battle's proceeding. His behavior was unnerving for being so distinctly human while his appearance was absolutely alien, monstrous. His eyes soon affixed themselves to where Anargen stood. The young Knight's fiery armor caused the creature's eyes to narrow. Canine lips pulled back to reveal teeth like daggers in size and sharpness.

One ear twitched as though he was listening for something. With a great huff from his nostrils, his lupine brow was set. Then he was a streak, too swift to be accounted.

Scattering Ecthels and Ords alike, the villain of lore swept towards the City of Ordumair. Not even slowing, he smashed through the gates, splintering wood, sending a shudder through the surrounding chamber. The beast barely slowed and rushed past the startled defenders within the city, not bothering to stop and malign a single home.

Everywhere the battle halted. "Where is he going?" Caeserus asked aloud, but probably didn't expect an answer. Any moratorium on fighting was ever so brief. Caeserus didn't notice a rapier's slash at his shoulder from an opportunistic Ecthel.

Anargen stepped in and deflected the Ecthel's blow. He needed only step aside to avoid the next strike. This Ecthel was wearied as well. Too worn to fight effectively. Battering aside the Ecthel's thin sword, Anargen broke the rapier. While the Ecthel gaped, Anargen dropped into a shoulder charge ending with a backhanded blow from his shield. He drew no satisfaction from seeing the rapier-bearer reel into a wall.

As the battle resumed its full intensity, Caeserus watched the

Grey Scourge disappear from sight. "That can't be good." Shouts from either side threatened to drown out the Knight as he continued speaking. "He is going to find the treasure — we have to stop him!"

"Sir Meredoch told us to stay here," Anargen disagreed, as he warily eyed those around them and occasionally blocked a glancing strike from nearby foes. "The City can't be further breached. Think of all the Ords who will be slaughtered!"

Caeserus had the same look in his eyes as that night when he burst into Anargen's home, insisting they leave. This time Anargen did not humor him. "No, I'm needed here. You—"

Even as he spoke, a beam of light pierced the gloom of the corridor. The light intensified quickly till it filled the whole passageway.

Squinting, Anargen could see through the formerly invisible haze of dust in the air that the light was pouring in through the opening the Ecthels had created. This was the first glimmer of something beyond the cold and dreary dark of these long days. A scene born of the sweetest reverie.

In a low but sweet tone, a horn's call rang through the air, demanding attention. Foreign, but not like the Ecthels'. This horn sounded pleasant, welcome if it could be logical to feel such.

There was a lull in the battle's intensity as the horn rang out again and again. The light grew brighter in the tunnel and there echoed after it the howls of werebeasts not yet entered. Those within the corridor growled, fur bristling. They barked to one another and after a few minutes of canine deliberation, charged back out whence they had come.

The disheveled offensive by the Ecthel's regulars now lacked their most formidable weapons. Distracted and out of step, many of their members faltered, unsure of how to proceed.

Finding their moment to turn the tide, one bold Ord cried out, "Ordumair!" and the others pressed the attack with newfound fury.

In a matter of minutes, the Ecthels were forced back out of the corridor. Incautious, the Ords pressed the attack, loosing a thunderous shout that evoked remembrance of the tales of their ancestors. Amongst those charging after the Ecthels was the elderly Orderer, wearing a gleeful grin.

Following them down the shattered corridors into the growing brilliance beyond, Anargen emerged into a portion cracked open by cannon volleys. A gust of air buffeted him. He looked out from the mountain side and could see the storm had broken. Sunlight pierced through the clusters of angry, ebony clouds. His eyes stung, but he fought to keep them open, to take in as much of the delicious light as possible. Anargen could almost feel the warmth of the sun burning away the chill that had clung to him for days.

In the valley below, moving across the glittering mounds of sun-caressed snow were hundreds of mounted warriors bearing a banner Anargen could not quite perceive from this distance. The sunlight seemed to dance with favor upon them.

Around the cavaliers marched dozens of darker clad foot soldiers. Friend or foe was not certain and even less material at this point. For the moment, these men had drawn the attention of the werebeasts and freed the defenders of Ordumair from the crushing onslaught of only moments prior.

Breathing in, Anargen closed his eyes in the warming sun. He longed to stay and cling to it, but he knew that as he had followed the werebeasts out, Caeserus had departed in the other direction. Caeserus had given chase to the Grey Scourge.

Anargen opened his eyes and took one last look at the daybreak, knowing it might be the last time he did so. The warmth chased out his fear, and his limbs felt renewed. Then he plunged back into the dim Fortress, sprinting as never before to save his friend.

44

TWISTS AND TURNS

ANARGEN'S BREATH came in smooth, even huffs like the billows of his father's forge as he neared the end of the largest tunnel of the secret passages. His friend was a fast runner, but Anargen was able to run distances far better, and the pursuit of the Grey Scourge proved to be a lengthy trek.

"Excuse me, sorry," Anargen said as he passed yet another wounded Ord being helped up. Any who barred the Scourge's path too long were battered aside. Even some buildings bore scars where his huge furred form tore through the city. Only an elite few knew about the secret vaults of Ordumair. Ironically, it was likely for their exclusive nature that the werebeast's keen sense of smell could find it. Did find it.

Inside the tunnels of Ordumair, the creature had left numerous torches snuffed out or knocked from their places on the walls. Taking things a bit slower as he replaced a few torches and lit them again, Anagen murmured, "What exactly is he after that he's in such a hurry? Does he think he'll lose the battle?"

At the end of the tunnels was a great archway and braced under it catching his breath was Caeserus. Before Anargen could call out to him, his friend ducked through, hands behind his head.

As Anargen passed under the arch as well, he saw the Grey Scourge had taken time to score five long trenches into a mosaic on the floor. A marred version of the High King's lion stared back at Anargen.

Swallowing uncomfortably, Anargen followed this final passage. Of all he'd seen it was the most intriguing, formed entirely from uncut stone. Anargen was treading on the dark, ancient face of the mountain.

Ahead a series of torches were lit in a natural cavern. At either side of its opening, however, stood two limestone pillars. Each bearing the ancient script of the Ords.

"The famed Knight Hall built around the dual springs that saved Ordumair the First," Anargen whispered with reverence.

Whatever the Grey Scourge desired within, it would certainly be something no one had seen in centuries. Despite his hurry, Anargen slowed to a walk. This was the sort of place which demanded respect.

Within the chamber beyond, he felt the ancient, damp air heavy on his skin. Almost like a garment of initiation dropped on him. Musty odors mingling with fresher gusts for the first time also greeted him.

"Woah," Anargen said as he stumbled. Layered over the cave floor was marble, exquisite in both design and polished veneer. It covered the walls as well and formed pillars laced with gold leaf swirls that continued on each side of the room. These soared up to the ceiling which must have been quite high.

From above hung dozens of huge lanterns and mirrors, ornate and effective at illuminating the space. Much care had been taken in positioning them so that the floor's smooth surface reflected some of the light, and the marble's colors helped to amplify the effect.

Two great fountains stood prominently near the room's center. From one sprayed forth a steamy rush of water reaching high into the air, though far short of the ceiling. The second fountain's waters arrived via an aqueduct which routed waters from somewhere higher on the mountain. This fountain's waters came together in a gentle cascading fall. Each spray found its rest in marble pools that kept the waters separated.

All the walls surrounding the room were carved and embossed in gold leaf with more ancient script. Though he couldn't translate it, he knew they were the words that adorned the Spiritsword. At the room's very heart, standing proud and sagacious in appearance was the statue of an Ord, his sculpted armor and clothing from a long past era.

Around him was planted a grove in two arcs, all of the tall trees bearing golden leaves. So beautiful were these trees, Anargen could not say he had ever seen such arboreal splendor in all the lands of his journey.

Though longing to touch the leaves, a low growl drew his eyes elsewhere. Beyond all these resplendent sights stalked the form of the Grey Scourge and around him those whom Anargen had come to aid.

"Better late than never," Caeserus whispered to him as he came to stand with the other defenders arrayed in a circle around the monster. Within the center the Grey Scourge seemed to see none of them. Quite obviously he was fixated on a dais behind Thane Duncoin, Viceroy Ecthelion, and Sir Meredoch. Atop it was a stone chest with a relief in the likeness of an Ord for a lid. A sarcophagus.

Behind this rose a still higher platform, with tables where the Knights of this hall would have gathered around in discussion and banquets. Around all the walls at the room's back arched a huge series of shelves wearing an inconceivable number of tomes like medals of honor. Such splendor was beyond words for the teen.

There was so much more to see here, but Anargen's attention was forced back to the standoff. "You will not pass, Scourge," Sir Meredoch announced to the wolf-like menace. Even from a distance, Anargen could see Viceroy Ecthelion's hands were shaking as he held a sword aloft in punctuation of Sir Meredoch's words. The expression on his face looked nothing like fear.

"We are Knights in service of the Great King of Light, and as his servants we will not allow you to claim any of the things he destined for his people."

There was such authority, such power in Sir Meredoch's words, Anargen felt himself pressured to bow before them. But the Grey Scourge did no such thing. Rather a sort of yipping and cackling sound emitted from its mouth, until a bizarre lilting voice could be heard. The voice of Mr. Keeper, only deeper. "Foolish child. You know nothing of my claim or what you defend. I was there when the Golden Forest burned, and these Ord filth destroyed the splendor of Ecthelowall. I was there when gutless men of Ecthelowall bowed and betrayed their own rather than fight. Centuries since have taught me well, your king has no claim over anything here."

Drawing his Spiritsword, the flames dancing over it in an instant, Sir Meredoch called out, "You have no strength to challenge the High King's claim upon this place. Leave now, return to the shadows and mire that are your home."

The Grey Scourge's tail lashing in what approximated an amused wag ceased. A feral snarl built in his chest till a roar echoed off all the walls, magnifying its sound to painful levels. The creature's claws ground into the marble, as he turned a furious gaze on each person arrayed before him.

As his roar faded, the Grey Scourge's muscles tensed, and he leapt in a single bound, swift as a candle is snuffed out by the wind, to land behind those opposing him.

Caeserus rushed forward as two Ord sentinels charged up the stone stairs on either side of the raised platform. Paying them no mind, the Grey Scourge bounded left from the raised position and battered down Thane Duncoin.

Before anyone could react, he had dashed to the other side of the group and battered aside three more Ords like a child scatters leaves by jumping among them.

By now, Sir Meredoch was on the creature's flank. Rather than strike, he waited for the beast to react to his move.

Finding Sir Meredoch's burning blade awaiting him, the Grey Scourge yelped in surprise and dodged to the side a fraction of a second earlier than Sir Meredoch's sword sizzled through the air.

As the beast landed agilely, its claws screeched along the smoothly veneered stones, and he lowered his scarred head. An instant later he charged and crashed against Sir Meredoch's shield, forcing the Knight away. The Grey Scourge hopped to the right, whirled round, and bashed the Viceroy aside as the Ecthel tried to mimic Sir Meredoch's flanking tactic.

Faster than conceivable, the Scourge streaked off. Anargen's eyes took a moment to track his movements, which led in a roundabout path to stand before Caeserus.

Before Anargen could shout a warning, the monster began raining down a hail of blows. Strain was evident on Caeserus's face as he barely held his fire-traced shield in guard against the crushing strikes.

Duncoin, nearest to Caeserus at that moment, tried to rush to his aid, but the Grey Scourge, aware of this, put all his weight on one leg, spun, and lowered his head, using it to lift the Ord clean off the ground and into the air.

As the Ord flew backwards like a leaf caught up by a storm's strong breeze, the Grey Scourge sprang to snag the Ord out of the air with his bared teeth.

Faster than anyone could have believed possible, Sir Meredoch leapt up and tackled the Grey Scourge out of the air, bringing him down and giving him a good jab from the white-hot tip of his Spiritsword.

A deafening howl ripped from the throat of the Grey Scourge, and he bucked violently, casting off Sir Meredoch to land hard elsewhere. Meredoch was slow in raising himself up to his elbows.

Anargen finally found himself able to move and rushed to

the side of his mentor. Sword gripped tight, with flames crackling in righteous anger, Anargen stood guard over Meredoch while two of the Thane's protection detail approached the Grey Scourge from either side.

Usually a clever tactic, but not this day. Bashing aside one with a clawed paw, the Grey Scourge padded around and grabbed the Ord's shield in his jaws, slinging him, still tethered to the shield, onto the ground. The sound of metal crying out in mourning echoed through the hall.

"Off him, mongrel!" Caeserus shouted as he and Anargen each charged to rescue the Ord.

Once again the evil thing's eyes turned toward the dais. Feinting a swipe, he bounded towards his objective, abandoning hope of conquering all his adversaries at once.

Awaiting him were the other two Ecthelish warriors, each standing their ground. Their courage managed to slow the Scourge's pace and force him to divert his approach.

The longer cut around the room to get the proper line of attack on the two Ecthels, though only a handful of seconds, allowed Sir Meredoch to get back to his feet and moving at a full speed. While each Ecthel, in turn, found himself being dashed against the stony coffin of the Ord ruler, Sir Meredoch came into position and swung his sword in a wide mid-level arc, forcing the Grey Scourge back.

"Come now, did you think it would be so easy?" Sir Meredoch huffed out, jibing at the creature through deep breaths.

Incensed, the monster struck back, but its claws could not prevail against Meredoch's steadfast *Thyreos Pistis*. A vicious dance ensued, of bared teeth and burning, snapping, and striking at a dizzying pace.

The Viceroy and Thane struggled to get into position about the scuffle to lend extra protection to the central point of the battle, the chest, which was the apparent thing of importance to the Grey Scourge.

Breathing unevenly as the duel lingered unresolved, Sir

Meredoch certainly was just a man, but he fought with skill and determination unlike anything Anargen had ever witnessed. There was no blow nor feint that did not bear a block or receive a worthy counter from the Defender of the Realm.

The perimeter around the battle of wills was tenuous, shifting as necessary to allow Sir Meredoch room to continue his defense. None knew how long he could maintain doing this and none dared step in and risk becoming a liability rather than rescuer.

Batting his paws at the Knights just enough to keep them all at bay, the Grey Scourge scanned the room. If possible, he looked conflicted. His prize must not have come as easy as he imagined.

A leap back from the guardians of the chest, gave him greater room for thought. Compulsion to retreat looked like it tugged at him. He expelled a frustrated huff, no weak spots had presented themselves. Then his eyes fell on Anargen.

There was a mad cast to the beast's glowering eyes. A low snarl issued from between his teeth as he looked on the young Knight. Anargen had bested the Scourge in his human form. With his friends he'd humiliated him in Bracken.

The Scourge's canine tongue ran over fangs, hungry for vengeance. Huge muscles bunched, and he was off charging towards Anargen at full speed.

A step before the monster reached Anargen's awaiting shield, Ecthelion plowed forward from his position and clipped the hind legs of the werebeast. There was a cracking sound as the Grey Scourge landed a glancing blow to Anargen's shield. The impact was enough to send Anargen skidding along the floor.

Looking over at where the Viceroy lay sprawled on the ground dazed, Anargen hoped Ecthelion's shoulder was only out of socket and not broken.

With a yowl the Grey Scourge's huge form bounced nimbly back to all fours. He rolled his shoulders as if shrugging off the setbacks. Once more he looked over the group.

From where he lay struggling to get back up, Anargen could see an Ord guard closing in on the Scourge's back. At the right, Caeserus made a cautious approach. To the creature's left was the solid marble of the Hall's platform and before him was the chest, his prize.

Before the encroaching wardens of the Hall could reach him, the Grey Scourge struck. Whirling around and grabbing hold of the halberd's head of the Thane's guard, he jerked the Ord round and with three deft shakes of his head sent the Ord tumbling in front of Caeserus, smashing him into the dais.

With these two downed he could have gotten to the box before anyone could reach him. Instead he turned on Ecthelion, his fearsome fangs bared, hovering inches above the Ecthel's face. Hot streams of damp fury huffed from the nostrils of the wolf-like snout. "Doom to all traitors," the creature snarled and slashed aside Ecthelion's arm held in defense.

From nearby, Caeserus was up again and ran past the crumpled form of the Ord-guard. His approach was too obvious, and the Grey Scourge, in his devious design, had awaited this.

Even as Caeserus prepared to strike out, the werebeast cunningly skirted the blow and struck Caeserus's shield hard enough to send him sailing backward. Crashing down a few feet away, the impact tore the Spiritsword from Caeserus's hand. The tinny sound of it clattering against the floor seemed to echo a thousand times magnified.

Suddenly the auspices seemed in the monster's favor, and he pressed his advantage. Stalking Caeserus, he raked his claws over the teen's shield again and again. Each hammering attack kept Caeserus burning all his energies on keeping one shield-block from disaster.

The Grey Scourge's tail lashed with delight over the strain evident on Caeserus's face. He could taste the fear in his prey.

"Off him, you fiend!" Anargen bellowed and launched himself at the creature.

He hadn't known it, but at the same moment Sir Meredoch

finished slinking into place for an attack of his own. There was no handling both Knights effectively, not in the mere seconds accorded by each Knight's pace, and so the Grey Scourge tried to dodge towards Anargen to fend him off first.

One step from impact, Anargen's sword flared with a brilliance neither had seen before. The werebeast skittered and lost his balance. Pouncing unopposed, Sir Meredoch put everything into his strike.

Such a cry went out from the monster's deepest inward parts that the room seemed to shake, and the combatants were forced to cover their ears. If pain itself had a voice, it could have uttered no sharper notes.

As he clamped his ears, Anargen saw why. Lying smoking on the floor was a forelimb of the beast. Sir Meredoch's blow had severed it cleanly. Within seconds, the limb caught flame and then turned to ash.

Before Anargen could properly register it, the fabled minion of darkness fled the room, staggering and wobbling into the stone of the narrow passages as he went.

No one moved. Within the chamber of the dual springs was a long silence only broken by the whisper of the fountain waters. To Anargen it was too much like a dream's fanciful flight. They had all survived, triumphed. At length, a series of sighs and mad laughs filled the stillness. Tensions carried for too long gave way to shouts.

Sir Meredoch called out, "Duncoin, brother, are you well?"

"Aye, though I've seen better days," the Thane replied and groaned as he made his way to his honor guard to check on them.

Some relief worked into Sir Meredoch's posture. "Good. The Grey Scourge took a particular dislike to you and the Viceroy. Ecthelion are you well, also?"

Duncoin wandered over and clapped his hand against Sir Meredoch's back, "Not such a dislike as could not be handled."

The Viceroy never answered. Ecthelion wasn't joining in the

celebrations yet. Anargen caught sight of Duncoin shooting furtive glances over at the Viceroy in the midst of making boisterous boasts and jokes.

A few seconds later, the Viceroy collapsed at the edge of the pool collecting water from above. His lanky frame stretched out limp and did not move again.

45

BINDING THE WOUNDS

ANARGEN RUSHED TO THE VICEROY. An immediate wave of revulsion struck him when he reached the Viceroy. Across Ecthelion's chest, dividing his green attire into tattered, brown-stained strips, were lacerations inflicted by the claws of the Grey Scourge. A strange putrid odor was already drifting off them.

The muscles around the terra cotta and carmine scoring of Ecthelion's torso spasmed. His face contorted, as though he wanted to scream but couldn't. Already he was growing pallid and beading with sweat. He stared up at Anargen and tried to peak. What came out was no more than a murmur, lost in the sounds of the fountain.

Grabbing some of the Viceroy's shirt, Anargen placed it over the wounds. "Sir Meredoch! Come quickly! The Viceroy is wounded badly!" Anargen tore free some more of the Viceroy's shirt and held it in place, causing the ruler to clench his teeth and moan.

Peering over Anargen's futile efforts, Meredoch scowled. "Anargen, please move aside." After a minute he looked up at Anargen and said, "These wounds are deep. They'll kill him if he's not treated right away."

From behind came a grunt of displeasure. The Thane stood not looking at anything in particular, but clearly irritated by the whole scene. "Let him alone. His is not the only blood spilt because of the Grey Scourge. Did he not will for such murderous acts to be visited upon us?"

Sir Meredoch ignored Duncoin. Taking in a deep breath, he looked up and saw the second fountain bubbling frothily nearby. Turning to Caeserus, who had wandered up, Sir Meredoch pulled away the stained strips of shirt and slammed them into Caeserus's hands.

Caeserus rocked back from the force of the delivery. Sir Meredoch commanded, "Get that over to the other fountain and dip in it in where the water first comes out, for a good while."

While Caeserus complied, Sir Meredoch grabbed a fistful of what blood-free fabric that remained of the Viceroy's shirt. Ripping it free, he turned to Anargen and said, "Take these and dip them in the cooler waters of the fountain here. Quickly!"

"You should not work so feverishly over him," Duncoin demanded. "He does not deserve any compassion for his part in the slaying of thousands of my people! Let him savor the reward due him."

As Anargen soaked the scraps of cloth, he saw Sir Meredoch rise slowly, his jaw muscles tense and eyes full of heat like live coals. "Perhaps then I should not have brought myself and these young Knights to your aid, Thane. If mercy isn't due him for his penance and sacrifice, why should we have placed ourselves in peril for your people? Didn't you abandon the High King and our Order? What fairness is there in that? Do not presume to know the intents of this man's heart, for I tell you now he is as much a servant of the King and entitled to the waters here as you!"

"These are my people's heritage! Forbearance is my own to bestow."

"Do not presume to lecture me about mercy and forbearance after all that has passed between us," Meredoch shouted. "All of this," he gestured to the room around them, "is just as much his heritage! Was it not a Knight Errant from Ecthelowall who led Ordumair I to become a servant of the High King? How many thousands over the centuries have benefitted from the King's benevolence at the hands of his ancestor that you now would see this man wither and die before your very eyes?

"Stand aside, Thane, and consider the stone of your own heart. It may be in greater need of aid than this Ecthel's wounds."

Careful to skirt around the intensely brooding Thane, Caeserus delivered the heated cloths. While they still exuded a steamy mist, Ecthelion writhed in pain and let out a gasp. The cloths lay heavily against the wound and quickly turned red.

Anargen held out the cloth soaked by the cool waters, so chilly they raised the hair on his arms. Tilting back the Viceroy's head, Sir Meredoch forced open the man's mouth and twisted the rag so that a steady trickle ran straight into his mouth and pooled. Without further instruction, Ecthelion swallowed with some noticeable difficulty. If these were magic cures, his face told nothing of their success.

Nearby, the guards, Ord and Ecthel alike, had assembled. Drawn by the argument and bustling.

Again Sir Meredoch sent Caeserus to the heated pool. As he departed the older Knight looked over the wounds and frowned. This was palliative at best. Looking around the room, he spotted the golden trees and suddenly his eyes brightened with a wild hope.

"Duncoin, he needs the golden leaves of that orchard. We can use them to treat his injuries!"

A gasp could be heard from the cadre of Ords who encircled their Thane. None of them must have understood these to be the golden trees from tales of the early years of their war with Ecthelowall. Then all at once, the Ords arrayed themselves like a wall in front of the trees.

Nobody moved for several long seconds. Anargen could

almost feel the heat radiating from the stares of the Viceroy's honor guard. If those Ords didn't move to help or at least step aside, blood would be spilled. Whatever good will that might have been fostered would forever be lost.

Duncoin spoke up. "We will give these in rescue of a fellow servant of the Great King."

The Thane gestured to his guards, "Gather some leaves, quickly."

His bearing was hard to read. Still refined and proud, but more passive than resigned. Anargen wanted to believe he had seen the wisdom, the merit, in forbearance. That Thane Duncoin was an Orderer once more.

When a small pile of leaves was gathered, Sir Meredoch began tearing them into tiny bits. Some of it he lined the heated rags with and applied to the wound. Again no instant relief. "Bring me a cup," he barked.

A few minutes later, they'd found a cup amongst the feasting effects atop the dais. Using it like a mortar and his sword pommel like a pestle, he ground the remaining leaves into a paste with some of the cooler fountains waters.

He grabbed the Viceroy's head, starting to force him to drink. Ecthelion was rigid, deathly pale and purpling as if he couldn't breathe. "No, no," Sir Meredoch said. Setting down the cup he began pacing.

"Were you too late, good Sir?" one of the Ecthels asked, his head already bowed as in mourning.

"Something is wrong. This isn't natural," Meredoch replied, looking around as though something in the room could help him and finding nothing.

"Nothing about this is natural," Caeserus said with a snort. "He was mauled by a monster born from utter darkness."

Suddenly Meredoch stopped pacing. "You're right. I hadn't considered it because no legends speak of it, but the beast's claws or saliva might have some poison in them."

"The leaves of the Golden Forest weren't well known for counteracting poisons of any sort," the other Ecthel lamented.

Sir Meredoch put a hand on the man's shoulder. "I might know of one. If everyone here will but trust me."

He didn't wait for assent. Pushing away from the man, Meredoch whirled around and drew his Spiritsword. As the flames traced up the sword's length, he swung the flat of it around and laid it against one of Ecthelion's wounds.

Everyone was too stunned to act, until a loud sizzling began and the comatose Ecthelion woke with a scream. His honor guard was in motion instantly, reaching for the weapons from the fight against the Scourge and closing on Sir Meredoch.

Anargen and Caeserus, likewise reacted quickly and drawing their own blades barred the path to their mentor. "Sir, we trust you, but what are you doing?" Anargen asked through his teeth.

"Drawing out the poison and cauterizing the wounds," Sir Meredoch replied. A smell describable only as horrid filled the air.

Gagging Anargen and Caeserus held position as long as they could but soon had to break away. The danger to Sir Meredoch was minimal, everyone in the room was covering their mouths and noses against the stench. All the while Ecthelion cried out in garbled fits of agony.

Muffled as he covered his face, Sir Meredoch said, "I'm going to move on to the next wound."

The torment seemed to last for an hour, though it could only have been minutes. At the end, Ecthelion was breathing heavily, but with even rises and falls of his chest. Sir Meredoch poured the special drink into Ecthelion's mouth and stood. Walking up to the others, he said, "Now, we wait and see if he lives."

46

SETTING BROKEN BONES

"SO, the legends of the Golden Orchard are true," Thane Duncoin remarked, filling the passageways leading back to the City of Ordumair with heretofore absent sound. He and most of the group watched Viceroy Ecthelion. Three hours ago he had been near death. Now he was slowly hobbling along with support.

"And it seems the stories of the Ords hording the trees and other treasures was true as well," Caeserus muttered to Anargen.

Anargen shook his head. Now wasn't the time to reopen old wounds. Not after they had just survived the Grey Scourge. Not before they had to rejoin the defense, which may well be near defeat all the same.

It did occur to Anargen that the Viceroy was perfectly entitled to point such a thing out to the Thane. But the other ruler made no comment of any kind.

"We will of course, restore you a yield of seeds from the trees to replant in your homeland," Duncoin added quickly, sounding out of step. Probably having realized the impertinence of such a comment.

"Only after yours," Ecthelion began and sucked in a sharp, pain-filled breath, "is freed from danger."

Anargen spared a glance at Sir Meredoch. He'd not said much since leaving the cavern of the dual springs. Though he had been pleased to point many things out to Anargen and Caeserus within it. The central statue was Ordumair I, discoverer of the cave, and first Ord to become a Knight. Beneath his venerable and austere gaze rested a raised seal of some valuable stone, the name of which had long since been forgotten.

Following the curve of the seal were etched words in a more modern tongue: "Thane Ordumair II, the Bear, Twelfth Greatson of Ornand the Orderer, Defender of the Realm, and his bride Lady Alessia of Ecthelowall. Long May They Rest Peacefully in the Shade of the High King's Golden Grace."

"This seal marks the burial place of the two lovers rent apart by the start of this war," he had summarized. To it, he had added, "See here the symbol? It is the same as the signet. The tree of Ecthelowall and the fountains of Ordumair. Ordumair II understood, even after his loss, that their great peoples needed one another."

Whether the Ecthels or Ords present at the time agreed or not, wasn't clear. The former was too busy tending to Ecthelion and the latter too distracted by examining the dais for signs of what the Scourge may have wanted.

What was found was an opulently adorned little chest held by the stony hands on the sarcophagus. Dark oak with gold facets, it had an ancient script on it. None of the Ords could read it. But Sir Meredoch recognized it immediately as a long past variant of the language used by ancient Knights. "The Oracle of Ornand the Orderer."

Ever since he read those words, Sir Meredoch had held tightly to the box and even tighter to his words. When the decision was made to leave the caverns, and return to the battle, he said nothing. It hadn't gone without notice, but no one seemed willing to venture breaking whatever enchantment the box had placed on him.

Approaching the end of the tunnels, Anargen and all in the

party exited into the forsaken Knight Hall. Several Ords from the farmlands were there, cautiously investigating the structure for the first time in decades. Men, women, and a few children scattered at the unanticipated emergence of their leader and his motley retinue.

Whether in too much hurry or finding them unworthy of his notice, the Thane marched past the farming families without a word for them. Once a few rounds up, his gait became stately, more of a march. Citizens they encountered gave way. In Ordumair the Thane was well recognized. Unlike commoners elsewhere in the Lowlands who seldom recognized their rulers. The greatest example being when the High King had stood amongst his subjects and displayed his splendor. Many still did not recognize him then.

Before the group could reach the twenty-fourth round, however, an assemblage of what appeared to be commanders in the Ord army approached in haste.

At their lead was Sir Orwald, trotting along at a pace much faster than his age would suggest reasonable. As the group neared, Anargen noticed Bertinand and Terrillian with them. Seeing his friends, Anargen's heart lifted and then sank. The presence of all those in charge of the defenses meant they had all been hemmed within the city! Ordumair was still destined to fall.

Sir Orwald spoke in a fast and serious tone. "Dear Thane, we bring good tidings from without the walls of Ordumair. The Ecthels have been defeated!"

Duncoin's mouth lolled open. Before he could rein in his expression and tone he blurted out, "What? How has this come to pass? The Grey Scourge fled, but what manner of cleverness and valor has expelled them wholly from our lands?"

Shaking his aged head, Orwald replied, "No, no, dear nephew. The High King has sent us his aid. Outside the walls of Ordumair are assembled a hundred Knights from Estonbury and a thousand soldiers from the Albarons!"

"They've already surrounded and overcome the Ecthels left behind after the werebeasts returned to their human forms!" Bertinand exclaimed, forgetting his place.

Caeserus, too, left protocol behind. "They reverted from their beast forms? How can that be? With the cover of darkness, they've been in that form for weeks."

"If you lads will let me speak," Orwald reproved. "I am trying to tell you the darkness has lifted!

"Our people have been saved! About that hour the sun broke through, there arrived the warriors of our aid. The fight intensified and the werebeasts began reverting to their human forms, with no small amount of pain! Those Ecthelish put up a fight, but their commanders waved the flag of surrender some time ago."

Looking ready to collapse, the Thane said softly, distantly, "Did you extend a welcome to those who fought on our behalf?"

At this Sir Orwald smiled ruefully. "I was in search of our Thane for that purpose."

"Bring them to my quarters, and have a meal prepared for them." Glancing from Sir Meredoch to Anargen and Caeserus to the Ecthels, the Thane added, "Have a place prepared for each of these with me as well."

47

THE ANNEALING OF ORDUMAIR

A STRONG BREEZE tugged at the parchments spread over Anargen's lap. He held them tighter as the temperate gust passed. As he looked out from his perch atop the shattered stones of Valesgard, the Valley of Ords stretched before him. The sun above was generous with its warming rays, and he drew in a breath for the simple joy of such a thing. He was coming to love this particular vista.

With the battle for Ordumair resolved, he savored the luxury of such a respite. This was the third time he had made the trek to the ruins, the first since all those struck down in its defense had received proper burials. Valesgard, much like the valley below and Ordumair in the distance, was scarred. Work had begun to heal those wounds, but their lingering presence still had a powerful impact on Anargen. That's why he was seated atop a rather large portion of the postern gate's housing, sketching what he saw, or rather what he imagined the scene below him would have looked like before.

Before monsters and machines of war brought all of it so near to utter ruin. Before an icy storm had so inundated the soil, it left huge swaths thick with intractable mud patches and fresh fens. Before a huge host of tents bearing the banners of their rescuers, the men of Albaron, had been pitched like a small city at the base of Ordumair. Their arrival had been pivotal in driving back the Ecthel forces. Had they not heeded Sir Meredoch's pleas for aid, albeit belatedly, all could have been lost.

We came so close...

The charcoal in Anargen's hand snapped. Anargen looked down and realized he had been rubbing too hard against the parchment and broken off the tip. Examining the overall picture closer, he could see the shadowing had grown very dark in his distractedness. Somehow, the sharp contrasts seemed to fit.

As he worked to better utilize his dark swaths, he glanced up. Making the trek up the hillside was Iaegon. The young Ord waved at Anargen, and he couldn't help but smile. Enthusiastic was the gentlest characterization for Iaegon's zeal for life since the fortress was liberated.

A little further down the hillside, just out of Anargen's range to comprehend, was another figure headed towards Valesgard. Probably someone coming to retrieve him for a task in the restoration work going on.

"Anargen! Hale morning!" Iaegon shouted once he was a dozen or so yards away.

"Hello, Iaegon. It is, isn't it?" Anargen replied, adding a few more quick strokes before giving the Ord his attention in full.

"A fine day for a duel," Iaegon observed, giving the area around them and sky above an appreciative look.

"Just like yesterday and the day before, hmm?" Anargen replied and went back to shading.

"Till I win, yes," Iaegon said, crossing his arms over his chest.

Under his breath, but intentionally loud enough for Iaegon to hear, Anargen muttered, "You will be waiting quite some time then."

"Ha! We'll see." Just then he seemed to notice the charcoal and parchment Anargen had been using. "Writing another letter to Seren, are you?" the young Ord teased, able to slip between the divergent impressions of the callow teen and stern heir-apparent to the Ord rule with remarkable ease.

Charcoal stopped in mid-sweep. "No." Feeling his cheeks warm, Anargen spun the artwork around for Iaegon to get a better view. "I wanted to capture the mountains and landscape as it must have appeared before the Grey Scourge and the siege."

Iaegon nodded, adopting the more somber airs of his station and scanned the sketch with great intensity. His blue eyes flicking from point to point, tracing every curve. "It does look remarkably accurate," he murmured.

While Iaegon examined the sketch, Anargen looked past him to the road up to Valesgard. The other figure he'd seen was much closer now and easily identifiable as Sir Meredoch. Before Iaegon finished his assessment, Meredoch was standing only a few feet away.

Anargen cleared his throat and pulled back the drawing, spinning it around to face him again. "I take it you like this?" He gave a quick bob of his head to indicate the Ord should look behind himself.

"You should show this to my Uncle Duncoin. It would do him good, I think," Iaegon said before turning to look to his back. "Hale morning, sir!"

A thin smile formed on Sir Meredoch's lips. He gestured towards the encampment of Albarons below. "Iaegon, your uncle has need of your service. Your guests are having trouble finding suitable grazing land for their horses. I'm sure you're familiar with Lowdrar's Knoll. Will you please escort them there? The knoll's grass had the best chance of surviving the storms."

"Yes, Sir Meredoch," the youth answered, though the look on his face as he passed the elder Knight made it clear he found the request odd. As though he wanted to reply, "Why didn't you take them yourself?" Iaegon certainly had better upbringing and diplomatic sensibilities than to do so.

Meredoch didn't appear to notice. Eyes sharp and fixed on Anargen, he seemed to know just when Iaegon had passed out of earshot near the base of the path up to Valesgard. "The lad is quite impressed by you, Anargen."

Shrugging, Anargen deflected. "He just thinks he can build up his skill fighting me till he can challenge someone of real talent."

"You sell yourself short," Meredoch admonished, surprising Anargen with the seriousness to his tone. "What you endured here, what has been accomplished here, is worth respecting. Iaegon knows that and you should too."

"Yes, Sir . . ." Anargen hesitated, finding himself yet again waffling between his mentor's familiar name of Cinaed and his true name.

"Call me whatever you like, Anargen," he said waving a hand dismissively. "You earned that right."

"Thank you, Sir Cinaed," Anargen answered. "You didn't search me out to bolster my self-worth, did you?"

"Nor to alleviate you of concerns about what to call me," he replied, a tight smile edging his words. "I thought you should be aware of what has transpired in secret council."

Anargen's eyes widened, and he found himself pushing off his stony perch. Setting aside his sketch, he walked closer to Sir Cinaed as if the other man were whispering. "Secret council? You mean about what's inside the chest we found?"

Cinaed nodded. In hushed tones, he explained, "The chest contained an oracle, recorded by Thane Ornand the Orderer. Son of Ordumair I."

"Thane twelve generations before the Ord and Ecthel whose love started the Three Hundred Year War," Anargen recounted and quickly quieted under the stern look he received.

"Time is short, so I must be quick, lad. That oracle is almost three hundred years old, yet bore incredible similarity to your friend Caeserus's dream."

Within his chest, Anargen's heart began to quicken its pace and his hair rose on end. Caeserus did have a vision!

"There were enough details in the oracle, however, to suggest what has transpired here was not the fulfillment of that dream. It seems past debate that the tower of light in both accountings must be further south. My feeling is the tower is in Kirke."

"The capital of Libertias?" Anargen found himself blurting and immediately regretting it.

Cinaed's annoyance was slight. "Yes. There is not time enough to better explain, but I think we should travel south and soon."

Thinking it better not to speak, Anargen nodded in a half-comprehending way. Kirke was south and east of Black River and one of the greatest cities of Libertias, perhaps the entire Lowlands. What wonders was the High King calling us to?

"Lad?" Cinaed enquired, gripping Anargen's shoulder.

"Sorry, sir," he replied, his idyllic imaginings of the great capital still lingering before his mind's eye. "How soon is 'soon'?"

A grunt escaped Cinaed's lips and made Anargen almost jump. Eyeing him with frustration clear in the draw of his mouth, Cinaed answered, "The first of spring, I'd wager. We cannot leave any earlier without depriving the Ords of much needed guidance."

"I didn't realize they were so willing to accept it from us. It seemed enough that they don't call us 'hungermen' anymore."

Shaking his head, Cinaed lifted his hand from Anargen's shoulder and ran it through his close-cropped hair. "Not ours. The Thane's. He and his retinue are coming. They're all coming."

Seeing Anargen's immediate confusion, Cinaed sighed. "The Albarons and Ecthels as well. Sir Bruce clan Loch, brother to the Laird of Albaron, brought news of simmerings in Ecthelowall. It appears, not long after I arrived in Albaron's lands pleading for aid and departed, an envoy of the Monarch of Ecthelowall arrived."

A significant pause allowed Anargen to quip, "I thought Ecthelowall was ruled by a Viceroy and Parliament of noblemen, not unlike Libertias and its Counts?"

"It is, or rather was," Sir Cinaed confirmed. "No ruler of Ecthelowall has claimed the title Monarch in three hundred years." Another meaningful silence ensued, but Cinaed continued before Anargen felt ready to ask after the insinuation. "There seems to be more to the betrayal Viceroy Ecthelion suffered than he knew."

"I see," Anargen stated, though he wasn't sure he was seeing all the pieces to comprehend the entire board. "How does that concern our quest though?"

"That is a good question. Chances are it does not. But, no one is interested in playing a game of chance." Cinaed bit at his lip for the first time since Anargen had met him, but the older Knight said nothing further.

"There is more, isn't there?" Anargen asked.

"Yes. But I'm afraid I cannot tell you any of it."

"Another exercise in trust?" Anargen asked benignly, to which Sir Cinaed nodded.

Anargen shrugged. "You know I will follow you. It's Caeserus who will take some convincing."

Sir Cinaed chuckled, a fresh mirth displacing the stony pall of their conclave. "How do you think I got these silver hairs?" He rubbed at the top of his head and then slapped Anargen on the back. "Thank you for your trust, Anargen." There was a change in Cinaed's demeanor. Hard to place, but he appeared lighter, satisfied. He began to walk away and added as an afterthought, "I will let you get back to your art. I can't remember the last time Ordumair looked so lovely."

Anargen smiled at his mentor till he knew the other was well out of sight. Sitting back down to his sketch, Anargen sighed. Whatever assurances he'd given Sir Cinaed, Anargen was still troubled. Having just escaped the shadow of secrets and questions, he was again being asked to follow his mentor near-blind. Except now, the journey had no true, fixed destination they could name. Kirke was only a guess at a piece of a puzzle. And if what had transpired at Ordumair had only been meant to obscure the pieces of greater significance, what evil lay ahead for them all?

Feeling a wave of anxiety strike him, Anargen decided he was done drawing and gathered his parchments into his leather satchel. As he stuffed them into the bag, his hand found the familiar contours of Seren's letter.

On impulse, he pulled it out of the bag and examined the still unopened envelope. Holding it between two fingers, he tapped a corner against his lips as he considered something he hadn't dared yet. The quest would be long. Much longer than he could know.

Setting his jaw, Anargen tore free the seal on the letter and opened it. His heart took a moment to skip to life as it realized what he was doing.

The letter was short, so short, it confused Anargen, and he found himself reading a middling sentence first and then circling back to the start of the letter. As he read the last sentence, his grip on the letter tightened, and he found himself sucking in a sharp breath. A tear formed at the corner of his eye.

He reread the letter again:

Anargen,

I do not accept your apology, because I do not see the need of it. Your sacrifice to serve is the same well from which I draw your love. Likewise, your absence is where you will find renewed drawls of mine. Life is filled with losses that are full of greater gains. And I shall be waiting for you to return.

Fondly,
Seren

FOURTH INTERLOGUE

"AFTER READING THE LETTER, Anargen drew his Spiritsword and watched its flames dance across the length of the blade. He resolved that he, Anargen, *Paladinus Lucis Aeternae,* would, by the High King's might —"

From somewhere at the room's back, another voice interdicted. "Stop right now, innkeeper! This is all quite enough."

Jason was jarred out of his intense focus on the story. He blinked and turned, along with everyone else in the inn's tavern, to see Councilman Erickson striding forward with two constables beside him. "I have given you sufficient warnings to cease and desist all your mad ramblings, this story among them. Regrettable as it may be, I'm afraid you are not of sound mind and will have to come with us, sir. On my authority, you are being committed to the provincial asylum."

"Asylum?" another voice, tremulous, inquired. Aria was standing a few feet away, tray in hand, eyes wide with horror.

"Aria, this does not concern you," her grandfather stated, giving her a reproving look. His stern gaze flicked to the councilman. "Take me, if you must. I trust you will better respect the rights of my patrons?"

The councilman looked at each of them, and his eyes

lingered on Jason. "All except him," he said and pointed to Jason. "He was overly enthusiastic for your tales. I'm afraid that makes him suspect of being party to your lunacy."

"Party to —" Jason gaped. "I don't even know this man! I just came into town to . . ." He had to stop. There was no good way to explain why he was in Brackenburgh.

He gnawed on his bottom lip and had just resolved to divulge the truth when the councilman waved a constable forward and said, "Bring him. The physicians will be able to sort out whether he suffers like delusions or not."

Jason could not even form words. All the relative ease of moments before was shattered. Surely he was dreaming. At his side, the old man, already cuffed, spoke up. "Mind the inn, Aria. When the day ends you can come to me."

A collection of tears was rolling down Aria's cheek as she nodded to her grandfather. When her eyes met Jason's, there was such a thicket of emotions in her gaze, he couldn't begin to untangle it all. Again, her grandfather spoke up. "All will be well, child. Trust in the Great King."

This earned a swift jab from the constable holding the old man, and the councilman motioned for them to proceed. Outside there was a brief respite in the rain, but it was still over-cast and from how dark it had grown, Jason guessed they were already in the thick of the night hours. He fought back the urge to curse his luck for having gotten caught up in an old fool's tale so much so that he overlooked the clear signs of danger. How had he survived on his own so long only to be caught up in this?

They had walked for about ten minutes, keeping to side streets, avoiding the main thoroughfares where traffic was begin-ning to pick up again. The new electric lamp posts every few feet gave off less light than Jason would have liked and by the time they reached some of the most underused alleyways, there was no additional light at all. What sort of criminal is this man that they would travel through the seediest parts of town?

Jason's question had an ominous answer. Ahead a dark

wagon awaited. From its size and construct, even in the dreariness, Jason knew it wasn't one of the new automotive police transports. This was the sort of treatment reserved for political prisoners who needed to disappear and stay that way.

"Where are we going?" he blurted out, for which he received a sharp smack to the back of his head. Stumbling, he bounced into the constable roughly leading the old innkeeper, who released his prisoner, turned, and gave Jason a hard shove into slick dark bricks of the building on the right.

Jason slid down the wall, unable to keep his balance even pressing against the wall because of his coughs and the wall's slimy coating. As he did, he noticed the councilman hand something to the innkeeper. Then a large form of a constable intruded, and Jason looked up with a sheepish grin. "Sorry, sir," he offered preemptively.

"You are a sorry sot!" the man who had shoved Jason snarled. "Anymore funny business from you and we'll be wheeling you to the morgue instead of jail. Understood?"

Though he nodded fervently, Jason did not understand. He knew that things in the towns were growing more hostile to those who held to fanciful old tales and resisted the district governor's laws, but there was a visceral hatred here. "I promise I —"

Jason never finished the sentence. Further down the alley, the councilman cried out in terror and suddenly slumped to the ground. As he did, the old innkeeper turned around. In his hand, he held what looked like a torch.

Where did he . . .

Were his hands not cuffed behind him, Jason would've covered his mouth to help stifle his gasp. The old innkeeper had a flaming sword. Fire traced around inscriptions on the blade and filled the enclosure with an increasingly bright light.

"What is that?" one of the constables screeched, his arm over his eyes.

"He has a torch," the other replied. "And he killed the councilman! Shoot him!"

Jason slid down to the street as he saw the wobbling way the man held the gun. Two shots were fired off. One missed wildly off the bricks to one side of the alley, the other seemed to be a direct hit to the old man's chest.

Impossibly, the storyteller just marched down the alley with a slow purposeful gait and brandishing his blade, swung the fiery thing round, burning the barrel off the pistol.

The other constable jumped forward with his billy club and made a wild swipe, throwing his whole body into it. For his trouble, the innkeeper stepped to the side, allowing the man's momentum to carry him harmlessly by. With a deft thump of the pommel to the man's back, he slumped to the ground, a moan slipping from his lips as unconsciousness took him.

By now the other constable was stricken with terror. Jason was shuddering himself. There was no way the old man from the inn, stiff and gnarled by age, should be moving so fluidly or quickly. He was faster than Jason. That was no small feat. Jason's speed had been a prized attribute through his life.

"Kneel, sir," the innkeeper boomed, his voice more commanding than the Mayor of Brackenburgh. "And this shall be swift as an eagle."

It must have occurred to the constable to run, because he began to pivot a foot as though to try. He wavered and dropped to his knees. The shudders running through his body were more visible as the old man approached with his burning sword.

Bending down, the old man whispered something to the constable that Jason could not hear and then thumped the back of his head with the pommel. The constable fell forward, out cold.

As the innkeeper stood erect he turned toward Jason. By the light of the blade Jason could see a faint sheen beneath the man's loose old tunic and duster around the spot the bullet had torn a hole. Jason had to squint, but he thought it looked like a thin plate mail from days of old covered the man's torso. More marvelous and terrifying was the fact that there was no dent or hole or remains of the bullet at all, only a faint haze of fire swirling beneath the fabric but not consuming it.

A grunt from the other end of the alleyway jerked Jason's attention off the old man, who stood still and calm as the air after a violent storm. Several feet away, the councilman stood, letting his dark jacket, which had a hole seared in it, drop away. He turned around to face the old man, stretching his arms in a disturbingly casual way after his constables had been felled like wheat before a thresher.

An eerie feeling of dread passed over Jason, and for some reason, he felt cold, colder than ever before in his life. Watching the councilman, the sensation deepened, as the official pointed at the old man, a mocking sneer highlighted by the flames from the sword and the pall of shadows. "You are Cinaed, aren't you? I wondered if I had found the right geezer or not."

Though Jason gaped and felt ready to curl in a ball, the innkeeper stood like a mountain. "And you are not Councilman Erickson. What have you done with the boy?"

"Shouldn't you be more concerned what I will do with you?" A dark grit had entered the councilman's voice, though with only faint light touching his face, he didn't look like the councilman after all.

"Humph, greater than you have tried to tell me the same and have so fallen." Cinaed, if that could be possible, shirked off his duster. It drifted to the ground and suddenly the white of his tunic could not contain the fiery sheen of his armor that had been hidden the whole time.

"Pride will get you killed, old man," replied the thing, which sounded nothing like Erickson nor seemed to hold a definitive visage beyond darkness and cruelty. Barely perceivable, it edged backwards.

"And we both know my pride does not rest in my prowess."

The old man's brows furrowed, sword held at the ready. "I do not fear you."

"Then I will amend your foolishness!" the dark creature leapt and kicked off each side of the alleyway, some kind of black dagger in hand. It came down inches from Cinaed.

The creature stabbed, missed, and then was a flurry of movements Jason couldn't quite sort for the war between firelight and shadows taking place. The creature had brought the dark with him.

After seconds, which passed like a single breath's lifetime, the thing stepped back, made a final charge, and then bounced back to the wall at left. It sailed past Cinaed and tumbled to the ground.

A bitter cry, sharp and painful to hear, echoed in the alleyway, and the thing clutched its abdomen. Little jagged lines of light and angry red patches were over various places on its body.

Glancing over to Cinaed, Jason saw the old man slump against the wall drawing heavy, jagged breaths, but they were becoming more even. His eyes were intent on the creature, filled with a tenderness that smacked of pity.

"I will kill you!" the thing screeched and writhed on the ground.

"Doubtful. You will be lucky to leave this alley," Cinaed replied, getting a hold of his breathing and still carrying that look of regret.

The creature moaned and wailed and began dragging itself toward the end of the alley, but not the one Jason would expect. He was dragging himself towards Cinaed.

Suddenly finding his feet, Jason ran over to Cinaed's side and cowered beside him, thinking this was all too like having a venomous snake at hand.

It passed by, without acknowledging Cinaed or Jason, and without the storyteller taking the chance to finish it off. Once the creature was a few feet past, Cinaed murmured, "He wants to return to the shadows. He thinks the dark will cure him."

From the tone of Cinaed's voice, Jason guessed this was not so. Indeed, still some feet away, the creature came to a stop and whimpered then moved no more.

"Is he . . . is it dead?" Jason asked, suddenly aware that some heat did radiate away from the old man's armor and sword, so much so that the cold of before had been replaced by an inviting but also worrisome warmth.

"Yes and no," was the cryptic reply as once more Cinaed seemed to remember his age and grunted over the effort of reclaiming his coat and putting it on himself. Without further explanation, he began walking back the way they had come.

Gripped by a wave of fear at the thought of staying alone with that thing, dead or not, Jason followed on Cinaed's heels. "Where are you going?"

"To get my granddaughter. If Councilman Erickson is gone then we have lost our only friend in this city. We will need to make haste. The time is upon us."

"The time? The time to do what?"

"More than just hide. To stand again. Light the tower."

"What are you going on about? Is this more of your story? Was this all planned?" Jason could accept this as an elaborate charade for entertainment more than a grim reality.

"It is more of the story," the old man replied, sounding pleased. "But none of this was planned by me. I do not make the plans, do I?"

Jason didn't know whether to answer or not. The remark had seemed like a soliloquy. "That thing called you Cinaed? Are you really him? I mean you would have to be over a hundred years old."

"Hundreds actually," the old man corrected without pleasure and left it at that.

Not sure what else to do, Jason followed along dumbly, half expecting something more from Cinaed.

After a few dozen steps, Cinaed sighed. "Help me get my

granddaughter and I will explain more. I will tell you of the travail."

For a moment, Cinaed lingered there, waiting on Jason. Jason, however, could think only of how impossible it was to put coherent thoughts together. Nothing made sense, nothing about it seemed believable. All of it was the stuff of legends, stories told without the courtesy of serious consideration.

Shrugging, Cinaed seemed to lose his patience and walked on. In his wake, Jason could feel the pull, like an undertow, to stay where he was, dark and unfamiliar as it was, because in a way it was more familiar. He could forget all this. Be about his business and never think about this day again.

But there was another pull, one strong enough to force one foot in front of another, that drug him after the old man. Carrying him along to see by the light of day what of this whole affair remained. Catching up, he told the old man, "Tell me everything."

NORTHWESTERN LOWLANDS
(JASON'S ERA)

KNORLAND

ECTHELOWALL COMMONWEALTH

VOGTEREMARK

REHALCYON EMPIRE

Hoarfrost
Caldoness
Flepin's Fjord
Langlan's Bay
Seabridge
Glowerrothes
Elkfolk
Suchester
Edynwrath
Sorgby
Wendelwell
Gamlin
Cuan Cove
Vadden
Hildecrest
Glastonae
Trevon
Daggerpointe
Estonbury
Lynchwood
Brisbay
Dellington
Narrowville
Grimndale
Brackenburgh
Ecthalon
Westerly
Port Valence
Fairwinds
Oakstead
Middleborne Islands
Merlais
Falconcleft
Kinsington
New Ecthelowall
Abarros
LeTalk Museum
Geisle
Durby Downs
LeTalk
Havenvar
Tenchford
Manaburg
Stormridge
Port Jarreth
Einwinsburgh
Youngston
Neresbad
Falkirke
Tynwood
Pierreville

BOOKS BY BRETT ARMSTRONG:

Destitutio Quod Remissio

———◇———

Tomorrow's Edge Trilogy

- Day Moon
- Veiled Sun (coming soon)

———◇———

Quest of Fire Series - Published by Expanse Books, an imprint of Scrivenings Press LLC

- The Gathering Dark
- Succession (novella)